CHAPTER ONE

LUCINDA. PICK UP. Lucinda. Pick up. Lucinda. Pick up.

Lucinda's fingers hovered over the keyboard keys right as the voice stopped, their ends tingling from typing ninety-plus words a minute.

She cocked an ear but couldn't tell where the voice had come from.

From her desk—aka The Guard Tower Blocking All From Entrance Into Her Boss's Sacred Space—she could see all the way from his corner office, down the hall past Reception to the lifts at the end, and there was no one nearby.

She went back to typing and…

Lucinda. Pick up. Lucinda. Pick up. Lucinda. Pick up.

With a huff, she lifted her fingers from the keys and zeroed in on the sound.

It was coming from her phone, which was lit up beseechingly by her elbow. Someone had added a new ringtone. The picture smiling back at her gave her a fair idea who was behind the deep, gravelly voice.

Biting her lips to suppress a scowl—or possibly a smile—Lucinda pressed the little red "end call" dot on the screen, flicking the call to voicemail. She was a busy woman. The man could wait.

Straightening her shoulders, Lucinda found her spot on the screen once more, pressed a quick finger to her earbud and picked up the trail of the conversation in her ear as Dahlia—Executive Assistant to the Head of Advertising at the Melbourne Ballet Company—continued her story about the man who'd stood her up for drinks the night before.

As Lucinda listened, mmm-ing in all the right places, she continued to type a bullet-point list of the day's top business-related headlines—trending brands, celebrity gaffes and wins, as well as a few choice titbits she thought might be relevant to her boss—a ritual she'd begun when she'd first landed a job at the Big Picture Group six-and-a-half years earlier.

Then her mobile started ringing again, the tone deep, resonant and insistent. Male. *Lucinda. Pick up. Lucinda. Pick up. Lucinda. Pick up.*

Lucinda did not pick up. She opened a drawer, tossed the phone inside, covered it in a pile of miscellaneous paper and shut the drawer once more.

Then into her mouthpiece she said, "Dahlia, you are a rare gem. Find a man who sees your worth. One who looks you in the eye. Who listens when you speak. Who shows up when he says he will. Find a grown-up. Do not waste another moment settling for anything less. You'll thank me."

Dahlia thanked her profusely and rang off. But not before promising to send Lucinda a dozen A-circle tickets to opening night of the Melbourne Ballet's next show. Lucinda didn't bite back that smile. She already had a couple of clients lined up who'd love her for ever for those tickets.

Though she did wonder—if only briefly—whether she was, in fact, the best possible person Dahlia, or anyone, could turn to for dating advice. At least she hadn't given Dahlia any advice she wouldn't follow herself.

"Probably why you've been single for so long," she muttered, before getting back to work.

Until her phone started up again. *Lucinda. Pick up. Lucinda. Pick up. Lucinda. Pick up.* Only muffled. By paper. And a closed drawer.

Lucinda slowly typed the last bullet point, saved the

file and sent it flying through the ether to her boss's computer, before turning on her chair to face the man himself.

Angus Wolfe, one of the top branding specialists in town, if not the country, sat on the other side of a wall of diffused, smoky glass that separated him from the rest of the world.

He leant back in his big leather chair, feet up on the decadently deep windowsill, face in profile as he looked out over the stunning view of the Melbourne skyline. The dying sun sparkled and glinted off the staggering shards of chrome and glass beyond but Lucinda only had eyes for the mobile phone pressed to his ear.

When the drawer began to vibrate a moment before her phone rang, she whipped it open, grabbed her phone and again pressed the little red "end call" dot. She then shoved back her chair, stalked to the discreet glass door that was hers and hers alone, opened it with a satisfying swish and strode across the acre of soft grey carpet to her boss's desk.

There was no way he wasn't fully aware she stood behind him. The man's ability to read a room was legendary. He noticed changes in temperature, pulse, breathing and tone of voice the way other people noticed being kicked in the shin.

Yet still she took a selfish moment to drink him in before officially making herself known.

For Angus Wolfe's profile was a study in staggering male beauty.

The man was all chiselled angles. Sharp jaw, close-shaven. Hair darkly curling and a mite over-long. The reading glasses he refused to admit he needed to wear did nothing to soften the impact of the most formidable pair of dark-hazel eyes that had ever been seen.

Even the tendons in his neck were a sight to behold.

Then he shifted. Slowly. Like a big cat stretching in the sun. The lines of his charcoal suit moved with him, cut as they were to make the most of his…everything. Each one cost more than she'd spent on her car. She knew. She paid his bills.

Then she spotted his socks. Peeking out from the top of his custom-made dress shoes was the merest hint of a wolf motif. She'd given him those socks for Christmas.

Her heart gave a little flutter, releasing a gossamer thread of lust that wafted from throat to belly to places less mentionable.

She squished the thing. Fast.

Angus Wolfe might be able to read a room, but if anyone dared claim that Lucinda Starling—his long-time executive assistant, his right-hand woman, his not-so-secret weapon—was a teeny, tiny little bit in love with him, he'd have laughed till he split a kidney.

Either she kept her cards closer to her chest than she realised or he had a blind spot when it came to her. The fact that he had no clue was a *gift*. And she planned to keep it that way.

For the sake of her job. Her self-respect. Her mental health.

When her phone went off in her hand—*Lucinda. Pick up*—she flinched.

Then she pulled herself together. She held her phone at arm's length and said, "Really?"

A beat slunk by before Angus turned in his chair, mouth kicked to one side in the kind of half-smile that always meant trouble.

"When did you even get access to my phone?" she asked.

He tapped the side of his nose. "I have ways," he said, his voice deeper in person than in the recording, the words unhurried, the effect magnetic. "Ways and means."

"So they say," she sassed.

No one else would have noticed Angus's pause. The infinitesimal shift in his eyes. But Lucinda noticed it all.

It was her job to do so. It was what made her so good at getting him what he needed before he even knew he needed it.

It was also why she mentally kicked herself for the flirty bass note in her voice.

Their relationship, as it was, was a finely tuned, perfectly balanced thing. There was sass, and plenty of it. And banter. There was also brutal honesty. And respect. A little flirtation was within the rules. Part of the game. For they worked really long hours and had to do what they had to do to keep it fun. It took work to keep the balance right. Work to make sure the guy had no clue how she felt about him.

Lucinda feigned resignation as she cocked a hip and waggled her phone in his general direction in order to deflect his attention. "Were you calling for a reason or were you just bored? Because I have plenty of admin I can sling your way if you're looking for something to do."

Angus blinked, breathed deeply through his nose and dragged his chair closer to his desk. "Thank you, but no. I wanted you."

"I was busy," she said, even while his words skipped and tripped through the unguarded parts of her subconscious.

"Doing what?"

She moved around behind his desk, turned the sleek monitor to face her and called up the screen that mirrored her own, where a bright-yellow computer-generated sticky note said, *Read me*.

Angus rubbed a single finger across the crease below his bottom lip. Lucinda tried not to stare at his mouth, she really did—but there she was, staring, as his face split into a grin. "Anyway, now I have you, sit."

His voice had dropped. A fraction. Enough.

She glanced up at his eyes. Imagined a bookshop full

of self-help books taking her to task for allowing herself even a brief moment of fantasy.

Gritting her teeth, Lucinda walked back round his desk, taking the time to change her ringtone to something less likely to make the hairs on the back of her neck flutter and tickle. Where was a funeral dirge when you needed one?

She pulled up her chair, the rose-pink velvet tub chair he'd bought her for Christmas. The fact he let her keep it in *his* office, the absolute best part of the gift.

She sat then pulled out the notebook and pencil she'd grabbed without thinking when she'd picked up her phone. She scratched the pencil a few times to warm it up and settled in preparation for Angus's labyrinthine mind to shift, sway and touch on more bright ideas than any one person had the right to keep in their head.

"Ready?" he asked, that slight lift on one side of his mouth.

"Always."

Angus clapped and like that he was in work mode. One hundred and ten percent. "Right. The Remède account."

For the next ten minutes, Angus went on a wild and woolly stream of consciousness about the rebranding of the Remède cosmetics company, once upon a time a global force, now attempting a last-ditch about-turn in its fortunes before it sank.

It didn't matter if it was a lipstick maker, a political party or a department-store chain. Angus knew what made people connect with a product. What made them want.

Angus jumped from thought to idea, from grand plan to fine detail. Pausing rarely, never forewarning the shifts. Using Lucinda as a sounding board, a mental stress ball, a repository for the pyrotechnics that had built up inside his brilliant head throughout the long working day.

And Lucinda wrote. The adrenaline high of keeping

up with Angus's mental gymnastics was cushioned by the tactile bliss of a dime-a-dozen 2B pencil tip gliding over quality note paper.

"And…?" she said, her voice a tad breathless, when he'd gone quiet for longer than a second.

"And we're done."

"Super."

She figured it would take about another half an hour to pour the notes from the page into the right files and to-do lists and then she could head home.

"Plans tonight?" Angus asked.

"Not much." Beyond the funny smell coming from the laundry that she'd promised herself she'd investigate.

Not that Angus would understand. His apartment was a sleek, temperature-controlled monument to earning big bucks.

While her cottage was…in need of a lot of TLC. But it was hers. Which made it wonderful.

"You?" she asked.

Again the small smile that tugged at the corner of his mouth. It told of fine dining, decadently expensive wine, all while looking across the table at a beautiful woman.

She rolled her eyes.

A well-timed reminder of the many ways in which she and Angus might as well have been different species.

He could survive on the barest amount sleep per night, and often did, while if she didn't get a solid seven in a row she woke up looking and feeling part-witch.

He had a kitchen he never used and didn't need, considering he ate out every night, while she budgeted.

She could count on one hand the number of times he'd mentioned his family in six and a half years. While he knew everything there was to know about hers and they were more important to her than breath.

Her life was…slower. More structured. A daily routine of shopping lists stuck to the fridge door and juggling responsibilities. He said tomato, she said… Well, she said tomato as well.

The point was, at work they fit like custom-made kid gloves but their paths divided the moment they left the office.

On that note… When she reached the glass door at the boundary of his office, she stopped. Clicked her fingers. "Oh!" she said, as if she hadn't been trying to find a way to bring up something all day long. "I have some leave saved up. Enough that Fitz and his HR army are getting twitchy. I've checked the calendar, and there's nothing pressing, so I'm taking this weekend off."

"Off?" he asked. "Or *off*-off?"

She had weekends off anyway, but working for Angus ensured that meant very little. The man never stopped working. He was a hustler at heart and the hustle knew no clock. And, as she was basically his computer, his sounding board and his answering machine, if he needed to get it out, she was the one who caught it.

"Off-off," she said, taking a small step towards her door. "Friday through Sunday."

"Why?" he asked, pulling himself to standing and stretching his arms over his head. His white business shirt clung to the acres of muscle and might, one button straining so far she caught a glimpse of taut, tanned skin.

Her voice was only a little husky when she said, "Does 'none of your business' mean anything to you?"

"Can't say that it does."

"I have plans."

"What kind of plans?"

Come on, Lucinda. This is not a big deal. Stop prevaricating and tell him!

"Just…plans."

"Plans!" a voice boomed from the direction of Angus's main office doorway. Lucinda spun to find Fitz Beckett and Charlie Pullman, Angus's business partners in the Big Picture Group, amble on in.

"I love plans," said Fitz—broad, dashing, a total cad, the Big Picture Group's partner in charge of Recruitment, and Angus's cousin—as he hustled over to Lucinda, took hold of her and twirled her into a Hollywood dip. "Plans are my favourite. What are these plans of which you speak?"

Charlie—tall, lovely, an utter genius and the Big Picture partner in charge of Client Finance—followed in Fitz's wake, giving Lucinda a shy smile before heading over to Angus's desk and launching straight into a story about financial irregularities in one of their client's accounts.

The three of them in one room was a formidable thing. The three of them in one company made for one-stop business branding, recruitment and financial strategy.

From her upside-down vantage point she saw Angus raise a finger to his mouth to ask Charlie to shush.

"Lucinda was just telling me about this weekend's plans," said Angus, his voice a deep rumble.

"Exciting plans?" Fitz asked as Lucinda slapped him on the arm until he brought her back upright.

"Do any of you men know the meaning of the word 'boundaries'?"

Fitz shrugged. Charlie blinked. While Angus's intense hazel gaze remained locked onto her.

When Fitz cleared his throat, Lucinda realised the room had gone quiet. How long had she been staring back?

In a panic, she covered herself by crossing her eyes. When she uncrossed them, she found the corner of Angus's mouth had kicked into a half-smile.

Her heart fluttered like a baby bird in her chest.

"Look it up," said Lucinda, not giving them even an

inch. "If I don't see you before I head off, have a good night."

Fitz shot her a grin. "Count on it."

Charlie lifted his hand in a wave.

Angus motioned the others over to the couches by the bookshelves and just like that he'd moved on to business. His one true love.

Lucinda turned and walked out of her boss's office, shutting the door behind her with a snick. She moved back to her desk where she sat and waited for the tremors in her hands to subside.

Why hadn't she just told him? Told all of them?

"Told them what, exactly?" she muttered as she put her notebook in her bag, deciding to type it up later that night, and closed up her desk for the day. "That you've been seeing a really fabulous man but you didn't tell anyone as you didn't want to jinx it? That, although he's absolutely perfect on paper, you know you've been holding back because of this hopeless crush you have on your unsuspecting boss that has kept you in an emotional wasteland for the past several years? So now, even though you haven't managed to light any real spark with Mr Perfect-on-Paper yet you've planned a dirty weekend with the guy because you're not getting any younger."

Yeah. She could just imagine their reaction.

Boundaries. Boundaries were a good thing. Angus did not need to know every minor detail of her life.

Lucinda slipped into her jacket, whipped her scarf around her neck, grabbed her bag and strode down the hall towards the bank of lifts, lifting a hand to wave to any stragglers still at their desks.

Lucinda pressed the Down button and waited, recalling another "minor detail" she'd kept to herself; the phone call she'd received just that day with a job offer most executive assistants would kill for.

What was the point? It was hardly news. Recruiters attempted to headhunt her all the time.

But, whatever challenging conditions came with their working relationship, she'd never leave Angus. Their connection was rare. The repartee, the respect, the shorthand, the success they shared. Every other assistant she commiserated with over then phone made her realise how lucky she was.

While without her he'd fall apart.

Being the best assistant Angus Wolfe could ever ask for meant she'd come to know the man better than she knew herself—literally.

His favourite colour? Charcoal grey.

Hers? Who knew? Bluish? Periwinkle? Was that more purple? She did like her yellow kettle a great deal.

She also knew he was even more hopeless when it came to romance than she was.

Though he'd say otherwise. He called himself a dedicated bachelor. A strident holdout when it came to romantic entanglements. Too busy. Too set in his ways. That not imposing those constraints on any one woman was a public service.

All of which meant that even if by some strange twist of fate Angus ever saw Lucinda in the same light in which she saw him, he would still not be the man for her.

For Lucinda liked entanglements. She yearned for constraints.

So, she, Lucinda Starling, planned to put an end to her self-imposed emotional wasteland.

None of which Angus ever needed to know.

"Honey, I'm home!"

Voice echoing down the hallway of her small cottage in suburban Abbotsford, Lucinda took off her jacket and scarf, not bothering to disentangle either from the handle of her bag as she dumped the lot in a heap on the hall table.

"In the kitchen!" called Catriona, Lucinda's big sister, housemate and godsend.

Lucinda sniffed the air in the hope there might be a little leftover dinner she could snaffle and caught a whiff of chicken and potato wedges—the good ones she'd found on sale. She hoped Cat had added a little chopped carrot for colour and health. Maybe some baby spinach leaves.

Then she sighed as she kicked off her heels and padded down the hall.

Cat was in the kitchen, one foot tucked up against the other knee, chomping down on a piece of buttery toast.

Her sister had inherited their dad's lanky genes. Lucinda was shorter and curvier, like their mum. She grabbed a carrot stick in lieu of the toast.

Thinking of her parents gave Lucinda a sad little clutch behind her sternum, as it always did, even though it was over ten years since the crash that had taken them.

Then she looked past her sister to the small room beyond. Her heart swelled, her lungs tightened and her head cleared of any and all things that had seemed so important only a moment before.

For there sat Sonny. Her beautiful boy. Hunched over a book at the tiny round table tucked into the nook beside the small kitchen, distractedly polishing off the last potato wedge. His plate was wiped clean bar a few spinach stems. *Go Cat!*

"Hey, sweet pea!" Lucinda called.

Sonny looked up from the adventures of Captain Underpants, hair the same dark brown as Lucinda's hanging into his eyes. A blink later, his face broke into a smile filled with gappy baby teeth, one wobbly. "Hey, Mum!"

She edged around the bench and pressed back Sonny's hair to give him a kiss on the forehead, making a mental note to book in a haircut. She caught scents of sweat and sunshine. "Good day?"

"Yup."

"What's the newsy news?" she asked as she headed into the kitchen.

Cat tilted her head towards the microwave, where a plate sat covered in a little mound of cheap, easy goodness. Lucinda nodded her thanks then plonked onto a chair tucked under the kitchen bench.

Sonny looked off to the side, searching his data banks for whatever snippet he'd tucked away, knowing she'd ask. "Mr Fish, the fighting fish that lives in the library, is missing."

"*Missing,* you say? That *is* news."

Sonny nodded. "Jacob K and I went to the library at lunchtime and saw the tank was empty. Jacob K asked if it was dead. Mrs Seedsman said, 'Many believe they know what happens when a creature is no longer with us, but nobody knows for sure'."

"Did she, now?" Lucinda looked to Cat who was biting back a laugh. "Quite the progressive, Mrs Seedsman."

"I like her hair. It has purple bits on the ends."

"Then I like Mrs Seedsman's hair too."

Happy with that, Sonny gave her another flash of his gorgeous smile before easing back into his book.

Lucinda turned to Cat. "Jacob K?"

"New kid," said Cat. "Sonny was put in charge of him."

"Of course he was. He's the best. Anything else?"

Cat finished rinsing the plates and popping them in the dishwasher, before reaching for a glass of wine she'd clearly had airing in wait for Lucinda to get home and take over Sonny duties.

"All good. Came home chatty. Didn't touch his sandwich again."

Lucinda sighed. Once he was down, she'd be online searching for lunchbox ideas for kids who refused to eat sandwiches, as heaven forbid Sonny eat something she could prepare and freeze in advance.

She glanced at the clock on the wall. "Bath time, kiddo."

"Okay," said Sonny, not moving from his book.

Lucinda considered that her five-minute warning, knowing by now she'd have to ask at least three more times before he actually moved. It gave her time to unwind and settle into the different pace and sounds at home compared to the office.

Time to shed her work persona—proactive, sophisticated, tough, respected—put on her Mum skin—reactive, threadbare, fingers crossed she was making all the right choices, and a massive soft touch when it came to her boy—and remember that, whatever worries she dealt with at work, they always came second to this.

And always would.

A half-hour later, Sonny was bathed and dressed, his hair a little wet from being washed, his pyjamas soft from the two nights they'd already been worn. She could get another night out of them. He only had one other pair that fit. The joys of owning a growing boy.

Once he'd given Cat a goodnight hug, Sonny ran back into his room.

Lucinda carried him the last few metres, just because she could. It might not be an option for much longer. At eight years of age, the kid's feet were nearly dragging on the floor.

Once Sonny was settled, Lucinda tucked herself up on his bed, making sure not to block his bedside lamp so he had enough light to read. They took turns reading and listening. When she dozed off for the second time, Lucinda gently closed the book and went through the rest of the night-time routine: butterfly kiss, nose-tip kiss and kiss on both cheeks, followed by a seven-second cuddle.

Special toys were found and tucked into their respective nightly positions—Dashy the Dog behind Sonny's neck, Punky the Penguin behind his knees. Blankets were moved up to the chin, star-shaped night-light put on low.

This was the time of day when she felt so lucky to have this all to herself—this routine, this sweetness, this boy. Her heart filled her chest. She loved the kid so much.

Though give it ten more minutes and if he called her name needing a drink, or a trip to the toilet, she'd wish with all that same heart that she had a partner to shoulder the load.

Such were the swings and roundabouts of single motherhood.

Lucinda made it to the door before turning to blow one last kiss. "Goodnight, little man."

"Night, Mum."

"Love you."

Yawn. Then, "Love you more."

She went to close the door before she was stopped by a, "Hey, Mum?"

"Yeah, buddy."

"Did Angus ring you today?"

Lucinda narrowed her eyes. "We work about three metres from one another all day long. We can wave from where we sit. So why would he…? The ringtone!"

Sonny tucked his sheet up to his nose to smother his laughter.

"Did you have a hand in that, little man?"

"Angus messaged last night to ask me how. Cat had let me use the tablet to research planets for homework," he added quickly. "Not playing games."

"Hmm. You are a rascal."

Sonny grinned. The sweetest, most good-natured kid in the world, he was the least rascally kid ever. He made better choices than she ever would.

She was working on improving that score.

"Goodnight, little man."

"Goodnight, Mum."

She closed the door then notched it open just a sliver before padding back to the kitchen to stare inside the fridge in hope of healthy inspiration.

All the while thinking about Sonny. And Angus.

She knew they not so secretly messaged one another. She'd been the one to set up the private account when Sonny had worn her down with begging. And only after Angus had insisted it was fine with him so long as Lucinda had full access to the conversations.

Not that she checked much these days. It was mostly links to "try not to laugh" videos. But it had all started after a less innocent incident a few years back.

Sonny had woken up feeling sick one day, and none of Lucinda's usual methods of cajoling, encouraging and downright bribery had convinced him to get ready for kindergarten. So, with a huge, unwieldy backlist of things to do waiting for her at work, she'd taken Sonny to the office with her for the first time.

Angus—completely up to date on every small thing—had shocked the living heck out of Lucinda when he'd offered to let Sonny hang with him in his office. After a good two and a half seconds of consideration she'd handed over Sonny's tablet—a necessary evil of modern parenting—and left the men to their own devices.

Less than an hour in, over a mid-morning fruit snack, Angus had wangled from Sonny the real reason behind the "sore tummy". The kindy group had spent time that week making Father's Day cards.

Sonny—being Sonny—had put up his hand to ask his teacher what to do if he didn't have a father to give a card to.

Lucinda had made it her life's mission to make sure Sonny understood that, whether a child had a mum and a dad, or two mums or two dads, grandparents, siblings or a mum and a super-cool aunt, every type of family could be as rich with love as any other.

Unfortunately, other kids had pretty set opinions on what a "family" ought to look like and had made it their mission that day to make sure Sonny knew it too.

When Angus had pulled her aside that afternoon, while Sonny had been learning how to use the photocopier with one of the guys in accounts, Lucinda had felt sideswiped. Not only that Sonny had gone through such an ordeal but that he'd spilled to Angus. And not her.

Angus had taken her by both hands—something he'd never done before that day—had sat her down, made sure she was looking him in the eye and explained that he'd told Sonny how he'd grown up without a dad too.

She'd learned more about his childhood and his motivations for why he worked so hard in that one conversation than she had in all the time they'd known one another. And, when Angus had assured her that his imperfect mother's love had been his north star, the guiding light that had kept him on the right path, she'd been hard pressed not to sob.

Things had changed between them that day.

In trusting Angus with her son, she'd given him the impetus to step out from behind the figurative wall from behind which he engaged with the world, leading to a moment between them that had been honest, raw and real. And the tiny, innocent glint of a crush she'd happily harboured had erupted, splintering off into a thousand replicas, spiralling uncontrollably into all directions like fireworks, too much, too many for her to have a hope of reining back in.

While Angus, with his vintage chess set and killer AFL handball skills, fast became Sonny's hero. The strongest—maybe the only—male influence in his young life.

She'd never told Angus that Sonny had come home from kindy that week with a card made out to him. It was another of those "minor details" she figured best to keep to herself.

She heard the water cooler talk. She wasn't alone in her crush. Every girl in the office was right there with her. Only, they talked about how infamously uncatchable he was. That he dated widely. And never for long. They called him the Lone Wolfe. If he knew how quickly Sonny had become attached to him it would have sent him back behind that wall.

As things stood, their friendship had grown. Evolved. Stretched. Become something important to them both. It was good. Just as it was.

Lucinda realised she was still holding open the fridge door. She let the door close, but not before taking out a small tub of chocolate custard.

Tossing the lid of the custard into the bin, Lucinda nabbed a spoon from the drying rack by the sink and went to find Cat in her usual spot, watching Netflix while typing away madly at the laptop balanced on a cushion on her lap.

A freelance journalist, Cat's life was a case of produce or starve. But it also meant that when Lucinda's husband had left, deciding marriage and parenthood was all too hard—while Lucinda had been cooking dinner and holding their toddler in her arms, no less—Cat had moved in the next day, more than filling the space Joe had left behind. Making Lucinda realise how little she'd asked of him. How little space she'd taken up herself.

Sonny had been thirteen months old. Earlier that day he'd walked for the first time.

That was nearly seven years ago now.

And it had taken that long for the regular routine, the comfort of home and the warm hum of work success to make room for other hopes and dreams that had begun to flicker at the corner of her mind's eye.

With a sigh, Lucinda sank into the lounge room chair.

"So," said Cat, *tap-tap-tap*. "Did you tell him?"

And, just like that, Lucinda's contented little bubble burst. "Hmm?"

"Angus. Did you finally tell him about this weekend?"

Lucinda wriggled on her seat, trying to get comfortable. "Yep."

Cat's fingers stopped tapping. "Really? Did you say the words, 'Mr Wolfe, sir, I am taking next weekend off because my man-friend, the estimable heart surgeon Dr Jameson Bancroft-Smythe, and I are going away to a fancy resort for some grown up time'?"

Lucinda's silence spoke volumes.

Cat snapped her laptop shut. "Seriously?"

"I said I was taking the weekend off. The reason why is *none of his business*."

Cat's nostrils flared. "You forced Angus to stay here, sleeping in your bed while you bunked in with Sonny after he had dental surgery, because the dentist said there was a chance of bleeding overnight. The two of you obsessively text one another through every new episode of that stupid Warlock school show. You both spend way too much time coming up with wilder and-or weirder gifts for one another, just because. Not to mention whatever went down at that crazy office Christmas party a couple of years back. You and I both know the lines are very much blurred between your boss's business and your own."

Lucinda's throat had gone dry at the mention of the office Christmas party. Cat must have been really agitated as she knew better than to bring it up. The events of that night had miraculously remained classified, locked in a vault ever since.

Moving on after a surreptitious swallow, Lucinda said, "What exactly do you want me to say?"

"I want you to admit to me why you didn't you tell him about Jameson. You didn't have a problem telling *me* all about it. If you and Angus are as tight as you claim to be, why not tell him?"

Cat was no idiot. Quite the contrary. She was a shark despite the fact that, modern journalism being what it was, she wrote as many stories about Instagram celebrities as she did about human rights violations. Which was why she said, "I need to hear you say the words."

Lucinda threw her hands in the air. "I don't know why! Maybe I've enjoyed keeping this part of my life just for me. Maybe it still feels precious, fragile and not quite real, and if I say it out loud it will pop. Maybe I'm slightly concerned if Angus knows then he'll come over here when Jameson is due to pick me up and answer the door with a shotgun in hand so Jameson knows not to mess with me. Maybe if I tell Angus he'll ask questions, and poke holes in my logic, and convince me I'm making a huge mistake."

Cat sighed. Dramatically. "Nobody but you can make you feel anything."

Lucinda dropped her hands and looked indulgently at her big sister. "I know that. I do. I'm just nervous, okay? I want this weekend to go as smoothly as possible. I *need* it to. I've already put so much effort into keeping things going this far, considering how often we've had to cancel our plans with his work and mine. And Angus is right in the middle of this huge account, working for a man he looks up to a great deal. It felt better not distracting him with things that don't matter."

Cat snorted, as if she didn't believe a word of it.

"He's sensitive," Lucinda attested. He really was. Highly attuned to people's needs and wants. It was what made him so good at his work. Judging from the little bits and pieces she'd picked up over the years about his childhood, staying hyper-aware had been the only way he'd survived.

"He's a man-child," Cat muttered.

"Cat!"

"He has a driver, a cleaner, someone else who answers his phone. No wonder *he* hasn't found his own girl to take away for a serious weekend—none of them could possibly live up to his contingent of carers. And, in that list, I include you."

"Thank goodness for that," Lucinda shot back. "Without my part as a cog in the Angus Wolfe wheel, we would never have been able to afford this beautiful little house in which we now sit, all cosy and warm."

What she didn't say to Cat was that she didn't see herself as one of his "contingent of carers". She was his outlet. His release. In the tough, hard-working, driven life of Angus Wolfe, she was unique.

"You really believe that, don't you?" Cat asked. "You sell yourself short. And the great and wonderful Angus does too. He so takes you for granted. I could…" Cat stopped. Shook her head. "Tell him. Tomorrow. Or you'll burst from holding it all in."

Lucinda left Cat's comment be. It wasn't the first time Cat had tried to convince her Angus expected too much. She'd learned to agree to disagree.

She'd been an exhausted, inexperienced mother of a toddler who had no clue if she could do the job, much less commit to the hours required, when she'd interviewed to work for him. But he'd seen something in her nevertheless. *Chutzpah*, he'd said. A raging desire to pull herself up by the bootstraps that he understood.

He expected her to work hard, but he worked harder. And he'd *never* made her feel as if he took her for granted. Despite all she'd given up in order to work with him— time with her family, romantic relationships…

She shook her head and settled deeper into the chair.

"What ifs" were never worth the time spent dwelling on them. Life was good. Her family was healthy and happy.

She loved her job. She had the security that came with having a roof over her head. What more could she want?

A devilish little voice whispered into her ear. *Love. Intimacy. Romance. Someone who puts your needs first.*

Hence the dirty weekend.

When her phone buzzed in her pocket, she found herself unsurprised to find a message from Angus.

She glanced at Cat, only to find her back typing at her ancient laptop.

The message asked if she was keen to start watching the final season of *Warlock Academy* on Netflix—a decade-old schlocky, supernatural teen drama they were both obsessed with. Another part of her job description—find TV shows just soapy enough to engage Angus and brain-numbing enough to let his active mind slow down so he could fall asleep at a reasonable hour.

She messaged back.

You bet.

Then she grabbed the remote, changed the channel, poked her tongue out at Cat when her sister groaned and settled in to watch teenaged witches and demons battle it out at a high school football match.

Though she kept shifting in her seat, unable to find a comfy spot.

For there was no denying that if she had to choose between her upcoming weekend away, with a handsome, eligible doctor who'd made it all too clear how much he liked her, or snuggling at home watching TV with a man who wasn't even in the room, she'd choose the latter. Every time.

Worse, this was the first time admitting as much actually unnerved her.

Cat was right about one thing. Something had to give.

CHAPTER TWO

ANGUS LEANT BACK in his office chair, finger tapping against his lips as he looked over the impressive wall pinned with striking images, word clusters and thought clouds framing the penultimate drafts of the Remède rebranding that the graphics team had moved into his office earlier that morning.

Louis Fournier, the venerable president of the Remède cosmetics company, was just outside, leaning over Lucinda's desk.

Angus didn't need to see Lucinda's face. From the way she sat forward in her chair, chin resting on her palm, chair swinging from side to side, it was clear she was flirting her heart out.

Angus felt the smile start in his throat before it even reached his mouth. *Atta girl.*

Fitz's assistant—Velma—was built like a German tank with the accent to match. She was stern, efficient and ferociously protective of her charge. Fitz claimed he couldn't be trusted with anyone more tempting under his nose all day long. Everyone knew he adored Velma as much as Velma doted on him.

Charlie's new right hand—Kumar—was only slightly more human than Charlie. But, as work mates, they fit together like two pieces of a puzzle no one else understood.

In fact, there was not one single staff member at the Big Picture Group who was carried by someone else. Fitz for all his insouciance, was a ruthless recruiter. They ran a seriously tight ship.

And yet none of them held a candle to Lucinda.

The way she went about things was instinctive. And tenacious. She knew when to be brusque, when to be dulcet, when to be straight down the line and when to bewitch until she had even the most difficult clients eating out of her hand in a matter of minutes.

She was out there right now, wearing Remède's Someday perfume. He'd seen it on her desk about an hour earlier. There was a story there, about her parents, both gone long before he'd met her. Lucinda kept a bottle in a drawer as a reminder of them, but she only pulled it out when Louis was on his way.

As if she felt his thoughts, Lucinda turned to look over her shoulder, the floppy frills at her collar framing her face, her long, dark hair swinging, her red lips curled into a half-smile.

The crack of the glass door created a slight distortion. He shifted slightly so he could see her whole face. It was a good face. Candid, spirited, empirically lovely and as familiar to him as his own.

A pair of small lines criss-crossed above her nose. A rare indicator of indecision.

Perhaps *rare* was the wrong word, for the criss-cross of lines over her nose had shown up more and more over the past weeks. Then there was that new lipstick. Darker, glossier than usual. She'd cut sugar from her coffee. Added infinitesimal pauses before each sentence. All of which, in Angus's mind, spoke to restlessness. To a change in the air.

And he was not a man who liked change.

She lifted a single eyebrow in question. *Ready?*

It took him a moment to remember what he was meant to be ready for.

Louis Fournier. Remède. Saving his old friend's business. He nodded curtly.

The criss-cross above her nose flickered off and on before she turned back to finish up with Louis.

Angus breathed out hard and rolled his shoulders.

His instinct for branding came from the ability to tap into the greater collective human subconscious. To mine people's baser urges in order to encourage—no, *demand*—that they look to his clients to fulfil those needs.

Tapping into Lucinda's baser needs to find out what was going on in her subconscious was not something he had any intention of doing.

Whatever was going on with Lucinda did not impact on her work. It would pass. Everything did. Eventually. And, if not, he'd drag it out of her when he had the Remède account off his plate.

Angus pressed out of his chair and moved to look over the mood wall one last time to make sure nothing had been missed. For nothing was ever perfect. Not for him. There were always improvements to make.

A childhood spent being told that he was a mistake by the procession of men in his mother's life, a blight, in the way, had not been pleasant. But there was no doubt his burning need to prove them wrong was the root of his success. The reason he never stopped striving to do better, to be better, to reach for more.

Without them would he have been standing there in his huge corner office? Would he have had the gumption to land Louis Fournier as a client? As a mentor? As a friend?

He heard Lucinda's laughter from beyond the glass wall and he turned away from the mood board. She'd pinch him if she heard him speak that way about the business. Literally. She'd growl at him to "chillax". To appreciate all he'd accomplished. To enjoy the spoils.

His partners had no problem revelling in the benefits of their success. The highlight for Fitz had been when they'd been written up in *GQ*. Charlie's highlight had come when the university from which he'd graduated with his doctorate in mathematics had enlisted him to manage their financial matters.

Angus's one bright, shining moment?

It hadn't hit him yet. Or, more precisely, for him it wasn't about a moment. It was about moving forward. Stopping to look back, even for a moment, could halt the momentum he'd worked so hard to achieve. So he'd keep working. Keep striving. Keep kicking hard beneath the surface to make sure it continued.

Voices drifted through the glass door leading from Lucinda's desk to his as Lucinda waved Louis into the office. Angus moved to meet them halfway.

"Gus," said the older gentleman, a glint in his eye, and a goodly dose of French still in his accent despite his years spent in Australia. "Good of you to squeeze me in this morning."

Angus's gaze slid to Lucinda who was quietly shutting the door behind her. "Did you flirt him into calling me that?"

She opened her eyes wide and mouthed, *"Who me?"*

At which Louis scoffed. "You do not answer to Gus? I am an old man. Anything I can do to save the time I have left…"

"Fair enough," said Angus. "Then I'd suggest you call that one Cindy. Every lost syllable helps."

Louis looked over his shoulder in time to see Lucinda scowl menacingly Angus's way. She tried to right herself, but only came across looking guiltier still.

Louis's resultant laughter was rich and deep, full of the smoke left by a lifetime of cigars. "You two. Even if I did not have a business to save, I would pay simply to watch you spar."

The guilt on Lucinda's face made way for chagrin as Louis reminded him of their Hail Mary attempt to right his company's ancient ship. For Remède, one of the world's most revered beauty brands, was on the verge of collapse.

It would not happen on Angus's watch. In fact, if he was on the hunt for a highlight, saving Remède from ruin would come close.

For, once upon a time, Louis Fournier had saved him.

Post-university, making waves as the youngest-ever junior partner in a whiz-bang upstart marketing firm, he'd met Louis at an industry night at which the older man had been a plus one.

They'd started up a conversation at the bar and found commonality in their disinterest in schmoozing and their love of French New Wave cinema.

The conversation had moved to the hotel lounge, leading to Angus missing the moment his team had won an award that night. Not that it had mattered. In the hour he'd spent with Louis he had already mentally moved on.

For Louis Fournier was the first man his senior who had seen straight through the cool veneer, the steely ambition, to the hunger beneath. The hunger to truly make a difference. And to show Angus that hunger had inherent value.

"Latte, Monsieur Fournier?" Lucinda asked, snapping Angus back to the present. "Milk, no sugar?"

"Oui. Merci."

Lucinda didn't need to ask for Angus's order. She knew how he liked his coffee, his steak, his calendar. She knew his shirt size, his in-seam measurements and his favourite underwear—having restocked the closet in his private bathroom many times over.

She also knew when to pass the team baton to Angus, to switch off the glamour and melt into the background.

When she returned a few minutes later, bringing the neat silver tray and comforting aroma of hot coffee into the room, Angus hid his smile behind his hand. He couldn't remember the last time Lucinda had brought him coffee rather than farming it out to an intern. The last time he'd asked if she'd be so kind, she'd laughed so hard he'd heard it even after she'd closed the door between them.

But Louis was old-school. The kind of gentlemen who would never enter a room before a woman, who smiled and nodded at every person who met his eye. And Lucinda had a huge soft spot for the man.

She placed Louis's elegant, heat-resistant, double-layered glass on the table at his elbow, alongside a plate of small French pastries.

"Ah," Louis said, eyes closing against the heavenly scent. *"Parfait."* Angus recognised his mug in an instant. She'd bought it for him for… Lent? The Queen's birthday? International Pirate Day? He'd lost track of the occasions once their gift-buying had become a blood sport.

He turned the mug. On one side it boasted his favourite Winston Churchill quote: *Success is not final, failure is not fatal; it is the courage to continue that counts.* The other side of the mug had a tacky photo of a penguin pushing another penguin off an ice shelf.

When he looked up, Lucinda was leaning over him, placing a smaller plate of pastries beside him. The frills trickling fussily down the front of her shirt weighed the fabric down, giving him a glimpse of white lace. The swell of female curves.

He tensed and looked up. Her eyes were on her work, a smile curving the glossy red of her lips. Definitely a new colour for her. It suited her. A great deal. So much so, he'd found himself staring. Considering.

Reminding himself this was Lucinda. His assistant. His right hand. His foundation. His conscience. The yin to his yang. The light to his dark. He could not do what he did without her.

Therefore, there was no staring at her lips. Or beyond the frills of her shirt. Or at any other part of her. No matter how inviting. No matter how lovely. Those were the rules he'd set himself from day one when he'd first seen her sitting outside Fitz's office waiting for an interview, foot tapping with nerves, the rest of her glowing with eagerness, charm and life.

Her eyes shifted to his.

"Appreciate it," he murmured.

"My pleasure," she replied, though the criss-cross of creases over her nose were back.

Damn it.

Angus schooled his features until he knew he appeared cool, unmoved, the very picture of ambivalence—an expression learned over many years at the feet of those who'd enjoyed it when he flinched.

It was an expression that had once made an intern cry. Not a deliberate move, but there you go. Lucinda, on the other hand, raised a single eyebrow. Slowly. As if she was bemused he was trying such a move on her.

"Need anything else?" she asked, under her breath.

I need you to stand up, he thought, his eyes starting to water with the effort not to stray. He wondered for a brief moment if Fitz's tank-like assistant Velma had a twin sister he could hire instead.

Lucinda righted herself—thank everything good and holy—her glossy dark hair swinging past her shoulders and showering him in the scent of her shampoo; coconut and lime, making him think of cocktails. Of holidays. Of Christmas parties. One in particular that he did his very best *not* to think about. Especially in the middle of important business meetings.

"Shall I leave you boys to it?" she asked, hip cocking, swinging her pencil-skirt-clad backside right into his eyeline.

Angus's gaze shot to the ceiling. Was that a spider's web on the light fixture?

"*Merci*, Lucinda," Louis said, saving Angus from having to answer. "You are not only an utter delight and a great beauty, with excellent taste in perfume, you can now add coffee angel to your list of super powers."

"And I shall."

"In fact, have you ever considered cosmetic modelling?"

Lucinda un-cocked her hip. "What's that, now?"

"Your skin is like satin, *cherie*."

"My *skin*?"

"Louis," said Angus, his voice a little gruff. "Are you making a move on my girl?"

At that Lucinda twisted and pinned Angus with a look he'd never seen before. Her eyes were wide, pink sweeping fast across her cheeks. Her mouth opened as if she was about to say something before she snapped it shut and turned slowly back to Louis.

"Monsieur Fournier, beneath the satiny veneer of my glorious Remède foundation is the lamentable skin of the mother of an eight-year-old who refuses to sleep past five in the morning."

Then she bent down and kissed the older man on the cheek.

"But you are sweet for pretending. Now, stop distracting me. I am an important person with important work to do." With that she stalked out of the room.

Both men followed with their eyes.

Louis broke the silence. "Never let that one go."

"Count on it," Angus promised, even if the amazing Velma did in fact have a nicer twin.

Then, putting all thoughts of red lips and white lace aside, Angus got to work.

For the next hour, and even after Louis had said his good-byes, Lucinda sat at her desk and vacillated between fuming and telling herself to stop being so ridiculously reactive.

But the moment Angus had said the words *"Are you*

making a move on my girl?" something had snapped inside her.

She wasn't usually so touchy. She knew it had been a joke. One she'd usually have played along with if it got the job done.

It was as if the conversation with Cat the night before had pried something loose. Then her earlier chat with Louis, in which he'd constantly joked about her being far too good for the likes of Angus, had further shifted whatever it was that now shook inside her.

The fact was, she was rattled. If she'd been in a mood like this at home she'd have found a way to distract herself while she got her head on straight. But, here, she couldn't hide behind her desk all afternoon.

She was a grown-up who'd been through plenty worse. So, instead of sending an intern to clean away the cups, she did her best to shake it off and headed into Angus's office.

"How'd it go?" she asked as she placed plates and coffee cups back onto the silver tray.

"As well as can be expected," said Angus from his leaning spot, sitting on the wide shelf that ran under the long window, legs stretched out before him, gaze caught on some paperwork he held in one hand. "He kept reiterating that he has faith in us. In me."

Words that would usually be music to Angus's ears, but she could tell from his tone that they hadn't been.

This, she thought, *is what I need to find my equilibrium again.*

Work talk. Pure, clear cut. Uncomplicated.

"But?" Lucinda said.

"He spent far more time talking about you. About how his perfume has never suited a woman more."

And with that his eyes lifted to hers.

With the sun behind him he was little more than a silhouette, but she felt the glance all the same. Felt it hit her eyes, before tracing the line of her cheek and landing on her mouth.

She wished she hadn't reapplied her lipstick as it suddenly felt too red. Too slick. And yet, conversely, as his gaze remained, she was also glad that she had.

Then he seemed to shake himself before he looked back down at the papers, lifted himself away from the window and tossed the papers onto his desk. "He also made it clear he believes that whatever I'm paying you it's not enough."

"He's right, of course."

"No doubt." Hands sliding into the pockets of his suit pants, he rounded the desk towards her, those long legs eating up the distance between them in three short strides. "But it was a distraction. I get the feeling things are worse than he's letting on."

And there she was, caught up in some throwaway line, while Louis was in actual trouble. Gripping the tray harder, Lucinda said, "Could you convince him to let Charlie weigh in on his financials? Say it's part of the service? No extra fee?"

Angus shook his head. "It was hard enough for him to come to me at all, and he could only do that by convincing himself he was doing me a favour."

"Would you like me to put it to him?"

She saw Angus allow himself a moment to consider the offer. She wished Cat could see him in such a moment. For all his genius, and his self-belief, he was always open to her opinion.

But then he shook his head. Which was wasn't uncommon either.

Yet, while any other time she'd have moved on, it turned out the rattle had not gone away. It trembled as she huffed out a breath filled with sudden frustration. "Seriously, I can sweet talk him into a meeting at least. I know I can."

"I'll handle it."

"Louis respects me. And likes me. But he also doesn't have to worry about keeping up appearances where I'm concerned. He won't fear that I will no longer look at him like he's my hero."

Angus shifted uncomfortably. "Leave it, Lucinda."

"But—"

"Enough." Angus ran a hand through his hair, giving the ends a tug.

Lucinda stilled. The only parts of her that moved were her shoulders, inching back, and her nostrils, flaring gently as she put the brakes on her temper. Barely.

Until his eyes once more snagged on hers.

"Was there something else?" he asked, slowly leaning back against his desk and folding his arms over his chest.

While he acted as if he hadn't just shut her down, as if they were in the middle of a regular conversation, the rattle inside her began to shiver and shake until it bumped against her ribs like a drumbeat. Like a call to arms.

"Actually, yes," she said before she even felt the words coming. "It's about this weekend."

"What about it?"

"My plans. I am going away with…" She stopped there. As if her words had smacked up against a stone wall. She ran her tongue over her bottom lip in an attempt to loosen them.

"Is this a guessing game?" Angus asked, his voice now edged with impatience. "You're going with… Catriona? The Easter Bunny? Elvis?"

And just like that the rattle stopped rattling. As if a storm inside her had stilled. And her voice was calm, even, as she looked her boss in the eye and said, "I'm going away with a man."

She watched Angus closely. As closely as one person could watch another. She noticed the flare of his nostrils.

The tightening of his jaw. The way the rest of his body went preternaturally still.

Then she did her very best not to read anything into it. To pretend she was simply an employee passing on a titbit of little interest to her boss.

"A man," Angus finally managed.

"Yes, *a man*. Not just any man," said Lucinda, the floodgates now wide open. "The man I've been seeing. For a few weeks now." Off and on. When he hadn't been called away to surgery. Or to phone calls with doctors in developing countries needing his advice *stat*. He was a doctor. Had she mentioned that?

"Sonny?" Angus asked, his voice a mite strained. But that part she understood. That part made her shoulders relax down away from her ears. Raised by a single mother himself, Angus took Sonny's welfare nearly as seriously as she did.

"Hasn't met him yet," she assured him. "But if this weekend goes well…"

Her boss blinked at her and said nothing. And now she couldn't get a read on him at all. Only the fact that he looked so utterly disinterested told her that he was trying too hard.

Which, in turn, brought the rattle back to life. With a vengeance.

"Would you like to know where we're going?"

There, a flicker below his right eye.

"A resort. Near Daylesford. Called Hanover House. It's gorgeous. Well, Cat says it's gorgeous. She did an article on it for a travel blog last year. Super-romantic."

His Adam's apple bobbed lightly before he said, "Sounds nice."

Nice. This from a man who put words together that took businesses from the verge of ruin to stratospheric.

From the outside, Lucinda was certain their conversation seemed reasonable. Polite, even. But she felt as if she was watching it unfold from another dimension. The air crackled between them, voices rippling, words they were steadfastly refusing to utter buffeting against them in steadily increasing waves.

"How about the man himself? Don't you want to ask who he is? What he does for a living? School grades? Parking tickets? How he votes? You're usually all over that kind of thing. Figuring people out. Putting them into neat boxes so you know how to deal with them."

A muscle twitched beneath his right eye.

What are you doing? a voice cried in the furthest recesses of her mind. *What do you want from him? Are you looking for a reaction? Are you baiting him to tell you, "no, you can't go"?*

Angus lifted a hand and ran it over his chin, then around behind his neck. "Lucinda," he said, "If you're thinking ahead to letting Sonny meet him, then he is no doubt the kind of man both Sonny *and* I should hero worship. Now, are we done?"

He glanced pointedly at the coffee cups on the tray. His eyebrows rose, as if to remind her what she should be doing with her time rather than nattering with him about her private life.

Wow. Harsh.

They clashed all the time. Telling it like it was was their dynamic. And it worked. In fact, they fed off it. She knew if she walked away things could settle. They always did after such electric, static-fuelled dust-ups.

But, rather than feeling invigorated, she felt twitchy, discomfited and strangely hollow.

She turned and walked towards the door, her feet numb, her face burning.

But when she reached the door she stopped, turned and gave Angus one last look. "One more thing," she said.

Angus breathed out hard. As if he was clinging to control by a fingernail. His voice was deep and tight as he said, "I think we've covered everything. You're going away. HR has signed off on it. It's done."

"Not about the weekend," she managed, even while storm clouds gathered about her head, lightning flashing with the darkness. "It's about today. When I asked if I might be given the chance to try to convince Louis to talk to Charlie about Remède's finances…"

She closed her eyes, shook her head and started afresh. "I get that you have the final word, that as your assistant it's my job to grease the wheels, keep you fed and watered so that you're able to perform at your best. But Angus?"

She waited, squeezing a breath into her tight lungs, as it took for ever for him to respond.

"Yes, Lucinda?"

"I'm not *your girl*."

With that she took his dirty plates and left.

CHAPTER THREE

I'M NOT YOUR GIRL.

Lucinda's words from earlier that day bounced off the inside of Angus's skull like echoes inside a bell tower.

He hadn't meant anything by it. She knew it, too. It wasn't like her to be so pedantic.

A voice that had emerged from the swampier parts of Angus's subconscious since he'd sat down at the bar around the corner from work said, *It's also not like her to go on a dirty weekend with some guy you've never heard of.*

A hand slapped down hard on Angus's shoulder, followed by Fitz's voice. "You look like hell."

Angus grabbed his cousin's fingers and pried them off his shoulder. "Appreciate it."

"I, on the other hand, am not sure how anyone survives a single day without getting a load of my handsome mug."

As he dragged out the stool next to Angus, Fitz caught the eye of the bartender, tapping Angus's drink and asking for one of the same. "So, what's the haps?"

"Does a man need a reason to have a drink with his favourite cousin?"

Fitz snorted. "Only cousin. And, yes, I don't think you've wasted a single minute in your entire adult life. Then there's the dark cloud hovering ominously over your head, and the fact your leg looks ready to take off…"

Angus looked down. His left leg was shaking so hard it all but crackled with excess energy. He stopped, only to find he couldn't, so gave up and let it jiggle for all it was worth.

"Did someone have a better idea than you at work?" Fitz asked.

Angus shot him a look.

"You're right. What was I thinking? So what? Designers no longer making suits? The cobblers of Spain all out of shoes? Lucinda mad at you?"

Before he could stop it, Angus felt a tightening around his left eye.

Fitz let go a long, high whistle between his teeth. "So, it's the lovely Lucinda who has you hunched melancholically over your scotch. Interesting. What did you do?"

"I didn't *do* anything."

Fitz snorted. "So what didn't you do? I know you didn't miss her birthday, what with the charming gift-a-palooza thing you have going between you. So what?" Fitz slammed a hand against his chest. "Was there another… *event*? Dare I say, Christmas party?"

A muscle flickered in Angus's jaw, while every other muscle in his body clenched. Hard. His glass paused before it hit his lips. When the liquid finally spilled down his throat, he relished the burn. "Nothing happened at that damn Christmas party, as I've told you a thousand times."

Yet, every time that night came up, something slippery and uncontrolled uncoiled within him.

"I could say the suspense is killing me, but the truth is I'm actually beginning to bore of—"

"Lucinda's gone and got herself a new man and they are going away together this weekend."

Fitz stilled, then burst into laughter. "That's it? That's why you look like your doctor just gave you bad news? Because Lucinda has a *boyfriend*?"

Angus shook his head. He had no better answer.

"Come on, mate. She's bright, bold and knows more

dirty jokes than any man I know. It's more of a mystery why she hasn't been snapped up already."

Angus gripped more tightly to his glass.

He'd thought about this—about why he was reacting the way he was. It wasn't the fact that she was seeing someone. Or even that she hadn't told him about it till now. He felt as if his tendons had frozen solid because she had never come close to introducing any man in her life to her son.

Well, his subconscious perked up and responded, *apart from you.*

That was different, he shot back.

The day he'd met Sonny he'd felt as if he'd been hit with a lightning bolt: this was his opportunity to be, for another kid, the kind of man he'd desperately needed in his own life at the same age. A man to encourage his curiosity, to welcome his boisterous side, teach him how to stand up for himself in the playground and to appreciate his mother.

When the day came that Lucinda introduced Sonny to a man in her life, the kid would be smart enough to understand what that meant. And, once that door was opened for Sonny, it could never fully be closed again.

It was his duty to make sure she realised how formative such a moment would be. To make sure, before she did anything she couldn't take back, that she was sure.

"The real question is," Fitz intoned, "why hasn't she nabbed herself a long-term fella? All she'd have to do is snap her fingers. The woman is smoking hot. Hair like a dark-chocolate waterfall. Skin like Italian marble. Those big, brown cow eyes that can see right into the depths of your deeply charred soul."

"You might want to tone it down."

"What? The smoking hot thing?" Fitz was clearly on a roll. "I'm not trying it on. It's an empirical fact. You must be aware that your assistant is as good as it gets.

Say it out loud so I know you are a human man: *Lucinda Starling is a glorious, gumptious, gorgeous specimen of womanhood*."

Angus took a long, slow sip of his drink, only to find he could no longer taste it.

Fitz tapped a finger against his lips. "No? Too busy drinking? Well, I'll say it—for a woman like that, every weekend ought to be a dirty weekend."

Angus turned to Fitz. Everything in him clenched, as if readying to take a swing.

By the glint in Fitz's eye, he knew it. Hell, he'd have welcomed it. As if it would prove a point. A point Angus had no intention of helping him make.

"Enough," Angus managed through gritted teeth. "You're talking about someone's mother."

At that, Fitz burst out laughing. He laughed until he had to grip the bar so as not to fall off his stool. "Man, you kill me. I gifted you so many other ways to defend her and *that's* where your mind went? I guess if a guy is in need of a bucket of iced water to toss over himself, that'll do it. Though, if the first thing you think of when you look at Lucinda is 'mother', then I worry for you and the future of our bloodline."

Angus flinched. As if their bloodline was anything to write home about.

His father had left when he'd been around Sonny's age. He still remembered the fight. The smash of glass. His mother's scream. The roar of the car engine and the squeal of tyres. And the relief, short-lived as it was…until the procession of men his mother had let into their lives as she'd searched for a way out of the poverty cycle in which she'd grown up. So she could give her son a different life. In the hope he'd be a better kind of man.

Fitz slid his phone out of the inner pocket of his jacket. "This guy of hers, who is he? Give me a name."

"I didn't ask."

Fitz blinked at Angus. "Your precious assistant told you she has a new man in her life and you didn't ask who he was? What he did for a living? What he ate for breakfast? How he voted? You, who creates mental portfolios of every person he ever meets in case the day comes you need to beat them in battle." Fitz clicked his fingers at the bartender. "Excuse me, good sir, did this gentleman ask you a slew of questions the moment he caught your eye?"

The bartender gave Angus a look. "No. I mean, kind of. We talked about uni. And which hospital I was born in. And that time I saw a UFO."

The bartender looked between them, suddenly rethinking his recent choices. Then he moved stealthily to the other end of the bar.

"What are you doing now?" Angus asked as Fitz continued typing madly into his phone.

"Messaging Cat."

"Lucinda's *sister*?" That was enough to snap Angus out of his funk, his senses coming back online with a crack. "How the hell do *you* have her number?"

Fitz shrugged. "We met at the work Christmas party we're not allowed to talk about. You drank your feelings. Lucinda wore that insanely hot green dress. Ring a bell?"

Too many.

Such as the large boardroom emptied of furniture. Cocktail tables laden with buckets of champagne. Walls dripping in sparkling lights and silver stars. Loud chatter and laughter.

In his mind's eye the crowd parted, which surely had not happened. And there, in the breach, Lucinda. A bare-armed, long-legged vision in a spring-green dress. Dark hair down and curled seductively over one creamy shoulder. Lips a slippery red.

He remembered blinking, as if the view had been too bright to believe. That dress, made from some witch-designed material that shifted and shimmered over her waist, her hips, her…everything as she walked. As she breathed.

Until she'd caught his eye, a smile like no other stretching across her lovely face.

Fitz broke in. "Turns out Cat had just written an article about female Viagra for some women's magazine. One thing led to another and…we hooked up. Before you go all Hulk on me, it was one time. She decided pretty quickly that, while I'm a tiger in the sack, I'm not nearly good enough for her. We've been friendly ever since."

Angus sank his head into his hand. His scoundrel of a cousin and Lucinda's terrifying sister had been "friendly" for over a year. Did Lucinda know? Did he want to be the one to tell her?

Fitz clicked his fingers at his phone. "Here we go. Cat said she's met him and he's awesome."

"Met who?"

"Lucinda's fella," said Fitz. Slowly. "Jameson Bancroft-Smythe."

"That's his name?"

"Every bit of it. Now, let the cyber-stalking begin. Okay, we have a skateboarder from Sydney. Looks about fourteen. A guy with about a hundred great-grandchildren. And…whoa. You need to see this."

I really don't, Angus thought, training his gaze to stare into the melting ice in his glass.

"Man, I'm sorry to tell you this, but the dude looks like Robert Redford."

"Now?"

"Uh…no. I'm thinking circa *The Way We Were*. Maybe even *Barefoot in the Park*."

Fitz held out his phone and Angus looked. *Whoa.*

"*Dr* Jameson Bancroft-Smythe," Fitz read. "Born in The Netherlands. Educated in London. Worked for Doctors Without Borders. Now head of Paediatric Surgery at Princess Elizabeth Hospital. And…there!"

Fitz held the phone under Angus's nose so he had no choice but to look.

And there he was—Robert Redford's doppelganger—decked out in a well-cut tux, surrounded by people in benefit black, including one Lucinda Starling who stood at his side, grinning from ear to ear, champagne flute clutched in both hands, Dr Jameson Bancroft-Smythe's hand resting possessively on her lower back.

Angus must have made a noise, as Fitz murmured, "Hmm?"

Though Fitz was already distracted by a pretty blonde making eyes at him at the end of the bar. His barstool scraped against the floor as he pushed it away. "Now, I've gotta go see a blonde about a phone number. Promise you won't do anything exciting till I get back?"

"Exciting?" Angus mumbled.

"Change company by-laws to insist upon seven-day working weeks. Dance on the bar. Track the good doctor down and declare pistols at dawn. Call Luc and make up some excuse as to why she has to work this weekend with you instead."

"Promise."

Fitz grinned then headed off.

While Angus leant his head into his palms, pressing hard into his eye sockets.

Because this slippery feeling in his belly, this discontent, wasn't him. Not since he'd been a scared kid who had no idea where he'd be sleeping or who he and his mum might be living with from one week to the next. Controlling his environment, or how he responded to it at the very least, was at the core of how he interacted with the world.

He was so good at it he'd made it his living, controlling how people responded to a brand by how it was packaged.

Maybe there is something in that, he thought as he lifted his head out of his hands.

In honing, in his own mind, the core promise of the Lucinda Starling brand.

He started at the beginning—the day they'd met.

Several years back she, along with a couple of dozen men and women, had come into the Big Picture Group offices to interview for a spot in the office pool.

The place had smelled like fresh paint. Half the furniture had yet to arrive. He, Fitz and Charlie had been up to their eyeballs in debt and they'd just had their first big win—a client whose rebrand had gone beyond viral. In order to keep the momentum going they'd decided to recruit: hungry, sharp, lateral thinkers who could help them take their business intergalactic.

Fitz had sent his assistant Velma to eyeball the line-up of hopefuls and weed out the chaff. Not that it had stopped Angus and Fitz from taking a peek, putting down bets as to which had faked their résumés, which would keep up with Fitz's famously twisty interviews, which would flounder and which might become a part of the Big Picture family.

To a one the interviewees had been a study in edgy, sleek, über-cool university graduates in a range of grey, white and black, prepared to claw one another's eyes out for a place in the booming start-up.

And then there'd been Lucinda.

She'd been wearing a whimsical floral dress, her dark waves of hair tumbling over her shoulders, her big, brown eyes wide with excitement, her toes wriggling in the ends of her summery high heels as she chatted brightly to a severe-looking girl who looked part-Dementor sitting beside her. She'd been like a sunflower among a field of thistles.

"Check out Snow White," Fitz had said. "A blue bird might land on her finger at any moment, right before she breaks into song."

Angus had laughed, as he'd been meant to do, but all

the while he hadn't been able to take his eyes off her. The way she'd charmed the people either side of her, making them relax, sit back in their chairs and laugh—even as they were all going for the same job.

For all that he'd been dubbed a wunderkind, the "people" side of things let Angus down. He struggled with levity. Small talk. Building client relationships. If his job had entailed no human interaction, it would have been perfect.

As such he had little need for someone with an honours degree and a well-curated LinkedIn profile. What he needed was softness. Laughter. Light. Warmth. What he needed was a sidekick who could make the clients loosen up and agree to do as they were told.

Very few times in his life had a clench in his gut meant something good. But this was one of them.

His message to Velma had read: *Dibs on Snow White.*

They hadn't had the easiest of starts. He wasn't proud of the moment he'd found out she was a single mum with a toddler at home. He'd reconsidered. For a week or two. Before giving her something his mother had rarely had—a real chance.

And, without the education or experience to fall back on, she'd made mistakes. Plenty of them. But she'd owned up to them. And had always endeavoured to do better next time. In Angus's book, when it came to people, that was about as good as it got.

For several years now, in his mind, Lucinda's "brand" had been his not-so-secret weapon. His counterpoint. The best decision he'd made as far back as he cared to remember.

But she was right. She wasn't *his girl.*

She was, by the look of things, someone else's. Some stranger by the name of Jameson Something-Or-Other-Smythe. The man taking her away to some romantic resort he'd never heard of.

Hand moving of its own accord, it reached into his

jacket pocket and pulled out his phone. With the barest sense of masochism, Angus said the words *Hanover House*—the name of the place Lucinda said she'd be staying.

Like a man slowing at the site of a car crash, he squinted as he flicked through the pictures—all misty vistas, glittery cocktails and flickering fireplaces, award-winning spa, business centre…

His thumb hovered over the screen as he processed the information looking back at him.

Then he looked up, into the middle distance, a tingly feeling at the back of his head telling him to swipe the page away and forget about what he'd just seen.

Another feeling—deeper, grittier, louder—told him to follow his gut.

Lucinda was as key to the future growth of the business as she had been to its past. The business that was now so tightly intertwined with Angus's very identity they could no longer be separated.

If Lucinda was considering introducing this man to Sonny, it had to be serious. Meaning everything was about to change.

And, for Angus, change was a four letter word.

He'd worked too hard, sacrificed too much—time, relationships—to create the life he lived. To ensure the success of the business. To show those who'd told him he'd never amount to anything how wrong they were.

He was about to find out just how far he'd go to protect that.

He glanced back at the phone and drilled in.

A few minutes later, Angus slowly slipped the phone back into his pocket then pushed his stool away from the bar.

He slammed a hand down on Fitz's shoulder as he passed, smiling for the first time in hours as Fitz flinched. "I'm off."

Fitz blinked. "And looking far more like yourself, I must say."

He had an actionable strategy now. So round and whole and complete in his head, he was shocked he hadn't thought of it sooner.

"Crisis over?" Fitz asked.

"No crisis," Angus said, offering the blonde a polite smile. "I don't do crises."

"He's kidding," Fitz demurred. "Crises are his bread and butter. Superhero complex, this one." Then to Angus he said, "Fun and games aside, if any one of us poor slobs deserves love and valentine hearts and eternal happiness, it's Lucinda. Am I right?"

"Rarely," Angus allowed, even as his mind was already ticking away in other directions. Then to the blonde he said, "Be gentle with this one. He's my favourite cousin."

"Only cousin," Fitz called as Angus strode purposefully out of the bar.

That Thursday, Lucinda wriggled her toes in her shoes as she stood waiting for the lift to take her back up to the office, the final minutes of her long-overdue lunch break ticking down.

It had been a huge working week.

The day after Lucinda had told Angus about her upcoming weekend, he'd come into work like a man possessed: snapping up three huge new clients and committing to insane deadlines on top of the Remède rebrand, which was due to be pitched to Louis Fournier and his board early the next week.

Lucinda felt breathless and stretched, like she couldn't stop, even for a second, or it would all collapse on top of her. It was the best natural high she knew.

The lift doors opened and she slipped inside.

Work had been great, but things between her and Angus? They'd been…odd.

Fitz often lamented she and Angus were like four-year-olds on the playground the way they kissed and made up after their feisty skirmishes as if nothing had happened.

Not that they *kissed*. Ever. Not even close. Well, there was that one time something *might* have happened. But it hadn't.

Lucinda shook her head. Hard. The point was, Angus had been weirdly polite. She'd even caught him whistling.

"What did you expect?" she muttered to her wavering reflection in the lift doors.

Well, her subconscious muttered back, *you expected him to be grumpy. Like a bear with a sore tooth. As if the fact that you were heading off on a weekend away with another man might matter. Might burn.*

The lift binged and she pressed the button for the Big Picture Group offices, waving to the receptionists, who happily waved back.

She took a left and strode down the long hall to her desk, which sat like a castle keep protecting Angus's office which took up the entire far corner of the second-to-top floor of the city building.

Once there, she tucked her shopping bag under her desk so that no one could see the distinctive label before she sat in her chair. Then she gave the bag an extra little shove with her toe.

She'd hadn't gone out with the express decision to shop, but when she'd walked past the slinky, black negligée in the store window a little voice in the back of her mind had told her that perhaps she ought to be making a bit more of an effort for bedtime than packing an old T-shirt, stretched-out yoga tights and her ancient tasselled pashmina.

A surreptitious glance through the smoky glass into Angus's office found him in the exact same position in which she'd left him—sitting back in his big, cushy office chair, easy smile on his face, hands moving elegantly through the air as he wooed some client on the phone.

Lucinda shifted on her seat as she felt the low-level hum that came to life inside her whenever she focussed on Angus for too long.

Her phone rang and she reached for it gladly, answering, "Jameson. Hi."

"Hey."

A busy man, he wasn't one to bother with endless small talk. It was one of the things she liked about him. His directness. The way he said what he meant and meant what he said. Not the fact that he was busy. Though, as a working mum, the fact that he didn't put much of a claim on her time *was* a bonus.

"All good to go?" she asked. As one of the top doctors in the city he was constantly on call. They'd barely made it through a whole date without him having to dash off to save an organ. Or a village.

"Good to go. You? Packed and ready?"

"Not even close! But I will be by seven tomorrow morning."

"I'll pick you up then." A pause, then, "I'm glad the fates have aligned and we are finally able to do this, Cindy."

Her nose twitched at the nickname. Not a favourite. Which was why Angus had told Louis Fournier to use it. The cad. She'd tell Jameson another time, when they knew one another a little better. And how they'd laugh!

She meant it when she said, "Me too."

"Until tomorrow," he said.

"Tomorrow."

When he hung up, Lucinda slid her phone back onto her desk with a sigh.

Jameson Bancroft-Smythe really was one of the good ones. He was kind, considerate, attentive—when he wasn't rushing off to tend to some major medical emergency or another.

He'd never once pushed her to go any faster than she was ready for, which she appreciated. Most of the time. Other times she wished he'd look at her in a way that told her he'd like to tear her clothes off and have his way with her then and there.

It had been a long time since a man had looked at her that way. In fact, she could count back to the actual day. It had happened at a certain Christmas party a year and a bit ago.

Lucinda closed her eyes tight, shoving the memory deep down into her memory banks.

Her smart watch buzzed against her wrist. Another gift from Angus—for her birthday this time. The leather band was her exact favourite tone of spring-green.

It was an hour till she was clocking off. A rare early mark on a Thursday afternoon. Her desk was tidy. Angus's calendar was up to date. Every one of her favourite 2B pencils was sharpened to a weapon-grade point.

"Lucinda."

Lucinda all but leapt out of her skin at the sound of Angus's voice. She was usually far more attuned to his movements. Not hard when the air all but shifted to make way for him as he moved.

When she turned to him, she found him staring under her desk, his gaze caught on the shopping bag.

Turned out, in attempting to poke it deeper under her desk, she'd knocked it over. The *Foxy Lady* logo was all too obvious on the sparkly hot-pink bag, its slippery black contents having spilled out of the tissue wrap and onto the floor.

"Oh, good Thor," Lucinda muttered, leaning down to shove the lot back in the bag.

When she looked up, she expected to see Angus smiling beatifically as he had been all week. But his jaw was tight, his eyes unusually dark. When his gaze lifted to hers, her heart knocked about behind her ribs.

His voice was no more than a rumble as he said, "I have some bad news."

"Oh?"

"It's about this weekend."

Angus's words took a moment to register, said as they were in a deep, rough voice that sent trickles of heat down her spine.

"I'm sorry, what?"

"This weekend. I know its last minute, but a conference opportunity has come into play. I need you and your 2B pencils there with me."

And just like that the trickle of heat turned into an inferno, sliding into her belly and radiating out to the ends of her extremities. No, no, no, no, no!

With tingling fingertips, Lucinda pushed back her chair, shoved her handbag over her arm, rummaged under her desk for the *Foxy Lady* bag and gripped the handle tightly in her fist. "Not happening. I'm on holiday. As of right now." Well, an hour from now, but a girl had to do what a girl had to do. "Take someone else. They can even use my pencils."

Lucinda looked at the jar filled with freshly sharpened nibs and felt a small jolt of disloyalty.

Until Angus said, "It's for Remède."

And just like that the raging inferno of self-will turned to ash.

Any other account and she'd have told him to suck it. But Remède?

For, just as Louis Fournier meant a great deal to Angus, the Remède brand meant so much to Lucinda. Her father had bought her mother a bottle of Remède's Someday perfume every year for Christmas.

She continued to keep a bottle nearby, rarely wearing it but liking the fact that she could open it up every now and then, dip her toes into the past and bring up so many more lovely memories of her parents long after they were gone.

And now that she'd met Louis Fournier her love for the brand was even more personal.

She knew how precarious things were with Remède. She'd been in the room that morning when Angus, Fitz and Charlie had called a special partners-only meeting to address the fact that even a successful rebrand might not be enough to save the company.

"Where is it? The conference?" she asked through gritted teeth.

Angus glanced past her a moment. "You won't believe me if I tell you."

She barely believed him as it was.

"It's at Hanover House."

Her eyes whooshed to his so fast they nearly rolled back in her head. "You have to be kidding me."

Angus shook his head. Slowly. Hypnotically. And she'd never before felt a stronger urge to smack him.

She barely managed to grit out the word, "How…?"

"Curious as to where you were heading, I looked up the place online. When I stumbled onto the business centre page, there it was. A conference the likes of which we've never attended before. A conference that may be just the thing we need."

Lucinda hardly heard the last words over the sound of her heart rattling around in her chest. All week long he'd acted as if he hadn't even remembered her telling him she was going away, yet he'd remembered the name of the resort. And he'd looked it up.

"You were there, Luc. In the Remède meeting. Things aren't looking good."

"With the company, yes. But that's why he came to us. Your rebrand, the social media, the print ads, the website—Angus, it's all gorgeous." The campaign was lush, elegant and aspirational while using hip, young influencers in an attempt to draw a younger, fresher audience to the brand. "It's some of the best work you've ever done. And it's launching next week. Surely there's nothing more that can be done."

He held her gaze a moment, then a few more, till she found herself drowning in the dark hazel depths. Then his gaze dropped to the bag in her hand. The bag they both knew contained a sexy black negligée.

Angus cleared his throat. "Forget it. I shouldn't have asked. I'll be fine. I can function without you."

She felt every strand of the cord handle in her tight palm, hoping her bravado covered up the fact that Angus had unwittingly just poked her greatest fear: that she was inherently dispensable. Her ex had certainly thought so. Not even their beautiful boy enough to keep him around.

Angus said, "Velma can organise a temp."

Before she even felt the words welling up in her throat, Lucinda countered with, "No. Don't."

And for a second, a flash, a smile lit up his face, one that made her knees turn to jelly and her head come over all woozy. She shook her head. Cleared the cobwebs. Made plans.

Okay. With the Remède relaunch imminent she'd never forgive herself if she didn't do all she could to help.

But this weekend was important. If it went well, if she and Jameson had the time and space to see if there was a spark amongst the rapport, it could change everything. For her and for Sonny.

Despite the little glitch in self-confidence as Angus had blithely claimed he could function without her, she knew she was not defined by the moment her ex-husband had left without a second glance. She was defined by decisions she had made since—raising a fantastic, healthy, loving kid and being the best damn executive assistant in town.

"I can do both," she said.

"Hmm?"

"I can have my weekend and I can help you out when you need me at the conference. That's it. That's the deal I'm willing to make."

While Angus considered, Lucinda held her ground. She imagined running from Jameson to Angus, Angus to Jameson, and felt a little ill. But it was what it was. She only hoped he didn't come back with a counter offer, as deep down in places she preferred not to visit she knew if he asked her to choose there was a good chance she'd choose him.

Then Angus nodded once. And Lucinda turned on her heels and walked away before he could change his mind. Or she changed hers.

Over her shoulder she called, "Have someone flip me the conference details."

"Will do," he called back. Then, "Until tomorrow," mirroring Jameson's exact words.

Until tomorrow, Lucinda repeated in her head. Wondering if two such innocent words had ever felt so ominous.

CHAPTER FOUR

WHAT THE HELL were you thinking?

Angus stood at the edge of the foyer of Hanover House's business centre, peering into its conference room to find women as far as the eye could see.

But no Lucinda.

He'd asked an unimpressed Velma to forward her the itinerary. And had heard nothing since. Forcing him to wonder if she was still on her way to the hotel, or if she'd arrived the night before. Alone. Or with Jameson Whatsit-Whatever…

"Hey, honey. You looking for your wife?"

Angus turned to find an older woman with a gravity-defying silver coif, a skirt suit so pink it burned his retinas and a name badge boasting a bright yellow gerbera and the words *South Victorian Regional Beauticians' Organisation* written thereon.

A conference dedicated to cosmetics happening in *this* hotel, *this* weekend, had felt like a sign, right when he was struggling with the Remède account and Lucinda's announcement. Now faced with the reality—booths draped in gauze and lace and velvet, tables covered with bottles and tubs and tubes, signs promising a life of no frizz, spot-free skin and youthful nails—he wondered what the hell he'd been thinking.

For a moment he considered going along with the woman's assumption, jumping in his car, heading back to Melbourne and leaving the future to fate. But in his experience fate was a mischievous, interfering dirt bag who made a habit of putting hardship in the way of good people.

Angus held out his hand. "Angus Wolfe, conference attendee."

The woman's eyes widened to the size of ten-cent pieces before she gathered herself ably. "Elena Zager, conference organiser."

She held out her hand for a shake. Or a kiss. Angus went with a shake and a slight bow, which went down just fine.

"Well, aren't you going to be a cat amongst the pigeons? Shake things up a little. Just what this conference of ours needs."

Soon, two other women approached. One had long, red dreadlocks down to her waist and what looked like henna tattoos winding from her neck to her wrists. The other was small—even in her sharp-as-a-blade black heels— and bone-thin with straight black hair that stopped a knife's edge before her chin.

Each wore badges showcasing their business names and how many years they'd attended the conference. Both looked him at him as if he was a hot lunch.

"Ladies," said Elena. "This here is Angus Wolfe. He's here to attend our little shindig."

"Happy day," said Ms Henna.

"Amen," purred Ms Black Heels.

Angus gave them each a smile, wondering how long it might take for Lucinda to swoop in and do the peopling for him so he could get to work. For, if they were going to save Remède, they would need more than the best branding revamp he'd ever pulled off—they would need a miracle.

Yet he had quipped that he could function without her so…"Not sure if you can tell," he said, "But I'm a first timer. I'd be grateful if someone could show me the ropes."

Elena muscled her way forward when it looked as though Ms Black Heels was about to leap in. "Mr Wolfe, I'm the president of this fine organisation, so I will make it my mission to take care of you this weekend. Let's go find your name tag and a map and then you can tell me what brings a tall drink of water like yourself into our oestrogen-laden midst."

After one last glance over his shoulder in the hope Lucinda would appear, Angus held out an elbow and Elena sneaked a possessive hand into the crook. "Let's do it."

Lucinda lay back on the sumptuous bed in her king suite with its glorious mound of velvety soft pillows on luxurious sheets.

Only problem was, she lay there alone.

For, when she'd rung Jameson late the night before to explain the turn of events, he'd been…fine. So fine he'd suggested they simply postpone. And, while she'd told him he was a saint and a gentleman and a star, in the back of her head she felt more than a little wounded.

She hadn't expected Sir Galahad but she'd have liked him to put up a little fight.

Maybe he was purloining mood-suppressors from the pharmacy at work.

Or maybe… She closed her eyes and shook her head but it wasn't enough to stop the little doubt demon from finding a way in.

Maybe she was effortlessly dispensable after all. As always, the sentiment made her flinch like the fast, shallow bite of a paper cut.

But maybe it was simpler than all that. Maybe she'd built this weekend up into something bigger than it was.

She *liked* Jameson. He was good and kind and handsome and successful. He didn't press claims on her time. He was easy to be around. He was comfortable.

He was the kind of man she'd be happy to have in her

son's life. Sonny was of an age where he noticed how many people in his life loved him. Where he needed a father figure.

He has Angus, a little voice piped up in the back of her head.

And he did. Sonny adored Angus. And Angus adored Sonny. They wrestled. They had a secret handshake Sonny flat out refused to share with her. And Angus always got Sonny the wildest presents for his birthday and Christmas. And just because. Volcano kits, Nerf guns, two hours with a reptile handler—things Lucinda would never consider as they were too messy or dangerous.

But, for all that she allowed herself the occasional fantasy of imagining how it might be if that was her life—for real, every day, every night—it was just that. A fantasy.

She and Angus were friends. Real friends. They bickered, they forgave, they had in jokes, they felt comfortable in their silences. They'd developed a shorthand, a trust.

But a romance? No.

Not least of all because it would change everything at work. Unlike the wild west that was single parenting, and the absolute quagmire of dating, work was the one part of her life in which she felt secure, in control.

But also because Angus wasn't a "for ever" kind of guy. Too many ghosts. Too many walls. If they tried and failed Sonny would never understand. Sonny loved Angus so much she quietly worried that he'd take Angus's side.

So for all that Angus had the ability to make her shimmer, writhe and yearn with a simple look—more than any other man, including the good doctor, had ever come close to—she had to shove it all down deep, deep, deep inside.

Growling out loud, she dragged herself to sitting, the bed so big she had to wriggle her way to the end before she landed on her feet.

Either way, no romance for her this weekend. Just work. She'd do it and she'd do it well.

Still, the thought of having to go out there, find Angus and tell him Jameson had happily told her to go ahead without him was crushing.

She glanced at her watch.

Assuming Angus had made it inside the business centre doors for the Market Stall Day, he'd have been there a good hour by now. On *his* own. At the South Victorian Regional Beauticians' Organisation Bi-Annual Conference. Without her to run interference. To look after the small talk. To be his bodyguard.

Meaning he'd have to talk, listen and engage with what she imagined would be a couple of hundred women in excitable first-day-of-conference mode as they talked about make-up.

Let him see how it felt to function without her.

The thought of it made her feel a little bit better.

Based on the bones of a one-hundred-and-fifty-year-old mansion, Hanover House's sprawling extensions touted a perfect mix of country comfort and purposeful elegance.

After getting lost—twice—in search of the meeting place Angus had texted to her, she was in desperate need of a strong coffee when she saw the gilt sign reading Bean and Brew Bistro.

The cosy booths were already taken and a bunch of boisterously loud women sat huddled around a few tables that had been pressed together.

Lucinda moved to the counter to order as she waited for Angus.

A voice—an all too familiar male voice—rumbled behind her. "And then Fitz tried to convince us it was his date's stay-fast lipstick. But, as any who visited Maude's booth this morning will know, the only way it would be on his mouth was if he put it there himself!"

A cacophony of feminine laughter followed.

Slowly, so slowly she could all but see the dust motes

floating around her head, Lucinda turned as someone, presumably Maude, said, "Exactly! It's the lack of wax that makes all the difference."

And, as if a ray of sun had poured through a gap in a cloud, Lucinda spotted a head of curly dark hair amongst the flock of female heads. Shoulders of Adonis. A blue suit she herself had made sure was back from the cleaners the day before because he'd needed it for that weekend. And it hit her. That meant he'd known about the conference days ago.

Before she even felt her feet moving, Lucinda was at the table. "Angus?"

As one, the women looked her way, each of them sporting a look somewhere between curiosity and suspicion.

Then her boss turned, his gaze landing lazily on hers. "Lucinda, hi. Nice of you to join us."

Don't you "Lucinda, hi" me, you self-serving, stubborn, interfering...

When Angus realised that she was struggling to speak, he glanced back at his flock of fans. "Everyone, this is Lucinda, my executive assistant extraordinaire."

She gave them a group smile, even as her skin felt as if it was stretched so tight over her face it was about to snap.

As one, the group exhaled. And then the questions came her way, thick and fast. "Oh, she does look smart. You never said she was so pretty! Is that your natural hair colour? It's gorgeous. Maybe a little dry. Have you tried a deep condition? Max-hydration would help too. Here's my card. But your skin! It's like a baby's bottom. What do you use?"

The talking suddenly stopped, the entire group waiting for answers.

"Oh. Uh…" she said. "Yes, it's my natural hair colour. Um…sure. Max-hydration sounds smart." Once she found out what max-hydration entailed. "And…goat's milk soap and water."

A collective gasp went around the table like a Mexican wave. Was that good? Bad? Ought she to be concerned?

Before anyone had the chance to tug her deeper down the rabbit hole, Lucinda planted a hand on Angus's shoulder, her thumb digging into the tendon between neck and shoulder, the place she knew he sent all his tension when the ideas didn't flow as fast as usual.

"Sorry ladies," she said. "Do you mind if I borrow him for a second? Boring work stuff."

Angus slowly pushed back his chair and sent the table a smile that had them all melting into puddles before holding out an arm and ushering Lucinda out of the café with a subtle roll of his shoulder as he went.

Finding they couldn't go ten feet without someone saying, "Hi Angus." "Having fun, Angus?" "See you soon, Angus.", Lucinda grabbed Angus by the arm of his suit and dragged him out of the bistro, around the corner and behind a lush, eight-foot-tall, fiddle-leaf fig tree that had been planted in a pot big enough to hide in.

He looked at a big broad leaf curling over his shoulder, then at her, one eyebrow lifting.

"Put that eyebrow back down. I'm the one who should be giving you the single-eyebrow-lift treatment. Angus, I am so angry with you right now I can't even… How long ago did you know about this conference? Days, right? It didn't occur to you it might have made my life easier if you'd let me know earlier? Or were you afraid if you gave me too much time I'd organise that temp for you after all?"

"The short answer: yes."

Oh. Okay then.

"Right. Next time you might want to give me a little more credit. Okay?"

When Angus had no response, she looked up to find him staring at her poodle sweater. Not a sweater made of poodles but black, knit, fitted, with a silver poodle motif on the front.

That plus skinny jeans and knee-high boots was miles from her usual uniform of pencil skirts and fancy tops, sleek hair that took far too long to do in the mornings and high heels that made the balls of her feet ache by the end of the day. The pains of looking professional. Indomitable. Indispensable.

But when Jameson had blithely agreed to postpone it hadn't occurred to her to repack until it had been too late, leaving her with a choice of outfits she'd now spend the weekend regretting. Especially if Angus kept looking at her the way he was now.

When Angus still hadn't blinked, she glanced down to realise he *wasn't*, in fact, looking at her poodle sweater — his gaze had snagged on the small, gold ladybird charm resting warm against the dip in her collarbone.

The one Angus had gifted her the first Christmas they'd begun working together.

Not long before, she'd told him the story of how Sonny's first sighting of a ladybird—the delight, the wonder, the utter joy—had been a turning point for her after her husband had left. How that day she'd known she could do it. Be a single mum. Raise a happy, kind, curious boy.

It was the gift that had started it all.

It hadn't occurred to her to leave it behind this weekend. To replace it with something less...*his*.

Feeling like Alice about to fall through the rabbit hole, she shook herself back to the present.

Then clicked her fingers in front of Angus's face to snag his full attention. "Angus. Eyes up."

He blinked, his jaw clenching for half a second before his expression cooled. His hands slid into the pockets of his suit pants, all ease and nonchalance.

"Where were you this morning?" he asked. His voice came out low, with the intimacy demanded of being shuttered behind the fronds of an over-sized house plant.

"Checking in," she said. "Settling in. As one would normally do when on holiday. Which I am. I checked the itinerary and figured you wouldn't need me for this morning's market stalls." She glanced in the direction of the bistro. "Seems I was right."

Not rising to the bait, Angus instead asked, "Where's what's-his-name?"

And her gaze slid right back to his. Still not settled on the least embarrassing way to tell him that what's-his-name had stayed home, she said, "You know what his name is."

The jaw clench was back. So maybe he wasn't as cool and nonchalant as he was making out.

But maybe it had nothing to do with her situation. Angus wasn't overly fond of crowds. Or people in general. Situations such as these were when he needed her most.

And, if the fact that that made her feel all warm and fuzzy wasn't a sign that she needed to be hit over the head with a frying pan, she didn't know what was.

This was her moment to let him know he could relax, that she was at his beck and call for the weekend. But some small part of her, possibly the part that had been rattling around in her chest the past few days, stopped her.

"Don't worry about Jameson, okay? He's a big boy. He can take care of himself."

At that, Angus's jaw clenched so hard he looked as if he might break a tooth. Meaning it wasn't the crowds that had made him so tense. Lucinda slowed her breathing and tried not to spin stories in her head.

"How did this morning go?" she asked, moving carefully into work mode.

"Good. How's your room?" he asked, his voice a little rough.

"Lovely. Yours?"

"Adequate."

"Just adequate? Who booked it? Velma?" Lucinda's

mouth twitched at the thought of Velma muttering away at having do work for anyone but Fitz, thus booking a broom closet when he'd be expecting a suite. "Look at you, making friends all over the place this week."

"Mmm. Look, can we find somewhere private? Quiet? I need to unload everything I saw this morning. And there's a lot to unload."

Angus ran a hand up the back of his head and shifted from foot to foot, bringing him deeper into her personal space. There wasn't all that much room behind the plant, as it turned out.

Lucinda pressed her back against the wall. "Can't get much more private than this."

"And yet, it's not what I had in mind." His eyes snagged on hers, all hazel and gorgeous, before sliding off to the side, allowing her the chance to breathe out.

"Okay. I'm fairly sure the French doors in my room lead to a small balcony, table and chairs." She remembered a moment too late he was expecting her to have her lover hiding in there. "But no. Not there. It's…um…too cold to work outdoors."

"Lucinda," Angus said, his voice deep, low, raw. "I know this is awkward. But I didn't come here to cramp your style."

"Whatever," she said, holding out a hand, only to find it hovering mighty close to his chest. Close enough she could feel the shift in the air as he breathed. "If it can help Louis, then it's fine."

It wasn't even close to fine.

Angus nodded. She could see the question in his eyes. But she found herself in a rare moment of having no clue what it meant or what to do with it. She only hoped he couldn't see the prevarication in hers.

"Good," he said, deciding to take her words at face value. "Because, while I had hoped that coming here might reiterate that our rebranding was right on track, after this morning I'm more confused than ever."

"How so?"

"I don't know," he said, his voice dropping, the sound scraping against her insides like sandpaper. "It's just… I've got this itch between my shoulder blades. Like we're close, but one wrong step and it will implode faster than we can clean it up."

Lucinda swallowed.

Angus noticed. His gaze on her throat, he said, "It was the strangest thing. When the conference appeared on the hotel website, it felt like I had to be here. Like I'd regret it if I didn't come. It felt like fate."

"First you asked Velma to book you into a conference, then you admitted you're not perfect. And now you're talking about fate? Who are you and what have you done with my Angus?"

Angus's eyes lifted back to hers.

What? Wait! No. My *boss*. She'd meant to say *my boss*.

Too late now. The air around them seemed to shift and shimmer as the words vibrated between them like a plucked wire. It put his "my girl" quip from the other day in the shade.

Feeling as if the small space behind the plant was about to run out of air, Lucinda said, "Anyway, let's go. We can do this. We'll find a room somewhere. I've got my notebook and pencils. You can give it to me there. Your ideas, I mean. Thoughts from this morning."

Stop talking now and get the heck out of here!

When Angus made no move to follow, Lucinda gave him a little shove, the feel of him—all hard, warm planes beneath his suit shirt—searing her palms. "Move."

He stepped away a smidge. Holding her breath, she slipped past the warmth of his body, ignoring as best she could the tingle of goose bumps popping up like burn blisters all over her body.

We'll find a room—and you can give it to me there?
her subconscious mocked.

If only she'd had her actual weekend date with her, the
one with whom she'd been hoping to summon up a spark,
that line could have gone down a treat!

Angus decided to stay for a moment, hand against the
wall, eyes closed as he packed away myriad conflicting
thoughts, revelations and sensations that had bombarded
him as he'd found himself sharing four square feet of
space behind a plant with Lucinda.

What the hell had just happened?

From the moment he'd seen his ladybird charm nestled
in the V of her top, the air around them had crackled with
electricity, with history, with possibility.

And now, despite his protestations to the contrary, seeing her in that playful little sweater, jeans that fit way
too well for comfort, her hair held back by a ribbon that
looked as if it would fall open with the slightest tug, in
rare flat shoes that brought the top of her head just to his
chin, the perfect height to tuck her in tight, his reasons
for being there at all felt decidedly muddied.

Was he there to work, making the most of a rare grass-
roots insight into the beauty business to shore up the
Remède rebrand?

Was he there to protect Sonny? To make sure Lucinda
didn't jump the gun on bringing him into any new relationship?

Was he there to protect his business? To do what had
to be done to secure the life he'd worked hard to build?

Or had the "superhero complex" Fitz insisted he harboured sent him there to look out for Lucinda? To make
sure this man of hers was good enough? Though any man
would be hard pressed to live up to that claim.

He knew why Lucinda was there, of course. In her
lovely room with French doors and a balcony. She was

there for *Jameson*—a big boy who could take care of himself.

As a primal growl built up at the base of his throat, Angus shook his head, his brain taking longer than he liked to stop banging against the side of his skull.

"Angus?" Lucinda's voice called from the other side of the plant.

"Mmm…?" he said. "I've lost…something. Just a second."

Lost something? Lost his mind, more like.

"I'll find us a room, shall I? So we can get your thoughts down before the next session?"

"Yep. Do that."

She was right. Whatever the reasons for coming, from this moment on it had to be about Remède. All he had to do was focus.

But all he could focus on was how, if he breathed through his nose, he could almost still gather the scent of her—apple and cinnamon and soft female skin.

Like Christmas. All that egg nog…all that bloody cheer. And don't even mention the mistletoe…

Angus groaned and ran a hand over his face.

Enough. All right? Enough.

It wasn't the first time they'd had such a moment. And chances were it wouldn't be the last. The important thing was they were always able to move through it. To work together despite it. Hell, maybe that constant tension was one of the reasons they got so much done.

But it could never…be anything.

They needed one another too much to mess with what they had.

She needed his constancy with Sonny, something he knew would crumble if anything ever happened between them. He'd been there, in Sonny's shoes. And when she realised she deserved more than he was able to give it would fall apart all too fast.

And he needed her to play her part in the business he and Charlie and Fitz had worked their downtrodden, working class asses off to build.

Feeling better—or at the very least as if he had a clearer vision of what came next—Angus gave his head one last shake before leaving the safety of the plant, hoping he'd never set eyes on the thing again.

CHAPTER FIVE

ANGUS SAT IN the back of the generous yet only half-full auditorium as a speaker talked animatedly about the "curly girl movement", losing him when the lingo headed down the lines of "squish to condish" and "scrunch out the crunch".

He turned to his right, ready with a joke for Lucinda, only to still when he remembered she wasn't there. She'd gone to another talk, one about the science of cruelty-free cosmetics, something he'd have been far more interested in than "deep conditioning".

It made him wonder if she'd ordered him to sit in on this one as some kind of punishment for making her come at all.

The woman three seats up blushed and gave him an encouraging smile.

He gave one back—though less encouraging—before grabbing his suit jacket from the back of the empty seat beside him and shuffling along the empty row to his left.

"Everything okay?" It was Elena Zager, conference organiser, exit gatekeeper.

"All good. Great speaker. Lots of personality. Your attendees are lapping it up."

"Curls are a booming industry right now. Hugely energised, grass roots, engaged social media community. Making big waves. So to speak."

Angus wondered briefly if Remède had any products that might be swept up by a grass-roots campaign but knew it wouldn't be enough.

Elena motioned to his own head of curls. "Do you oil?"

Angus blinked. "Wash and wear."

"Mmm…"

Before she began to dole out advice, Angus crossed his arms and leaned against the door, positioning himself as her partner in the line of defence against room-leavers. "How are things going? With the conference."

"Brilliantly!" Elena looked around. "Though it would have been nice to have a few more attendees. Our speakers are world class. Those who come rave about the events in the feedback sheets. Time was we'd fill a room like this, but our numbers are slipping, especially as we struggle to drum up fresh faces. Present company excluded, of course."

Angus smiled, his eyes roving over the stage set-up, the banners, the promotional signage. It all looked a little tired, no doubt due to funding restrictions that came from diminishing numbers. A vicious cycle he and Lucinda saw time and again when clients came to him, feeling at the end of their rope.

"Have you ever had professional help, branding-wise?" he asked.

Elena leaned away. "Whatever do you mean?"

"Logo refresh, colour choice, website SEO audit, advertising buy-ins, social media spreads, creating viral headlines…"

When her eyes began to glaze over, Angus swallowed the lingo and thought about how Lucinda might put it. "Uh…how do people know about the conference?"

"My nephew made our website, and this year he started a Facebook page. It's quite good. We advertise in trade magazines, but that gets more and more cost-prohibitive each year. And we do a mail-out to our list. I think that's all."

Before he even felt the words forming, Angus heard himself say, "If you'd like me to put together some ideas, ways to invigorate interest, I'd be happy to offer up some thoughts."

Elena blinked, splotches of colour rising beneath the thick layer of make-up she wore. Damn it. He'd offended her. When he'd only been trying to help.

This was why he needed Lucinda. She was the one who usually drew the client in, for she was honest and real. You felt it the moment you looked into her eyes.

But she wasn't around, so he had no choice but to fend for himself.

Angus lowered his voice, found what he hoped was a warm smile and said, "Just between you and me, I'm not actually in the beauty industry."

"Oh?"

He leaned in conspiratorially. "Updating business brands, helping companies connect with the people who need them, is what I do for a crust. And I'm quite a big deal in my field, if I do say so myself."

"Oh! Well, then, I guess if you have any advice, I'd be amenable to hearing it."

Angus gave her a smile. A real smile. Clearly, he'd picked up some of Lucinda's skills after having watched her in action over the years.

Elena patted him on the hand before heading back down into the auditorium.

Angus leaned back against the door, the realisation of what he'd just offered to do slowly sinking in. He didn't have the time for this. Or the head space. The answer to Remède's very big, very real problem was the only thing he ought to focus on.

Especially when it felt so close. As if the answer was right under his nose.

Where *was* Lucinda when he needed her?

With her discount-store pencils and fancy notebooks in hand, she'd have the idea out of his head and into a user-friendly plan in no time at all.

It was a hell of a thing, the way she did that. Head cocked so her dark hair swung over one shoulder, soft brown eyes narrowed as she pierced him with a laser look. It was as if she could see right inside his head, to his very core.

A place few people had ever seen.

Client relationships never went beyond the professional. Other friendships—neighbours, work acquaintances, old uni friends—were peripheral. The women he dated remained at arm's length. Allowing them any closer would mean giving them the power to move him. Affect him. It would mean risking loss of control.

Having watched his mother let man after man into her home, into her heart, he'd also had to watch them leave, every one of them taking a piece of her with them until by the end he'd barely been able to recognise the woman who'd promised she'd give him a better life no matter what.

Of all the life lessons she'd tried to impart, the most lasting was one she'd never said out loud. She'd lived her life wide open and it had changed her. So, he lived his as a closed book. Invulnerable.

To everyone…except one.

Pressing himself away from the door, he slipped through. His steps ate up the miles to the small single room Velma had booked to grab a stash of hotel stationery.

Needing to keep his mind busy, to keep his thoughts from straying, he chose the accoutrements necessary to whip this organisation into the best shape of its life.

It would be like sorbet for his creative brain, leaving a clean slate on which a moment of clarity might shine, lighting the way to bring the Remède rebranding together.

After the Science of Cruelty-Free Cosmetics session, Lucinda had sent Angus a message to say she'd meet up with him later in the afternoon for a debrief.

If he took that to mean she was spending time with Jameson, then surely that was on him?

Instead, she spent an hour wandering the grounds of Hanover House, breathing in the fresh air, literally smelling the roses. Grateful to have some time to herself. Time on her own was at a premium, what with her long work hours and her beautiful boy to take care of.

When she found herself wandering aimlessly in and out of a series of tall conifers, her first thought was that they were the perfect size for a man to tug his woman behind and kiss her till her knees gave out. Taller than a fiddle-leaf fig, in any case. Denser. More private.

Thought what did a fiddle-leaf fig have to do with anything? It was Jameson who should be dragging her behind a bush and kissing her senseless, not…anyone else.

And he would. When they rebooked their weekend away. She'd make sure of it! Though the handful of kisses they'd shared so far hadn't boded all that well for the promise of swooning and watery knees.

Suddenly, the thought of lining up a weekend when they were both free, booking the time off and getting Sonny used to the idea of another weekend without her felt all too hard.

Her phone vibrated silently in her pocket.

She stopped walking and made a deal with herself. If it was Jameson checking in, calling to whisper sweet nothings and tell her how much he wished he was there with her, alone, she'd make it happen. And soon. But if it was anyone else…

She lifted the phone from her bag, her shoulders slumping. In disappointment? Or relief?

Phone at her ear she said, "Hey, Kitty Cat."

"Loosey-Lu," her sister sing-songed. "You free to talk? Not handcuffed to the bed? Swinging from a chandelier?"

"I'm free."

"How's the good doctor?"

Okay, so she might not have told her sister her weekend plans had changed either. She'd have to do a lot of nice things for a lot of people to balance out the karma her recent decisions might unleash.

Eyes closed, she tore off the proverbial Band-Aid. "Don't know. He's not here."

Silence.

"Didn't I mention? Turned out I had to work this weekend. A conference. At Hanover House, of all places. But when I told Jameson that I could do both—weekend with him and work a little—he blew me off."

"The villain," was Cat's flavourless response. Then, "So you're at the resort. Only not with Jameson. With instead, I'm presuming, your dashing boss?"

"Mmm-hmm."

Speaking of Angus, Lucinda took the phone away from her ear to check the time. Time to head back. She was joining said dashing boss in fifteen minutes in the small meeting room they'd nabbed within the business centre.

"You sound out of breath," said Cat. "Are you certain you're alone?"

"I'm walking. Fast."

"Right. Sure."

"Okay, I have to go. You know Angus—work, work, work. Remind Sonny when he gets home from school that he can call me any time."

"Are you sure? I know you no longer have hanky-panky as your primary mission this weekend, but you don't want a blackout period? A metaphorical tie hanging from the hotel door? Just in case?"

"He can call me any time."

"Okay, then. Bye."

Lucinda hung up without saying goodbye, threw her phone into her hand bag with a little more force than necessary and grumbled and muttered all the way back to the hotel.

She was getting a little sick of her sister's passive-aggressive commentary on her relationship with Angus.

Though for a moment or ten, behind the fiddle-leaf fig, it had felt…new. Hot. Breathless. The way he'd looked at her. Holy-moly. His body had vibrated with a level of tension that was quite something, even for him. As if it was taking Angus as much effort not to touch her as it was for her not to touch him.

To run a hand up the back of his neck and another up the front of his business shirt, sliding a finger beneath a button until it popped free of the hole. To press herself against him until she felt the hard press of his…

"Argh!" she cried when she realised where her mind was going, scaring a pair of topknot pigeons who leapt squawking from the lawn into the air.

She pressed her hands against her eyes as if that might wipe away the vision now burned into her retinas. "Okay. Pull yourself together. You just need to get through this weekend, do all you can for Remède and, come Monday, everything will be back to normal."

As pep talks went it was a bit of a fizzer. For the first time "normal" didn't sound like everything she'd ever wanted.

But it got her feet moving again. So, by the time she found her way back to the meeting room she was ready to work. Or ready to fake it, at the very least.

She lifted a hand to knock, then shook her head and opened the door. Angus was already there, sitting at a small round table which was covered in pens and paper.

His curls showed signs of having been raked with frustrated fingers. His left cheek was a little pink, as if he'd been leaning on his fist. His tie was missing, as was his jacket. His shirt was wrinkled and rolled up to the elbows. His right leg jiggled like crazy under the table. He looked raw, ravaged. Like a boardroom warrior.

When he realised he was no longer alone and looked

up at her, his eyes a little wild, intense, glinting behind his reading glasses, Lucinda had to shake her head in order to stop staring.

"Hey," she said, moving to dump her bag and jacket on a spare chair before grabbing a notebook and pencil and carefully shoving papers aside to claim a small corner of the table.

He blinked, a small measure of the heat in his eyes dimming as he said, "Where's Dr Whatsit?"

She waved a hand in the direction of the door. Or Melbourne. "Probably on a call."

There was a good chance. When they were together he was always on the phone. Which, come to think of it, was actually pretty frustrating.

She'd brushed it off, putting it down to the fact he was an important man who did important work. But would she be happy to be second fiddle to a man's work all the time? If she ever opened her heart truly, all the way open, it would be because she trusted the man in her life would be there for ever. For her. For Sonny. For them.

Angus cleared his throat again. Probably because she was staring at him. Again.

She shook her head. "Sorry. A million miles away."

Angus did not look impressed. In fact, he looked mighty uncomfortable. As if he imagined she'd been daydreaming about Dr Whatsit and what they might have been up to together behind the conifers.

Finding herself rather enjoying seeing Angus flummoxed, Lucinda opened her mouth to fan the flames with some carefully chosen words then snapped it shut.

Enough. Really, enough.

She brought her notebook onto her lap. "Before we get to work, I have a confession."

He frowned. "I prefer the 'get to work' part of that sentence."

"And yet I'm telling you anyway. It's about Jameson."

Angus sat back and held up a hand, the column of his throat turning patchy. "Lucinda—"

"He's not here. In the hotel. He was never here."

He stilled, his hand still hovering in mid-air. "I don't understand."

"He was *meant* to be here. This weekend was a real thing for us. A big thing, or so I thought. But, when I rang and told him I had to work a little while we were here, he bailed."

Angus slowly sat forward and ran a hand over his chin. After a few long beats, in which the only sound was the ticking of a clock on the wall overhead, he said, "Luc, I'm sorry. Truly. I didn't mean for that to happen."

Didn't you? a small voice piped up in the back of her head. Thankfully she stopped it from escaping through her lips.

"You led me to believe he was here."

Lucinda held up a finger. "If you think back, you'll find I never once said he was here, I simply didn't let on that he was elsewhere."

Don't ask why. Don't ask why. Don't ask...

"Why?"

Ah, the eternal question. There were many reasons. She chose one. "I was embarrassed. After making such a big deal about this weekend and the thing that spilled out of the shopping bag. The ease with which he took the news was less than flattering."

The look in Angus's eyes was telling. But telling of what? There was a quiet intensity about him, a sense that all kinds of big emotions rippled beneath the surface.

His voice was so quiet when he said, "He's a surgeon," that Lucinda jumped.

"Yes."

"Meaning he is on call a fair bit."

"Yes. Often."

"Having your time together cut short is one of the joys of dating a doctor."

Snort. "Like you'd know."

"I did, in point of fact, date a doctor once."

"A doctor of what? Astrology?"

The intensity in Angus's eyes changed. Shifted. Warmed. "No," he said, his voice dropping to a purr. "Vivian was an actual medical doctor."

Lucinda opened her mouth with a qualifier, but Angus got there first, "Who doctored on humans. From memory, I quite liked the fact she was constantly on call. It meant she had so little claim on my time. I wonder what happened to her?"

"I bet you do."

His smile was wide. With teeth. And, oh, the things it did to her insides. And outsides. All over.

Lucinda frowned down at her notebook to find she hadn't made a single note.

Then Angus asked, "Do you want to talk about it? About him?"

"With you?"

He looked over his shoulder as if checking to see who might be lined up behind him.

"Funny," she deadpanned. "We don't do this. You and I. We don't talk about the people we…date." She might as well have used a number of other terms, given how the temperature in the room seemed to rise.

"We don't, do we?"

She shook her head. Slowly. Feeling more than a little mesmerised by the look in his eyes. "Best we keep it that way, don't you think? I know we don't have much in the way of boundaries but the people we date…maybe that should be one of them."

"Maybe. But, while we're considering that, tell me this: is there anything I can do to make it up to you both, if you imagine you'll be…dating him again any time soon?"

A second or three went by before Lucinda realised she was still shaking her head.

"No, I can't help, or no, you're done with him?"

Her voice cracked a very little as she said, "Both." And she meant it. For, if he'd let her go all too easily, the truth was she was glad he wasn't there.

"Good," Angus said, the edge of his mouth kicking into a slow-burn kind of smile that made Lucinda's insides melt.

"Good?"

"You deserve the kind of man who'd stand up and tell you no."

"Ah, what now?"

"Along the lines of no, you can't work this weekend, as I have plans. Plans that won't work if I don't have you all to myself. All weekend long."

Lucinda tried not to swallow. She really did. But if she wanted to get the words out she had no choice.

"I'll keep that in mind. Now, what's going on here?" She flapped a hand at the table to distract him. "Did a stationery shop crash-land on your table?"

She was gifted a slight tilt of the head—the equivalent of giving her a C+ for her distraction efforts—before he nudged his glasses higher on his nose and his attention slid back to his work.

"I'm helping the committee rebrand before their next event."

"What committee?"

A muscle ticked in his jaw. "The, ah, committee who organised the conference. That we are attending."

"Elena and her lot? They *hired* you?"

"I volunteered."

"You volunteered. To help them. For nothing."

This from a man who let his underlings deal with small-fry accounts such as cinema chains and TV stations as he was too busy catering to airlines and media conglomerates. This man who equated success with the number of multinational clients on his waiting list.

She popped out of her chair and placed the back of her hand on his forehead. "Are you okay?"

Feeling warmth, feeling her skin tingling where it had met his, she curled her fingers away and sat back down. "Do they have something on you? Please tell me you won a free makeover and there are photos to prove it!"

Angus slowly leant back in his chair, long legs sliding deeper under the table until one of his feet brushed against hers. She quickly crossed her ankles and tucked her feet back as far as they would go.

"Can't a guy just do something nice for a bunch of beauticians with it not having to mean something?"

"Not you."

Something flashed behind his eyes.

"Angus, I didn't mean…" Lucinda leant forward. "Remède, Angus. You're here, rather than having a much-deserved weekend off, because of Remède. Right?"

It took a few beats longer than it should have for him to nod.

"Then do you even have time for this?"

"Probably not. But I was looking for a win."

Oh? *Oh.*

Lucinda's heart gave a little kick.

The guy was the most winning person she'd ever met. Some campaigns were more successful than others, but they were always baseline successful. For him to be *that* worried about Remède's account? For him not to have complete faith in himself? Boy, that must be messing with his head.

And she felt more than a little silly for harbouring a teeny, tiny thread of hope in the back of her head that the reason he was here was for her.

Agreeing to a quickie pro bono for a non-profit, that was way out there for him. And it was her job to go there

with him, to make sure he made it back to safe ground.
Meaning it was time to go to work.

"Okay. Let's do this. A genius fix, but on a low bud-
get. Feels like how it used to be back in the beginning.
Remember?"

The moment she said *okay*, Angus looked slightly less
haunted. "It was the Wild West—scrounging for time,
pulling in favours, like digging for diamonds in the back
yard. Bloody hard work, but fun, right?"

She couldn't help but grin. "The *funnest*. Now, while
it's terribly cute that you tried to do this without me, let
me sort out the crazy you have going on here."

It took Lucinda about a minute and a half to have Angus's scattered notes in neat piles. Another ten—during
which she kept shushing him when he tried to interject—
to read through the piles, pick out the thread tying it all
together and annotate.

Once done, she sat back with a happy sigh, flush with
the sense of accomplishment.

When she caught Angus's eye, she found him watching her with a darkly indulgent smile.

She glowered. "Now what?"

"You made the noise."

"What noise?"

"The happy 'humph' you make whenever you're feeling particularly pleased with yourself. You make it a lot."

"I do?" She licked her lips which suddenly felt preternaturally dry.

He nodded, his gaze dropping to her mouth. And suddenly it felt as if they were back behind the fiddle-leaf
fig again. As if there wasn't enough air. As if they were
saying more without words than with.

"Then I must be pleased with myself a lot. Which
makes sense. Because I'm awesome."

Angus's smile stretched. "And no matter how busy
we are, how tight the deadlines, how much work I pile

on your plate, that noise always tells me you're happy where you are."

"Where I am?" she said, her voice light.

"Working with me."

Her chest tightened pleasurably.

With him, he'd said. Not *for* him. Whenever she found herself particularly frustrated, when he was grumpy or stubborn or locked away in the impenetrable mental cave in which he lived much of the time, it was moments like this, when he treated her not just as another employee but as his partner, that turned it all around.

That made her tingle. And sparkle. And wonder. And hope.

And yearn.

Look away! her subconscious cried, and for once she did as she was told, picking up a piece of paper from the table and staring at it as if it was the most interesting thing she'd seen in a long time.

"'South Victorian Regional Beauticians' Organisation'," she said, reading the conference package he'd scribbled all over. "*That* has to go."

"Right there with you." Angus pulled out a sheet of paper he had tucked up inside the conference folder, on which he'd sketched out a new business name and logo.

"When did you come up with this?" she asked.

"Five minutes before you stormed in and I let you pretend you'd taken over."

She shot him a look before her gaze was pulled back to his sketch.

It was simple, elegant, aspirational, feminine, strong and dead on target. The colour was not the usual cosmetic pink, but a sweet, wistful spring-green. Extremely close, in fact, to the colour of her watch band. Her reusable takeaway coffee mug. Her favourite dress.

Another woman might have imagined that was because

he'd been thinking about her as he'd worked. Lucinda steadfastly refused to imagine any such thing.

"Are you sure you're not a woman?" she asked.

The curl of his smile, the gleam in his eye, the roll of his shoulder, were all so very male that Lucinda's ovaries hiccupped.

"So, what about…? Where's that bit with the membership restructuring…?"

They both leaned forward to reach for a piece of paper at the same time. Lucinda grabbed it, Angus's hand closing over hers.

She glanced up, finding herself close enough to see all the colours in his magnetic eyes. To see stubble darkening the edges of his hard jaw. To watch him attempt to control the measure of his next breath.

She ought to have pulled some ninja move and unglued her hand from his before he even knew she was on the move.

But, while she was considering, he lifted her hand to have a closer look. Sonny had drawn on the back of her hand before she'd left, so she'd "remember him" while she was away. It was a now faded lopsided heart.

Angus sniffed out a breath, his eyes creasing into a smile as he ran this thumb over the drawing. Then, as if he was in some kind of trance, he turned her hand over, distractedly watching his thumb as it traced her lifeline. Or was it her heartline?

Lucinda could not breathe. She could barely think. Every nerve, cell and emotion centred on the gentle swipe of Angus's grazing touch.

When he reached the tender underside of her wrist, it became too much and she jerked her hand away.

Hope, confusion and years of pressing her feelings deep down inside mixed into a tempest inside her, pushing her to her feet so fast her chair scraped sharply against the floor before teetering and tipping over.

She spun and crouched to pick it up, right at the same moment that Angus came round the table to do the same. Her eyes snapped to his to find them dark and bottomless.

Lucinda slowly pulled herself to her feet, her legs shaking with the adrenaline coursing through her body.

Angus stood by her, the chair in one hand. He gently placed it back down. And stayed where he was, breathing hard enough that she could see the shape of him beneath the constraint of his shirt.

"The next session starts soon," Lucinda somehow managed to croak out.

"Right."

"I think I'll go freshen up before heading to…whatever it is I'm heading to."

"Okay. I need to track down some coffee and then I'll come back here. Keep working on this. Can I grab you a cup? To take with you?"

Now he was asking if he could get her a coffee? Lucinda really needed him to say something smug. Or arrogant. To restore balance to the galaxy.

She shook her head then leaned around him to reach her bag, holding her breath so as not to swoon as she brushed so close to him she could feel his body heat.

Somehow her feet remembered how to walk, admirably carrying her to the door. Where she stopped. Turned. She couldn't leave with that kind of tension pulling between them or she'd not hear a word of the next session.

"Will you be okay? Doing this on your own? Because I can stick around…"

"I'm fine. This feels…good." The warmth that lit the edges of his smile made her wonder if he was fully aware of the butterflies smacking into her ribcage. Then he said, "I'm sorry about Dr Whatsit. Truly."

"Yeah," she said. "Me too." For she was. It should have been so easy to fall for him. To fit him into their lives.

Then, "And, should you have a Dr Whatsit in your life one day, you can talk to me about it, you know. Any time. Boundaries, schmoundaries."

Something dark swirled behind his eyes. "There'll be no Dr Whatsits for me, Luc. You know better than anyone that my mother taught me the benefits of a life of solitude. Which either makes me a very lucky man, or it's the great tragedy of my life."

Lucinda gave him a smile, as was expected.

All the while, as she headed back out into the hotel and walked unseeingly towards the conference rooms, her heart twisted so hard it hurt.

She'd lost loving parents while still relatively young. Her husband had left her when they'd had a beautiful thirteen-month-old boy.

And yet, Lucinda thought with a heaviness settling over her like a rain cloud, the fact that this man flat out refused to move beyond the ghosts of his boyhood might yet turn out to be the great tragedy of her life as well.

CHAPTER SIX

"WHAT THE HELL are you doing at a beauty conference in the same hotel in which your assistant is meant to be having her dirty weekend but now isn't because she's stuck working with you?"

Fitz's voice rattled through the phone pressed to Angus's ear as he leant against the cold concrete balustrade outside the Bean and Brew Bistro, watching the trees below sway in the moonlight.

He nursed the end of a strong, post-dinner coffee, one he'd begun just before Lucinda had given a good impression of a fake yawn before claiming exhaustion and heading to her room. Alone.

"Who told you?" Angus growled.

"Who *hasn't* told me? I had questions. About things. And you're not here to answer them. To stop me whinging about it, Velma informed me where I could find you. Then the lovely Cat, in a scratchy mood I must say, called to demand I do something about it. About you."

"Me?"

"Apparently everything in the world is your fault."

"I see. What was so important you had to track me down?"

A pause. "Can't remember. But, now I have you, anything you need to get off your chest? About the amenities, perhaps? The chamber maids? How you and the lovely Lucinda are getting along out in the blustery wilds?"

"It's Daylesford, not the Outback. And, like the many conferences we've been on together over the years, we're getting along just fine. And trying to get a deeper insight into the industry in the hope it gives us another angle to add to the Remède rebrand."

"Fair enough. Any highlights thus far?"

When it came to Remède? No.

As for the weekend, so far it had all the hallmarks of a roller coaster.

Dinner had been…polite. Lucinda had met him after the conference day was done. Had kept her eyes on her notes as she'd talked through a series of neatly written bullet points. Had recited a phone conversation she'd had with Sonny that afternoon, word for word. Then bolted.

Whereas in the meeting room, earlier that day…

Angus closed his eyes against the memory of Lucinda sitting before him, her brown eyes huge as she watched him trace his thumb down the soft skin of her palm, her throat working, her cheeks pinking. He'd all but seen her light up from the inside out.

He shook his head. He couldn't possibly say what he'd been thinking. He'd seen the drawing on the back of her hand and had pulled it closer to find the endearing love stamp from her son.

As for the rest? Something had come over him when he'd felt the warmth of her hand curled beneath his. The erratic pulse beneath the skin. Something primal and deep.

But Lucinda was out of bounds.

No. She was the one person in his life with whom there were no "bounds". She called him out when he was too demanding. Rolled her eyes when he refused to budge. She knew when to give him space. She had even more faith in him than he had in himself.

She knew him. The good bits and the bad. And she stuck around anyway.

Then there was the fact she'd let him into her family. Gifted him the friendship with her son. No limits.

No rules. She trusted him to have Sonny's best interests at heart.

For a guy like him, who pushed back against anyone who tried to get close, that was exceedingly rare.

Never in his life had a person been as important to him, to his success, to his self-worth, to his mental health.

Messing with that would be self-defeating. And Angus was no masochist.

As such, he recapped all he'd seen and heard in case Fitz saw something he didn't.

Apparently, Fitz saw no such lightbulbs, as he said, "So, nothing to hang your hat on so far. Bar scaring Lucinda's guy away. Probably a good thing there, right? Last thing any of us need is for Luc to turn into a love-sick muppet. The woman runs the whole ship. We'd be dead in the water without her."

"Dead," Charlie's voice agreed amiably. "In the water."

"I'm on speakerphone?" Angus asked, coming to a halt.

"Always. Now, why did I call you again?" Fitz asked.

"Heaven only knows."

"Is Lucinda there?" Charlie's disembodied voice asked in the background. "Can you get her? I wanted to ask her something."

"She's not with me," Angus answered.

"Why not?"

Fitz piped up. "Probably avoiding him."

"What am I missing?" Charlie asked.

"The twenty-first century," Fitz answered. Then, with exaggerated patience, he went on. "Okay, here's the sordid tale in a nutshell. Angus, pipe in if I miss something. Lucinda was all set for a dirty weekend with some hot doctor. Until Angus found out and went all superhero and figured out a way to be there to save her from herself. So, though they are there together, the lovely Lucinda is not *with* Angus. And that, dear friends, is the issue of the day. Now, if our erstwhile hero would only man up and admit that he and our gorgeous girl are—"

Angus didn't bother saying goodbye. He simply hung up.

Lucinda stood in her hotel bathroom, hands gripping the edge of the sink. Not feeling anywhere near as tired as she'd made out.

In fact, she felt wired. Too much cheap conference coffee? Too much Angus?

Which was ridiculous, considering the time they spent in one another's company at work. And yet somehow this weekend she'd found the usual methods she employed to keep her feelings at bay just weren't cutting it.

During the afternoon's laugh-out-loud session spent guessing famous perfumes while blindfolded, then shouting out the scent ingredients that stayed with them the most, she'd managed not to think about Angus's thumb grazing her hand. Much.

But the moment she'd walked into the bistro, seen him sitting by the large picture windows, the dusk light playing over the angles of his face, her heart had raced so hard she'd felt as if she was about to go into full-blown panic.

She'd never eaten dinner faster.

Glancing up, she caught her reflection in the mirror. The slinky black negligée she'd slipped on after the cool shower she'd taken gleamed in the down-lights. She'd also touched up her make-up. Even dabbed on a spritz of perfume in unmentionable places.

For nothing. For no one. Just because.

She turned her face this way and that. Not yet thirty, her skin was pretty good. She liked her nose. And her crooked smile. She'd always thought her eyes a little dark, but it was a good face.

She stood, turned side-on. Lifted onto her toes to see as much of herself in the bathroom mirror as she could. Having had Sonny young, there were few signs on her body that she'd ever given birth. A little roundness in the belly. A couple of stretch marks that gleamed in the right light.

She was attractive enough. Funny. She liked talking. She was a great listener. Good at reading between the lines. Working for Angus as long as she had, it was a skill that came in handy on a daily basis.

So, with all that going for her, what about her had made it so easy for Jameson to say, "No worries. Weekend away postponed. Easy-peasy"?

What made not one of the men she met at work gatherings, parties or those she passed in the fruit and vegetable aisles at the supermarket fall madly, irreversibly in love with her?

What about her had made her husband able simply to walk into the kitchen one day and say, "I can't do this any more"?

True, she and Joe had not had an easy time of things. She'd met him not long after her parents had died suddenly. He was a man with itchy feet and little to hold him down. Everything her regular suburban life had not been up to that point. She'd fallen hard. Followed wherever he'd led. They'd married fast, a baby already on the way.

But it hadn't taken long for him to tire of their life after she'd made them stop and put down roots. For at heart she was that kind of girl. A home girl. A stayer. A believer in for ever.

Would she ever find someone—not Jameson but someone better? A stayer, like her? Someone who made her heart race, her toes curl, her cheeks hurt from laughing, someone who made her tell Angus *no*?

Angus. A man to whom it was nearly impossible to say no. Whom it was nearly impossible to sway. Nearly impossible to resist.

But there was still an inner wall she'd never made it beyond.

It was that wall that made it easy for her to harbour her secret crush. She could never truly lose her heart to the man as his wasn't up for grabs.

Realising her hands were sliding over the slinky fabric while she thought of Angus, she lifted them away, curled them into fists and walked away from the mirror, turning the bathroom light off behind her.

She climbed from the end to the head of the bed before falling in a heap on the right-hand side. She'd never migrated to the middle of the bed by habit as, after Joe had left, Sonny occasionally made his way into her room when he was sick or had bad dreams.

She lay on her back and flung an arm over her eyes. Hoped sleep might take her so the dangerous thoughts still swirling behind her closed lids could be excused as dreams.

Her phone buzzed on the bedside table.

This time she knew who it was before she even checked. When Angus's face showed above the message he'd sent, her limbs came over all warm and her breath released on a sigh:

They have Netflix. Should I keep going with Warlock Academy or wait for you?

Knowing sleep wasn't coming any time soon, she sent back her response.

She put her phone aside, grabbed her fluffy old pashmina and dragged it with her under the covers, pulling the blankets up to her chin and stretching out her arm for the remote.

Lucinda was in reception the next morning, struggling not to yawn as she made sure she and Angus had access to their small meeting room for the next two days, when a familiar voice rent the air.

"Mum!"

Lucinda spun nearly a full circle before she saw her boy rushing her like a whirling dervish. He leapt into her arms and she twirled him around. "Hey, baby boy! What on earth are you doing here?"

"Cat brought me. As a surprise. She said your friend couldn't come any more so you'd be really sad. And lonely. So we came to keep you company!"

Lucinda scanned the foyer to find her sister swanning across the floor, dragging two small battered suitcases behind her. "How wonderful," she said, while she glared at Cat for all she was worth.

"Really? You don't sound like it's wonderful."

Snapping her gaze back to her son, she let him drop to the ground then took his adorable face in her hands, knowing that only this face would save her from strangling her sister. "Really. Every moment I have with you is my best moment ever."

Sonny grinned. "Mine too."

Lucinda held Sonny tight to her front as she straightened and faced her sister. "Kitty Cat."

"Loosey-Lu. Sleep well?"

"Very well." At the thought of sleep, Lucinda's yawn could no longer be denied. Her nostrils flared from the effort at swallowing it down. She'd asked for dreams and she'd got them. Racy, lusty, hot, sweaty ones.

Cat's smile was all too knowing.

"Go look out that window," Lucinda said, pointing to a window seat near the front doors. "They have the most beautiful, fluffy white clouds out here. Come back and tell me what shapes you can see in them."

Sonny bolted for the window, leaving Lucinda to turn to Cat with hands on her hips. "What on earth are you doing here?"

"Sonny already hit the high notes."

"I'm working, Cat. I can't hang with you guys. Does Sonny understand that?"

"We've made plans. Marco Polo in the heated pool. Skimming stones by the lake. Jurassic Park marathon."

All things they could have done in and around home. So why were they…?

"Are you *babysitting* me?" Lucinda asked, her voice rising enough that the guy behind reception gave her a look.

"Something's different," Cat said. "I can smell it. I'm here to make sure you don't do something you can't take back."

Lucinda's mind went instantly to the hand-holding incident the day before. Put like that, it sounded so innocent. But it wasn't. It hadn't been. It was out there now. Woven into the fabric of their story.

"I am a grown-up person, Cat, if you hadn't noticed. I've managed to survive thus far without an overseer."

Cat glanced towards Sonny. Making the point that he was the result of a time in Lucinda's life when her decision-making had been less than stellar. Falling for Joe, sticking with Joe, marrying Joe. Not that she'd have changed a single moment. Not when it had brought her her beautiful boy.

But she got it.

"Do you have a room?" Lucinda asked. Her mind went to her beautiful big suite, with its huge bed, lounge, desk and balcony. They could make it work. Before buying her cottage, they'd lived together in smaller digs.

"All good," said Cat. "After I wrote that article on the place, they offered me a room for a night, so this is my chance to take them up on it. And I know you're working, so Sonny will stay with me." Cat moved a little closer, her eyes downcast, her foot nudging against the wheel of a suitcase. "Look, I probably shouldn't have sprung this on you, but I felt like I had to. When I moved in after Joe left, you asked me to help make sure you never fell for someone so wholly wrong for you again. So this is me. Helping."

Cat moved to the desk to check in, while Sonny's footsteps slapped against the floor as he came bolting back from the window. "A chicken. A flamingo. And a pair of yellow gumboots."

"Yellow?" Lucinda asked, her skin feeling as if it was burning at Cat's insinuation that she was in danger of falling for Angus. Who was, according to her sister, wholly wrong for her. "How could you tell?"

Sonny shrugged. "Just could."

"How was the drive? What's the newsy news?" Lucinda asked.

"Traffic was bad. Cat thinks it's going to rain, but I told her there are no cumulonimbus clouds so it won't. And she said the S-word."

"Did she, now?"

"She said it was okay because you can use that word in the car. When drivers are being…you know. Because they can't hear you. And because it's true."

"Stupid," Cat called out. "The S-word was 'stupid'. And that driver was stupid. Right, Sonny?"

Eyes wide, Sonny nodded. "He really was, Mum."

Then suddenly Sonny tugged his hand from hers and bolted, right as Angus's deep voice boomed across the lofty space, "Hey! Kid!"

"Uncle Angus!" Sonny cried as he threw himself at Angus's suit-clad leg.

"Speak of the devil," Cat murmured as she sauntered up to stand by Lucinda, arms crossed.

Freshly shaven and in a dark charcoal suit, the man did look as if he could charm anyone out of anything. Then, with a growl, he leant over, grabbed Sonny by the waist and flipped him upside down till Sonny's laughter bounced off the walls.

If Cat's intention had been to use Sonny as a prophylactic, it wasn't working, as Lucinda's heart clutched so hard she winced. But it was a good kind of pain. As it always was watching her two favourite guys together.

Sonny was so thirsty for a good man to look up to and Angus, though he'd never admit it, more in need of a family than anyone she'd ever met.

Then Angus looked up, searching the vast lobby till his gaze landed on hers. And caught. All hooded dark eyes and simmering charisma.

Then Angus ambled her way, slowly tipping Sonny the right way up. And Lucinda felt herself catapulted right back to the night before, standing in the bathroom, hands running over her sexy negligée, thinking about him.

"You need a tissue? To wipe up the drool," Cat said, right in her ear.

"Oh, shut up."

"Morning, Catriona," Angus said as he came to a halt before their little tableau.

"Angus," she said with a nod.

"This is a nice surprise."

"Is it?"

Angus had the good grace to grin. Then he turned to Lucinda. The impact of those deep, clever eyes of his made her come over all fluttery. "I found this pet monkey roaming the lobby. Any clue who it belongs to? Or should I give it to lost property?"

"I'm her son!" said Sonny, jumping up and down, trying to catch Angus's eye.

"Her son?" Angus asked. "Well, hello, Her Son."

Sonny laughed so hard he clutched his side. "It's *Sonny*."

"Sonny, you say? Well, that's a far better name." Angus held out a hand. "I'm Angus Wolfe."

Sonny flopped a hand into Angus's.

"This way, remember?" said Angus, catching Sonny's eye. Then he shifted the limp hand into the proper grip, waited for Sonny to grip harder and they shook three times.

Angus smiled at Sonny. Lucinda smiled at Angus. And Cat groaned as if she was in physical pain.

"Look, Angus and I have about half an hour before we need to get to work." She could grab a pastry from the conference coffee-cart. "Would you like me to help you guys find your room first?"

"Yes!" Sonny yelled.

"Okay, then. Let's get this show on the road."

Lucinda held out her hand to Sonny. He took it, then held out his other hand to Angus.

S-word, S-word, S-word.

When she looked up at Angus he was watching her, his face inscrutable, before he took a subtle step back. "Go on, kiddo. I'll catch you later, okay?"

"Okay," said Sonny, his shoulders rounding tragically.

"Oh, good gravy," Cat muttered. "We were up with the sparrows this morning. I need a lie down. And a coffee. Let's check out our fabulous room, hey kid? Goodbye Angus."

"Catriona. Lucinda."

"I'll make it quick," Lucinda promised.

Angus nodded and Lucinda felt the burn of his eyes in the middle of her back until they turned the corner leading to the lifts.

"Do *you* think it's going to rain, Mum?" Sonny asked.

Lucinda smiled down at him. "Not a chance."

CHAPTER SEVEN

By six o'clock that evening, Lucinda's nerves were shot.

Not from the conference, which was fantastic, and they'd really hit their straps. By then most of the attendees knew who they were—who Angus was, at any rate—had heard that he'd volunteered to help them update their brand and someone had researched him enough to know he was doing the same for Remède.

As big fans of the venerable label, so many came forward with thoughts, advice and stories about the times Remède products had marked different periods of their lives.

Angus had insisted they stick together for the day—take the same sessions, sit in on the same conversations, two heads being better than one. Meaning she'd had to cope with his hand at her back as they'd all snuggled into a lift, the brush of his arm as he'd reached for a pen, the constant hum of his body heat simmering away beside her.

Add the fact that Sonny kept messaging from Cat's phone asking when she'd be done.

She'd originally booked dinner for two: romantic corner booth in the resort's premier restaurant. The chef was famous. He'd been on TV. Now, with the conference awards dinner later that night, and her little boy to consider, she'd changed to a table for three at six pm, at the family restaurant with the kids' play room. That phone call to change the booking had physically hurt.

But she'd long since chosen places to eat according

to what Sonny might like on the menu. Turned out, that night it didn't much help. He was not in an amiable mood.

Sonny was tired of wandering around the hotel. Bored. He didn't want to answer questions about school the day before. Or how his junior AFL team might have gone without him—probably quite well, as he still preferred making shadow puppets to actually getting his hands on the ball.

By the time they finished dinner, Lucinda had bribed him with promises of hide-and-seek. Later, in her hotel suite. And only if he used his real voice, not the one that came with a pouting bottom lip.

No doubt keen on a break herself, Cat had taken off to the powder room about ten minutes before and was taking her time returning.

It was a blessed relief when Angus appeared in the restaurant.

It was short-lived, though, as a dark-haired woman came walking in beside him. Laughing, touching him on the sleeve.

Lucinda readjusted herself on her seat, tugging on the neckline of her spring-green dress, feeling more than a little over-dressed for a date night at a family restaurant with her son, but her suitcase boasted limited options.

Sonny said, "You feel sick, Mum?"

"Hmm?"

"You're frowning. Is it food poisoning?" Currently, one of his favourite books was about the human digestive system. "Or gastro?"

"What? No. I'm fine," she lied as her gaze tugged back to the bar.

To Angus. And his mystery companion. Was she someone from the conference? A random hotel guest, perhaps? She'd been with him once when a random gorgeous woman had walked up to him in the middle of the street and given him her card, saying, "Call me."

No wonder. He was a gorgeous man. All broad shoulders, strong jaw and dark curls. His hand waved elegantly as he spoke and he had one foot hooked on the small ledge beneath the bar, his body turned towards the woman, who looked at him as if her bones were slowly melting in his presence.

"Uncle Angus!" Sonny cried, leaping from the chair and bolting around the tables.

"Sonny!" Lucinda called, but it was too late.

Angus turned, smiling in genuine joy when he saw Sonny rocketing up to him. He caught the kid mid-fly and held him at eye height to ask him a question. Sonny pointed. Angus lowered the boy to the ground, his gaze searching the restaurant.

Lucinda held her breath until his eyes found hers. They were dark in the low light, his face more familiar to her than her own.

Then something in his expression changed, hardened, smouldered. Even from that distance she felt it like a sunburn across her cheeks, her bare shoulders, the backs of her knees.

He said something to his lady friend. She nodded, grabbed their drinks and headed towards the other end of the restaurant, away from the kids' room. While Angus wound his way through the tables to Lucinda.

She was standing before she even realised she'd moved.

"Sorry," she called when he was close. "I see you're busy. I tried to stop him."

He shrugged, just the one shoulder, until his eyes landed on her dress. After a beat or two he looked away, to anywhere but at her. She felt like jumping to catch his eye.

"Enjoying your dinner?" he asked.

"Yes," said Lucinda, right as Sonny said, "No."

Lucinda waggled her hand towards Sonny, who was gripping Angus around the middle, trying to drag him away. "Sonny. Sit. Leave Angus be. He has company."

"Company?" Angus's gaze narrowed and finally connected with hers, before gliding over her face, no doubt taking in her warm cheeks, her tight jaw, the flicker of a pulse at her throat. "Ah. Griselda is on the conference committee, just arrived this evening. Elena asked if I could catch her up, so I talked her through what we had so far on the way here, as the committee are meeting for drinks."

"Oh!" Probably best not to sound quite so relieved. "How did she like the sound of it?"

"As expected," he said with a smile and a quick half-wink to surreptitiously thank her for her help.

"So, they're talking sainthood?"

He chuckled, the sound low and deep and intimate. She could feel it travel over her bare shoulders before diving into her belly.

Then his gaze dropped back to her dress and a muscle ticked in his jaw. His eyes seemed to darken a few degrees. And then…

"When they say it's a small world, they really have no idea," said Cat as she appeared from nowhere, arms crossed, eyes alight with malevolence.

While Angus came over cool as a cucumber.

Chance were, she'd been projecting anyway. With a jaw like that, muscles were sure to tic. And his eyes were always smoky and dark. It was no wonder she felt constant hot flushes.

"Don't let us keep you, Angus," said Cat.

Lucinda shot her a telling glare, but Cat just poked out her tongue.

"No!" Sonny said. "He's playing hide-and-seek."

Sonny reached out and slid his hand into Angus's. Without even seeming to realise it, Angus closed his fingers around Sonny's.

"You promised," Sonny said, as if knowing a no was on its way. "You've finished dinner. It's nearly bed time. Hide-and-seek."

Officially out of the energy to deny him, Lucinda lifted her eyes to Angus.

"He's wilful," said Angus.

"He's eight."

"He's you."

If Lucinda hadn't already had feelings for the man she might have fallen head over heels for him right then and there. As it was, it took every ounce of that wilfulness of hers not to melt into a puddle at the sight of the big man holding her son's hand. Not to imagine giving in, telling Angus how she felt, him smiling at her and saying he'd been waiting to hear those words since the day they'd met.

But Angus began bouncing on the balls of his feet and stretching his arms over his head. "Haven't played in years but I was neighbourhood champ when I was the kid's age. Keen to find out if I've still got it."

And Lucinda breathed again.

"Okay, then," she said. "The rules. We team up. That way nobody gets lost for good. We'll have time limits to each 'hide'. Grown-ups keep phones on. No hiding outside. No getting in people's way. This floor only. Once you hide, there's no moving. It's not a race. Sonny and I can be on one team—"

"No," said Sonny. "I want Auntie Cat on my team."

"Oh."

If Lucinda sounded a little rebuffed, Angus looked it. She caught Sonny's eye only to find his jaw was set. "Are you sure? You can go with Angus, if you'd like?

"You always tell me what a good team you and Angus make, when we go through that list you have of what makes a good friend."

Cat laughed, though there was no humour in it. Then she reached out and took Sonny by the shoulders, moving him into her corner. "Well, I give up. Let's get this show on the road, shall we?"

"Fine," Lucinda gritted out. She looked at her watch. "So, who's it?"

Sonny stuck his hand in the air. "Us. We're counting to one hundred. Go! Mum, hurry, hurry, hurry."

"Right. Um…okay." Lucinda grabbed her bag and her phone and checked the table to make sure she'd left nothing behind. She checked her memory to make sure they'd paid.

"Come on, *Mum*," said Angus, his voice low, his hand held her way. "Hurry."

Competitive spirit lit, Lucinda took it and together they fled.

"Excuse me. Sorry. Excuse us." Lucinda was near breathless with laughter by the time they'd squeezed through the tightly packed tables of the family-friendly restaurant and burst out into the hall.

"Which way?" she asked, turning back to Angus. When she realised she was still holding his hand, she let go and made as if she needed that hand to hitch up her bag. "What do you reckon?"

"I've got an idea," he said, taking her by the hand once more.

It would have been impolite to pull away a second time.

"Where are you taking me?" she asked, her high heels tap-tap-tapping as she jogged to keep up with his long, loping strides.

"Our tree."

"*Our* tree?" she asked. Only to pull up short when they rounded a corner to find themselves facing the humungous fiddle-leaf fig behind which she'd dragged him the morning before.

Before she could demur, Angus grabbed her by the hips, spun her about and pressed her behind the big, fat leaves of the fiddle-leaf fig.

She turned at the corner to complain about the manhandling only to have him place a hand flush over her open mouth while he held a finger to his own.

Then she heard it: Sonny barking orders, his voice growing in volume as it neared. "This way!"

"Slow down, mate."

"Come on!"

When the voices neared, instinct had Lucinda grabbing Angus by the shirtfront to pull him closer, using him and his big, dark form to shield her. She pressed her head into his chest and locked her knees to stop them from jiggling away the excess of adrenaline pouring through her body.

"Run, Auntie Cat!" cried Sonny, close by now. "Angus is really fast."

"How would you even know that?" That was Cat.

"He told me. It doesn't matter if you're wearing the wrong bra, you have to run!"

When Sonny's voice faded into the distance, Lucinda began to laugh.

Angus removed his hand from her mouth and rubbed his thumb against his palm as if rubbing away a tingle. Her head still against his chest, his deep voice rumbled right through her as he said, "That was close."

Lucinda looked up. The fact that she still had a handful of shirt and was using it to pull him to her was clearly not lost on either of them—Angus's eyes were pitch-black, his jaw as hard as granite, his heart thunderous beneath her hand.

"Too close," she said, waggling her eyebrows in an attempt at levity, but the huskiness of her voice gave her away.

Slowly, she unpeeled her fingers, one by one, before leaning back into the corner, as far as she could go, until none of her was touching any of him.

His usually perfect shirt was all squished and messed up, so she gave it a tug, lining up the buttons before ironing the crushed sections with her hand. She could feel the bumps of his chest, his ribs, his abs…

Swallowing hard, she carefully lifted her hand away.

"So," he said. "What now?"

On any other man that deep, devilish tone would have made her sure it was an invitation. Lucinda looked anywhere but at Angus, lest he see it in her eyes.

"Should we move? It's pretty tight back here."

"Can't. You made the rules. No moving."

Right. She and her rules had a lot to answer for this weekend. "Then we wait."

But not like this. Not face to face.

So, she sat, sliding ungracefully down the wall, knees bent up to her chin, dress tucked discreetly behind her thighs.

After a beat, Angus turned his back to the wall and did the same.

"Lift," he said.

She let out a little whoop when he grabbed her by the ankles. Then, realising what he was trying to do, she held onto the feathery layers of her skirt as he stretched out his long legs beneath hers before gently lowering her legs on top of his. He held her ankles a moment before sliding his hands away.

Then he closed his eyes and let the back of his head hit the wall behind him.

"You okay over there?" she said, her voice sounding strangely intimate in their little tree cave.

"Big day."

"Was."

"This is the first time I've been able to catch my breath."

"Comes from being a wanted man."

Eyes still closed, Angus's smile grew. Slowly. Enticingly. "It is nice to be wanted."

"I'm sure." She'd meant it as a joke, but even she heard the caustic edge.

She regretted it the moment Angus opened his eyes and tilted his head her way. Shadows poured over his strong features, creating hollows beneath his jaw, his bottom lip. Their faces were so close, she breathed in the air that he breathed out.

"Don't tell me you're still smarting about Dr Whatsit?"

"Nope," she said, shaking her head. "Last night I got to thinking. There's a pattern. With the men in my life."

She caught his eye, waited for him to say the word "boundaries", but he simply waited for her to go on. And, shrouded by the intimacy of their strange, leafy hidey hole, she found herself saying, "I can't seem to keep them. The men in my life. They seem to find it all too easy to leave."

A tempestuous expression came over Angus's face as he imagined the men who might have slighted her. He grew bigger, like a bear about to attack. But he never came close to the brink.

The man pained himself to be civilised, never burdened others with his emotions. But his emotions were big. Deep. Raw. If he ever let them free, boy that would be something to see.

"Luc, come on."

"I mean it. Look at Joe. I put that down to the fact the man was as deep as a puddle. Cute—sure. Swaggering—you bet. But vapid. I should have seen that coming. I've dated since. Chosen better. And still I'm single. Then Dr What's—*Jameson*. He had all the hallmarks of the kind of man who'd stick. Yet here I am."

"Stuck with me instead."

Lucinda coughed out a laugh, even while her belly flip-flopped at the multi-layered truth behind those words.

"What's wrong with me?" she asked, letting her face fall into her hands with a comic whimper, even while she didn't feel much like laughing.

"Not a single thing."

Lucinda stilled. Not only at Angus's words, but the ragged tone in which they'd been said. Little spot fires burst into life all over her body, making her face burn, and she wondered how hard it might be to live the rest of her life with her face in her hands.

Too hard, she thought, taking a deep breath before lifting her face. Lifting her eyes to his.

Angus's mouth lifted gently at one corner. Then he said, "You, Lucinda May Starling, are good and clever and brave and adventurous and charming and honest and lovely, and for a man to have had the chance to be with you and not do everything in his power to make it work makes him a schmuck."

Lucinda wished she'd been recording all that on her phone. It could keep her warm through many a future winter. "Even Dr Whatsit? He once saved several boys who got lost hiking by rappelling down a cliff to pluck them off a ledge."

"Not even Dr Whatsit. You hold yourself to a higher standard than most. That's not something to feel ashamed about. It's admirable. You do it because you know your worth. And you do it for Sonny."

"I do it for Sonny."

"He sounded just like you right now," Angus said, his hand dropping to rest on her knee.

"Hmm?" she said, having forgotten what it was they were talking about as every cell focussed on his hand.

"Sonny."

"Oh. Right. We do sound a little alike."

"I meant the fact that he's a total bossy-boots who has no qualms about telling his betters exactly what to do."

Lucinda narrowed her eyes. "If the kid knows best, why hide his light behind a bushel?"

"Why indeed?" he said, his voice low in the shadows.

"For the world would be a far darker place without the Starlings in it."

Lucinda swallowed as Angus's words washed over her like a balm.

He never baulked at showing his appreciation—with thanks, with praise, with the thoughtful gifts he'd given her over the years in their nutty contest to one-up one another.

But this felt different.

This whole week had felt different. From the moment she'd told him she wasn't "his girl". As if by looking him in the eye and saying out loud to his face that the flirtation that added sparkle to their work-laden days wasn't serious— the game-playing and the gift-giving—she'd peeled back one extra layer, pressing one step closer to the heart of him.

And that step closer made her yearn so badly to go one step more. And another and the next. Until she alone was allowed to see all the way to his broken, beating, beautiful core.

"Rest assured, Angus," she said, her voice soft, light as a cloud, "we Starlings count ourselves ever so lucky to have a Wolfe in our midst too."

His smile kicked up at one side, his gaze locked on to hers for a few long beats before it dropped slowly, achingly slowly, to her mouth.

What was he thinking when he looked at her that way? Did he have a single clue what that look did to her? Could he hear the revving of her heart? Was it even possible he was imagining stripping *her* layers back?

She heard the double entendre inside her head and her imagination ran with it. She pictured him shifting his hand, just an inch, until his little finger tucked beneath her skirt. Then a second finger. And a third.

She squirmed, shifting so that the back of her knees rubbed against the pants of his suit. Nerves now on high alert, the friction sent a shiver through her from tip to toe.

"Need me to move?" he asked.

She shook her head. The only thing that could fix how she felt in that moment was for him not to exist.

"Then what now?"

"Shall we talk about work?"

Angus shook his head. "Worked enough today."

"Okay. Then shall we talk about why you feel like you're struggling with Remède?"

A grimace came over Angus's face before his expression cleared, as if the grimace had never been. "I think you'll find that's work."

Lucinda shifted and turned, her knees brushing higher against Angus's thighs. But, now she had something concrete to focus on, she was sticking with it. "I don't believe you."

"You don't believe me."

"I've never seen you like this. Erratic. Doubting. It's as if your very foundations have been given a good shake. This isn't just about work. So what's wrong?"

Angus breathed in deeply, breathed out hard, his face a study in broody suspense. Then he said, "You know that Louis is more to me than a client."

"Of course. He's the one who convinced you to leave your marketing job and go out on your own."

"He was also the first person who looked at me and didn't see a punk kid."

"Angus," she chided. "I don't believe that."

The first time Lucinda ever set eyes on Angus had been only a few months after his infamous meeting with Monsieur Fournier. She'd been sitting in Reception on the top floor, waiting to be interviewed by the head of HR, one Fitzgerald Beckett. The business was so new, the place had smelled of fresh paint.

She'd been surrounded by smart-looking people, most of them younger than her and far more savvy, many of them tapping away on their phones as if they were already running the world. The only reason she'd been given a shot at an interview at all was because Sonny and Fitz had the same dentist. Fitz had mentioned to his dentist they were hiring the same week she'd joked that she needed a better job to pay her dental bill.

Fitz had made an entrance as Fitz was wont to do—welcoming them all and warning them the process was about to be brutal and only the toughest among them dared stay. Angus had slipped quietly into the room, leaning unobtrusively against a wall near the door.

He'd been no "punk kid" even back then. He'd seemed nerveless, riveting, hungry, his laser focus taking them in one by one, as if weeding them out before any of them had uttered a word.

"You might have been a little incorrigible back then, but only because you had ambitions. You were hungry. But you were never a 'punk kid'. I know. I was married to one."

Angus's gaze landed back on hers. "Then you were one of the only ones to see that. Not that you'd have ever had the chance to come to that conclusion without Louis Fournier's interference. If not for him, I'd have likely been a marketing cowboy at some slick, soulless firm. And I'd be going home at the end of the day feeling… empty. Whereas now…" He sighed. "This isn't a game to me. Or a puzzle to figure out. We change people's lives. I am so very grateful to be able to do what we do, Luc. Right, deep down inside."

Lucinda smiled and nodded, struggling not to burst into tears. For she felt moved. Moved that this man could admit such things to her.

To think of all the things that had to align to get her to that moment. To get them both to that moment. Joe and Sonny. Fitz and his dentist. Angus and Louis. Without every piece of that puzzle she'd not be sitting on the floor behind a humongous plant, her legs draped over Angus's while his finger traced gentle circles over her knee.

"Have you heard of a thing called *kintsukuroi*?" she asked.

Angus shook his head.

"It's a Japanese art of repairing broken bowls, plates, vases, whereby they use lacquer mixed with powdered gold so that when the pottery is fixed the repairs are obvious, like veins of gold. The breakage is seen as part of the history of an object, rather than something to hide."

Angus watched her, saying nothing.

"That's what Louis saw in you, Angus," she said, her voice husky. "Not just your potential, but the breaks along the way, and the determination to get back up, to repair."

Angus sat forward and lifted his hand from her knee to rub both hands over his face before letting out a primal growl. "A man like that should not have to step over the crumbled remains of his once great company on his way to forced retirement."

Lucinda reached out, peeled his hand from his face and held it in both of hers, battling to hold in her feelings as she sat witness to a rare tumult of emotions Angus could no longer hold in.

"And that's why," she said, "He came to you."

Angus's gaze cleared. Slowly. Until he was more like the man she was used to. But the shadow of his shaken confidence remained.

"You don't need to do that, you know," he said.

"What's that?"

"Be my cheerleader. I'm a big boy. I can take a hit."

"Yeah, you are," she said. "*Such* a big boy."

A slow smile spread across his face, even as his eyes narrowed. Even though he'd known more success than most men saw in a lifetime, that hunger still remained. It was a part of him. And when he switched it on it always made Lucinda burn.

Then his gaze began to roam. Over her hair, snagging on the swathe that never stayed put. Over her cheeks, her jaw, pausing once more on her mouth, before travelling down the twist of a spaghetti strap, over the criss-cross at her décolletage, her bare shoulders.

Lucinda's heart picked up pace and the hairs at the back of her neck prickled. She'd seen the same predatory gleam light his eyes as clients had signed contracts. Well, not exactly the same look. For there was heat here, ferocious and deep, that would send most clients running for the hills.

He shouldn't be looking at her that way.

And she shouldn't be relishing the fact that he was.

"Were you really going to introduce Dr Whatsit to Sonny after this weekend?"

The change of subject nearly gave her whiplash. "Yes. But what does that have to do with—?"

"I didn't only sign up to the conference for Remède. I couldn't stand the thought of you being here, with him."

Oh, help. "Angus…"

She didn't even realise she still had hold of his hand until he used it to pull her closer, wrapping his other hand over hers. Enveloping her in his warmth. His strength. His fingers sliding over hers, making her belly quiver. Her heart squeeze. Her lips part.

"When you told me you were hoping to introduce him to Sonny, I saw red."

Lucinda blinked.

What the…? Was he really looking at her like that, her hands in his, telling her his only concern was for her *son*?

Anger, mortification and heartache —deep, haunting heartache—rose in a maelstrom inside her. Her voice rose with it, getting louder and higher with each word as she nearly shouted, "Are you flipping kidding me?"

"Luc, you know my background. I can't say strongly enough what a game changer that will be for the kid."

Lucinda yanked her hands away from his so fast he nearly fell on top of her. Scrambling to her feet was no mean feat, with the tangling of limbs, the shortness of her dress and the fact she felt so close to tears she could taste them.

"Why am I so surprised? For such a smart guy, you really are the dumbest man I know. Seriously. Of all the conceited, idiotic, selfish—"

Then, close enough to have Lucinda flinch, Sonny's voice split the silence. "I'm gonna check the café! Mum's always saying she needs a coffee, they're totally in there!"

"Sure thing, bud," Cat's voice followed. Then, "I'll wait right here so don't go where I can't see you." Then, to empty air, "Jeez that kid can run."

"I'm calling time," Lucinda said, just above a whisper. "This game has gone on long enough."

Angus pulled himself to standing far more gracefully than she had.

When Sonny's voice called, "Auntie Cat," Lucinda grabbed the trunk of the plant and shook it for all she was worth.

"Wait a second," said Sonny, before he peered through the leaves, then, "Found them!"

Lucinda reached through the leaves and roared. Sonny jumped out of his skin before bursting into tears. And Lucinda's shoulders slumped.

Seemed she couldn't do anything right tonight.

"Lucinda…" Angus said, tracing a hand down her arm.

"Goodnight, Angus. I'll see you in the morning."

"But the awards dinner…"

"No one will miss me. You'll do just fine without me. I'll be there tomorrow, for the keynote at nine."

He stood back, an inch at most, and waved his hand for her to go first. She slid past him, brushing against his side, feeling too big a fool to get any kind of kick out of it at all.

Then she wrapped Sonny up tightly in her arms, holding him close, wiping his tears as she walked Cat and her boy back to their room without once looking back.

CHAPTER EIGHT

WHEN LUCINDA TOOK a right, Angus took a left, heading back towards Reception. Then out of the front door and down the steps, with no idea of where he was going, only that he needed space. And air. And room to breathe.

He was halfway towards the lake when it started to rain. Big, fat drops that had him soaked in half a minute. Not that it helped cool him down. His internal engine was running at maximum speed, his thoughts spinning too fast to catch, bursts of adrenaline pumping through him.

For he knew. Big time. He knew that he'd just screwed up the way he knew when a campaign hit that sweet spot where colour, tagline and key image all came into perfect sync.

But he didn't feel himself, his emotions slipping about inside him, unable to find purchase, his head too foggy to figure out why.

He'd only been trying to help. To tell Lucinda she deserved better. The best. She and Sonny. Because her kid was great and she was an amazing mother—loving, honest and fierce. She was also a brilliant administrator. And a loyal friend.

Fitz had been dead right. If anyone deserved love, Valentine hearts and eternal happiness, it was Luc.

She'd looked so sad when talking about the band of idiots she'd allowed into her life, he'd have done anything to help her lose the doe eyes. They made him ache. And growl.

And want to kiss everything better.

To place one hand against the wall right by her neck, trapping her in place. To run the other down the length of the delicate green strap barely holding her dress in place. The same dress she'd worn to the damn Christmas party a year and a half ago, when she'd appeared on the other side of the crowd looking like temptation in heels.

He pictured her face tilting up to his, those warm brown eyes melting as he showed her just how heart-stopping he thought she was…

Angus's feet squelched to a stop as he balled his hands into fists.

He had to stop. Stop thinking about her that way.

But he couldn't, not since he'd seen her standing in the restaurant wearing that dress. In an instant, tension had coiled around him like a spring. When she'd slid to the floor behind their tree, and wrapped her legs over his, his entire body had felt trapped in a vice. As though he'd implode if he couldn't touch her, feel her, be with her.

The rain really began to bucket down, the noise thunderous. He tugged his suit jacket over his head, preparing to head for a nearby copse of conifer trees, before he gave up, held his arms out and let it lash him. Cleanse him. Beat down against his skin until the strange, frenetic heat pulsing through him abated.

Finally, after a few minutes, he felt as if he could hear himself again.

When the rain made no sign of slowing, he turned and headed back towards the hotel at a walk, tipping an imaginary hat towards the doorman, who batted not an eyelid at his bedraggled form.

He'd finished the conference rebrand before dinner. He'd called in help from the graphics team back home, getting in touch with a couple who were always happy for overtime and sending them photos of his ideas. He'd worked hard, and it felt good. Like sorbet for the mind.

With that clarity it was time to get the real work done.

To look back over the Remède rebrand with new-found knowledge of the industry, through the eyes of long-time consumers, lapsed consumers and competitors.

He just needed one idea. One lightbulb. One—

Angus came to a sliding halt when he saw Charlie and Fitz walking through Reception. Charlie looked just as soaked as he was, while Fitz was bone-dry and sporting enough matched luggage to be heading off on the Orient Express.

"Angus!" Fitz spotted him, holding his arms out as if for a hug.

"What the ever-loving hell are you doing here?"

Fitz did his best super-hero impression, even flicking out a pretend cape. "We're here to save you from yourself!"

Angus growled.

"Oh, put your claws away, sunshine," Fitz scoffed. "I was bored, and Charlie was sitting next to me while I was bored, so I convinced him to keep me company on the drive here. We've booked into this conference of yours too, to see what all the fuss is about."

"All that's left is the awards night and a final speech over breakfast."

"Perfection! Speaking of perfection, where's Lucinda?"

His jaw clenched before he admitted, "With Cat. And Sonny."

"Cat. And Sonny. They gate-crashed too? Well, the gang really is all here!"

"Go home, Fitz. Take Charlie with you before you lose him."

"And miss the big party?"

"Awards dinner."

"Awards dinner? Never! We're not going to miss that. Are we, Charlie?"

Charlie glanced away from the TV over the bar off

to the right of the front desk. He'd somehow made them change it to the business channel.

"Come on, cuz." Fitz flung an arm around Angus's neck. "Let's show these ladies of lipstick how it's done."

The awards dinner was long over, the after party in full swing. The DJ played "Celebrate" for the seventh time and Fitz stood on stage, singing his heart out. Charlie had lost his shoes and shirt and was dancing with Ms Black Heels, Ms Henna and about a half dozen other women.

While Angus sat at a table by the doors, checking his watch or checking the hall in case Lucinda came looking for him, now Sonny would be down. If she'd cooled off.

Elena took the seat beside Angus. "Darling boy."

"Elena."

"Why so glum? This is a party. And a great one. Thanks in no small part to you and your friends."

"Not glum," said Angus. "Designated driver. It's my fault they are here so it's on me to get the boys back to their rooms in one piece."

"Mmm… And the lovely Lucinda?"

"Her son is here and her sister. She's spending some time with them."

"Her son? So, she's married, then? I thought—"

"Not married. Very much single." Angus shook his head, wondering why he'd felt the need to be so vociferous.

"I see. Then I'd be remiss in not saying the two of you complement one another very well." With that cryptic comment, Elena looked out over the happy crowd. Her crowd. "I don't know what I did to deserve you, Angus Wolfe, but it must have been spectacular. Even without all the amazing work you have done for us this weekend, this party is going down in history. Half those here have already paid deposits for the next conference and that is unheard of. Please tell me you'll come?"

Angus went to shake his head, before realising it wasn't a hard no. He'd had a good time this weekend. Broadened his horizons. Looking up and out suited him. "I'll sign up to the mailing list. Then we'll see."

Elena reached out and put her hands over his. Her skin was paper-soft. "I know how busy you are. You're a darling for even pretending. This isn't my first rodeo. I looked you up five minutes after we met. I'm well aware how lucky we have been to have you. I know you've been talking to a lot of the other girls about Remède. How is old Louis? Is he well?"

Angus coughed out a laugh at the thought of anyone daring to call Louis "old". "Ah, he's…keeping on."

"I'm glad. What a dear man. My first job was working one of his counters in David Jones back in the day. The lushest, loveliest product I've worked with then or since. The kind that makes every woman feel special, despite their scars, their worn-off edges."

Angus stilled as a small flame flickered to life in that place inside where ideas were born.

Elena went to take back her hand before Angus turned his over and captured it. "Special? How?"

Elena blinked. Thought. Then said, "My favourite lipstick—back when I was young and married, a zillion lifetimes ago—was a coral gloss by Remède. I'd wear it day and night, even while washing the dishes, knowing that when my husband came home from a long day at work I'd feel pretty for him. After he passed, I continued to put on that lipstick every time I washed the dishes as it reminded me of all the good. I know it sounds very old-fashioned but it's a rare product that can make queens and housewives alike feel like royalty. Then again, Louis Fournier is a rare man."

She squeezed his hand before letting go, then glanced over her shoulder to the double doors. "Why don't you head off? I'll make sure your boys get home safe."

Angus didn't need to be told twice. He kissed Elena on the cheek before taking off.

His mind was like a wildfire of ideas, burning up everything in its path.

He needed Lucinda.

He needed her with her cheap pencil, her fancy notebook and the way she understood what he meant. Her ability to put his thoughts into words the world would understand.

Something Elena had said tugged at a loose thread inside him and, the more it tugged, the more the way he'd been thinking about Remède's rebrand unravelled.

They'd gone high-concept. Crisp, aspirational glamour. Because Remède was a quality brand. Celebrity endorsements. A string of lean, tanned, beautiful social media influencers all lined up at the ready.

He'd gone for big when he should have been going *in*. Tapping into how to make every woman feel beautiful. Honest. Special.

But how could he do that if he hadn't been able even to convince Lucinda of the same?

Suddenly it was of supreme importance that he did so. That he made Lucinda understand what he'd been trying to say, badly, behind their tree. How special *she* was. And not just on occasions when she allowed herself to wear her mother's perfume.

If he could make Lucinda see it, and believe him, then maybe the rest of the world would too.

Lucinda woke with a start.

Feeling disoriented in the strange, dark room, she glanced at the clock to find it was a little after ten. After saying her goodnights to Sonny and Cat, who'd been tucked in watching *Jurassic Park*, she must have come back to her room and fallen asleep. Fully dressed.

Pulling herself to a sitting position with a groan, she

ran a hand over her hair to find it knotted on one side. She gave her face a good stretch, as if shaking off a mask she'd been holding in place for months.

But couldn't find the wherewithal to get up. Get changed.

Had Angus made it to the awards night? Probably. Despite all the whammy errors of judgement, thought and deed he'd made over the past weekend, he was a big one for keeping his word.

"Gah!" she yelled, and fell back on the bed.

What would it take for her to remain angry with the guy? Right now, she could really do with a good head of steam where he was concerned. Some deep-rooted, stomach-churning loathing would be great.

What a rotten thing to think.

Angus Wolfe had never let her down. He'd given her opportunity, support, kindness and space, galvanising her need to work into creating a career she could be proud of. One she was mighty good at.

Just thinking about the man—the way he'd looked her in the eye and said he'd followed her to the hotel because he was worried about Sonny—made her feel as if her insides were on the outside, as if her nerves were exposed. Every movement scraped. Every feeling ached.

Lucinda turned her head towards the door, thinking she'd heard a gentle knock. Nothing. Even her ears were playing tricks on her.

It sounded again.

"Cat?" she muttered, rolling off the bed and trudging over to the door.

When she whipped it open, she found Angus standing in the hall.

His eyes were preternaturally bright, his hair tightly curled as if it had recently been wet. His tie was skew-whiff.

He opened his mouth to say something before his gaze

dropped to her dress. And something seemed to come over him. A kind of mental fugue that made his eyes go dark and his jaw clench.

"Angus," she snapped. "What's going on? Why aren't you at the awards dinner?"

He shook his head. "May I come in?"

Like a vampire; unable to enter without explicit invitation. And just as dangerous. Especially when she was feeling so wobbly. But if they were going to move beyond this weekend, if things had a hope of going back to normal come Monday, it had to start some time.

So, with a sweeping arm, she invited her boss into her hotel bedroom.

"What's so important it couldn't wait until tomorrow?" she asked, closing the door and padding over to the couch in the corner where she'd flung a bra. She tossed it into her open suitcase which she then shut with a toe.

When she looked back, it was to find Angus standing at the end of her bed, staring at the mussed-up blankets on which she'd been sleeping.

"Angus? What's going on?"

His gaze swept to hers, before sliding back to her dress. "I wish you hadn't worn that dress."

"This dress?" Why on earth not? "It's a gorgeous dress. And I look mighty fine in it, thank you very much."

Something in his eyes told her he agreed. And yet he looked pained.

She went to him. "Angus, are you okay? You look unwell. Have you been drinking?"

"Not a drop."

"Okay then, how about you fill me in on whatever was so important you had to come to my room at ten o'clock at night."

"Is it that late?"

"It's that late."

His mobile rang. He ignored it. He didn't even glance at it to see who it was.

"Angus, your phone."

"They can wait."

"It's okay."

He looked into her eyes, believed her, then with a nod grabbed his phone out of his pocket and answered it with, "Fitz, are you bleeding? Have you been arrested? Then don't call me. I'm otherwise engaged." With that he turned off the phone. All the way off. His eyes on her the whole time.

Feeling like she was having some kind of out of body experience, Lucinda said, "If Fitz needs you, take the call."

"He can wait," Angus said. "I'm here with you."

Lucinda curled her feet into the carpet in an effort not to sway straight into the man's arms.

Good gravy, are you so hard up for a man who'll stick, you're getting all woozy over crumbs?

But even as she thought it, she knew it wasn't that.

Despite the times she'd had to leave at the drop of a hat for Sonny. Despite the tough first months when her need to be liked had clashed with his need for personal space. Despite the fact that she stood up to him on a regular basis, refusing to back down when he was in a bolshie mood. Or when he was flat-out wrong.

Angus had stood by her through thick and thin.

He'd never left.

In fact, he'd done the opposite. He'd followed her here. Not for some small-fry conference with a tenuous link to a favourite client. Not because he feared for Sonny's mental health.

He'd followed *her*. She knew it. Right deep down in that most feminine place inside.

The question was, why?

Slowly she uncurled her toes from their grip on the carpet.

"Angus, what's going on?"

"What's going on? Fitz thought I should know that Charlie is currently leading a conga line at the party downstairs."

"I'm sorry, *what*? Why the heck are *they* here? Did you invite them?"

His left eyebrow notched. "Fitz claims they're here because he's bored and never met a conference he didn't love."

"Why are they really here?"

"I think it's to stop me from doing anything stupid."

"Such as?"

He wouldn't say.

But she knew. Deep within a moment of true clarity, she knew.

For he was looking at her in a way that told her he'd like to tear her clothes off and have his way with her then and there. It was the look she'd been waiting for her whole life. Untempered, unmitigated and all kinds of trouble.

"Why are you really here, Angus?" Her mouth was so dry it was a miracle she found words at all.

He glanced towards the door, as if trying to remember himself. "Remède. Back at the party—the dinner —I'd had a breakthrough about Remède."

"Not here, to my room. But to the hotel." She took a step his way. His gaze dropped to her bare feet. When she took another step, he slid his phone into his pocket and waited.

"What really sent you to the hotel website? And don't tell me it was Sonny because, while I know you love my kid, you know I'd never do anything that wasn't in his best interests."

"I may have had other reasons." His eyes slowly lifted back to hers.

"Such as?"

"Fear."

Well, that was not what she'd expected him to say. "Of *what*?"

"Of Dr Jameson What's-His-Name-Smythe. Of the way he looked at you in a picture Fitz found on Facebook. That he'd marry you and have three more kids."

"Oh."

"And—" He cut himself off.

Lucinda took another two steps his way. "And?"

"Your priorities would change. And you'd…leave me."

She couldn't help it. She laughed. The thought of her *ever* leaving him was ridiculous.

Angus's face grew stony. Some instinct had her reaching out and taking his hand.

"I wasn't laughing at you, Angus. I promise. The thought of ever leaving you is laughable. You know how much I love my job. How important the Big Picture Group and the motley crew who run it are to me." She swallowed. Then said, "How important you are to me."

He took a step her way.

Not expecting it, she rocked back, but he reached out, slid an arm around her waist and hauled her against him. It took everything she had not to swoon.

She waited for him to let her go. But he didn't.

Instead, his voice came to her, rough and low, as he said, "How important?"

She lifted a hand and held her forefinger and thumb an inch apart. "This important."

"Well, that's something." His eyes, dark now, not a glint of light within to be seen, moved slowly between hers. "Did I ever tell you how much I like this dress of yours?"

"That would be a no."

"Enough that I'm especially glad Dr Whatever-the-Hell-His-Name-Was never got the chance to see you in it."

Lucinda breathed out hard as Angus did more than nudge at the line between them. "Angus," she warned, "It's okay. I know I had a moment there, behind our tree, when I was feeling a little sorry for myself, but I'm tough. I don't need you to be extra nice to me."

He reached up and ran a finger over one twisting strap, his finger sliding beneath it as he traced it over her shoulder and down the blade. "The last thing I'm feeling right now is nice."

The line blurred a whole lot more.

And then he went ahead and obliterated it when he said, "The night of the Christmas party, I was hiding at the edge of the makeshift dance floor as Dean Martin crooned about a winter wonderland, while outside in downtown Melbourne it had been a sweltering thirty-five degrees Celsius. I'd been waiting a good half an hour for you to arrive so you could save me from all the small talk when the crowd cleared and there you were. Looking like you'd stepped out of a flower patch. All glowing and fresh and bright as a star. The feeling that came over me—I'd never felt anything like it before. A heaviness in my limbs. A hollowness behind my ribs."

Lucinda knew how that felt, for she was feeling that way right now. "You say that to all the girls."

"Never," he claimed. "They'd laugh in my face."

"Are you kidding? They'd quiver in their heels."

His gaze warmed and his touch moved south, his palm sweeping down her back, sending goose bumps in its wake. "Is that what's happening to you right now, Lucinda?"

Somehow she managed to say, "I'm not wearing heels."

He laughed, the rumble travelling through him into her. And pulled her closer still.

Feeling reckless, she said, "You wore your navy suit that night, the one with the fine pinstripe. No tie. I remember thinking, *wow, Mr Casual even has his top button undone.*"

He cocked his head. "It was a party, after all."

"True. But it's not the suit I remember most from that night so much as the—"

"Mistletoe," they said at the same time.

Lucinda felt herself transported back to that moment. Coming out of the store room with a roll of paper towel to mop up a spill, right as Angus had come in. They'd both ended up in the doorframe. Toe to toe. His hands at her elbows. Laughing at the near-collision.

Then someone—a disembodied voice—had headed past them in the hall and shouted, "Mistletoe!"

And they'd looked up.

When Lucinda had dared look down, dared make eye contact with Angus again, he'd already been watching her, chest rising and falling as if he needed more air. The fingers holding her by the elbows had tightened. Just enough to tell her she wasn't alone.

"So," he'd said, eyes flickering to the offending greenery above that was holding them both to ransom, before dropping back to hers, so dark and saying so much without saying a word.

"So," she'd said, her voice cracking, her heady gaze dropping to his decadent mouth.

She remembered thinking, maybe she could do this. Maybe this would be her only chance to see what he tasted like. What those lips would feel like on hers. To slide her hands into his dark curls and kiss the man till they both forgot who they were to one another.

Whether she'd lifted onto her toes, or he'd done it for her, she remembered how they'd edged closer, the air heating, shimmering, the sounds of the party dropping away.

Until the roll of paper towel she'd been holding had fallen out of her hands and rolled down the hall, breaking the spell. Reminding them both of who they were. What they were meant to be doing. And not doing.

"I'd better go clean up the mess," she'd said before all but bolting out into the hall.

It turned out many people had hooked up that night. So many, Fitz had put out a memo saying he hoped they'd all had fun and let off some steam but now it was time to get back to work.

There'd been no recriminations. No complaints. It was the kind of work place where respect, work ethic and good nature prevailed. A couple of short-term relationships had been born before fizzling out, and a couple of long-term ones were still going strong.

While Lucinda and Angus had pretended that their "moment" had never happened.

"I thought you'd forgotten," she said. "Or I'd dreamed it. There had been a fair lot of bubbly thrown around that night. Did I? Dream it?" Her voice was soft, husky.

Angus breathed in deep. "If not for that roll of paper towel, I'd have kissed you then and there."

Lucinda's chest hurt as so many feelings rushed through her body. Good and bad. Dangerous and hopeful. The ache of wasted time. The feeling that the future was concertinaing too fast for her to keep up.

"You never said," she said. "Never even a hint. The rest of the night you were impossible to catch, then come Monday it was business as usual."

"You didn't mention it either. So I deferred to you."

He'd wanted her, but he'd deferred to her. What a heady thought. To actually have a *say* in the affairs of her heart rather than feeling like flotsam tossed about on a great stormy sea.

She lifted a hand to rest against his heart only to find it thunderous, erratic. As if he was fighting some mighty, invisible, internal battle behind his cool facade.

And his hand swept the stray swathe of hair behind

her ear, his palm resting against the edge of her jaw. "I didn't want things to change between us."

"I didn't want things to change between us, either," she said, noting they'd both used past tense.

For deep down inside it was what she wanted more than anything else in the world. When she blew out candles on her birthday cake, when people asked what she wanted for Christmas, in her head she always said the same thing.

She wanted to be cherished. She wanted to be seen. She wanted to be important to someone. More than anything, she wanted all that from Angus.

Their friendship, their working relationship, had survived so much already.

He'd seen her premenstrual more times that she could count. He'd forgiven her short temper after a week of little sleep when Sonny had had the croup. She'd seen him quietly distraught when he'd lost his grandfather's watch. Heartbreakingly stoic when he'd lost his mother.

But never, in all the years she'd known him, had she felt this close to the man. This close to doing something truly reckless. Like leaning her cheek against his shoulder. Tipping up onto her toes and kissing the edge of his chin. The glasses dent at the top of his nose. Bussing her lips against his.

And, as her heart sent blood around her body before drawing it back again, she knew—knew right, deep down in places primal and eternal—that she wasn't alone.

Angus's eyes were so dark they were now devoid of colour. His jaw so tight she could make out the shape of every muscle under the skin. If he tucked her hair behind her ear again, she'd jump him. Then and there.

Six and a half years of working for the guy be damned.

She'd find another job. Agencies tried to headhunt her all the time.

But she didn't want to walk into another job. She

wanted *her* job. The thought of not going to the Big Picture Group every day made her heart hurt. She'd helped build that place—created connections with amazing businesses, grown a network of favours, been instrumental in helping the clients leave better off than when they'd arrived.

But it felt as though all of that was happening in another dimension as she melted in his arms. Caught as she was in the maelstrom in his eyes. Mesmerised by his thumb caressing her cheek. By the supremely male evidence he could not hide.

The only reason they'd gone no further was because he was stronger than she was. He'd practically spelled it out for her. He would never make the first move.

For he deferred to her.

Knowing she was about to leap into unchartered territory without a map, a guide or an escape plan, Lucinda wrapped her hand around the knot of his tie and pulled him towards her.

"By something stupid," she said when his face was near level with hers, "do you think Fitz meant this?"

She lifted up onto her toes and placed a light kiss on his cheek. His skin was warm, if unexpectedly rough. He smelled like heaven.

Then she moved to the other cheek, her touch almost reverent, the grip on his tie strong.

When she moved back to her flat feet she looked into his eyes. They burned like a long-dormant volcano rumbling back to life. As if he was barely holding himself together.

"Don't do that unless you mean it, Luc," he said again, his voice coming from somewhere deep and private, making her feel as if she were trespassing some place in which another living soul had never been. A place she ought to think very carefully about trespassing on now.

"Never," she said.

"Luc…" he said, his voice fuelled with warning, even as he pulled her up against him so she was in no doubt how tempted he was. The way he said her name—the longing, the history, the regret—tipped her over the edge.

With an outshot of breath, like a sigh she'd been holding onto for several years, Lucinda grabbed Angus harder by the tie, pulled him down to her level and kissed him.

She felt him still, as if he were holding the entire universe at bay, before he wrapped both arms tightly about her and kissed her like a man starved.

It was crazy. Wild. As if they'd both been clinging to civility for so long that now it had been stripped away, they were left stark, bare.

He tasted of heat. And cinnamon. Of tenderness and chance. And she couldn't get enough. Needing more, needing to climb inside the man's very skin, she leapt into his arms, wrapping her legs around his hips.

He laughed against her mouth.

"Luc," he said, his hands trying to get purchase on the layers of tulle as he held her to him, "are you trying to give me a heart attack?"

"Yes," she deadpanned. "Now that I finally have you where I want you, what I really want is to put you into decommission."

"Now?" he said, pulling back far enough to look deep into her eyes. "Now that you finally have me?"

What could she possibly say bar, "Angus, I've wanted this for longer than I can remember. And if you didn't know that already then you're not half as smart as you think you are."

At that he said nothing. At that he leaned into her and kissed her again. Slowly this time. Achingly slowly. Sweetly, deeply. Till her lungs collapsed and her bones dissolved and she no longer cared if she came back together in one piece again.

She was only half-aware of the jolt as his knees hit the

bed. As he laid her carefully on the soft mattress. There he took his time, swiping her hair from her face, first one side then the other. She ducked her cheek into his hand. Her eyes closed as she all but purred.

When her eyes opened it was to find his roving over her hair, her cheeks, her mouth, as if he was committing every angle, every freckle, every smile-line to memory.

She lifted a hand, only to find it shaking, and pressed it against his cheek. The scrape of his stubble sent shivers through her. The reverberations, she was sure, would never quite go away.

"Finally," he said.

It was like coming home.

Only to a home she'd never known. One of ease and bliss and the sweet ache of longing.

"Don't stop," she said, eons later, breathless, no longer herself. "Don't you dare stop."

"I won't," he promised. "Not for all the world."

And he didn't. Not until later again when, replete to their very marrows, neither of them could move, talk or fathom how it had come to pass.

Or how it hadn't happened sooner.

CHAPTER NINE

LUCINDA LAY ON her side, the sheets pulled up to her chin, the blissful, cool, soft cotton of the hotel pillow against her cheek. She couldn't keep the smile from her face even if she wanted to.

For after the bed there'd been the shower. Angus had joined her there and… *Oh, my.*

Once he'd dried her off with a big, white fluffy towel, the friction making havoc with her already overloaded senses, he'd found an old T-shirt in her suitcase—as if he knew the black, lacy ribbon thing wasn't really her, and helped her into it. Then he'd proceeded to lift her onto the bathroom bench and… *Oh, wow.*

Lucinda felt the side of the bed depress as Angus sat beside her. Barely able to keep her eyes open, she managed a, "Mmm…?"

She waited for him to kiss her on the shoulder before making a stealthy exit. She'd always imagined that would very much be Angus's MO: no sleepovers, no false expectations. But all her imaginings so far had not even come close to the reality.

Instead, he lifted the sheet, tucked himself in behind her, bare bar his black boxer shorts, slid his arm over her and pulled her close.

She was spooning. With Angus. And she decided then and there that reality was far better than fantasy.

"Angus?" she said, her voice hoarse.

"Hmm," he hummed against the back of her neck.

"Why did you come here last night? There was something you were in an all-fired rush to tell me—"

"Right. It was Remède," he said. "I'd forgotten... Distracted as I was by other things."

"Really. I hadn't noticed."

He nipped the tendon between her neck and shoulder, and when she cried out, he kissed the spot till she was purring once more.

"I'd had a breakthrough," he murmured.

"Tell me about it."

"Now?" he asked, and she could hear the smile in his voice.

She turned onto her back so she could look him in the eye. "I'd like to know."

He nuzzled his nose into her hair before lifting up onto his elbow, his head resting in his palm. That face, she thought, her heart stuttering at the sight of him. His nearness. The unusual ease of his expression, the full glory of the man behind the mask.

"Elena, of all people, said something that reminded me of something you'd said," he murmured, his finger now tracing the edge of her arm, the curve of her shoulder, the rise of her neck. "The Japanese pottery tradition where they use gold dust to highlight the repairs, not conceal them?"

"Kintsukuroi." She loved that fact. It had helped her through so many of the mistakes, the bad times, the regrets—imagining the mental scars healing with rivers of gold.

"Taking Remède back to its core construct, that's what it's all about. It isn't about covering up a woman's flaws. Hiding them behind a 'dewy glow' or fancy 'protein bond repeating serums'."

Wow, he really had been paying attention at the conference.

"So what is Remède about?"

"You."

"Me?"

"You and your mother's perfume. It's about making a woman feel special while also feeling very much herself. Whether by way of a scent that sweeps her back to sweeter times, or a lip colour that makes her feel loved, makes her remember to smile. Remède—with its tastefulness, its poignancy, its longevity—is the gold dust, the through line, that holds their best memories together."

It was a wonder that this big, quiet, self-possessed giant of a man could think that way. It took tenderness. It took heart.

Lucinda reached up and slid her hand behind his neck, pulled him down to kiss her.

Goodness knew how much later, voice croaky, he murmured against her mouth, "I take it that means you think I'm on the right track?"

"You, Angus Wolfe, are a wonder. When, hundreds of years from now, you finally depart this mortal coil that brain of yours ought to be bronzed. Or, better yet, studied. No, replicated. For the betterment of mankind."

"Only my brain?"

"Well, I can think of some other parts of you that are pretty good too."

Angus settled himself over her, his gaze boring into hers, his expression so sincere it took all her power not to burst into tears.

Then he said, "I'm not sure what I did in a past life to deserve you, Lucinda Starling, but whatever it was I'm very glad I did it."

And then he kissed her, and held her, and cherished her. And when she finally fell asleep she didn't dream. She didn't need to.

Angus shut the door to Lucinda's hotel room with a soft click. Then he closed his eyes and leaned back against the door.

The hall was thankfully quiet, the guests no doubt all enjoying a Sunday morning lie-in, as dawn only just peeked over the hills beyond.

Watching Lucinda as he'd dressed, the pre-dawn light shining softly golden over the familiar curves of her face, the urge to wake her with a kiss, a touch, a caress—to make love to her again, or simply to see that look in her eyes when she saw him there—had been so strong he'd had to breathe his way through it.

Strong feelings were not his forte. Not when it came to his private life. They confused, they encouraged bad decisions. So, he'd left her be.

Leaning against the door he took a few moments to think. To plan out what steps to take next. For there was no map for where he'd just been. No tried and true strategy to fall back on.

Only, his mind remained blank. Empty. He felt light, washed clean. The kind of clean that meant he could smell flowers from a mile away. Could see colours he'd never seen before. Like the world after a storm.

Lucinda's *I've wanted this for longer than I can remember* ran on a loop inside his head. She'd wanted it. Wanted *him*. Said if he didn't know it already he wasn't as smart as he thought he was.

What he hadn't said was, "Right back at you."

From the very first moment he'd seen her waiting to interview at the Big Picture Group offices, he'd known she was different from anyone he'd ever met. Her light had been bewitching. He'd felt he had no choice but to invite her into his life.

But even as their friendship had deepened, even as she'd become intrinsic to his life, he'd held back that one last part of himself. Broken, burned and unwilling to burden anyone with his scars, he'd held back—especially from someone as light and lovely as Lucinda.

Until last night, seeing her walk towards him in that dress, he'd given in. Given up. Given over to her.

A shiver rolled down his back, landing with a hot thrum of energy in his gut, as he imagined a life in which he'd resisted. In which he'd never known the taste of her, the feel of her, the sounds she made when she was really happy.

Then he heard a noise somewhere down the hall.

Within a second he recognised the pair of people hunched over against the wall several doors down.

Cat—hair wild, barefoot, wearing what looked like a onesie—was down on her haunches, her hands resting on Sonny's knees as he sat leaning against the wall. Crying.

Without thinking, Angus jogged their way, calling out, "Cat?"

Cat stood, groaning as her knees cracked.

Sonny shot Angus a wet glance before wiping his eyes with a sleeve.

"Everything okay?" he asked Cat as he neared, keeping his voice down.

"He took off out of the room while I was in the bathroom," Cat said, looking chagrined. "Bad dream. Not like him. Could be something he ate. The strange room. Or the dinosaur movie marathon we watched last night."

Angus shot her a look.

Cat shrugged. "Either or."

"Mmm… Hey, bud," Angus said, crouching down but glancing past the kid, trying to look as casual as all get-out. For he'd hated being fussed over when he had been upset at that age. It had only made him feel as if he was under a spotlight. As if showing how he felt had been wrong somehow.

Sonny sniffed.

"Bit early for a hike, don't you think?"

A quick glance saw Sonny's mouth doing its best to turn down. "I wasn't hiking. I was looking for Mum."

"She's asleep, bud. But you know she'll come see you the minute she's awake."

He glanced up at Cat to find she was glaring down the hall in the direction whence he'd come. She then gave him a swift once over, no doubt taking in the crumpled suit, the time of day. Her eyes narrowed as she put the pieces together with ease.

Then she crooked a finger at him and took a few paces away, tapping a foot on the floor till he joined her.

Her voice lowered to a hiss. "Please tell me I did not just catch you on a walk of shame…from my sister's room."

He slid his hands into his suit pockets. "Not sure that's any of your business."

Even while he could honestly have said *no*. For he felt no shame. No regret.

"What the hell were you thinking?" Cat asked, her voice rising.

"Cat," he warned. "Not the time or place." Angus looked to Sonny, whose tears had dried up and who was watching them carefully over the tops of his knees.

But Cat, who looked as if she'd had about as much sleep as Sonny, wasn't having it. "And I thought you were smarter than this. Well, I hoped, and prayed and begged whatever gods might be listening that even if she drank the Angus Wolfe Kool-Aid, you were experienced enough to make sure nothing ever happened. Why couldn't you have just left her the hell alone this weekend?"

Wasn't the first time Angus had been told point blank he wasn't good enough, but it was the first time in a long time, and the inviolable walls that usually buffeted such assaults, had been put away for the night.

Glaring at Cat, he kept his voice low. "Because she deserves better than some schmuck who cancels dates, spends half his time on the phone and says 'fine' when she tells him she might have to work instead of go away with him!"

"And you think that you can do better?"

Angus ran a hand through his hair.

"That you can be there for her, heart and soul, one hundred percent?" Catriona laughed, the sound completely lacking in humour. "Luc is your assistant. And that's it. Weird crush dynamic you've had going on for years notwithstanding. Her real life is with us. Me and the kid. The people she can count on to be there for her. Always. Unless you can promise me right here and now that you're in it for the long haul, for better or worse, putting her first, before the job, then cut your losses and move on now."

Angus's gut churned at Catriona's demands. And, while his usual method would be to rock back, to make it clear how little he cared, how little he could be impacted by the whims of other people, this time he leaned in.

"Luc means the world to me, Cat. Her happiness, Sonny's happiness, are more important to me than my own. And you know it."

Cat's eyes flared. Surprisingly in triumph.

But he was too riled to make sense of it. "She's the closest thing I have to family. I can't lose her. I won't. It would do me in. What I've achieved, what I've earned, what I've learned...without her none of it would be worthwhile."

The world was quiet for a beat, before Catriona coughed out a laugh. Then she crossed her arms and said, "Well, it's about time."

While Angus tried to figure out why Cat was looking so bloody smug, Lucinda's voice floated towards them. "What on earth's going on out here?"

Angus turned to find Lucinda padding down the hall, wrapping herself in an old, tasselled, dark-green pashmina that fell below her knees. He'd seen her wearing it more than a dozen times before when they'd shared suites at conferences. After she'd taken him in when he'd been sick. In hospital when they'd thought Sonny might have had pneumonia.

He'd thought seeing her in her magical green dress for the first time had been a watershed moment. But this… watching her walk towards him in that ancient wrap, looking flustered, soft and well-ravished—by him—made looking at her in that dress feel like a walk in the park.

He felt himself smiling from way down deep inside. If only she'd look his way, she'd know it. She'd feel it. That everything had changed. And it was all okay.

But, before Cat or Angus could fashion a sane answer to her reasonable question, Sonny was on his feet, bolting into her arms.

Lucinda held the kid tight, running her hands over his head and down his back, before leaning down and lifting his face to hers. Checking with her special mother powers to make sure he was in one piece before planting a big kiss on his hair.

Then she looked up at the grown-ups and mouthed, *"What happened?"*

Cat moved towards Lucinda and Sonny, putting a hand on the kid's shoulder. "Sonny came looking for you. I went looking for him. And found Angus. Skulking down the hall."

Lucinda's brow furrowed, her hands moving to cover Sonny's ears. But she still wouldn't look Angus's way.

"You okay, buddy?" she asked, attention back on her son. "Did you want something? Or did you just miss me? You know if you wanted me you only had to ask Auntie Cat to call and I'd have come to you in a heartbeat."

"I had a bad dream. That friend of yours, the one who was meant to come away with you, was chasing me and tried to eat me."

Lucinda's eyes were wide as she looked at Cat, who bit at a fingernail.

"He asked. When you told him you were going away for the weekend, he asked why he couldn't come too. I told him you had a friend staying with you."

"Cat. Seriously?

"I panicked!"

Lucinda held Sonny tighter. "My friend Jameson doesn't eat meat, so you're perfectly safe."

"I don't want him to be my new dad."

"Oh, honey bunny. That's just fine because he won't be. Is that what you thought was happening this weekend?"

Sonny nodded, fresh tears pouring down his sweet face. "If I have to have a new dad, why can't it be Angus?"

All three adults held their breath as Sonny's bombshell landed with what felt like a sonic boom.

"Angus?" said Lucinda, recovering quickest. "Sweetie, Angus can't be your dad."

"But why not?" Sonny begged, his bottom lip quivering as he looked to Angus with eyes filled with wishes and tears.

Angus had long since had a zillion reasons lined up as to why he would never be a father, for not a single "father" who'd waltzed in and out of his life had made the job seem appealing, but in that moment he couldn't think of one. Not when the urge came over him simply to step in, wrap them both up tightly and vow to protect them from anyone who made them sad. Anyone who dared make either one of them cry.

But it was not Angus's place to have a say. Angus who was now pulling his leg hairs through the pockets of his suit pants to keep from doing something or saying something. It was Lucinda's job. Only Lucinda's. If he'd learnt anything from being in Sonny's shoes, it was that.

"Why?" Lucinda repeated, her face collapsing as she saw the earnest plea in Sonny's expression. "Because he's

Angus. He, um… He doesn't cook, for one thing, and a dad needs to be able to cook."

"*You* don't cook."

"I do! Just not very well. I'd bet the house that Angus can't boil an egg. And he…ah…he certainly doesn't clean. And you know how much cleaning I have to do. A dad would have to help me with that. What else? Angus never buys his own groceries. Or answers his own phone. He's too busy to coach your footy team. Or read to you every night. Angus can't be your dad, hon, because he's practically a big kid himself."

Angus knew Lucinda was trying to soften things for Sonny, to bring him down from the ledge, yet with every reason she gave it felt like death by a thousand cuts. Everything she said was true. To a point. But the fact that the litany of reasons why he could never take on that role in their lives had been on the tip of her tongue spoke volumes.

Sonny sniffed. "But you tell me all the time the most important ingredient in making a family is love. And you love Angus. And I love him. And Cat loves him."

Cat snorted.

"We do, hon," Lucinda said, flicking her sister a look. But not Angus. If only she'd look at him. Just for a beat. Her smile could include him, temper her words. Maybe this was salvageable. But no. Her attention went right back to her son. "Angus is one of our very best friends. But it takes more than tickles and bad jokes and a mad footy boot to be a dad. It takes patience and compatibility and commitment. He would have to want it more than anything else in the world. And you know how much Angus loves his job and his nice clean apartment and his me-time. Besides, Uncle Angus has to learn how to take care of himself before he can be entrusted to take care of anyone else."

Even Cat flinched at that last twist of the knife.

While Lucinda smiled down at Sonny as if delighted at having navigated a potential disaster.

"Come on, kid," said Cat, holding out a hand to Sonny before leading him down the hall to their room. "Let's order something gross and sugary from room service. Mum will be along in a minute."

And soon it was just the two of them. Angus and Lucinda. And finally, she looked his way. Her eyes heavy. Her mouth soft. The weight of the night before once more wrapped itself around him like a siren song.

"I'm so sorry about all that," she said, twisting and untwisting a corner of her wrap.

"You have nothing to apologise for," he said, his voice sounding as if it was coming from someone else.

"Yeah, I do. I ought to have seen that coming. And I never wanted you to feel uncomfortable, or beholden, or put in a position where—"

"I didn't. I don't. He's a great kid, and I… I love him right on back." The moment the words left his mouth, Angus felt light-headed, as if he'd been blowing up a balloon for too long. But he was still grounded enough to see Lucinda startle.

"I know," she said. "I know you do."

But when she smiled he saw only flashes of the Lucinda from the night before. Heat and desire and such sweetness it made his skin hurt. And the deeper feelings they'd both secretly held onto for years.

But there was a resoluteness there now as well. Her mind was with her son now, or it very much wanted to be.

Her son. Her number one priority. From day one she'd made that clear. And it was one of the reasons he was so taken with her.

Long-ago promises he'd made to himself and to his own mother kicked in, and instead of hauling Lucinda into his arms and attempting to unravel all that he was feeling, sensing and experiencing that morning he did what he'd always done.

He deferred to her.

He slid his hands into his pockets and causally leaned against the hallway wall. "You're okay for a lift home?" he said.

He hated himself when she flinched. When she finally seemed to pick up on the coolness in his voice.

"I drove, remember?" she said. "Cast aside last minute, as I was, by my date."

He nodded. "Head off early, if you'd like. I can finish up here. Sonny looks like he needs you."

"Right. Thanks. No reason to stick around any longer now, I guess."

No, he thought, with chagrin, *none at all. Not the fact you admitted that you've wanted me for a long time. Not the fact that we just spent all night in one another's arms. And not the fact that it's taking every single ion of power I have not to haul you into my arms and beg you to stay.*

But no one would be any the wiser. For he was an expert at concealment. At hiding such strong feelings. It was safer that way. Easier for all.

"I'll leave you to it, then, shall I?"

She swallowed, her eyes bright, conflicted and beautiful.

They could get past this. They were friends. They were practical. They were too enmeshed in one another's lives for it to be any other way.

"See you tomorrow?" she said.

"Tomorrow," he returned, then he pushed away from the wall and strolled away.

CHAPTER TEN

ANGUS COULDN'T GET his head straight on this, the day he needed to more than ever before.

He'd been back at work for a couple of days, every second spent implementing the complete about turn on the Remède rebranding.

Louis Fournier and his team were due at the Big Picture Group offices in less than two hours. And he had to convince them to throw out the ideas they'd okayed a week before.

He knew he was right, his instincts on song. The *kintsukuroi* method was a perfect fit for the Remède ethos, as well as following the current trend in beauty being all about wellness and authenticity. It had real potential to turn the company around.

It was just every other single aspect of his life that felt jagged, ill-fitting and wrong.

And if he couldn't focus, couldn't demonstrate absolute certainty, couldn't be the man in whom Louis had seen all that potential and convince them that they were right to put their faith in him, to trust him, it could yet all go up in smoke.

The phone rang on the other side of the smoky glass and his gaze was drawn that way as it had been a hundred times a day since he and Lucinda had come back to work a few days before.

Who was he kidding? His gaze had always been drawn that way. He'd convinced himself it was because Lucinda was his good-luck charm, his guard at the gate, his anchor.

When the truth was, she *was* all that and so much more.

Lucinda was also strong, soulful, warm and kind. She was trusting, unsure, loyal and lovely. She was his friend, his confidant, his favourite person on earth.

And when she'd taken him by the tie, pulled him in and kissed him every fibre of his being had cried out in relief.

This, a voice had whispered inside his head. *This is everything you have worked towards. Everything you've ever wanted. Being the kind of man Lucinda Starling could want.*

Then Lucinda had taken such pains to explain to Sonny why Angus was her friend, her confidant and one of her favourite people on earth and why he could never, ever be more.

He'd had no armour to protect himself. He'd felt the slice of every word—just as he had as a kid, told constantly by his mother's line-up of deadbeat boyfriends that he didn't matter, that no one would care if he'd never been born. That he wasn't enough.

And now she was out there, smelling of that damn Someday perfume that made his head spin. Wearing that skirt that fit so right it looked as if it had been sewn on. Her hair was tucked over one shoulder, sleek and dark and tempting. He remembered how it had felt sliding through his fingers…

Damn it.

Angus sat forward, sinking his face into his palms, then he gouged his finger through his hair, tugging hard enough to hurt.

This was why he'd resisted all these years. This ache. Deep. Physical. Knowing her, being with her, opened up in him wants and desires he'd never let himself entertain. Hopes of a future, a partnership, a family—managing to carve out a life his own parents had never been able to.

He'd followed her to the damn resort for fear of losing her and somehow it felt as though it was happening anyway. Leaving him brimming with a kind of psychic pain he couldn't control. Or name. And sure as hell didn't want.

Well, enough was enough.

"Lucinda!" he shouted, forcing himself out of his chair.

He saw her shoulders square. She took a moment before slowly pressing her chair back and making her way through the smoky glass door between her world and his.

Without saying a word, she stood there with her fancy notebook and her cheap pencil, chin tilted, knees locked. She appeared cool. Unmoved.

And utterly lovely.

But, the closer he looked, he could see how her ankle jiggled. How she nibbled at the inside of her lip. The smudges under her eyes.

If he was disoriented in this new landscape, then so was she.

The only way forward, as he could see it, was the one that had got him where he was today. Disengagement.

His strength was in his ability to compartmentalise. It had helped him through the very worst parts of his childhood. And it had helped him deal with the temptation of having this woman sitting just outside his office for the past six-and-a-half years.

It had to help now.

"Angus?" she said. "Did you actually want me, or were you shouting my name for the fun of it?"

"I wanted you," he said.

Some strong emotion fluttered across her deep, brown eyes.

But she pulled herself together, moved to the pink velvet chair he'd bought her as a gift, sat on the edge, crossed one ankle over the other and held her pencil over her notebook. "Shoot."

Angus moved more slowly to the front of his desk, his feet knowing what his mind refused to admit—that more than anything, more than having things back to the way they were, he wanted to be near her. Needed to be. And he always had.

She looked up, her brown eyes wary. And beautiful. And sad.

It was the sadness that finally got him—as if she too was battling with the knowledge that a seismic shift had happened this past weekend. It shook him. Made him buck up and damn well pull himself together.

"Remède," he said, his voice so gruff he barely recognised it himself.

She lifted her chin. "The boardroom is set. Food is on its way. Champagne is chilling. The IT team are working on the last layout changes to the website. It'll be close but they'll get it done in time. They have tickets to Comicon riding on it."

"Great."

"How about you?" she asked. "Are you ready?"

And despite the fact they'd tiptoed around one another for days, far more clumsily than after the Christmas party, the care in her voice—honest, real and clear as day—shone through.

And Angus's heart dropped into his chest as if it had fallen into a well.

"I am," he said. "You?"

She blinked. "Me? Ready to flirt and charm and flitter about? Always."

"You do more than that, Luc."

Her face crumpled at his use of her nickname. "I know," she said, voice soft. "I was kidding."

"No. You weren't."

She swallowed. A conversation like this would have felt different a week before. Full of banter, sass and good-natured ribbing that would have left them both feeling as if they were floating an inch off the ground.

Now every word had weight. Now every word mattered. Stacking up against him, building a wall so large soon neither would be able to see past it.

Before he could kick the damn thing down, Lucinda was already on her feet, heading back towards her door.

If this was the way things were going to be from now on it would be untenable.

"Luc," he said, stopping to clear his throat. "Lucinda." She stopped, turned. "Mmm?"

I want you. I adore you. I need you. I can't lose you. You are a part of me. The best part of me. You took a shell of a human being and made him whole.

Some deep, undamaged part of himself, some sliver of light and good, took him by the throat and gave it a squeeze. Made him check himself. To be truly sure. For Cat was right—there was no lower scum on earth than a man who would mess with a single mother unless he was in it for the long haul.

"You know I couldn't do any of this without you," he said.

Lucinda looked at him, right at him, her warm brown eyes like a laser.

"I know you say that, Angus, and some part of you might even believe it," she said, with a flicker of a humourless smile. "But the truth is, you always could."

Lucinda stood looking down at her desk, at the tub of sharpened pencils, the pile of pretty notebooks.

The joy that it had given her—the sense of ownership, of purpose, of self-respect—felt like something that had happened in a movie she'd once watched.

It was ruined. She'd ruined it. Making love with Angus, telling him she'd wanted him for the longest time…

He looked so pained every time they made eye contact now, as if he was choking on something. It had to be regret.

Not that *she* knew what to say. Whether to apologise

or make light. To tell him she was struggling too. To agree to pretend it had never happened. They'd made it past the Christmas party near-kiss and managed to work together just fine. If anything, the sexual tension had upped their game.

So long as they'd stayed either side of the immovable, inviolable line they'd kept between them, she'd been allowed to exist in a kind of perfect balance between working with Angus in a job that fulfilled her more than she ever would have thought possible and basking in the presence of the smart, sharp, talented, determined man she adored.

Only it hadn't been balanced. It had been emotional purgatory.

And now the line was gone, obliterated, she was totally untethered, her feelings all over the place.

Maybe she should just look Angus in the eye and tell him she'd thought herself a little bit in love with him before and now she was drowning in it.

Every time she looked at him, she saw not her boss, or the man she'd had a secret crush on for years, but his bare chest as he'd hovered over her, the dark heat in his eyes as they'd made love. She felt again the tenderness in his touch, the way he'd relaxed in a way she'd never seen in him when he'd cradled her as she'd fallen asleep. As though protecting her was his happy place. As though something that had kept him chained all these years had finally broken free.

Then she'd woken up. Alone. In every possible way that could mean.

Reaching out and finding him gone, her heart had stuttered in her chest. She'd told herself it was okay. That he hadn't said goodbye before leaving her room because it wasn't goodbye. That they'd be together again at breakfast. And beyond.

Only to slowly begin to panic about what came next.

Would they head into work on Monday holding hands, gazing into one another's eyes over the boardroom table, co-signing Fitz's form that people had to sign when they started seeing one another at work?

Then, with all that piling up in her head, when she'd found Sonny in the hall and been forced to answer why Angus couldn't be her boy's dad...

He'd been so good to Sonny, and for Sonny. If Angus was keen and ready and wanted it too, he'd be a wonderful father. Kind and fun with solid boundaries and strong arms.

But he'd made it so clear over the years that fatherhood was not for him. That he believed no man should come close to that job without a medical, a police check, a licence and a wide-open heart.

So she'd brought out every lame thing Cat had accused him of in order to distract Sonny from the idea. She'd gone into pure self-defence mode.

But then, so had he.

Leaning against the wall in the hall, the very picture of causal indifference, offering her an early mark. Pushing her away. The wall that kept him separate from the world all but rebuilding before her very eyes.

She'd had Angus but she couldn't *have* him.

He was too flawed, thorny, demanding and damaged. She'd spent too long making sure other people were happy, as if doing so was the only way to make them stay.

But what if staying wasn't always the right answer? What if sticking, depending on her roots, believing in for ever, was the problem rather than the solution?

Before she was fully aware of where she was going, Lucinda walked down the hall, feeling as though she was on her way to her own execution. Yet at the lift she didn't even hesitate before pressing the button to head up to the HR floor.

* * *

Fitz's office was a mirror of Angus's only it was plush and brash and noisy and messy, where Angus's was spare and neat and still.

Lucinda gave Velma a wave. Velma nodded, letting her know she could head right on in.

Fitz glanced up, serious face on, as Lucinda entered his office. It softened when he saw it was her.

Taking off a pair of red tip-tilted glasses he'd clearly borrowed from Velma, he leant back in his chair. "You coming in or are you just going to stand there all day?"

"Stand here?"

"Sit," he insisted clicking his fingers. "Now."

Her feet dragged as she took the last few leaden steps towards the chair by Fitz's desk. When she sat, her breath left in a sad little whoosh.

"I was wondering when you might show up."

She blinked at him.

"You, Lucinda Starling, are a mighty oak, putting up with that fool of a boss of yours for as long as you have. And coming back to work, being your usual amazing self after what happened over the weekend…"

She leant forward, her head dropping to her knees. "You know? How do you know?"

"Sweetheart. It's my job to know. Besides, I was there. I was stumbling back to my room the morning after the party—boy can those women dance—right as Angus was checking out. Looking like a big, broken bear with a storm cloud over his head."

Lucinda lifted her head. The thought of Angus, broken, made her heart hurt. The thought he might feel that way because of her? How had she let things get so out of hand?

Because you love him, you goose!

Well, she thought miserably, there was that.

Fitz checked his nails as he went on. "I bugged him till he told me why. No details, unfortunately. Just the bare bones. But I'd figured it out. There's only one person in the whole world who can bring out that kind of emotion in our boy."

He pointed a finger Lucinda's way.

"I can't," she said, barely able to string more than two words together. "I can't do it any more, Fitz."

Fitz stopped fussing and looked at her. Then he hopped out from behind his grand desk, came over to her, lifted her out of the chair and pulled her into a hug.

"Of course you can. You're in love with the guy. Anyone with two eyes and a brain like a steel trap could see it."

Something in the back of her head, some last remaining thread of a survival instinct, told her to baulk, to scoff, to poo-poo Fitz's suggestion. But, sounding and feeling like a kicked puppy, she murmured, "Does he know?"

"My cousin?" Fitz snorted. "Smartest guy I know, bar Charlie, who doesn't count because he's not human. But when it comes to the workings of the heart, Angus is as clueless as they come."

"It's not his fault."

Fitz laughed softly. "Only a woman in love would look at Angus Wolfe and believe the reason he hasn't settled down with a good woman—or a bad woman, for that matter—isn't entirely his fault."

With a groan, her face fell against Fitz's chest, her neck no longer able to hold up her head. She felt as if she had the flu. The love flu. The *unrequited love* flu. The Angus Wolfe strain.

"How did you two finally crack?" Fitz asked, his voice lacking its usual bolshie tone.

She knew what he meant. And she knew the answer. "He looked at me."

"Hmm," said Fitz in mock seriousness. "He has a way of doing that. What the hell does that even mean?"

She laughed, despite herself. The Angus Wolfe love flu was making her light-headed. "You know—the *look*. The kind that makes you see exactly what's going on in the other person's head and it's enough to make your knee-caps melt clean away."

"Ah, that look."

Lucinda lifted her head.

"He'd given me the look once before, you know? At that crazy work Christmas party a couple of years back. All that bubbly and dancing and mistletoe, someone was always going to do the walk of shame that night."

"Right," Fitz agreed, shifting from foot to foot, making Lucinda wonder for a moment who *he'd* walked from that night.

"The look that night—it was hot. And lingering. And brimming with the promise of sweaty limbs and torn clothing and regret." Lucinda laughed, though it felt more like a whimper, and stepped out of Fitz's hug. "And why am I telling you any of this?"

"Because you need to let it out or you'll implode. And you know there's not a single thing you can say that will change how deeply I adore you."

She nodded. He was right. She looked down at her hands. "Nothing happened between us at that party. Nothing anyone else would think was inappropriate. HR, for instance."

Fitz breathed out. Hard. "But last weekend? Sweaty limbs, torn clothing…"

"And regret."

"Luc. Honey."

"It's okay. I'm a grown-up. I knew what I was doing. And I knew no good would come of it. At the very least I'll be able to live off it for a long, long time. Perhaps even until I'm old and grey, and Cat and I are still living together in my sweet little cottage, watching Netflix and bickering."

"Sounds like a plan." Fitz reached out and put a hand on her shoulder as if he could tell she might well collapse to the floor otherwise. "So, I'm assuming you didn't come up here because you knew I have no filter and would happily listen to any details you might impart as to your dirty weekend with my stupid cousin?"

"I can't believe I'm about to say this out loud, but I need you to tell me what to do so that I can officially resign."

Fitz didn't even stiffen, as if he'd seen this coming a long time before she had.

She'd be fine financially. Her little cottage was all hers, Sonny was in a great public school and she'd get another job with a single phone call. She knew the kind of money she'd get offered from other firms.

But she'd miss this. She'd miss *him*. The thought of turning up to work for anyone but Angus made her feel physically ill.

She'd seen the man nearly every day for the past six-and-a-half years and had loved him for almost as long.

"He loves you too," said Fitz, as if he'd read her mind. He went to his desk to sort out the required paperwork. "In his own way."

"I know," Lucinda said. "But if he taught me anything these past few years it's that I'm worth more than that. Angus's way of loving just isn't enough."

And there it was. The truth she'd steadfastly avoided admitting to herself. For it meant no longer having a crush on her boss to keep her safe from truly opening herself up to the possibility of the kind of love her parents had. The kind of love she'd feared she'd never find if she ever really went looking.

She knew Angus would be side-swiped. For all that he'd shut her out over the past few days, he wasn't lying when he said he didn't want to lose her.

"Don't tell him," she said. "Remède will be here in an hour. And there's nothing more important to him than that."

"Nothing?" Fitz said, looking at her over the red sparkly glasses.

Then, muttering to himself about how he should have been a shrink or a psychic, Fitz printed out the necessary forms.

Lucinda stood outside her little cottage looking over the duck-egg-blue front door, the cream eaves, the gardenia bushes that had bloomed for the first time ever last spring.

Trying to reconcile herself with the fact that she was home. At two in the afternoon. Not because she'd had to pick up Sonny sick from school but because she no longer worked for Angus Wolfe.

She'd somehow made it back to her office after she'd finished hashing out her exit with Fitz. Then waited in the ladies' bathroom until the last possible moment before slipping into the back of the room for the Remède pitch.

Angus had sat at the top of the room beside Louis Fournier, foot resting casually on the other knee, finger playing lightly over the seam of his mouth. A picture of cool ease, when she knew how important it was to him that this meeting went well.

Angus hadn't looked her way, but he'd known she was there. She'd seen it in the way he shifted on his seat, the way his other hand clenched, as it had been doing all week.

She'd spent the meeting feeling as if she was on the other side of a mirror as his band of dashing, clever, talented marketing and graphics geniuses had played their symphony of social media spots and print ads and the complete overhaul of the website relaunch of the Remède brand.

It had been all she could do not to blub when Angus had explained the theory of *kintsukuroi*, not even pausing before crediting it to her. How Remède was a celebration of women—of mothers, daughters, sisters, friends—at every stage of life.

She hadn't been even the slightest bit surprised when Louis had pulled Angus into a bear hug, muttering praise and thanks into his ear while he shed a tear.

The Big Picture Group team had been on a total high after all the last-minute work they'd put in, yet the moment the meeting was done Lucinda had slipped out through the door—only to hear Angus's footsteps meet hers as he'd jogged to catch up.

"Hey," he'd said, his voice a little rough. "Hey, slow down. What's the big rush?"

"Stuff to do."

"So that was wild in there."

"It was amazing. You were amazing." Her voice had caught as she'd said, "I'm so proud of you, Angus. Not many would have gone to the lengths you went to in order to get that so right."

Lucinda had picked up her pace. Or she'd tried to, until Angus's hand had clamped around her arm.

She'd stopped and turned to find herself toe to toe with her boss. Her brilliant, impossible boss. Close enough to catch the scent of his soap, the fresh cotton of his shirt, to see the thread unspooling from a button hole. She made a mental note to remind him not to buy that brand again, before remembering that wouldn't be her job any more.

"Lucinda," Angus had murmured, his voice scraping her insides in a way that had her curling her toes into her shoes so as not to shiver.

Pulling together every ounce of self-protection she'd had at her disposal, she'd dragged in a short, sharp breath and looked up into his eyes. Warm, hazel and far too astute for comfort.

"What's going on?" he'd asked.

She remembered looking down the hall to see who might be watching. Who might note them standing closer than two work mates ought to stand. But everyone was busy chatting, laughing and moving in and out of one another's offices, the hive all a flutter after the successful meeting.

Then she'd moved to Angus's office, pushed open the door and crooked a finger his way.

A smile had hooked at the corner of his mouth. A smile so cocky, familiar, so beloved, she'd felt it as an ache deep down inside. Then he'd sauntered after her.

Expecting…something better than what he was about to receive.

But Lucinda had known, if she hadn't done it then and there she might not have done it at all.

So she'd pulled a single sheet of white paper out of her notebook and held it out to Angus—

The front door of the cottage swung open and Lucinda near leapt out of her skin.

Catriona poked her head around the door, a piece of toast poking out of her mouth. Then she glanced at her watch. "I thought I heard a funny noise out here. What are you doing home so early?"

Lucinda found her feet and walked up onto the porch. Swinging past her sister, she said, "I quit."

"You *what*?" Cat cried, then stopped to choke on a crumb she'd inhaled.

Lucinda had time to unwrap her scarf and hang it on the hall stand before Cat came hustling inside, her socks shuffling on the wooden floor. "Please tell me you're kidding."

"I thought you'd be happy."

"Why the hell would you think that?"

"Because it means I won't be working with Angus any more."

Cat flapped her hands, her eyes near bugging out of her head. "Why would that make me happy?"

Lucinda turned to face her sister. "You don't like him. You've never liked him."

"First, that's not true!" Cat cried out. "And second, when did you suddenly care about that?"

"So, you *like* Angus?"

"He's a freaking gem! No other boss would pay you as much as he does. Or give you the time off you need."

Lucinda stood wearing one high heel as she'd already kicked off the other shoeoff. And she breathed deep. "Can you just…not. Today. Or ever again. I'm not in the mood for games."

"Luc, I'm not playing. I promise. I'm too shocked. Seriously. I feel as if there's been a tear in the space-time continuum. You can't quit Angus."

"I didn't quit Angus. I quit my job."

"Same thing."

Lucinda glanced at her sister to find her standing in the middle of the hall looking…lost. "Come on, Cat."

"I mean it. I'm worried right now. I'm the quitter. I've quit a million jobs, a million men, but you? You're the 'for ever' girl. It's probably why I've never been able to hate Angus, even though he's so annoyingly good-looking and confident and brilliant. Because from day one he knew you were the for ever girl too. Just like he's a for ever guy."

Lucinda closed her eyes against the memory of that final moment. He'd refused to take the piece of paper, so she'd opened it up and read it out loud.

"Stop," he'd said, his voice rough when she was about half way through.

She'd looked up, expecting refusal, an argument, maybe even some kind of revelation. But she'd never seen him look so empty, so cold.

"I don't need notice," he'd said.

"What do you mean?"

"Go." He'd cocked his head towards the office door. "If you don't want to work here any more, just go."

She'd recoiled physically, taking a step back. "You don't mean that."

"When have you ever heard me say something I don't mean?"

And so, without another word to the man she'd worked alongside for the past several years, she'd walked out of his office on boneless legs, cleared out her desk, packed her meagre possessions into her big handbag and left. Nobody had noticed. Everyone had been too high, celebrating the Remède success.

Lucinda tuned to her sister. "If he's a for ever guy, Cat, then why did he let me go?"

Cat took her by the hand, wrapping it up tightly between hers. "He's hurt."

"*He's* hurt? I'm the one who's had to deal with his moods all week. With the fact he could barely even look at me. As if I'd done something unforgivable. We were both there that night." Oh, wondrous night.

Cat snorted. "I'd put money on him looking at you. The man can barely stop looking at you. If you guys weren't both equally mad about one another, it would be creepy how much the man looks at you."

Lucinda's lungs started to tighten with the effort of trying to hold in the words that were so desperate to come out. "What do you mean, he looks at me?"

"Are you kidding? The man could be the poster boy for longing."

Lucinda slowly kicked off her other shoe and leaned against the hallway wall.

"And don't get me started on how he looks at you when you're with Sonny. It's heart-breaking. Like watching a little homeless kid standing outside a candy shop window."

"Why would he do that? He's not a family kind of guy. You know his background. You know how hard he had it as a kid. His dad leaving, his mum and her string of appalling boyfriends. Family to him is a four-letter word."

Cat crossed her arms, no longer looking lost so much as mad. "Are you telling me, seriously, that you don't consider Angus family? That you'd let anyone else come into this house, sick, when your boy is here?"

"Well, no."

"Is there anyone else you'd text before watching a new episode of *Warlock Academy*?"

"Never."

"Has he seen you cry? Snort-laugh? Trip over? Swear? Has he seen you without make-up? In that God-awful green pashmina wrap thing? Has he ever played a board game with you, seen what a bad loser you are and come back for more?"

Lucinda nodded.

"And yet, with all that evidence to the contrary, he looks at you as if he's stumbled on a fairy princess in a secret, magical glen."

Lucinda leant harder against the wall and slowly slid down to the floor, letting her bare legs kick out in front of her.

Cat, her annoying, clever, difficult, stubborn, wonderful sister, slid down next to her.

"That's not normal, is it?"

"For a mere boss and employee? Ah, no. Have you ever seen any of my editors over here? Have they ever followed me away on a holiday weekend?"

"Why didn't you ever point this stuff out to me before?" Lucinda asked.

"I did. In my way. I say the grass is blue, you agree, saying it can look bluish in the right light. I say night is day, and you agree it can seem that way when the moon is bright. But, when I even think about saying something against Angus, you bite my head off and proceed to wax lyrical about how amazing the man is. I picked on him because I hoped you'd one day notice that the only time you stop trying to please everyone and simply tell your truth is when you're defending him." Cat nudged her with her shoulder. "I could stick a mirror up to your face, but what can I do if you refuse to open your eyes?"

Lucinda thought about it. Really thought.

Watching him struggle over the Remède account had changed things for her. The man had created a shiny, incisive, clean, fresh rebrand over which any company would salivate. It would have won awards, no doubt. But he'd known it wasn't right, had known it had missed the heart of the business. The soul. So he'd gone deeper, pushed himself outside his comfort zone, talked to people on the ground level, immersed himself in the product—learned the difference between lipstick and lip-gloss, for goodness' sake—to make it right.

Throughout, there had been no hiding the fact that beneath the Angus Wolfe mask was a man with a heart of gold. Not gold powder, or veins of gold, but the pure, twenty-four-carat good stuff.

Yet, so afraid of being left was she, she'd made a habit of pushing, of making it impossible for most men to bother. All men, bar Angus. He'd refused to budge. Refused to be disappointed. Refused to let her down.

And, the more she'd grown to care about the man, the more terrified she'd become of losing him. Losing him as she'd lost so many of those she'd cared about most.

When she'd felt things turning, changing, when a chance to find out what might actually be possible between them had presented itself, she'd pushed him away. Telling herself she was protecting her son when really she'd just been using his love as a shield.

"I was eighteen when I met Joe, can you believe that?" Lucinda heard herself say. "Mum and Dad had died not that long before. You were living overseas and I was at home. Alone. When Joe came on the scene, I saw him as my out. A chance to not be the good girl, to run away, to quit being me for a while. I think I was so happy when I found out I was pregnant, not because it was Joe's baby, but because it was mine. Because there'd be someone to love who would love me best."

Lucinda didn't realise she was crying until she tasted a tear on her bottom lip.

Thinking of Sonny, she wanted to crawl into his bed and gather up his toy fish, donkey and the headless rabbit. How long had it been since *he'd* even cuddled those toys? He was more into more grown up toys now. Transformers. Superheroes of his own.

She could learn from that. From Sonny. The way he loved. And forgave. Forgave Cat when her patience ran thin. Forgave Lucinda when she ran late from work. Forgave Angus when he forgot the name of a Pokémon.

Lucinda dropped her head into her hands.

The fact that Angus Wolfe knew the name of even one Pokémon should have been a sign. One of those huge, flashing road signs you can practically see from space.

He loved her. Angus *loved* her. And he'd done so for a very long time.

"But I've quit," she said, tears now flowing freely as it fully hit her what she'd done.

"So, un-quit."

"I'm not sure I can. I'm not sure I should. I'm not sure he'd take me back. You're right. I hurt him. The one person he knew he could count on walked out, right when he was enjoying the biggest high of his career. I should have talked to him. Told him how I feel. Instead I treated him as if his opinion about us didn't matter. I let him down so very badly."

"Fitz is right. You two doofuses deserve each other, you really do."

"Fitz?" Lucinda said, the weirdness of that statement

somehow making its way through the fog. "When have you been talking to Fitz?"

Cat looked down at her toes, wriggling them back and forth. "We…may have hooked up at that Christmas party of yours a year or so ago. And a handful of times since."

Lucinda gawped, then realised she didn't have the energy to care.

"Come here, you," Cat said, holding out an arm.

And Lucinda leaned over and rested in her sister's embrace.

Tomorrow she'd deal with tomorrow.

CHAPTER ELEVEN

"Whoa, hold up, there, cowboy."

Angus pulled up outside Fitz's office when Velma positioned herself bodily between him and the glass door.

If she'd been anyone else he'd have feinted left and cut round her, but rumour had it Velma had wrestled in her youth, and even in the heightened state he was in his self-protective instinct kicked in just in time.

"I need to speak to him," Angus gritted out. "Now."

"Honey, what you need to do is take a breath. Calm down. And remember that boy in there is family. He loves you. And he only has your best interests at heart."

All Angus knew right then was that he was wound so tight he could feel his blood stuttering through his veins. "Fine," he managed. "I'll give him a head start."

Velma's cheek twitched before she knocked on the door and called out, "He's here."

"I can see that," Fitz's voice called back. "Send him in."

Velma moved aside and slowly opened the door for Angus, who burst through it like water through a crack in a dam.

Fitz sat behind his desk, feet up on the table, ridiculous red glasses on the end of his nose. "Sit," he said.

"I'm not going to bloody well sit."

"Sit. Or I'll get Velma to escort you from the room."

"She can try."

"Whatever."

Fitz dropped his feet to the floor then came out from behind the desk. The man clearly had a death wish.

"I'm assuming you're here about the lovely Lucinda," said Fitz as he sat on the edge of his desk, crossed his arms and glared at Angus.

"She quit."

"Yes."

"And you let her."

"What are you suggesting I should have done? Tied her to the chair? Blackmailed her? Stuck my fingers in my ears and said 'la-la-la-la-la' till she gave up and went back to work?"

"You could have called me. Let me know what she was thinking of doing."

"And what would you have done? Ridden up here on your white steed, thrown her over the saddle and swept her off to the top of a high tower?"

Angus gritted his teeth so hard he swore he heard a crack.

Fitz breathed out, long and slow, then said, "She can't work for you any more, Angus. Not after what happened. Hell, I should have split the two of you up years ago. My reasons were purely selfish, and for that I apologise. Together you guys make the rest of us a ton of money."

"Nothing happened. Before last weekend. Nothing had ever happened."

"Angus, mate, every time the two of you are in the same room something happens. The air crackles and heats up several degrees. A yeti could walk through the middle of the office and you wouldn't notice. Knowing that, I should have moved her to another department, if only because it would have given you both one less reason not to go for it."

Angus went to say, *"Go for what?"* but he knew. It seemed everyone but him had been aware of it for a long time. He slowly lowered himself into Fitz's spare chair, his head falling into his hands. "Where is she now?"

"My spies told me she left a little while ago."

"Was she okay? When she left?"

"What do you think?"

Angus didn't need to think. Not after the way she'd looked at him when he'd told her to go.

She'd looked as if she'd been slapped.

If he'd been attempting to redraw the line between them—after she'd made it clear at the weekend that despite their night together she didn't see a future between them—he'd gone about it the right way. For he'd turned a fluid line in the sand into the Grand Canyon.

"How about you?" Fitz asked. "Are you okay?"

Angus rubbed his hands over his face. "I don't know. I truly don't. I can't imagine going back down there and doing what I do without her beside me."

Neither could he imagine looking up and seeing someone else sitting in her chair. Or going a day without talking to her, hearing her stories about Cat and Sonny. Without watching her work a phone, or seeing her smile.

Life without Lucinda was a life he truly couldn't fathom.

Angus grabbed hold of his hair and tugged, the pain barely registering.

But life with her, really *with* her…

Lucinda had told Sonny that he wasn't ready for fatherhood. That he couldn't take care of anyone else until he learned how to take care of himself.

But he'd been playing father to Sonny for years.

He'd been ready for Sonny. But the truth was, he hadn't been ready for *her*. That was why he'd deferred to her. Why he'd never put his own needs first where they were concerned.

But that didn't mean Angus didn't *know* what he needed.

He needed for his work to be satisfying.

He *needed* Sonny. For he loved that kid as if he was his own.

And he needed Lucinda. He needed her like he needed air. It wasn't the dodgy, supernatural teen TV shows on Netflix he loved so much, it was having an excuse to talk to her late into the night. She sustained him. She challenged him. She had taught him how to live, how to laugh and how to love.

And, as if the wheels and cogs of the universe that had ground harshly and noisily around him his entire life were finally slipping into their rightful place, silencing the constant burr in his head and dissolving the shackles around his heart, Angus knew what he had to do.

He stood. The wheels and cogs were now spinning in the opposite direction and spinning fast. "Her letter of resignation. It was addressed to me. Not to Big Picture. Meaning, while she no longer works for me, she could still work for the company."

Fitz scoffed. "Um, yeah. I might have taken longer than I ought to split the two of you up, but you don't think I was stupid enough to let her leave altogether? Oh, Angus, you might be the star of this operation—the Dorothy, if you will—but I am the great and powerful Oz."

Angus let Fitz's waffle slide. He was already too deep inside a plan. A plan to fix things. Fix everything. By pulling off the most important rebranding of his life. His own.

"Where have you put her?" His voice dropped to a growl. "She's not working for you."

"You kidding? Velma would curl up and die if she didn't see my gorgeous face every day. We hadn't hashed anything out yet. I told her to come back tomorrow and we'd work it out."

"Good. Because I have an idea."

"Do I need to write this down? I feel like I need a notebook and a pencil. I know I won't look nearly as gorgeous as Lucinda in one of those skirts she likes to wear, but I'll try."

Angus shot him a glare, but it was barely half-strength. He was too charged to pretend to be offended. In fact, he was done pretending altogether. Any more pretending, he'd get a stomach ulcer.

Holding back his feelings as a kid, when he'd been scared or lonely or worried about his mum, had meant those hurting him had left him alone. It had helped him get through the rough.

But he wasn't in the rough any more. He was in the prime of his life.

He'd achieved everything he could ever have dreamed of.

Only to realise he'd not been dreaming big enough.

"Get that pencil and notebook," he commanded. "I'm ready."

"You ready?" Fitz asked after rapping noisily on Angus's glass door.

"Ten seconds," Angus said, holding up a hand as he went over the plan in his head, double checking he hadn't missed anything, so used was he to having Lucinda there to fill in the blanks.

It felt like months since he'd seen her, not days. Months in which he'd had to answer his own phone and schmooze his own clients. Call IT for help when he couldn't open his email.

He would hire another assistant, but right now he needed the clarity of remembering what it was he loved about his work. The rush of being in the trenches.

And now it was Lucinda's first day back. She'd taken a week off. Time owed, Fitz had said. Time to think about the offer he'd made regarding a new position in the company.

A promotion, actually. A big one. She was taking over Charlie's job as Manager of Financial Affairs.

Charlie was brilliant, and a big part of their success,

but the guy couldn't lead. When Fitz and Angus had discussed the idea with Charlie, he'd near wept with relief. He and Kumar would continue to pound away at their calculators, making money for their clients and the Big Picture Group, while Lucinda would be the new face of the department. And the boss.

Angus's gut had hurt when Fitz had told him her first question before accepting had been to make sure Angus would be okay with it. He wished he'd seen her face when Fitz had told her it was all Angus's idea.

"Now or never," Fitz said.

Yeah, that was what he feared.

Angus stood, looking around him for what he might need to take to a staff meeting.

"Come on! Hurry up! No resting on your Remède laurels, mate. Boardroom. Now." With that, Fitz strode away.

Angus left through the small door that took him past Lucinda's old desk. It looked eerily tidy. There was no paper, no pencils. The back of the chair sat perfectly parallel with the desk.

He opened a drawer and found it empty too. Until, when he closed it, there came a tell-tale sound just before a cheap 2B pencil rolled towards the front.

He picked it up and ran a thumb over the black and red stripes along its length.

A smile stretched across his face. Knowing how much she liked pretty notebooks, one of the first gifts he'd ever bought her was a very expensive pen. It had sat in the back of the same drawer for years while she'd continued to use her discount store pencils instead.

No airs. No graces. She was who she was. Thank the gods for that.

Holding the pencil tight, like some kind of talisman, Angus made his way down the hall towards the boardroom.

When he arrived, Fitz was talking with Velma, who

tried to look stern but couldn't contain the flicker at the corner of her mouth.

Charlie and Kumar sat against the wall, watching a video on Kumar's phone—no doubt a stock fluctuation. Or a UFO sighting. Hell, maybe it was a kitten lost down a well.

Angus moved to his seat at the far end of the table and sat, feeling as though fireworks were going off in his belly.

"Sorry!"

Angus stilled as Lucinda hustled breathlessly into the room, tucking a stray strand of dark hair behind her ear. The same stray strand that never stayed put.

He sat taller in his seat, his nerves un-pinching, his muscles relaxing, his bones yielding.

It had been a week since he'd seen her. A week more than he ever wanted to go without seeing her again.

"Sorry. I couldn't find…a thing. Sorry."

She shot Fitz a chagrined smile. He gave her a big thumbs-up.

Then she moved over to Charlie and tapped him on the knee. She looked nervous, as if he might be upset that she was now his boss. But, Charlie being Charlie, he grinned his sweet grin and gave her a hug.

After which Lucinda looked around before picking out a new chair. Her chair. At the table. Where she deserved to be.

As she fussed, fixing her skirt, cricking her neck, trying to get comfortable in her seat while she chatted with Fitz, Angus sat forward, leaning his chin on his hand.

He couldn't have recounted afterwards exactly what it was that she was wearing, only that she was put together in a way that was perfectly Lucinda. Professional, yet whimsical. Neat, yet sassy. Elegant, and as sexy as all get-out.

She glowed. Surely everyone else could see that? Her

aura must have been made of spun gold. Or perhaps the sun simply hit her at the exact right angle. Whatever it was, he couldn't take his eyes off her.

"Okay," said Fitz, clapping his hands. "Charlie. Kumar. Save the soft porn for upstairs. Everyone ready?"

"Sorry," Lucinda said again. "I was looking for a pencil and couldn't find the right one… Which sounds ridiculous. Because a pencil is a pencil is a pencil, really. Am I right? It's not as if there's only one perfect pencil for me. In fact…anyone got a pen?"

Angus cleared his throat.

He saw her brace herself, as if she recognised the noise as his. Just as he'd recognise her scent in a crowd. Her laugh among a million others. Her sad smile from her tipsy smile from the smile she saved for those for whom she cared most.

As if the world was in slow motion, Lucinda looked his way. Not smiling. Not a bit. Her mouth was pursed. Her cute little frown lines entrenched above her nose.

When her eyes snagged on his—those gorgeous, big, warm, clever, brown doe-eyes—he felt as if he'd been sucker-punched.

In fact, the entire table seemed to hold its breath, waiting to see what either one of them might do and say.

Then Angus slowly held up the pencil he'd found in her drawer.

Her old drawer. Her ex-drawer. For she no longer worked there, just outside his office where he could look up and see her all day every day. Where he caught the occasional burst of her laughter through the thick glass, which made the world feel brighter, lighter, no matter how much work was on his plate. Where he saw her head bent over her work and knew she was on his side.

Louis Fournier might have been the first man who'd looked at him as though he wasn't some punk kid, but

Lucinda Starling was the first woman who'd looked at him and seen him for who he was.

Not a meal ticket or a good time. Not a party invite or a business opportunity. Not someone to ignore, or use or degrade. But a man in his own right. Flawed, damaged, stuck back together a little wrong but stronger for it. A man who saw the world not as it was but as it could be.

And she saw him as hers.

For he was her guy. And she was his girl.

"Oh, for Pete's sake!" Velma cried out, her strong voice booming across the room. "Stop mooning over the man and take the damn pencil so we can get on with this farce. The rest of you may feel as if time is on your side, but I have work to do."

Angus came to and found Lucinda staring at him, her cheeks pink, her eyes wide, unable to hide the cocktail of feelings he now realised he'd seen there before. Many times. For years, in fact.

He'd ignored them in the past—no, he'd *denied* them—fearful that if he'd claimed those emotions she'd spook, or deny, or eventually see that he was not worth it and he'd end up losing the most important person in his life.

He placed the pencil on the table and rolled it her way. She watched, a kick catching at the corner of her mouth as the pencil came to a stop right in front of her, before she blinked, caught herself, slowly gathered up the pencil, and looked down at her notebook.

Fitz clapped his hands. "Hear that everyone? My Velma has work to do so let's get this meeting under way."

"Meeting," Velma said, scoffing, before she pressed back her chair and lifted her exuberant frame out of the seat with a grunt. "We all know there's no meeting. No minutes to take. No decisions to make. Nothing bar the fact we need to settle the Lucinda-Angus issue once and for all."

"Excuse me?" Lucinda said, perking up. "There is no issue."

"*Pfft*. There's an issue the size of Fitz's ego."

"Huge!" said Fitz, holding his arms out wide.

"Enough," said Angus, silencing the room. *Now who's Dorothy and who's the great and powerful Oz?* he thought. "Velma is right. There is no agenda, bar getting Lucinda in here with me, so the rest of you can vamoose."

Lucinda's eyes couldn't have gone any wider if she'd seen a ghost.

The rest of the team, cool-headed in the face of drama and excitement, happily packed up their stuff and herded chattily from the room.

Once everyone was gone, and it was just the two of them, Lucinda's shoulders slumped and she looked his way.

"Congratulations," he said.

She winced. "It's not why I left—"

"I know. But this is a good thing. The finance team have skated for years. You'll turn our smallest department into a juggernaut in no time."

She smiled and it nearly reached her eyes. "I think you're right. I can't believe it, but I also can't wait. So, thank you. Fitz told me it was your idea. Charlie needs me. While you…" She took a breath. "You don't need anyone, Angus. It's your defining characteristic. It could be written on your tombstone."

For a very long time he'd thought so too. Otherwise everything his mother had done, everything she'd sacrificed, the times she'd left him to his own devices, would have been for nothing.

But none of that mattered now.

The only thing that mattered was sitting far too many chairs away.

He pushed his own chair back and strolled towards

her. He wondered if she even realised that she turned her chair to face him, a north to his south.

"You're wrong about one thing," he said.

"What's that?"

"You're wrong about what I need." He stopped a couple of metres away. If he came any closer he'd not be able to resist touching her. And first there were things to say. "I have something for you, Lucinda. A gift."

She sucked in a breath, her hand going to her neck. And then he saw it: the ladybird necklace he'd bought her all those years ago. And any concern that he was going too fast, that he might be over-reaching, disappeared.

"But it's not my birthday. Or St Patrick's Day. Or Sunday Funday."

"And yet…" Angus glanced through the glass walls of the boardroom and nodded.

Having been given the signal, Louis Fournier entered the room.

Lucinda stood. "Monsieur Fournier. Is everything okay?"

"Everything is wonderful," he said, giving Angus a smile before turning to Lucinda and handing her a small spring-green bag with a white satin ribbon.

She reached out and took it, glancing at Angus.

"Open it," he said, his voice rough.

He saw her hands were shaking, as she did just that, pulling out a small bottle of perfume.

A very special bottle of perfume. For Angus had had Remède's Someday perfume—the perfume her father had bought for her mother every year for her birthday—rebranded as a special edition. It had been a rush job, using glass makers in Venice, printing out of Sydney. It had cost him a personal fortune. And Louis Fournier had been behind him all the way.

The shape of the bottle was the same—a smooth, curving twist. Though the new label was shaped like the leaf of a fiddle-leaf fig, the colour the same spring-green as his favourite dress.

"Someday" was written in the same sweeping script font, only the words "Every Day" were now written beneath in neat, clean silver.

Lucinda's hand fluttered to her mouth as she sat back in her chair with a thud. When she looked up at Angus, her eyes filled with tears. Then she looked to Louis who was watching her with pure adoration in his eyes. "Monsieur Fournier?"

"Don't look at me, this is all Angus. The design, the colour, the shape, the name. It took some doing, but he can be a very convincing man when he's on a mission. Especially when his mission, dear girl, is you."

Her eyes swung back to Angus's.

No longer able to stay away, he moved in beside her and dropped into a crouch.

"What is it? What's in the bag?" Kumar whispered from the doorway.

It seemed the gang hadn't blithely gone back to work after all.

"Shh!" Velma. "Don't distract him. Kid's finally stepping up."

Angus ignored them. It was easy when Lucinda was looking right into his eyes. "Hey," he said.

"Hey." She sniffed.

"Do you like it?"

"I don't…" She gulped. "I don't even know what to say."

"Usually I can't get you to shut up."

She laughed, then hiccupped. And this time the smile came from her eyes before it lit up the rest of her lovely face. "You really had this made. For me?"

Angus nodded.

"But you told me to go. When I tried to resign. You didn't give me the chance to say why."

"You told Sonny I had no desire to be his father, without giving me the chance to answer that question for myself."

Her mouth dropped open. It would have been funny if Angus wasn't already on emotional overload.

She swallowed, licked her lips then said, "I did do that. And what would your answer have been?"

"That having the both of you in my life is the best part of my life. And that, if you didn't know that already, then I have been remiss. And I will make sure, from this day forward, that not a minute goes by that you don't know how important you are to me. How necessary. How much I love you. And how much I *will* love you. Every day."

"You do?" she asked, her voice like a breeze. Then she hit him. A slap to the chest. After which she gripped her hand into his shirt. "So why didn't you say something? Why didn't you haul me up, tell me off? Tell the truth?"

"I deferred to you. Sweetheart, I've always deferred to you. But I'm not going to do so any more. Now it's my turn to take what I want."

With that he reached out, cupped her face in his hands and kissed her.

"I'm not sure that's appropriate," said Velma from the doorway.

"She doesn't work for him any more," said Fitz, waggling his eyebrows.

Velma scowled. "I meant to be kissing in front of a client."

The CEO of Remède waved an elegant hand in their direction. "I am French. Let them kiss."

And kiss they did. Until Lucinda dropped from the chair onto her knees so that she was flush against him. He tasted her heat, her desire. When he tasted her tears, he moved to kiss them away, each and every one.

She pulled away suddenly and blurted, "I love you too. You know that, right?"

"I do."

"You said it, and I said nothing when I should have said—I love you, Angus. I've loved you for years. For ever. I was happy loving you in silence. But I can already tell I'm going to be a whole lot happier loving you out loud. You're my pencil," she said on a burst of laughter. "The one and only pencil for me."

"What did she say?" Fitz asked.

Louis shook his head. "Something about a pencil?"

"Staff meetings here sure aren't like staff meetings at my old job," said Kumar. "They had donuts, for one."

"Enough," said Fitz, reaching round them to take hold of the door. "Get back to work, the lot of you."

When the door shut with a snick, Angus breathed out. Finally. Finally, it was just Lucinda and him.

He disentangled himself from the delicious warmth of her arms, stood and held out a hand.

"You ready for this?" he said when she stood by him, toe to toe.

She grinned. "I was born ready. You?"

"You'd better believe it."

EPILOGUE

LUCINDA CAREFULLY HELD three coffees in paper cups high over her head as she edged her way past the multiple sets of knees, shivering to fend off the Melbourne winter chill, before taking a seat on a cold wooden bench behind the boundary fence at the local AFL field.

Tilda and Francine—mums to kids on Sonny's footy team—made room for her to sit then gratefully took the hot drinks.

"What did I miss?" Lucinda asked, backside slightly lifted off the seat as she spotted Sonny running down the left wing, calling for the ball.

"Much running in circles by most of them," said Tilda.

"Bastian spent quite some time staring at the clouds."

"One did look like Iron Man, so can't blame the kid."

Lucinda laughed as she planted her backside and took a moment to notice just how much her life had changed over the past few months.

Who knew that simply deciding not to be scared any more would make room for so much other stuff? Good stuff. Amazing stuff.

Taking on the position of Manager of Financial Affairs had given her far better hours at work, giving her the chance to do some school drop-offs, and pick-ups. Giving her the chance to make mum-friends—women who struggled with mothers' guilt while trying to forge a life for themselves, just as she did.

The extra time at home had given Cat more breathing space too. She was in London now, writing for an airline magazine, and ignoring Fitz's irregular pleas to come home because he was bored without her.

And Sonny had never been happier. Half a football field away, she could *feel* how utterly joyful he was.

It didn't take long for her gaze to seek out another figure on the field.

For Sonny's coach was hot stuff. Backwards cap, track pants that did nothing to hide the glorious male form beneath. Long-sleeved T-shirt rolled up at the elbow and covered with a lime-green coach's smock.

Arms outstretched, Coach Angus—*her* Angus—herded the boisterous bunch of under-nines into free space and reminded them to call for the ball, to look out for their team mates, then waited patiently for one of the girls to take her kick.

Step, step, drop the ball and thwack. It actually hit the kid's boot, which earned a clap from the crowd. Then the funny-shaped ball spun off sideways before rolling towards Sonny. And, boy, if the kid didn't swoop on it, keeping his feet in a move taught by none other than the coach himself while playing in the back yard every afternoon after school.

Sonny burst down the centre, heading straight for the open goal. Then he stopped and passed the ball to another team mate, who ran in and kicked a goal.

"Woo-woo-woo!" called Tilda. "Go, Bridget!"

Francine glanced up from her phone. "Oh, no. Did my girl do something good?"

"Ripper goal. With an excellent assist from super Sonny." Lucinda's heart, thumping in her chest, swelled with pride. And hope. And relief. And all things good, warm and wholesome.

Then the half-time buzzer rang out and the kids came running over to the fence line in their long shirts and falling down socks, sweat dripping from their hair, hands reaching for their water bottles.

After having a quick chat to the fifteen-year-old referee, Angus came jogging after them, the sharp wintry sun catching on the angles of his face as he loped their way.

Tilda and Francine let go of a tandem sigh.

"Have we ever thanked you properly?" Tilda asked.

"For?" Lucinda asked, her voice a little dreamy.

"Him," Francine answered. "Last year's coach was an absolute dud in comparison."

Tilda leaned around Lucinda to hit Francine on the arm. "Your husband is a doll."

Lucinda lifted her coffee and squeezed out from between them. "I'm outta here before this turns ugly. And you're welcome."

The women laughed and watched as Lucinda edged her way along the fence line to where the team sat in a circle, eating orange quarters.

"Hey, bud," she said, holding a hand to her eyes to block out the sun.

Sonny turned to find her, an orange peel stuck behind his lips to look like a big tooth. He pulled it out and the grin remained. "Did you see that?"

"Did I ever! Awesome team playing."

A shadow fell over her, blocking the sunlight. She dropped her hand and looked up into Angus's face. A halo of sunshine trimmed his gorgeous form.

"Hey, coach," she said.

"Hey, yourself."

He leaned over and kissed her, a devastating mix of heat and chill, yet somehow totally PG.

"Ew!" Bridget called out, and soon a chorus of "Ew!" and "Yuck!" followed.

Angus's lips smiled against hers before he pulled away.

"Having fun out there?" she asked.

He grinned, all beaming teeth and hot hazel eyes. "Yeah, actually. It's such a kick to see them improving. Did you see Sonny's assist?"

"I saw."

"That kid," he said, shaking his head in amazement. "The way he handed that off. He kills me. Comes down to some kick-ass parenting."

"Coach said 'ass'!" Milla cried.

Angus laughed. "That I did. And when you're as big as me you can decide if it's a word you want to say—or not. Till then, let's see who can think of the best word ever invented. Like…"

"Bubble gum!" Milla said.

"Chocolate!" said Bastian.

Angus grinned down at his team, his gaze lingering on Sonny. Lucinda saw the hitch in his chest and felt her own hitch in response.

She tipped up onto her toes, reached over the fence and wrapped her arms around Angus's neck, her hand landing on his chest. She whispered, "Thank you for loving my Sonny."

"Thank you for letting me."

How could she not? "Did I tell you today how much I love you?"

"Once or twice," he murmured. His hand lifted to close around hers, his thumb running up and down the sensitive middle of her palm.

She snuggled closer until her entire body seemed to sigh from an overload of pure bliss.

"Now you're just showing off!" That was Francine.

Lucinda buried her face in Angus's neck. "You have a fan club, you know?"

"Yeah," said Angus. "At training they threatened to bring placards. I told them to bring orange quarters instead."

"It worked."

"I'm very convincing."

"So I've heard."

He turned his head just enough to smile into her eyes, then gave her a quick kiss on the nose.

With a sigh, Lucinda let him go.

Now she had him for real, she found it all too hard not

to hold tight. Only the belief that he would indeed love her for ever made her able move away. To stand alone.

Angus clicked his fingers. "And I've had thoughts on how with a few tweaks the club could make some serious dosh."

"Sponsorship deal?"

Angus looked at her in wonder. "You. Me. It's like we have one brain."

"Two brains," she said as he backed away to join his team, now squeezing their water bottles at one another. "It's more fun that way."

A haze came over Angus's eyes and she knew he was trying to figure out a client for whom the line might work as a strap line. For, while his hours had also cut right back, ever since he'd moved in and they'd begun working on adding a second floor to her little cottage the guy never switched off.

As she made her way back up to the stands, her phone rang.

"Lucinda, pick up," crooned the ringtone of her phone in a deep, sexy voice, delivering a message that told her exactly what he'd like to do her when a certain someone was asleep that night.

She quickly pressed the button to hang up the call before it went further than PG. Then, grinning and blushing, she looked over her shoulder to find Angus with his phone to his ear.

She gave him a quick thumbs-up, a "yes, please" to every plan he had, before sliding her phone into the back pocket of her jeans.

While it was the kind of ringtone that would get her sideways looks at the supermarket, she might keep it for a while.

Maybe she'd keep it for ever. She was a for ever girl, after all.

* * * * *

SECOND-CHANCE SWEET SHOP

ROCHELLE ALERS

Give her the fruit of her hands; and let her own works praise her in the gates.

—Proverbs 31:31

Chapter One

The chilly February temperature and lightly falling rain did little to dispel the excitement coursing through Sasha Manning. She'd lost track of the number of times she had glanced at the wall clock. It was a week before Valentine's Day and the grand opening of her patisserie. Sasha's Sweet Shoppe was located on Main Street, in the heart of Wickham Falls' downtown business district. The mayor, several members of the town council and the chamber of commerce had promised to be on hand at ten for the ribbon-cutting photo op.

"You can keep staring at that clock, but it isn't going to make the hands move any faster."

Sasha turned to look at her mother. Charlotte Manning had worked tirelessly alongside her over the past four months to get the shop ready. And Sasha knew Charlotte, who'd had a mild heart attack nearly a year ago, could not continue to put in such long hours. Several days ago, she'd posted a help-wanted sign in the front window.

"I keep wondering if they're going to cancel the photo shoot because of the weather." The words were barely off her tongue when the town's photographer knocked lightly on the door. Sasha pressed her palms together to conceal their trembling. The door chimed when she opened it.

"Good morning, Jonas."

"Good morning, Sasha. Charlotte."

Jonas Harper, performing double duty as the photographer for the town and *The Sentinel*, Wickham Falls' biweekly, set his leather equipment bag on the floor and then walked over to the showcases filled with colorful confectionaries. "They look too pretty to eat."

Sasha smiled at the middle-aged man with a salt-and-pepper ponytail. She'd spent the past two days putting together an assortment of tarts, tortes, cookies and pies. Earlier that morning she'd baked several loaves of white, wheat, rye and pumpernickel bread. "I've put aside samples for you and the others."

Jonas unzipped his bright yellow waterproof poncho. "Is there someplace where I can hang this up?"

Charlotte stepped forward and held out her hand. "I'll take that for you."

Sasha watched her mother as she took Jonas's poncho, offering him a bright smile. At fifty-six, Charlotte was still a very attractive woman, despite what she'd had to go through during her volatile marriage to a man she was never able to please. Her blond hair was now a shimmering silver and there were a few noticeable lines around her bright blue eyes.

As the youngest of three, and the only girl, Sasha would cover her head with a pillow to drown out what were daily arguments between her parents. She had counted down the time until she graduated high school and could leave Wickham Falls, as her brothers had done when they enlisted in the military. It had been more than a decade since she'd called Wickham Falls home, but now she was back to stay.

"This place is really nice," Jonas said, as he glanced around the bakery. "It reminds me of some of the little bakeshops I saw when I visited Paris."

Sasha nodded, smiling. The colorful wallpaper stamped with images of pies, cakes, muffins and cupcakes provided a cheerful backdrop for twin refrigerated showcases, recessed lights, a quartet of pendants, and a trio of bistro tables and chairs. She had also purchased a coffee press, a cappuccino machine and a commercial blender to offer specialty coffees.

"That's what I had in mind when I decided to open this place." Although she'd never been to Paris, she had watched countless televised travel and cooking shows featuring French cooking to know exactly how she wanted her patisserie to look. Her mother had teased her, saying perhaps the residents of The Falls weren't ready for fancy tarts and pastries with names they weren't able to pronounce. But Sasha refused to let anyone dissuade her from her dream of starting over as a successful pastry chef.

When growing up she hadn't known what she wanted to do or be. Everything changed, once she left Wickham Falls and moved to Tennessee to accept a position as a companion to an elderly woman. Adele Harvey, the former English teacher and reclusive widow of a man who made a fortune buying and selling real estate, had become the grandmother Sasha never had.

Sasha saw the ad online for a live-in companion and filled out an application, despite not having any experience aside from occasionally babysitting her neighbors' young children. Two weeks following her high school graduation Sasha boarded a bus for a trip to Memphis, Tennessee, for an in-person interview with Mrs. Harvey and the attorney overseeing the legal affairs of the childless widow. It had taken the older woman only ten minutes to announce she was hired, and when Sasha returned to Memphis in mid-August it was as a first-class passenger on a direct flight, followed by a chauffeur-driven limo to what would become her new home.

The bell chimed again, breaking into her thoughts, and the editor of the newspaper walked in. Langston Cooper had left The Falls to pursue a career as a journalist. For more than a decade he had covered the Middle East as a foreign correspondent for an all-news cable station before returning to the States to write several bestselling books. His life mirrored Sasha's when he married a popular singer, but the union was dissolved amid rumors that she'd had an affair with an actor. Langston returned to Wickham Falls, took over ownership of the dwindling biweekly and within two years had increased the newspaper's circulation and advertising revenue.

Taking off his baseball cap, he smiled at Sasha, exhibiting straight, white teeth in his light brown complexion. Growing up, Langston and her brother had been what folks said were as thick as thieves. You'd never see one without the other.

Walking over to him, she pressed her cheek to his smooth-shaven jaw. "Thank you for coming."

Langston dropped a kiss on the mass of curly hair framing Sasha's round face. "Did you actually think I would miss the grand opening of The Falls' celebrity pastry chef?"

Sasha blushed to the roots of her natural strawberry-blond hair. She'd dyed the bright red strands a non-descript brown following her divorce to avoid attracting the attention of eagle-eyed paparazzi who'd hounded her relentlessly once the word was out that she was no longer married to country-music heartthrob Grant Richards.

"Have you forgotten that I'm not the only celebrity in The Falls?" she teased with a smile. "After all, you are a *New York Times* bestselling author."

Langston nodded. "I didn't come here for you to talk about me, but about you. After photos and the speeches, I'd like you to schedule some time for an interview for *The Sentinel*'s Who's Who column."

Since coming back to The Falls Sasha had discovered her hometown had changed—and for the better. The list of those returning to Wickham Falls to put down roots was growing. Langston had become editor in chief of *The Sentinel*, Seth Collier was now sheriff, and Sawyer Middleton headed the technology department for the Johnson County Public Schools system. And for Sasha it was a no-brainer. The Falls was the perfect place for her to start over with a business where she did not have a competitor.

"Can you call me in a couple of weeks?" she asked.

"You've got it." Langston leaned closer and kissed

her cheek. "Good luck and congratulations," he said as he left.

She hoped the samples she planned to offer those coming into the shop for her grand opening would generate return customers. A nervous smile barely lifted the corners of her mouth when she spied the mayor, several members of the town council and the head of the chamber of commerce through the plate-glass window.

"It's showtime, Natasha," Charlotte whispered.

"Yes, it is, Mama." Her mother was the only one who had refused to call her by her preferred name. When her mother brought her home from the hospital, her three-year-old brother could not pronounce Natasha; he'd begun calling her Sasha and the name stuck. She walked over to the door and opened it.

Sasha let out an audible sigh when the town officials filed out of the shop, each with a small white box, stamped with the patisserie's logo, and filled with miniature samples of red velvet, pumpkin spice, lemon-lime and chocolate hazelnut cupcakes. Cupcakes had become her signature specialty.

She pushed her hands into the pockets of the pink tunic with her name and the shop's logo stamped over her heart. "Even though Mayor Gillespie was a little long-winded, I think it went well."

"It went very, very well," Charlotte said in agreement. "Jonas took wonderful shots of the shop, and after your interview with Langston I'm willing to bet that you won't be able to keep up with the demand for your cupcakes."

Charlotte gave her daughter a reassuring smile. When she had come back six months before she had felt like crying when she opened the door to see her last born appear to be a shadow of the young woman who had come to her father's funeral what now seemed so long ago. The bright red hair was a mousy brown, and she had lost a lot of weight. At five-nine she'd appeared almost emaciated and it took Charlotte all her resolve not to become hysterical. It was only after she revealed the circumstances behind her marriage and subsequent divorce that Charlotte understood what Natasha had gone through.

Sasha pulled her lower lip between her teeth. She wanted to sell not only cupcakes, but also specialty cakes, breads and made-to-order elegant desserts. Wickham Falls wasn't Nashville, but she didn't plan to offer the small-town residents creations of a lesser quality than those in the Music City. The doorbell chimed and within minutes there was a steady stream of curious potential customers. She'd sold out of fresh bread before the noon hour.

"May I help you?" Sasha asked an attractive teenage girl with large dark brown eyes and neatly braided hair ending at her shoulders.

"Yes. I've come to apply for the part-time counterperson position."

"Are you still in school?"

"Yes, ma'am. I'm finished with my classes at noon, so I'm available from one on."

Sasha didn't want to write the girl off before she interviewed her, although she would've preferred someone more mature. "What's your name?"

"Kiera Adams. My dad is Dwight Adams," she said proudly.

The moment Kiera mentioned her father's name

Sasha realized she was the daughter of the local dentist. "Does your father know you're applying for the position?" She had asked the question because she did not want to have a problem with parents questioning the number of hours their son or daughter were committed to work.

Kiera shook her head. "Not yet. I figured I'd tell him once you hired me."

Sasha bit back a smile. The young woman did not lack confidence. "Mama, could you please cover the front while I talk to Miss Adams?"

Charlotte nodded. "Of course."

Sasha led Kiera to the rear of the shop, where she had set up an area for her office. She glanced over her shoulder. "Please sit down, Kiera. I've made up an application and I'll give you time to fill it out before we talk."

The help-wanted sign had been in the window for three days, and Kiera was the first person to respond. Sasha frosted several dozen cupcakes while Kiera filled out the application.

"I'm finished with the application, Miss…"

"You may call me Sasha," she said when Kiera's words trailed off.

She took the single sheet of paper from the teenager's outstretched hand. It took less than a minute to review what Kiera had written. Although Sasha hadn't included a category for age, Kiera indicated she was sixteen and a junior at the local high school. She was available to work every day beginning at one in the afternoon, and all day Saturday. Her prior work experience was as a temporary receptionist the previous summer at her father's dental practice.

Sasha revealed, if hired, what Kiera would be responsible for. She would need Kiera to work four hours every afternoon from Tuesday through Friday. And if needed, one or two Saturdays each month. "If I hire you, will it interfere with your studies?"

"No, ma'am. Even though I'm enrolled as a junior, I'm taking senior-level classes." She flashed a demure smile. "I took a lot of AP courses when I went to school in New York."

It was apparent Dr. Adams's daughter was very bright, and it was the third time Kiera had referred to her as "ma'am," which made her feel much older than thirty-two. "You are the first one to apply for the position, and I'm going to keep your application on hand. I plan to wait a few more days, and if no one else applies, then I'll contact you. Please keep in mind if I do decide to bring you on that initially you'll start at the minimum wage."

Kiera stood up. "Does that mean I'll get the job?"

Sasha felt as if she'd been just put on the spot. "I'm going to be up-front with you, Kiera. You're still a student and I don't want you to compromise your grades. And because of this I'd like your permission to talk to your father."

Kiera tucked several braids behind one ear. "I don't mind, Miss Sasha." She paused. "Will you call me if you decide not to hire me?"

"I will send you an email."

Leaning down, Kiera picked up her backpack. "Thank you."

Sasha smiled. "You're very welcome. I still have a few samples on hand I'd like to give you from our grand opening. Are you allergic to chocolate?"

A smile spread across the girl's face, softening her

youthful features. "Thank goodness, no. I love chocolate."

Sasha scrunched up her nose. "It's my weakness, too." She walked over to a refrigerator in the prep kitchen and took out a candy cane–striped box and filled it with chocolate crinkle cookies, brownies, a cup of chocolate mousse topped with whipped cream and grated chocolate, and the last chocolate hazelnut cupcake. "Enjoy. And thank you for coming in."

Kiera's smile was dazzling. "Thank you so much, Miss Sasha."

There was something about Kiera's youthful enthusiasm Sasha liked.

Dwight Adams's head popped up when he heard the light tapping on the door to his office. He had a two-hour wait before seeing his next patient. He hadn't expected to see his daughter until later that night, but her coming to his practice was a welcome surprise. He came around the desk to hug her as she dropped the backpack filled with books on the carpet and set a red-and-white-striped box on a side table.

"What are you doing here?"

Kiera rose on tiptoe to kiss her father's cheek. "What happened to 'nice seeing you'?"

"Of course I'm happy to see you. It's just that I didn't expect you to come here instead of going home. And, by the way, how did you get here?"

"I asked Grammie to drop me off. She has a luncheon meeting with the Ladies Auxiliary."

Dwight studied the teenager who was the mirror image of her mother at that age. The exception was her complexion and height, which she had inherited from him. Kiera, at five-six, was four inches taller than her petite five-foot-two mother. The school bus picked up and dropped off Kiera at the house; Dwight's widowed mother lived in a two-bedroom guesthouse Dwight had built on the property.

Kiera rested her hands on the thighs of her denim-covered jeans. "I applied for a part-time job at the new bakery."

Dwight went completely still. "You did what?"

"Please don't lose it, Daddy."

Extending his legs, he ran a hand over his face. "I'm not losing it, Kiera. I just need to know why you feel the need to get a job when you should be concentrating on your schoolwork. And it can't be about money, because I give you an allowance."

Kiera slipped her right hand in her father's left, threading their fingers together. "I need something to beef up my college applications, either work or community service. A lot of kids at school have already signed up at the church, town hall and other businesses in Wickham Falls. And besides, Miss Sasha said I was the first one to apply, so there is a good chance she might hire me."

"What about your working here?" Dwight questioned.

The summer before Kiera had worked for him when the permanent receptionist went on vacation. As a divorced father, he shared custody with his ex-wife, Adrienne; for years Kiera lived in New York with her and spent one month every summer with him in The Falls. He had made it a practice to visit his daughter several times a year, and whenever he returned home, he'd experienced a modicum of guilt that he bore some responsibility for ending his marriage when he'd been away in the military, which resulted in his not being there to see his daughter grow up. However, everything had changed this past summer when Kiera announced she did not want to return to New York to live with her mother and stepfather, and preferred spending the last two years of high school living with her father and grandmother in Wickham Falls.

Dwight had a lengthy conversation with his ex-wife and convinced her it was time for him to have his daughter for more than a month or a brief visit on school holidays. She finally agreed, with the provision that Kiera vacationed with her during the month of July. Assuming the role as a full-time father had also impacted his obligation as an army reservist. Serving his country for almost two decades while attaining the rank of major was now relegated to his past.

"That's nepotism, Daddy. I can't put down that I worked for Dwight Adams, DDS, and not have someone question our relationship. Miss Sasha said she wanted to talk to you beforehand if she decides to hire me. I guess she doesn't want my having a job to mess with my grades."

"Good for her." Dwight liked the idea that Kiera's potential employer was concerned about her education.

Although he was five or six years old than Sasha Manning, Dwight hadn't had much interaction with her when growing up in The Falls. He and two of her older brothers had attended high school at the same time. But he'd heard a lot about Sasha when she became a celebrity chef and then married platinum-selling country singer Grant Richards. He was as surprised as most in town when she returned to The Falls to set up a bakeshop in one of the vacant stores at the far end of Main Street.

Kiera pointed to the box. "She gave me samples of chocolate desserts. I was going to leave it in the break room until I remembered Miss Chambers is on a diet and doesn't want to eat anything with sugar, so I'm going to take them home for Gram…" Her words trailed off when her cell phone rang. Reaching into her jacket pocket, she stared at the phone. "It's Miss Sasha. She said she would email me if she wasn't going to hire me."

Dwight pointed to Kiera's death grip on the small instrument. "Are you going to answer your phone?" He noticed her expression of apprehension when she put it to her ear. Her expression changed quickly as she covered her mouth with her free hand. "Yes. My dad is here with me." Kiera extended the phone to him. "Miss Sasha would like to speak to you."

He took the phone. "Hello."

"Dr. Adams, this is Sasha Manning. Your daughter applied for a part-time position at my bakeshop. Although I told her that I'm waiting to interview other folks, I've decided to hire her, and I would like to talk to you because I need your reassurance that her hours won't conflict with her schoolwork."

Dwight smiled. His priority for his daughter was maintaining her grades so she could gain acceptance into at least one or two of her colleges of choice. It was apparent Sasha was of like mind. They discussed the details of the position. Dwight agreed to let her take the job but warned that if her grades slipped, she'd have to quit.

"I understand that, Dr. Adams. If it's all right with you, I'd like her to start tomorrow. I'm going to need a copy of her immunizations because she'll be working in what we call food service, and her Social Security number."

"I can get those to you later this afternoon after my last patient. What time do you close?"

"I draw the shades once I close at six, but I'll be here later than that. Does that work for you?"

Dwight nodded although she couldn't see him. "Yes." He was scheduled to see his last patient at 5:30. Then he would have to go home and get the documents Sasha needed to place Kiera on her payroll. "I'll probably see you after you close."

"I'll be here." There came a pause before Sasha's voice came through the earpiece again. "Thank you, Dr. Adams. I hope you don't mind my saying, but your daughter is a delight."

Dwight stared at Kiera staring back at him and winked at her. He had to agree with Sasha. There was never a time when he did not enjoy spending time with his daughter. And now that she was living with him, they had grown even closer. "I know I sound biased, but I have to agree with you. She is pretty special."

"I'll see you tonight?"

"Yes," Dwight confirmed.

"Dr. Adams, can you spare a few minutes of your time when you come because I'd like to talk to you about something other than your daughter's employment."

He paused, wondering what it was Sasha wanted to discuss with him. "Yes," Dwight repeated, now that she had aroused his curiosity. He ended the call and handed the phone back to Kiera. "It looks as if you're hired."

Kiera clasped her hands together in a prayerful gesture. "When do I start?"

"Tomorrow."

"Instead of the bus dropping me off at the house, I'll get off with some of the other kids on the other side of the tracks."

Dwight nodded. The railroad tracks ran through the downtown business district. "What about lunch?" He knew Kiera left school early because lunch was her last period of the school day.

"I get out at twelve and by the time the bus drops me off it will be about 12:30. Instead of going home to eat, I'll ask Grammie to help me make lunch and I'll eat it here before walking down to the bakery."

He smiled. "You have it all figured out, don't you?"

"Daddy, aren't you the one who told me to have a strategy before I execute a plan?"

Dwight managed to look sheepish. "Yes, I did." He'd lost track of the number of forewarnings he'd given his daughter over the years, and it was apparent she remembered most of them because she could repeat them verbatim.

Dwight found a parking spot behind the bakery and walked around to the front. He'd dropped Kiera at home and told his mother not to plan for him to eat dinner with her and his daughter. He had no way of knowing how long his meeting with Sasha would take.

The woven shade on Sasha's storefront had been pulled down, as had the one covering the front door.

Dwight tapped lightly on a square of the door's beveled glass insert, and seconds later he saw Sasha as she pushed aside the shade and then opened the door. He

was just as shocked as many in the town at the word
that Sasha Manning was back in town, and without
her superstar country-artist husband. She'd kept a low
profile until the town council approved her opening
a bakeshop in the downtown business district. Questions about her marriage were finally answered when a
photographer captured photos of Grant Richards with
a woman who was purported to be his new girlfriend.
And when reporters asked Grant about his relationship
with Sasha, he'd admitted it was over.

Smiling, Sasha opened the door wider. "Please come
in."

Chapter Two

Sasha successfully smothered a gasp when she greeted Dwight Adams. He was more than gorgeous. He was beautiful. His balanced features in a lean sable-brown sculpted face, large dark penetrating eyes and dimpled smile were mesmerizing. His buzz-cut salt-and-pepper hair was a shocking contrast to his unlined face. Dressed entirely in black—sheep-lined leather bomber jacket, pullover sweater, jeans and Doc Martens—he was unequivocally the epitome of tall, dark and handsome.

Six years his junior, she'd had little or no interaction with him when growing up. By the time she entered the first grade Dwight was already in middle school. Even if they had been the same age, they might not have traveled in the same circles. Wickham Falls, like so many small towns, was defined by social and economic division. His family lived in an enclave of The Falls populated by those who were middle- and upper-middle-class professionals and business owners, while she had always thought of her family as the working poor, because her father always said he was one paycheck away from the poorhouse. Despite Harold's claim they were poor, Sasha never felt as if they were. Her parents owned their house, there was always food on the table and, as the only girl, she hadn't had to wear hand-me-downs.

She'd overheard some of the girls that were in her brothers' classes whisper about how gorgeous Dwight was, but talking about cute boys or fantasizing about teen idols with her girlfriends had not been reality for Sasha. She'd never wanted to host a sleepover, because what happened in the Manning house stayed within the Manning household. Neither she nor her brothers ever publicly spoke about their parents' toxic union.

What she had never been able to understand was why her parents had married in the first place because they could not agree on anything; and yet they'd celebrated their thirtieth wedding anniversary. Two days later her father passed away from a massive coronary. He was only forty-nine. That was seven years ago, and the first time Sasha had returned to The Falls since leaving at eighteen.

"Congratulations, Sasha. You managed to add some class to The Falls," Dwight said as he glanced around the bakeshop.

She forced a smile she did not quite feel. She had spent more than a year planning to open a bakeshop, several months awaiting the town council's approval, and then even more time until the contractor finished renovating the space to make it functional for her to furnish it with prep tables, sinks, industrial ovens, mixers, blenders, deep fryers, food processors, bakeware and utensils.

"You don't think it's too fancy?"

Dwight turned and met her eyes. "Of course not. It's charming and very inviting." He smiled. "And I like the alliteration of Sasha's Sweet Shoppe."

She nodded. "It took me a while to come up with a catchy name. My first choice was Sasha's Patisserie, but changed my mind because I didn't want to have to explain to folks what a patisserie is."

Dwight walked over to the showcase and peered at the colorfully decorated and labeled pastries. "All they have to say is 'I want one of these and two of those.' By the way, how was your grand opening?"

Sasha moved over to stand next to him. "It went well enough. I gave out a lot of samples, and hopefully it will be enough to induce folks to come back again."

Dwight gave Sasha a sidelong glance. He had been more familiar with her brothers than their little sister. It wasn't until she had become a contestant in a televised baking competition that he, like most living in The Falls, tuned in to watch and remotely cheer her on. The camera appeared to make love to the tall, slender pastry chef with a wealth of red-gold curls, sparkling green eyes and an infectious laugh. Although she did not win the competition, her appearance was enough to make her a viewer favorite. Her star continued to rise when she became the personal baker to several celebrities and married a popular country singer, and then without warning walked away from the bright lights to come back to her place of birth.

It only took a quick glance for Dwight to notice lines of tension around Sasha's mouth. As someone responsible for managing his own practice, he suspected she was apprehensive about making her new business a success.

"I don't think you have anything to worry about. I ate a piece of your chocolate-and-pecan cheesecake and wanted more."

Sasha flashed a relaxed smile for the first time. The gesture softened her mouth as her eyes sparkled like polished emeralds. "I'll definitely put that on my cheesecake list."

Dwight reached into the pocket of his jacket and took out an envelope. "I brought you a copy of Kiera's immunizations and her Social Security number."

Sasha took the envelope. "Come with me. I'm going to scan both and then give them back to you. The less paper I have to file, the better."

He followed her to the rear of the shop, where a spacious immaculate commercial kitchen was outfitted with industrial appliances. His gaze was drawn to a built-in refrigerator/freezer, and then to dozens of cans and labeled jars of spices stacked on metal shelves that spanned an entire wall. Sasha had set up a desk with a computer, printer and file cabinet next to the exit door leading out to the rear parking lot. Bills and invoices were tacked to the corkboard with colorful pushpins affixed to the wall above the desk.

"So, this is where the magic happens."

Sasha nodded, smiling. "Disney may take offense, but this *is* my magic kingdom." She sat on the office

chair in front of the computer and patted the straight-
back chair next to the workstation. "Please sit down."

"When did you know you wanted to be a baker?"
Dwight asked, as he sat where Sasha had indicated.

She swiveled on her chair to face him. "I never
wanted to be a baker."

His eyebrows rose slightly. "But don't you bake?"

"Bakers make pies, while pastry chefs make desserts."

Dwight inclined his head. "I apologize and stand
corrected." Sasha's low, sensual laugh caressed his ear.

"There's no need to apologize, Dr. Adams."

He gave her a pointed look. "It's Dwight. I'm only
Dr. Adams at my office."

Sasha paused and then nodded. A beat passed.
"Okay, Dwight. I suppose you're wondering what else
I wanted to talk to you about?"

Dwight, sitting with his hands sandwiched between
his knees, watched as Sasha inserted a thumb drive
into a port. "I must admit I am curious." The seconds
ticked as she saved what she'd scanned and handed the
papers back to him.

"How difficult was it for you to set up your practice
here in The Falls? And how long did it take before you
knew it would be viable?"

Her query caught Dwight slightly unawares. He
thought Sasha would've established a detailed business
plan before deciding to open the shop. After all, she was
selling goods that relied on supply and demand, while
he offered a specific service.

"Well, it was somehow different for me because
there was no dental office in The Falls. I remember
my mother complaining about having to drive to Min-

eral Springs and sit for hours to be seen because the office was always overcrowded and overbooked. And once they added an orthodontist it became bedlam in the waiting room with kids falling over one another. Once I decided I wanted to be a dentist I knew beforehand that I would set up a practice here."

"How long have you had your practice?" Sasha asked.

"This coming October will be eight years."

"Did you know the first year that you would have enough patients to sustain your practice?"

"I knew that only when my patients returned for their sixth-month checkup. My mother was semiretired, so she filled in as my receptionist until I was able to find a permanent one, and after I hired a hygienist, I didn't have to micromanage, and everything fell into place. A couple of months ago I added a dental assistant to our staff who performs some of the duties the hygienist had assumed. Initially, most of my patients were kids who needed to have their teeth checked for school, a few for sleepaway camp, and then after a while I was able to sign up their parents."

"What about your hours?"

"At one time they varied because I was in the reserves and had to serve one weekend a month and two weeks during the summer. I resigned my commission last summer once Kiera came to live with me. Currently, I'm open Mondays and Fridays nine to six, and Tuesdays and Thursdays from one to seven. Even though I no longer go on maneuvers for the two weeks, I still close the office."

"What happened to Wednesdays and Saturdays?"

"Wednesday is designated golf day for doctors even

though I don't golf," he admitted, smiling, "and because I have two late nights, I can spend Saturdays and Sundays with my daughter."

Sasha inhaled a deep breath, held it before slowly exhaling. "I debated whether to close for one day, and then decided on two because I don't have an assistant. Mama had a mild heart attack last year and her cardiologist has cautioned her about overtiring herself. She's been working nonstop helping me to get this place ready, but by afternoons she's so tired that she must get off her feet. Most nights she's in bed by the time I get home. I wanted to wait to see how many more would apply for the part-time afternoon position before I made a decision, but because Kiera was the first to come in, I decided not to prolong the process."

"What time do you come in?" Dwight questioned.

"I get in around six and I'm usually here a couple of hours after closing."

He whistled softly. "That's a long day." Sasha nodded. "I really understand your apprehension, but this isn't the first time you've gone into business for yourself." He wanted to remind her that she had earned the reputation as a celebrity chef.

"That's true, but the difference is I'd worked out of my home and only when I was commissioned to design cakes for special occasions. I'm not questioning my ability as a pastry chef, but whether folks in town are willing to spend money on freshly made baked goods."

Dwight curbed the urge to reach out and take Sasha's hand when he noticed its trembling. "You're experiencing what every other start-up business faces. We don't know how it's going to turn out except that we must take the risk and hope we'll be successful. I had to withdraw money from an annuity to buy machines and equipment to set up the office, and it took me three years before I was able to put it back."

Sasha suddenly felt as if she was being a Negative Nelly. Unlike Dwight, she didn't have to borrow money to set up the bakeshop. She'd earned enough money from designing cakes for A-list celebrities to become financially comfortable, and she'd also inherited a small fortune from her former employer. Luckily, she'd signed a prenup before marrying Grant with the stipulation he wasn't entitled to her earnings, just as she wasn't entitled to what he'd received from his recording contracts. She'd had Adele Harvey to thank for the advice as to how she should protect her money.

"I'm sorry to bend your ear about…"

"Stop it, Sasha," Dwight said softly, cutting her off. "There's no need to apologize. You're not the first and won't be the last person to experience preopening jitters. I'm willing to bet you'll have a line out the door like the ones in Brooklyn when folks order cakes from Junior's for Thanksgiving and Christmas."

Her expression brightened noticeably. "You know about Junior's?"

Grinning from ear to ear, Dwight chuckled softly. "One of my army buddies was a native New Yorker and he knew every popular eating spot on Long Island and the five boroughs. The first time he took me to Junior's for dinner and suggested I try the cheesecake, I was hooked. I try to visit Junior's at least once every time I go to New York."

"Do you go often?"

"I used to go back three or four times a year when Kiera lived with my ex-wife."

The mention of an ex-wife had Sasha wondering if Dwight had remarried, despite his not wearing a wedding band. However, his marital status was of no import to her at the moment. Her sole focus was making a go of her patisserie.

"After I graduated from culinary school, I took a two-month break and treated myself to trips to DC, New York and Boston to visit a number of restaurants who'd earned a reputation for their signature desserts. Junior's was on my list for cheesecakes once I got to New York City. Everything I'd heard or read about their cheesecakes could not accurately describe what I'd eaten. I'd become so obsessed in attempting to duplicate their recipe that I gave up and now use a basic recipe and slightly tweak it to make it my own."

"Your cheesecake is spectacular."

A rush of heat suffused her face. "Thank you."

Dwight stretched out long legs and crossed his arms over his chest. "You can count me as a regular customer if you send me an email whenever you bake bagels, ciabatta, focaccia, cinnamon raisin or Irish soda bread."

Sasha felt a rush of excitement for the first time since sitting down with Dwight. She was looking forward to foot traffic for special-order items. "I'll definitely add your name to my mailing list. I plan to alert everyone on the list of the day's special." She pushed to her feet, Dwight rising with her, and extended her hand. "Thank you for the pep talk. I left a pad at the front of the shop for you to put down your contact information."

Dwight took her hand, his larger one closing over

her fingers. He went completely still. "Why is your hand so cold?"

"I've always had cold hands."

"Cold hands, warm heart?" he teased.

"You've got it," Sasha countered.

Once her marriage soured and she felt comfortable enough to disclose the details to her mother, Charlotte had accused her of loving with her heart rather than her head. She didn't want to tell the older woman that she did not want a repeat of her marriage, where every day was filled with hostility, so she'd bitten her tongue in order to keep the peace. However, in the end she knew she could not continue to put up with a man who was continually threatened that her popularity was surpassing his, as he constantly reminded her. It had taken more than six months for her to finally tell Grant it was over and that she wanted out. Much to her surprise, he agreed, and less than a year later they went their separate ways.

Dwight increased his hold on her hand, his thumb caressing the back and adding warmth not only to her fingers but adding a rush of warmth through her whole body. Though undeniably innocent, the motion elicited shivers of sensual awareness coursing through her. Sasha could not believe she was reveling in the feel of a man holding her hand.

"May I please have my hand back?" A teasing smile tilted the corners of her mouth.

Dwight dropped it as if it was a venomous snake. "Sorry about that."

I'm not, Sasha thought. She wasn't sorry because it had been much too long since she'd found herself affected by a man's touch. Now that she looked back on her relationship with her ex-husband, Sasha knew she had been in denial when she refused to see what had been so apparent from her first date with Grant. He was a narcissist. It had to be all about him.

Despite what she'd felt when Dwight held her hand, Sasha knew there was no way she could allow herself to be swayed by romantic fantasies. Her sole focus was making certain she remained in business. She had invested too much time and money in the bakeshop to have it fail. Dwight stared at her, and suddenly she felt like a specimen on a slide under a microscope.

Without warning, a wave of exhaustion washed over her as she tried unsuccessfully to stifle a yawn. "It has been a long day, and as soon as I let you out, I'm going to head home. I'd planned to put up a batch of dough for bread, but that's something I'll do when I come in early tomorrow."

"I'll wait and walk you out."

Sasha shook her head. "Thank you for offering, but I believe I can find my way to the parking lot rather easily."

"I'll still wait and walk you to your car."

"If you say so."

"I do."

There was something in Dwight's voice that indicated no matter what she said she wouldn't be able to dissuade him. She showed him where he could put down his contact information before returning to the kitchen to turn off lights and retrieve her tote from the lower drawer in the file cabinet. Dwight met her as she armed the security system, opened and locked the rear door behind them.

Sasha pointed to the van parked several spaces down

from the bakeshop. The parking lot was brightly lit with newly installed high-intensity streetlamps. A rash of burglaries and break-ins had prompted shopkeepers to get the town council to approve improved lighting to protect their businesses.

"The white van is mine."

Dwight walked her to her vehicle and waited for her to unlock the doors. "Do you want to give me a hint about tomorrow's special?"

"Red velvet cheesecake brownies. I'll put aside a few and give them to Kiera when she comes in. One of the perks will be she will get samples of the day's special." Dwight's dimples reminded Sasha of the indentations in thumbprint cookies when he smiled.

"That sounds like a plan."

Sasha got in behind the wheel and started up the van. "Get home safe," she said before closing the door. Dwight hadn't moved as she put the vehicle in Reverse and drove out of the lot. Talking to him had offered Sasha a modicum of confidence that she could have a successful business offering the residents of Wickham Falls fresh baked goods.

Ten minutes later, she maneuvered into the driveway of the three-bedroom house where she'd grown up, and where her mother still lived. It wasn't until she'd returned to The Falls and moved back in the house that she'd realized how small it was. Eleven hundred square feet was a far cry from the six-thousand-square-foot home she'd shared with her husband in Nashville's tony West End neighborhood. Sitting on three acres of prime real estate, the house was so large the builder had installed intercoms for her to communicate with Grant whenever they were in opposite wings of the mansion.

Sasha had given all of it up—the guitar-shaped in-ground pool, the horses she'd loved to ride, and rubbing shoulders with Nashville's country royalty—in order to control her destiny. The first night she crawled into the bed in her childhood bedroom, she slept for twelve uninterrupted hours and woke feeling as if she had been reborn. It took two months for her to put together a business plan to start over in a town she'd fled fourteen years before. Not only had she changed; the family dynamics had also changed. Her father was gone, and her brothers were lifers in the military, which left just her and her mother.

She parked the van beside Charlotte's brand-new Corolla. Sasha had purchased the vehicle as a birthday gift a week after returning to The Falls, because her mother's car had spent more time in the garage than it had on the road. She ignored Charlotte's complaint that she didn't need a new car, now that she was retired, and that a used one would suffice. Sasha had had to remind the older woman that she was entitled to own a vehicle that hadn't belonged to someone else first.

She got out, unlocked the front door, walked into the house and was met with mouthwatering aromas wafting to her nose. "Mama, I'm home," Sasha called out as she dropped her tote on a bench seat and left her shoes on the mat inside the door.

Charlotte came out of the kitchen wearing her ubiquitous bibbed apron. Sasha could not remember a time when her mother did not wear an apron when cooking. "I thought you were coming home much later."

Sasha ran her hand through the curls falling over her forehead. "I changed my mind."

"Are you feeling all right?"

She registered the concern in Charlotte's voice. "I'm just a little tired." The apprehension coupled with euphoria she'd felt earlier that morning had dissipated like air leaking out of a balloon. "I'm going to eat with you, then take a long soak in the tub before going to bed."

"Did you talk to Dr. Adams?" Charlotte asked.

Sasha smiled. "Yes. He gave me the papers I need to put Kiera on the payroll. I asked him about him setting up his dental practice, and he gave me some good advice. He also promised to become a steady customer if I bake some of his favorite breads."

Charlotte wrapped an arm around Sasha's waist. "Come. We'll talk in the kitchen. I still have to whip up the mashed potatoes."

Sasha sniffed the air. "You made meat loaf." Her mother nodded. Charlotte knew meat loaf with mashed potatoes was her favorite comfort food. There had been a time when as a wife and mother Charlotte made it a practice to make her husband and children's favorite dishes once a week. For Sasha it was meat loaf. Fried chicken for her brother Philip, grilled pork chops for Stephen and beef stew for her father.

"Yes. And it's time I take it out of the oven." Reaching for an oven mitt, Charlotte opened the eye-level oven and set the hot pan on a trivet.

"I'm going to wash my hands, and then I'll finish the potatoes," Sasha volunteered.

"Are you sure?" Charlotte asked.

"Yes. Sit down and put your feet up."

She did not want to remind her mother that she had been up before dawn and needed at least eight to ten hours of sleep to keep up her stamina. But Sasha hoped things would change with her new hire. Now Charlotte

would be able to leave the shop midday and return home
to rest before starting dinner.

"I'm not an invalid," Charlotte argued softly, as she
opened the refrigerator and took out a bowl of Greek
salad and a cruet with dressing.

"I know that, Mama. But remember what the doctor said about overtiring yourself. You have a follow-up
medical checkup next month and I know you're looking
forward to good news."

"I am. But I feel more like a toddler than a grandmother having to take naps in the afternoon."

Married at eighteen, Charlotte had delivered Philip
at nineteen, and he, following in his mother's footsteps,
married within days of graduating high school. He made
Charlotte a grandmother before her fortieth birthday.

"You'll be back to your former self when you least
expect it."

After laying out another place setting, Charlotte sat
down. She smiled. "That's what I'm hoping. And what
about you, Natasha?"

Sasha halted washing her hands in one of the twin
sinks. "What about me, Mama?"

"Do you resent having to come back to The Falls
after living the high life in Nashville?"

Sasha went completely still before reaching for a
paper towel to dry her hands. "Why would you ask
me that?"

Charlotte shrugged under a flower-sprigged blouse.
The tiny blue flowers were an exact match for her eyes.
"There are times when I see so much sadness in your
eyes that I believe you'd rather be somewhere else."

Pushing her hands into a pair of oven mitts, Sasha
picked up the pot of boiled potatoes and emptied it into

a large colander, steam temporarily clouding her vision. "If I'd wanted to be somewhere else, I never would've come home."

"I hope you didn't come back for me."

Sasha closed her eyes for several seconds as she carefully chose her words. She didn't know what had triggered her mother to question her motive for returning to her hometown. "I came back for me *and* you, Mama. I was so sick of the so-called high life that there were days when I didn't want to get out of bed. There was a time when I couldn't wait to leave The Falls, and then fast-forward fourteen years and I couldn't wait to come back. My only concerns are you getting well and making certain the bakeshop will be successful. When I mentioned my apprehension to Dwight, he reassured me what I'm feeling is normal for anyone opening a new business."

"I'm surprised he's going to allow his daughter to work for you."

"Why would you say that?"

"Everyone knows he's very protective of that girl. That's probably the reason why he hasn't remarried."

"How long has he been divorced?"

"Kiera may have been in the second grade when his wife left him."

Charlotte mentioning Dwight's marital status stirred Sasha's curiosity about the attractive dentist. "Why did they break up?" She riced the potatoes, added milk, unsalted melted butter, garlic powder, fresh chives, and then whisked the mixture until it was smooth and fluffy.

"I don't know if there's any truth to it, but folks were saying Adrienne didn't want him to set up a practice in

Wickham Falls and she gave him an ultimatum. In the end, she left, and he stayed."

"But didn't she know when she married him that he didn't want to leave The Falls?" Sasha asked. There were very few people in town Charlotte wasn't familiar with. After thirty years as a cafeteria worker for Johnson County Public Schools, she had come to know every student from kindergarten through twelfth grade during her tenure.

"I don't know. The only thing I can say is the Wheelers spoiled Adrienne because she was the only girl in a family with four boys, and with her looks she knew she could have any boy she wanted. And once she set her sights on Dwight it was all she wrote. Would you mind if I open a bottle of that fancy wine you sent me?" Charlotte asked, changing the topic of conversation. "After all, we are celebrating your grand opening, and there are a few bottles chilling in the fridge."

"You're right about that, Mama." Once Grant went on an extended ten-city tour, Sasha had shipped her clothes, wine collection and personal possessions to Wickham Falls. She had become quite the wine connoisseur once she learned to pair those which complemented fish, red meat and poultry. "Red or champagne?"

"Champagne."

Before moving to Tennessee, Sasha rarely had mother-daughter dates, but since returning, she had come to see another side of Charlotte's personality. As a young wife and mother, Charlotte had sought to shield her children from her husband's temper tantrums, while taking the brunt of his constant bitching and moaning about how much he hated his job as an orderly at the county hospital. Sasha expertly removed the cork from the bottle and filled two flutes with the pale bubbly wine. She touched her glass to Charlotte's. "A toast to Sasha's Sweet Shoppe."

Charlotte smiled. "Hear, hear!"

Between sips of champagne, bites of succulent meat loaf and garlic-infused mashed potatoes, she felt completely relaxed for the first time since getting out of bed earlier that morning. And once she recalled the events of the day, Sasha knew her grand opening had been a rousing success.

She peered over the flute at the updated kitchen. When she'd returned to Wickham Falls for her father's funeral, it was as if she saw the kitchen and bathrooms in the house where she'd grown up for the first time. Had they always been that outdated, or was she comparing them to the ones in the ultramodern mansion she'd shared with her then-husband?

Charlotte refused to accept money for the renovations, so Sasha contacted a local contractor and had him send her plans to redo the kitchen, full bath and the half bath off the mudroom. When the contracting crew showed up to begin work, her mother called and read her the riot act. Sasha hung up, waited a week and then called Charlotte back. She could not stop talking about how much she loved her new kitchen.

The money for the renovations hadn't come from what she'd earned as a pastry chef, but from an account Adele Harvey's financial manager had established for her following the older woman's death. No one was more shocked than Sasha when she had been summoned to the reading of Adele's will and informed she'd been left enough money to take her into old age, if she didn't squander it.

After her second glass of champagne, Sasha was unable to smother a yawn. "As soon as I help you clean up the kitchen, I'm going upstairs to take a bath and then turn in for the night."

Charlotte touched the napkin to the corners of her mouth. "You don't have to help me. I took a nap this afternoon, so I'm good."

Sasha stared across the table at her mother. She'd styled her hair in a becoming bob that showed her delicate features to their best advantage. Although she'd been widowed for seven years, Charlotte had never spoken about dating or the possibility of marrying again. However, it was different with Sasha. At thirty-two, she hoped she would find someone with whom she could fall in love, marry and have one or two children. Thankfully being married to Grant had not turned her off of marriage as a whole. If or when she did decide to date again, she was certain to be cognizant of the signs she'd chosen to ignore with Grant. She had been so blinded by love that she'd surrendered her will and had permitted her husband to control her very existence.

He had insisted she travel with him whenever he was on tour, attend his recording sessions and of course all the televised award shows. She had smiled pretty for the camera even if they'd had an argument earlier that night. After a while Sasha had had enough and decided she wanted out.

Here in The Falls, she did not have to concern herself about being dressed just so or going out without makeup to conceal her freckles. It had taken her living in a plastic world where she always had to be perfect for the camera for her to appreciate the laid-back comfortability of a small town in the heart of West Virginia's coal country.

"Are you sure you're up to it, Mama?"

Charlotte smiled. "Of course I'm sure. I don't need you working yourself down to the bone where you won't have enough strength to bake or even run a business. You've just begun putting on weight and I don't want folks saying that my baby girl looks like a scarecrow."

Sasha rolled her eyes upward. "Thanks, Mama." Pushing back her chair, she stood up. "I think I'm going to take a shower, because once I get into the tub, I won't be able to get out."

"Do you want me to come up and check on you?"

"Nah. I'm good." Rounding the table, she leaned down and kissed Charlotte's cheek. "Thank you for dinner. It was delicious."

"I'm going to put some away for tomorrow's lunch."

Turning on her heel, Sasha walked out of the kitchen, through the dining room and up the staircase to the second story. Charlotte had become a lifesaver and her lifeline. She had become her unofficial sous chef; she brought her lunch so she wouldn't have to leave the shop for a meal; and she'd been there for her to greet town officials and the walk-ins.

Sasha didn't know what she would've done if she hadn't had her mother. She entered her bedroom, stripped off her clothes and walked naked into the bathroom across the hall. She managed to brush her teeth and shower in under fifteen minutes. Within seconds of her head touching the pillow, she closed her eyes and fell asleep.

Chapter Three

Sasha woke early and was in the shop before five. She'd put up enough dough for marble rye, multigrain and several loaves of *pain de campagne*—a French country-style bread with a sourdough starter. She had also sent an email to the local church's outreach director that she had planned to donate any leftover baked goods for their soup-kitchen lunch program. There were several families in towns that had fallen on hard times and had to depend on the generosity of others to keep from going hungry.

Charlotte arrived twenty minutes before seven and checked the contents of the refrigerator showcase. She walked to the entrance of the kitchen. "Is the day's special ready for me to put in the showcase?"

Sasha's head popped up. "They're cooling now." She knew the red velvet cheesecake brownies would become a customer favorite because of the popularity of red velvet cake and brownies. And she hoped pairing them with cheesecake would take anyone that ate it by complete surprise.

She glanced up at the wall clock and realized she had less than forty minutes to make a dozen blueberry and oatmeal raisin muffins. It took muffins about fifteen to twenty minutes to bake and about five to cool. Sasha wanted to wait until she was certain she would have steady customers before she advertised for an assistant to help her in the kitchen. Creating specialty cakes required only one person, but it was not the same when she wanted to bake breads, pies and tortes. Sasha carefully placed slices of the cheesecake into a box and set it on a shelf in the refrigerator for Kiera, before putting the rest on a large baking sheet covered with paper doilies. She had cut small pieces as samples before she slid the sheet into the showcase.

Charlotte clasped her hands together. "That looks delicious."

Reaching for a toothpick, Sasha speared a sample and handed it to her mother. "Tell me what you think."

Shaking her head, while chewing and rolling her eyes upward, Charlotte moaned in satisfaction. "That's incredible. The raspberry drizzle really offsets the sourness of the cream cheese. This is a real winner. And I'm willing to bet folks will ask for it again and again."

"That's what I'm hoping."

"It's almost seven, so do you want me to raise the shades?" Charlotte asked.

"Yes. I'm going to bring out the muffins." While her mother manned the front, Sasha planned to bake small batches of Madeleine cookies, snickerdoodles, ginger, chocolate chip, sugar and cinnamon hazelnut biscotti. If or when they sold out, then she would know whether to increase the quantity or eliminate them from her list.

The morning passed quickly, and the chiming of the bell indicated a steady stream of customers. A few times Sasha had to come from the kitchen to assist Charlotte. She wore disposable clear plastic gloves when selecting the baked goods, and then removed them when handling money or credit cards. The transfer was rote for Charlotte, who'd spent thirty years working in food service. They both wore bouffant caps to prevent hair falling into the food.

Kiera arrived fifteen minutes early. Punctuality was a good sign for Sasha that she could depend on Kiera. "Come with me in the back and I'll show you where you can put your things." Kiera followed her to the kitchen, where she hung up her jacket. Sasha pointed to the teenage girl's three-inch booties. "Do you think you'll be able to stand comfortably in those, because you're going to be on your feet the whole time."

Kiera looked down at her shoes. "I can walk around in these all day."

Sasha wanted to tell her there were times during her school day when she was seated but decided to hold her tongue. And it was apparent Kiera was very confident with the heels that put her close to the five-ten mark. Sasha was five-nine in bare feet, and whenever she wore a pair of four-inch stilettos she towered over her ex—which was a bone of contention between them when she refused to attend a formal affair in ballet-type flats.

Sasha pointed to one of the three sinks she'd had the contractor install. "You can wash your hands over there. I'm going to give you something to cover your hair because we don't want our customers complaining of finding hair in their food. After that my mother will show you what to do."

She discovered Kiera was a quick study. Charlotte had stayed an extra hour to show the teenager how to man the front of the shop, and by the five o'clock hour Sasha had joined her taking and ringing up orders.

Kiera's dark eyes sparkled with excitement. "I can't believe you almost sold out everything."

"It was a good day," Sasha said in agreement. And that meant she had to come in even earlier the following morning.

"What do you plan to make tomorrow?"

"Cupcakes and mini pies."

"What about bread?" Kiera asked. "Because there's none left."

"I plan to always have fresh bread." And she knew she had to increase the quantity because she wanted to donate it to the church's soup kitchen. "It's time for you to leave. How are you getting home?"

"Daddy's going to pick me up. He doesn't see patients on Wednesdays."

Sasha nodded and remembered Dwight talked about Wednesday being golf day for doctors. "Why don't you go into the back and get your things? And don't forget to take the box with your name on it from the fridge."

The words were barely off her tongue when Dwight walked in. Her heart rate kicked into a higher gear as she stared at him. Today he was casually dressed in a pair of jeans, a gray sweatshirt stamped with the US Army insignia and Dr. Martens. He'd covered his head with a well-worn black baseball cap.

There was something intangible about the single dad

that pulled her in and refused to let her go when it hadn't been that way with other men, and that included Grant. Her ex had worked overtime to get her to go out with him, and at the time it fed her ego to have a man chase her. Dwight wasn't chasing her, didn't even appear to be interested in her, so she couldn't understand her reaction to him.

"How was her first day?" Dwight asked.

Resting her arms on the top of the showcase, Sasha smiled. "She's a pro."

"So, you're going to keep her?" he teased.

"I'll fight anyone trying to lure her away."

Throwing back his head, Dwight laughed. "That's serious."

"She's in the back getting her things." Sasha sobered. "You're very lucky, Dwight. Your daughter is a natural when it comes to interacting with the public."

"I must admit she had some experience last summer when she filled in for my receptionist."

"Do you expect her to work for you this summer?" Sasha was hard-pressed to keep the panic out of her voice.

Dwight shook his head. "No. If anything unforeseen comes up and my mother isn't busy, then she'll fill in."

Sasha rested a hand on her chest over her tunic. "Thank you."

Dwight gave Sasha a lingering stare, wondering what was different about her other than the hair bonnet. Suddenly it dawned on him that she wasn't wearing any makeup, unlike the day before, which had artfully concealed a sprinkling of freckles over her nose and cheeks. Her fresh-scrubbed face made her appear natural and wholesome.

Kiera emerged from the back of the shop, smiling and holding a red-and-white-striped box stamped with the shop's logo. "Daddy, I'm glad Miss Sasha saved some red velvet cheesecake brownies for us, because they were all sold out."

Dwight inclined his head. "I thank you, Miss Sasha, for you being generous *and* thoughtful."

Sasha, blushing, waved a hand. "There's no need to thank me. I should be the one thanking you for allowing Kiera to work here."

He noticed Kiera lowering her eyes, and it was apparent Sasha had embarrassed her. Even though he hadn't spent as much time with his daughter as he'd wanted, Dwight had come to recognize a certain shyness in her. He'd noticed boys her age staring at her while she pretended not to notice them. Maybe he was biased but there was no doubt she would become a beautiful woman like her mother. And it had been Adrienne's beauty and outgoing personality he hadn't been able to resist. They'd begun dating in high school and married within days of their respective college graduations.

"Daddy, I need to get home and do homework," Kiera said softly. Her head popped up. "I'll see you tomorrow, Miss Sasha. And thank you for the brownies."

"Tomorrow it is."

Dwight winked at Sasha and dropped his arm over Kiera's shoulders. He'd picked her up from school after her last class and drove her downtown. His mother had prepared a lunch for her granddaughter to eat before she began working. Victoria Adams had declared there was no way she was going to permit her grandbaby girl to miss a meal because of a job. She'd promised to pick her up from school on the days Dwight couldn't.

He knew his mother was overjoyed having her grand-daughter close to her every day instead of a month during the summer, and occasionally when she'd ac-companied him during his trips to New York. Dwight was more than aware that his mother had never ap-proved of his marrying Adrienne, and although her daughter-in-law had made her a grandmother, even today Victoria's impression of Kiera's mother hadn't changed.

Dwight pressed the remote device to the Jeep and opened the passenger-side door for Kiera. He rounded the vehicle and slipped behind the wheel. "How was your first day?"

Kiera ran a hand over her braided hair. "It was good except my feet hurt from standing up so much."

He glanced down at her shoes. He could not under-stand why his daughter insisted on wearing high heels, and when he'd questioned her, she claimed she liked standing out from among the shorter girls who'd treated her as if she was carrying a communicable disease.

That was the first time Dwight realized his daughter was regarded as an outsider in a school system where most of the kids had grown up together. Not only had Kiera acquired the sophistication of someone who'd grown up in a cosmopolitan city like New York City, but she'd also favored the ubiquitous black worn by many New Yorkers. She must have confided this to her grandmother when Dwight overheard his mother tell-ing Kiera, "Don't concern yourself about those jealous little snits, because they know you're better born and better raised."

He had his mother to thank for telling Kiera what was so obvious, because it would not have come out like that if he'd had to say it. There were a few occasions when he'd waited to pick Kiera up from school and he'd noticed several boys staring at her. This had obviously annoyed some of the girls with them, and when he'd mentioned this to Kiera, she stated the girls did not have to worry about her coming on to their boyfriends because all of them were stupid. Dwight agreed that some teenage boys were stupid, but there would come a time when they became mature young men. However, his daughter was having none of his talk about boys and so he dropped the subject.

"Maybe you should bring a pair of tennis shoes with you that you can change into before you start working."

Kiera nodded. "I'm definitely going to do that."

Dwight drove out of the parking lot and came to a complete stop at the railroad crossing as the gates came down. The sound of ringing bells and flashing red lights indicated an oncoming train. "How was school today?"

Kiera shifted on her seat. "Daddy, remember you asked me that when you picked me up?"

He smiled. "My bad. I forgot about that. Your old man must be getting senile."

"You're not old and you're a long way from being senile. Maybe you need to take up a hobby."

"I have a hobby."

"What's that?"

"You, baby girl, and fishing." He'd become quite an adept at fly-fishing.

Kiera laughed. "I can't be your hobby." She sobered. "Have you thought about getting a girlfriend? Mom's married, so what's stopping you from marrying again?"

A frown found its way over Dwight's features. "I

don't have time for a girlfriend. Maybe after you go off to college I'll consider dating again."

"But that's not for more than a year, and you'll be too old to hit the clubs looking for a girlfriend."

His frown grew deeper. "What do you know about trolling clubs looking for dates?"

"I heard Mom say that you look for women in clubs."

Dwight felt a surge of rage he found hard to control and counted slowly until he once again felt in control. Adrienne had a tongue that was lethal as cyanide and sharp as a samurai sword. He had dated a few women since his divorce, and fortunately, he hadn't had to resort to going to clubs to pick them up.

He chose his words carefully, because the last thing Dwight wanted was to belittle Kiera's mother. It was enough that she didn't get along with her stepfather. "Your mother is wrong."

"Then why would she say that, Daddy?"

He forced a smile. "I don't know."

Kiera met his eyes. "Don't you want a girlfriend?"

Kiera was asking him questions he'd asked himself over and over since his divorce, and he knew if he hadn't a daughter he would've considered marrying again. There was one woman who lived in the state's capital that he'd dated off and on for nearly a year. She'd accused him of talking incessantly about his daughter and decided to end their liaison because she wasn't able to compete with her for his attention. One thing Dwight had promised himself was that he wasn't going to hide the fact that he was a single father and his daughter came first in his life.

"It's not that I don't want a girlfriend. It's just that I haven't met someone I want to spend time with."

"Does she have to be pretty?"

Dwight shook his head. "No, Kiera, looks are nice, but they're not everything. I'd like her to be well-rounded so we could have intelligent conversations. And it would help if we both like the same things."

"Are you saying she would have to be a dentist, too?"

"Oh, no," he drawled. "That definitely would be a deal breaker. I don't want someone where we'd spend all of our time talking about deciduous, cementum and molars." The last car on the train passed and the gates lifted, and Dwight drove over the tracks.

"What made you fall in love with Mom and marry her?"

Frowning through the windshield, he held the wheel in a death-like grip. "What's with the twenty questions, Kiera? Have you been talking to your mother and she's been interrogating you about me?"

Kiera stared straight ahead. She was so still she could've been carved out of stone. "The last time I spoke to her she did ask me if you had a girlfriend."

A muscle twitched in Dwight's jaw as he clenched his teeth. "The next time you talk to your mother and she asks about me, I want you to say, 'No comment.'"

"You know how Mom is. Grammie says she's like a dog with a bone."

"Well, this big dog isn't having it. I meant what I said about feeding her information about me."

He wanted to tell Kiera that if her mother was so interested in his love life, then she should've never divorced him. After all, she had moved on with a new husband in a new city and loved her work, and from what he could see, she was having the time of her life.

"I know she's going to get mad at me if I say that to her."

"Let me handle your mother, Kiera. We're both adults and I can say things to her you can't or shouldn't. Your mother legally handed over custody of you to me, so that means I'm totally responsible for you until you're twenty-one."

Kiera rested her left hand over his right on the steering wheel. "I'm glad I'm living with you. Thank you, Daddy."

He smiled. "You're welcome, sweetie."

He would never forget the sound of his daughter's sobbing when she called to tell him her mother had made plans to send her to a Connecticut boarding school because Kiera had talked back to her stepfather. The tables were reversed because Adrienne's husband had issued his own ultimatum: him or his stepdaughter.

Dwight had canceled all his appointments and flew up to New York with the intent of causing bodily harm to the man who'd promised him he would always protect Kiera. By the time the jet landed at LaGuardia Airport his temper had cooled considerably, and he was able to sit down and convince Adrienne their daughter would do well living with him.

It was his ex-wife's husband who convinced her to agree to Dwight's decision. Initially, Adrienne had balked because it meant losing child support, despite her earning a six-figure salary, but in the end after meeting with her lawyer, she signed the papers.

"I love you, Daddy."

Dwight smiled. "Love you more."

And he did. He could not imagine loving Kiera any more than he did. Although he and Adrienne had taken precautions to prevent an unplanned pregnancy, he never regretted becoming a father. He'd loved her just that much. However, it wasn't the same with Adrienne. Motherhood changed her into a sullen woman who resented having to stay home with a baby while he attended dental school. Dwight had promised his wife that as soon as he passed the dental boards and set up a practice, she could return to grad school to get her MBA.

No one was more shocked than Dwight when she filed for divorce because she didn't want to be the wife of a small-town dentist. He'd told her repeatedly that he didn't want to or could not afford to set up a practice in New York City. Blinded by the bright lights and mesmerized by the hustle and bustle of the Big Apple, where she'd attended college, Adrienne couldn't get it out of her system.

He drove into the driveway of his house, tapping the remote device on the visor to open the garage door. Kiera kicked off her booties and unbuckled her seat belt. She was out of the Jeep before Dwight shut off the engine. Shoes in hand, she walked gingerly up the stairs and opened the door that led directly into the mudroom. He followed, removing his boots and leaving them on a mat next to a slop sink.

"What's up with her?" Victoria Adams asked Dwight when he entered the kitchen.

"Her dogs are barking."

Victoria slowly shook her head. "I told that girl that she can't look cute standing around for hours in those heels."

He tried not to smile. "Hard head makes for a soft behind."

"Either it's a soft behind or bloody toes," Victoria drawled. She lifted the lid on a pot of rice. "I can remember the days when I used to go to dances in spikes and thought I was really cute until I had to walk home with my shoes in my hands."

Dwight handed his mother the box from Sasha's Sweet Shoppe. "You're still cute, Mom." He had always believed his mother was one of the most beautiful women in Wickham Falls. Tall, slender, with delicate features in a flawless sable complexion, she had been voted the prettiest girl in her graduating class. The once curly hair falling to her shoulders reminiscent of clusters of black grapes was now snow-white and styled in a pixie cut that hugged her head like a cap. "You don't have to make dessert because Sasha has promised to give Kiera whatever she offers as the day's special." He handed her the box with the cheesecake.

Victoria's large dark eyes, eyes Dwight had inherited, were bright with merriment. "Well, bless her heart. That's so nice of her. I need to stop in and buy something. The last time I was downtown she still wasn't open for business."

"Maybe you could get the ladies at the auxiliary to order dessert from her. After all, we need to do our part to support our local businesses."

"I'll definitely suggest it." She glanced at the clock on the microwave. "It's going to be another thirty or forty minutes before I finish dinner."

Dwight dropped a kiss on his mother's hair. "Do you need help with anything?"

"No, I'm good here."

"Are you sure?"

"Of course I'm sure, Dwight. Go and hang out in the family room until I call you."

Even though his mother had her own kitchen in the guesthouse, she preferred using his. He didn't complain because it reminded him of the times when he'd come home from school as a young boy to find his mother puttering around in the kitchen while preparing the evening meal. As an OR nurse, she had worked the 7:00 a.m. to 2:00 p.m. shift. Her shift never changed because she had to be home in time for her son at the end of the school day. His mother dropped him off at his paternal grandmother's house the night before and picked him up there when the bus dropped him off at the end of the day.

He rarely saw his special-agent father when he was assigned to the FBI's Behavioral Analysis Unit in Norfolk, Virginia. After a decade, Mathias requested a transfer and was approved to work closer to home for the Bureau's Criminal Justice Information Services in Clarksburg, West Virginia. Although he'd traded fieldwork for a desk assignment, the two-hour drive between Clarksburg and Wickham Falls was worth the sacrifice if only to see his wife and only child more often. Mathias's dream of retiring and taking his wife on an around-the-world cruise vanished when the car he was driving was hit when the driver of a tractor trailer fell asleep behind the wheel. He'd died instantly, and even after twelve years Victoria continued to mourn his passing.

Dwight had just folded his body down to his favorite chaise when he heard Kiera screaming, "Daddy, I can't find my cell phone!" He didn't bother to move because Kiera misplacing her phone had become a regular occurrence.

"Where was the last time you saw it?" he asked when she raced into the room.

"I know I had it when you picked me up from school, but…" Her words trailed off. "I must have left it at Miss Sasha's."

"Are you sure?"

An expression of uncertainty flittered over Kiera's face. "It's not in my backpack, so I had to put it in my jacket pocket."

"Check your pockets again."

"I did, Daddy, and it's not there."

"You know what this means if you can't find it." Kiera closed her eyes and bit her lip. Dwight knew she was trying not to cry. "Why don't you call Miss Sasha and ask her if you left it there?"

Kiera held out her hand, and rising slightly, Dwight gave her the cell phone he'd set on a side table. He waited, watching her expression brighten when she spoke quietly into the phone. "Thank you."

"What's up?" Dwight asked when she returned his phone.

"She said she's talking to a client. As soon as she finishes, she's going to look for it. And if she finds it, she'll text you, and bring it over later because she's very busy right now."

He didn't want to tell Kiera that she just might be putting others out of their way because of her carelessness. But he knew she felt bad enough without him reminding her of how many phones she'd lost or misplaced over the years.

"I promise not to—"

Dwight held up a hand, stopping her entreaty. "Please, Kiera, don't say anything else. I'll cancel your account if Sasha doesn't find your phone, but it's going to be at least three months before you get another one."

"You can't do that, Daddy!"

"Did you forget what you agreed to when you lost the last one?"

"No, but…"

"But nothing, Kiera. You've had three cell phones in less than six months."

Kiera stomped her foot in frustration. "That's not fair!"

"Life is not fair, baby girl," Dwight countered. "Once you're old enough to have your own account, then I don't care how many cell phones you lose," he said as she turned and walked out of the room. Picking up the remote device resting on a side table, he clicked on the television, channel surfing until he found one of his favorite sports programs. The ringtone on his phone indicated he had a text message.

Sasha: Found the phone. Will bring it over after 9.

Dwight: I will come and pick it up.

Sasha: Don't bother. I'll drop it off. I'll get your address from Kiera's application. Later.

Dwight was really annoyed that Kiera had been less than responsible with her phone. She claimed she needed one to maintain contact with her mother and some of her former New York City classmates. But that was not going to happen if she continued to lose phones. And if she wanted to call her mother or friends, then she would have to use her grandmother's landline or the one at his office. His daughter had always had a penchant for losing things when she was younger: mittens, gloves, hats, scarves and now phones. He used to tease her that she would lose her head if it hadn't been attached to her body.

When she'd misplaced her last phone, they'd made a pact that she would have to wait at least three months before he bought her another one. Fortunately, Sasha found it, so this time Kiera managed to dodge a bullet.

It was close to ten when Dwight stood on the porch as he waited for Sasha's arrival. She had sent him another text saying she was on her way. Lightly falling rain had changed over to sleet once the temperature dropped fifteen degrees in two hours, and he'd turned up the thermostat and started a fire in the family room's fireplace to ward off the sudden chill.

He saw a sweep of headlights as her van maneuvered into the driveway. He came down off the porch to meet her when she alighted from her vehicle. She'd exchanged her tunic for a white T-shirt. The scent of her perfume wafted to his nostrils with her approach as she rubbed her bare arms. He couldn't believe she'd gone out without a coat. A rising breeze lifted the curls framing her round face.

He cupped her elbow. "Please come into the house, where it's warm."

"I had no idea it was this cold until I left my house."

He opened the front door, standing off to the side to let her precede him. "You should always leave a jacket in your car."

Sasha turned her head so Dwight wouldn't see her gaping as she walked into his house. The two-story farmhouse with a wraparound porch was filled with furnishings for maximum comfort and practicality. She thought of the style as casual country that made her feel immediately at home with a desire to stay and put her feet up. The open floor plan with a great room and a combination of the kitchen, living, dining and family rooms allowed light and air to flow unchecked.

Warmth and the smell of burning wood enveloped her like a thick blanket. "It's nice and toasty in here."

"What if I make you a hot chocolate to warm you up?"

Sasha turned to find Dwight standing several feet away, hands clasped behind his back. Her intention was to come and drop off Kiera's cell phone and then leave, but now she wasn't so certain she wanted to go back home. "I'd like that, thank you." Reaching into the pocket of her jeans, she handed him the phone. "She left it on a chair."

Dwight set it on the glass-topped coffee table. "Do you take your chocolate with whipped cream?"

Sasha smiled. "But of course."

He reached for her hand and led her into the family room. "Sit and warm up. I'll be right back."

She sat on a cream-covered upholstered armchair stamped with jade green leaves. Kicking off her flip-flops, she rested her bare feet on the matching footstool. Sasha did not know what had possessed her to leave the house in mid-February wearing only a T-shirt, jeans and summer footwear. Pressing her head against the back of the chair, she closed her eyes. She'd prided herself on being levelheaded, rational and always assessing a situation before acting. But somehow all was forgotten whenever she and Dwight Adams occupied the same space. Sasha did not know what it was about the man that had her reacting to him like a starstruck adolescent.

When he'd offered to come over to pick up his daughter's phone, Sasha had refused because curiosity overrode what was easier. He'd been divorced for more than a decade and she wanted to know if his home reflected his life as a bachelor father. However, his furnishings suggested a preference for a home filled with the interaction of family and friends.

Shifting on the chair, she studied a group of photographs on a side table. There was one of Dwight's parents in their college graduation finery and another of Dwight in his dress army uniform. The oak leaves on his collar identified him as a major. She smiled when staring at a photo of a younger grinning Dwight holding Kiera, who'd pressed her mouth against her father's cheek.

Her gaze shifted as she stared at the flickering flames behind the decorative fireplace screen. Nowhere in any of the photos had there been an image of Kiera's mother, and she wondered if Dwight's ex-wife had been responsible for decorating the house, and if he'd elected not to change it because it was a constant reminder of the woman he'd loved and married. Her musings about the man were interrupted when he returned and handed her a mug of steaming chocolate topped with a froth of whipped cream.

Sitting straight, she took the mug, her fingers brushing against his before he took a facing chair. "Thank you. Aren't you going to have some?" she asked.

Dwight stared at her under lowered lids. "No. I had a cup of coffee just before you got here."

Sasha tightened her hold on the hot mug. "Your home is beautiful."

He inclined his head. "Thank you."

She took a sip and the warmth in her throat and chest had nothing to do with the heated liquid, but with the way Dwight was looking at her. Why again, she thought, did she feel like a specimen under a microscope?

"Was this the original design when you moved in?" Sasha asked. She had to talk, do something other than stare at Dwight staring back at her. "I have never been in any of the homes on this side of town," she explained. Wickham Falls had a population under five thousand, yet the social lines were as clearly drawn as borders separating one state from another.

Stretching out his legs, Dwight crossed his feet at the ankles. "I had a contractor remove the walls after my divorce."

Dwight mentioning the divorce gave Sasha the opening she needed to delve into his personal life. "Do you miss being married?"

Inky-black eyebrows rose slightly with her question. "No. In fact, I like being single. But how about you, Sasha?"

"What about me, Dwight?"

"How difficult was it for you to give up your celebrity lifestyle and marriage to one of the biggest country recording stars on the planet to come back to a place with two stoplights and railroad tracks running through the middle of the downtown business district?"

Chapter Four

Sasha stared at the rapidly fading whipped cream before she looked directly at Dwight. "It was the easiest decision I'd ever had to make in my life."

"So, you don't regret coming back?"

"Not in the least." She took another sip of the semi-sweet liquid and then set the mug on a glass coaster on the table. She stood up. "It's getting late and I've taken up enough of your time."

Sasha did not want to tell Dwight that she wasn't ready to bare her soul about the details of her failed marriage. She did not know why it mattered, but she didn't want him to think of her as a small-town girl who'd allowed herself to get bedazzled and sucked in by the hype and glamour of America's Music City, where she'd married Nashville's hottest singing sensation after a three-month whirlwind romance.

Dwight also stood. "Don't leave yet. I want to get something for you." He walked out of the family room and returned minutes later with a military fatigue jacket and a small folding umbrella. "Please put on the jacket. We can't have you getting sick and having to close down so soon after your grand opening."

Sasha held out her arms as he helped her into it. The lingering scent of his cologne clung to the fabric. She wondered if his concern was because he was a doctor or a father. "I'll give it back when I see you again."

"You can keep it. I happen to have a few of them."

"If that's the case, then I'm going to leave it in the van in case I again decide to challenge Mother Nature."

"And don't forget a pair of shoes," Dwight teased with a wide grin.

She wiggled her bare toes painted a vermilion red. "I must be a country girl down to the marrow in my bones, because I love going barefoot."

Dwight slowly shook his head as he handed her the umbrella. "Even country girls know to wear shoes in the winter."

Going on tiptoe, Sasha kissed his cheek. "I really appreciate your concern."

Turning on her heel, she made her way to the front door, waiting for him to open it. She opened the umbrella, raced down the porch steps and over to her vehicle. A light layer of ice had covered the windshield. Touching the handle on the driver's-side door, she unlocked it and slipped in. As she tapped the start button, the engine roared to life. She closed the umbrella, leaving it on the mat behind the seat, and then turned the heat to the highest setting. She peered through the side window to find Dwight standing under the protection of the porch, watching her. It took several minutes to defrost the windshield before she fastened her seat belt and backed out of the driveway.

It wasn't until she turned off onto the road leading to her house that she chided herself for kissing Dwight. It hadn't mattered that it was a chaste one; she still shouldn't have done it.

"I'm losing it," she whispered to herself.

There was no doubt she wouldn't have had any interaction with the man if his daughter hadn't come to apply to work in the bakeshop. The only other alternative would have been if she became one of his patients. She had another month before her semiannual checkup and she planned to call the dental office in Mineral Springs, where she'd gone as a child, for an appointment.

Sasha continued to ask herself what it was about Dwight Adams that made her heart beat a little too fast to make her feel completely at ease around him. It hadn't been that way in the past when he'd come to her house to pick up her brother, because she knew he had a steady girlfriend. Even if he hadn't been dating Adrienne, she doubted whether Dwight would have asked her out because of their six-year age difference. That was then, but this was now. And it wasn't that there weren't mixed-race couples in Wickham Falls, and if she did date Dwight, they wouldn't turn heads if seen together. If folks did whisper, it would be about her capturing the attention of one of The Falls' most eligible bachelors. She didn't want to overthink or indulge in what she deemed fantasy, because there was no guarantee anything would come from her association with her employee's father other than friendship.

She made it home, unlocked the door and tiptoed

up the staircase to her bedroom so as not to disturb her mother. Sasha left Dwight's jacket on the back of a chair, slipped out of her clothes and pulled a nightgown over her head. After brushing her teeth, she set her alarm for five, got into bed and pulled the blankets up and over her shoulders. The incessant tapping of sleet against the windows was the perfect antidote to lull her to sleep. Morpheus claimed her, as she shut out the image of Dwight's dimpled smile and penetrating dark eyes that appeared to look not at her but through her to know what she was thinking, and that she liked him the way a woman liked a man.

Leaning over his reclining patient, Dwight used a light touch as he drilled a young boy's tooth. The four-year-old appeared totally oblivious to the sound of the drill as he concentrated on the images on the virtual-reality headset. Although his shingle advertised family dentistry, he counted more children than adults among his patients, which had earned him the reputation as the most popular pediatric dentist in the county. Children looked forward to sitting in his chairs. Video games and headsets were the perfect solution to distract kids if they required a local anesthesia, while a trio of wall-mounted televisions in the waiting room tuned to cooking, cartoon and all-news stations kept most of his patients occupied while they waited to be seen.

He removed the decay and then placed a sealer on the tooth prior to filling it with a tooth-colored composite resin to protect the tooth and minimize sensitivity. Rather than traumatize the boy with an injection of procaine, he'd applied a numbing gel to his gum, lip and cheek. Dwight checked to make sure the boy's bite was okay and adjusted the filling. He took off the latex gloves, discarding them in a designated container, and nodded to the assistant to finish up with the patient.

Dwight found it disturbing to treat a patient as young as four with cavities in his primary teeth. It indicated either poor dental hygiene or a diet of sugary foods in which plaque built up on the tooth and caused decay. Although he'd spoken at length to the child's mother about brushing his teeth after each meal and limiting his intake of candy and pop, it was obvious his advice and recommendations had fallen on deaf ears. This was the third tooth he'd filled for the child. His practice's motto was: Good Dental Health Is A Family Affair, and fortunately, most of his patients had embraced it.

He returned to his office and discovered the blinking red light on his private line. Tapping the button, he listened to his mother's voice-mail message. It was a rare occasion that Victoria called him at his office.

Picking up his cell phone, he scrolled through the directory until he found her number. "Yes, Mom."

"Are you still going to your lake house this weekend?"

"I've been thinking about it. Why?" Dwight had purchased the cabin in the gated community touted as a fisherman's nirvana. All the modern cabins claimed central air and heating and had direct paths that led to the lake. It was where he'd spent most of his weekends relaxing, fishing and occasionally socializing with a few retirees who lived there year-round. The weeks had passed quickly, and it was now late March, and spring had come to West Virginia with warmer temperatures and a profusion of flowers, lush lawns and verdant valleys.

"Kiera invited Sasha and her mother over for Sunday dinner."

Dwight sat straight. He'd asked Kiera if she wanted to go with him to the lake and she'd said she would have to think about it. Well, it was apparent her thinking about it meant she'd had other intentions.

"What did you say?"

"I told her I'm open to it, only because she can't stop talking about how much she likes Sasha and Charlotte, and also loves working in their shop."

Dwight focused on the framed diplomas, degrees and licenses on the opposite wall. He had made the decision, following the night Sasha came to his house to return Kiera's cell phone, to limit his contact with her. There was something about the redhead that stirred feelings he did not want to feel, and he knew becoming involved with his daughter's employer would not be to their advantage. Not only did they live in the same town, but they were also highly visible as downtown business owners.

What he could not deny was his attraction to the bubbly pastry chef. He liked her smile, infectious laugh and her generosity. There were times when she exhibited a modicum of shyness and vulnerability that appealed to his protective nature. However, it was never far from his mind that Sasha had earned a reputation as a celebrity chef who had become the wife of Nashville royalty.

What he did not understand was why she had given it all up to come back to a town that barely made the map. A town whose history was filled with generations that had worked in the coal mines under the control of unscrupulous owners that preferred closing the mines to installing government-mandated safety equipment, leaving workers without an alternative source of income.

In later years, career day at the high school was a boon for recruiters from every branch of the armed forces who enticed graduating seniors with offers of signing bonuses to join the military. Dwight graduated Texas A&M, attended dental school and then set up his practice in The Falls while serving in the army reserves as a dental corps officer. As a US Medical Department officer and as a reservist, he was required to attend the Ordnance Basic Officer Leader Course for two weeks rather than the ten to fourteen weeks for active duty officers. He'd been fortunate enough to combine his passions for the military and dentistry, but recently had to sacrifice the former to become a full-time dad.

"What do you want me to say, Mom? Uninvite them?"

"No, Dwight. I expect you to say yes. After all, we'll be eating at your house."

Dwight shook his head. "What's wrong with your house?"

"Nothing, except that I like cooking in your kitchen."

Dwight did not want to believe what he was hearing. Although the kitchen in the guesthouse was smaller than his, Victoria had insisted it be equipped with top-of-the-line appliances. "If that's the case, why don't you consider moving in with me?"

"I told you before, I like living by myself because I don't need my son monitoring my whereabouts."

"It wouldn't bother me if you got a boyfriend," he teased.

"Bite your tongue, Dwight Mathias Adams. I was married too long, and more importantly, I don't have the patience to put up with another man. You're the one that should be dating. After all, you're not getting any younger."

Dwight sobered. "I told you before that I can't afford to get serious about anyone until Kiera goes off to college."

"I hope you're not suggesting you need her permission to take up with a woman."

"Of course not, Mom. Right now, she needs to know she has a full-time father, and not some man who has been in and out of her life for the past sixteen years."

"You really don't give your daughter enough credit," Victoria said. "She knows you love her and that you would do anything for her, but I'm willing to bet that she doesn't want you to sacrifice having a relationship with a woman because of your obligation as her father."

A beat passed, before Dwight said, "It sounds as if you two have been discussing my love life."

"Correction, son. Lack of love life."

He had to agree with his mother, but he wasn't about to admit that to her. "I don't have a problem with Sasha and her mother coming for dinner," he said instead.

"Good. I'll tell Kiera to let them know we'll be expecting them."

Dwight ended the call somehow feeling he'd been set up by his mother and daughter as they attempted to play matchmaker. He then wondered if Sasha had intimated to Kiera that she was interested in her father. When he recalled their few encounters there was nothing in her actions that indicated that she wanted anything beyond being acquaintances. He was Kiera's father and Sasha Kiera's employer, and that was where their association began and ended.

* * *

Sasha bit back a smile when she heard Charlotte's intake of breath as she drove her mother's car into the driveway leading to Dwight's home. It had been more than a month since their last encounter, and Sasha wondered if she'd crossed the line when she'd kissed him. He hadn't been repulsed or appeared shocked by the gesture, but that did not stop her from mentally beating up on herself for initiating it. After all, she did not know whether he was involved with or committed to another woman, which could have explained his keeping his distance. She finally had to remind herself that she was a thirty-two-year-old divorcée with a business to run, and that had to be her sole focus.

"The doctor has a very nice house," Charlotte whispered softly.

"Yes, he does," Sasha agreed. Navy blue siding, white trim and blue-and-white wicker porch furniture made the structure a standout among those on the block. The United States and Go Army flags suspended on a flagpole fluttered in the warm air. It had become a tradition for those serving or who had served in the military to fly flags and pennants representing their branches to proudly display them on lawns or porch posts.

Charlotte made a guttural sound, as if clearing her throat. "I don't understand what would make a woman walk away from all of this to live in a city with folks falling over one another just to exist."

Sasha came to a complete stop and shut off the engine. "Different strokes for different folks."

Charlotte unbuckled her seat belt. "Like you, Natasha? Don't forget, there was a time when you couldn't wait to leave town."

She got out of the Corolla, opened the rear door and picked up the large shopping bag with boxes of tarts, tortes and an assortment of mini cakes and pies. It was apparent Charlotte had forgotten and Sasha did not want to remind her mother that the constant squabbling between her and her husband had forced their children to leave home as soon as they'd graduated high school.

Sasha waited for Charlotte to alight from the car, and together they walked up to the porch. The front door opened, and she came face-to-face with Dwight for the first time in more than a month. An unconscious smile parted her lips as he stared at her as if she were a stranger. She knew he was taken aback by her metamorphosis. A sleek hairstyle, the black sheath dress, with an asymmetrical neckline, ending at her knees and a pair of matching kitten heels had replaced the tunic, loose-fitting pants and comfortable clogs she wore in the bake-shop. Sasha had also subtly made up her face to bring attention to her green eyes and mouth with a smoky-grayish eye shadow and a burnt-orange lip color. Taming her flyaway curls had proved challenging until she'd exchanged the blow-dryer for a flat iron. She'd rationalized that she was going to someone's house for Sunday dinner; therefore, she needed to step up her game.

Dwight smiled slowly as his gaze shifted from Sasha to Charlotte. He opened the door wider. "Welcome."

Sasha handed him the shopping bag. "I brought a little something for dessert."

Dwight peered into the bag. "It appears to be more than a little something."

"Grammie, they're here!" Kiera shouted as she raced

over to greet them. Sasha noticed the slight frown furrowing Dwight's forehead, but it disappeared quickly when Kiera clapped a hand over her mouth. "Sorry about yelling in the house, Daddy," she said, apologizing.

He handed Kiera the shopping bag. "Please take this into the kitchen." He returned his attention to his guests. "Please come in and sit down. My mother is just finishing up with everything."

Sasha followed him through the great room, noticing that the dining room table had been set with china, silver and crystal; a vase overflowing with an abundance of white roses and tulips served as the table's centerpiece.

Charlotte touched Sasha's arm. "I'm going to the kitchen to see if I can help Mrs. Adams."

"Do you think that's such a good idea?" Sasha whispered to Dwight as he cupped her elbow and led her over to a sand-colored sofa. "Cooks are usually very territorial when it comes to their kitchens." She sat, and he took the cushion next to her.

"It'll be all right. My mother doesn't want anyone to share her kitchen, but it's different with mine."

Sasha stared at him, seeing laughter in the dark eyes. "Your mother doesn't live with you?" She'd asked the question because Kiera would talk about her grandmother as if they all occupied the same house.

"My mother lives in a guesthouse at the back of this one. Once my father passed away, I'd invited her to live with me, but she claims she likes having her independence to come and go by her leave. So, when I suggested she sell the house where I'd grown up and let me build something practical for her on the half acre at the back of the house, she finally gave in. I must admit that it's quite nice. She has two bedrooms, a full bath, galley kitchen, and a living and dining area that overlooks the back deck. Last year she planted a flower and vegetable garden."

Sasha stared at the beige-and-teal woven area rug rather than the man sitting only inches away from her. The warmth of his body intensified the masculine scent of his cologne, which only served to trigger the erotic thoughts she had managed to repress during their separation. At that moment she had to question herself lusting after a man who didn't seem even remotely attracted to her, and knew it was hopeless to even conceive of a possible relationship with Dwight Adams.

"How's business?"

His deep sonorous voice had shattered her musings. "Didn't Kiera tell you?" she asked.

He shifted on the sofa, the motion bringing them even closer together. "Tell me what?"

"That your mother stopped in one day to order tea cakes for the Volunteer Fireman's Ladies Auxiliary. The women liked them so much that a number of them came into the shop during the week to place orders for other pastries."

"Word of mouth does go a long way in a small town," Dwight said. He paused. "Right now, I'm willing to bet that my mother is trying to get yours to join one of her civic organizations. Victoria Adams is one of the best when it comes to recruiting folks to join local clubs. She complains that most have the same members year after year, because many of them aren't willing to accept new people with new ideas."

"It's called control, Dwight. They don't like relinquishing their power to others they may deem outsiders."

"Perhaps you're right."

"I know I am," Sasha countered quickly. She did not want to tell Dwight that most of the women that belonged to the civic and social organizations had a lot in common. Practically all were college educated, and their husbands were either businessmen or had attained some political standing in Wickham Falls.

"Hopefully my mother can convince yours to join the Ladies Auxiliary, because they'll be hosting a fundraiser in a couple of months to raise money for a new ambulance for first responders."

Sasha knew the group met at noon on Wednesdays, and if her mother did become a member, then she would have to man the front of the shop until Kiera arrived at one. The more she thought about it, the more she warmed to the possibility of Charlotte becoming involved with a local civic organization. It would give her mother something else to do other than work in the bakeshop.

"I think it would do Mama some good to get involved in things affecting The Falls." Secretly Sasha hoped Charlotte would meet a man who might respect her more than her late husband had.

"Now that you're a business owner, do you plan to join the chamber of commerce?"

Sasha nodded. "It's funny you ask, because one of the members came into the shop the other day and left an application and a ticket for their annual dinner dance. He did apologize for the short notice because the event is next weekend."

"Do you plan to attend?"

"No," Sasha replied. "I'll pay for the ticket and probably give it to one of my regular customers."

"You can give it away if you want, but I'd like you to go with me."

Sasha went completely still once she realized Dwight was asking her to be his date for a semiformal affair. "You have two tickets?"

He smiled, flashing dimples. "Yes. I always buy two because it's for a good cause."

She blinked slowly. "You don't have a date?"

"No. I usually take my mother, but this year she agreed to stay home with Kiera. She's trying to cut down on the number of social events she attends during the year. She has the Ladies Auxiliary and she's also involved in several military causes that include the Wounded Warrior Project."

"Don't you have someone else who can go with you?" Sasha knew she was asking a litany of questions, but she had to know if there was another woman in Dwight's life before agreeing to be his date for the night.

"No. That's why I'm asking you. But if you don't want to be seen with—"

"Don't say it," she said, cutting him off. "I'm truly honored that you asked me to be your date."

And she was honored. He was the first man she'd found herself liking enough to date since her divorce, and now that Dwight had asked her to go to the fundraiser with him, her fantasies were about to become a reality. There had been men who had come on to her before and after her marriage, but Sasha always felt that they had an ulterior motive. Before marrying Grant, she'd believed it was because they'd recognized her from the televised cooking competition, and once she was divorced it had been her high-profile marriage to a recording superstar.

But none of that appeared to faze Dwight. To him, she was a small-town girl who'd become a popular celebrity chef, but then left the bright lights to return home and to open a sweet shop. She had lost count of the number of folks who came into the bakeshop to either stare at her or ask about her failed marriage whenever she manned the front. It was as if they were more interested in her personal life than in making a purchase.

"Folks are really going to be shocked to see us attend together."

Dwight chuckled under his breath. "You're right about that." He paused. "What do you think about giving them a preview?"

Vertical lines appeared between Sasha's eyes. "A preview how?"

"Come with me tomorrow night to the Wolf Den for Military Monday. We can hang out for a couple of hours to give folks an opportunity to see us together. I can pick you up at seven and have you back home around nine, because I know you get up very early."

It was Sasha's turn to laugh. "I'm willing to bet gossip will spread throughout The Falls like a lighted fuse. If *The Sentinel* had a gossip column, we certainly would be included."

Dwight nodded, smiling. "And like the song, we'll give them something to talk about."

Sasha leaned to her right, their shoulders touching. "You're so bad," she teased.

"Guilty as charged, as long as it's a good bad."

For a reason she did not want to understand, Sasha was looking forward to being seen in public with Dwight

Adams. Aside from his good looks, she admired his unwavering devotion to Kiera. When living in Nashville, she'd met and socialized with divorced and single fathers whose priorities weren't their children but chasing the next woman. And based on their behavior, she had come to believe just paying child support was not the benchmark for being a good father. Her parents may have argued constantly as if their very existence depended upon it, but there was never a time when her father hadn't been there for his children.

"Isn't good bad an oxymoron?" she questioned.

"It all depends on the context."

Dwight covered Sasha's hand resting on the cushion with his. He threaded their fingers together. Her hand was cool, but not as cold as when she'd admitted to having cold hands and a warm heart. He knew he had taken a chance and risked being rejected but hoped beyond hope that she would agree to go to what had become the social event of the year. Everyone who owned a business in Wickham Falls would be there. And having her agree to go to the Den with him would be an extra bonus.

The fund-raiser gave folks a reason to dress up and let their hair down once dinner was over and dancing began. The local dry cleaner did a brisk business cleaning tuxedos and dress suits, while women made certain not to be seen in the same gown or dress they'd worn the year before. Dwight always enjoyed the gathering because residents were more than generous when it came to support of their local businesses.

He gave her fingers a gentle squeeze before releasing them and stood up. "Don't move. I'm needed to help carry the food to the table."

He walked past the dining room and into the kitchen and picked up a large platter with fried chicken. Victoria, after viewing an infomercial, had purchased an air fryer and sang its praises in her attempt to fry chicken without using oil. Not only was the method faster but also healthier than frying it on the stove. After that it had become her go-to appliance for cooking chicken and meat. Dwight set the platter on the dining room table. Kiera joined him as she filled goblets with sparkling water.

"I think Grammie cooked too much food," she said sotto voce.

"Not to worry, sweetie. None of it will go to waste because we'll be eating leftovers for the rest of the week."

"I heard that, Dwight," Victoria called out.

He gave Kiera a sidelong glance. "Your grandmother must have ears like a bat," he said between clenched teeth.

Kiera nodded. "I know, Daddy," she whispered.

Dwight returned to the kitchen and picked up two more platters, one with braised beef short ribs and the other with caramelized pork chops. Whenever Victoria volunteered to cook Sunday dinner it wasn't the ubiquitous Southern menu of fried chicken, sweet potatoes, collard greens, corn bread and pound cake or peach cobbler for dessert, but a variety of meats and sides that would become leftovers for lunch and dinner for several days.

Today she'd prepared her celebrated potato salad, sautéed carrots and garlicky spinach, and a field-green-and-apple salad. Victoria had taught Dwight to cook as soon as he was tall enough to look over the stove. She'd said she did not want her son to depend on a woman to feed him because he was unable to put together a palatable meal for himself. He opened a bottle of red wine and a rosé to allow them to breathe before filling the wineglasses. A carafe of sparkling lemonade was positioned at Kiera's place setting. Dwight seated his mother at the head of the table, and then Charlotte at the opposite end. He sat on his mother's right, while Kiera and Sasha sat together.

Victoria raised her water glass, everyone following suit. "Here's to friends and family. May this not be the last time we eat together."

"Are we going to do this every Sunday, Grammie?" Kiera asked.

"We certainly don't want to put your grandmother out every Sunday," Charlotte said before Victoria could answer her granddaughter. "I'd like to host next Sunday—that is, if you don't mind. It's been many years since I've cooked for more than one person. And that only changed recently since Natasha's come back."

Victoria looked directly at Dwight. "I can make it, but you'll have to ask Dwight about his intentions, because now that the weather has changed, he spends most weekends at his lake house."

"Daddy says once he gives up drilling teeth, he's going to become a professional fisherman."

"What happened to Dwight and Daddy speaking for himself?" Dwight questioned as he glared at Victoria and then Kiera.

Kiera ignored his slight reprimand when she said, "He's tried to teach me to fish, but the only thing I want to do with fish is eat it."

Sasha's pale eyebrows rose slightly. "What do you catch?"

Remnants of his annoyance with his mother and daughter lingered around the fringes of his mind when he shifted his attention to Sasha. "Rainbow trout and smallmouth bass."

"Do you clean and cook your catch?"

He nodded. "What I don't cook I clean and bring home and freeze."

"Daddy, can Miss Sasha come with us the next time we go to the lake house?"

Suddenly Dwight felt as if he was being put on the spot. First his mother had disclosed his future weekend plans and now his daughter was asking if he could include her employer. The few times Kiera had accompanied him, she complained about having nothing to do or no one to talk to. She didn't like getting up early to stand in water waiting to reel in fish, and she'd complained incessantly about cleaning their catch, but then said it was worth it when she sat down to eat grilled fish.

"That's something I'll have to discuss with Miss Sasha, because she just may have plans for her weekends." His explanation seemed to satisfy Kiera when she picked up the glass of lemonade and took a long swallow.

Dinner continued with Charlotte complimenting Victoria on her amazing buttermilk air-fried chicken, molasses-braised short ribs and potato salad. "I don't know whether I will be able to come close to matching this scrumptious feast."

"Mama's being modest, Miss Victoria. She's also a great cook."

Victoria winked at Sasha. "I'm sure she is."

Charlotte sat up straight. "Does this mean we're on for next Sunday?" Everyone sitting at the table nodded.

"What time should you expect us?" Dwight asked.

A network of faint lines fanned out around Charlotte's blue eyes when she smiled. "Four. Is that too late for you?"

"Not at all," he replied. "It's just that the chamber's dinner dance is the night before and I'll probably need time to recuperate from the festivities."

"Dwight and I are going together." Sasha's announcement appeared to stun everyone as a swollen silence ensued.

Dwight peered at her over the rim of his wineglass at the same time amusement shimmered in his dark eyes. Well, he thought, the cat was truly out of the bag. Sasha accompanying him as his date was certain to have tongues wagging. The only and last woman he'd dated from Wickham Falls he married. And he'd been forthcoming with Sasha when he told her he liked being single. But even more important, he had no intention of contemplating getting serious with a woman until his daughter left for college.

He also did not want a repeat of his last relationship, where he had been forced to choose between her or Kiera. It had been the second time in his adult life where a woman had issued an ultimatum. The first had been when his daughter's mother wanted him to choose between living in Wickham Falls and New York.

Victoria pushed back her chair and stood. "It's going to be a while before I bring out dessert and set up the

Viennese table, so I'm going to show Charlotte my place and the gardens." A slight blush suffused Sasha's face at the mention of the number of desserts.

Dwight also stood. "I'll clear the table and put away the leftovers."

Sasha rose to her feet. "I'll help you."

Kiera drained her glass of lemonade. "Daddy, can I go to Alexis's house to study for our chemistry test?"

"Okay. Just don't come back too late." She and the next-door neighbor's daughter had played with each other whenever Kiera had come to spend the summers with him. Dwight waited until he was alone in the house with Sasha and said, "I do believe you shocked everyone when you mentioned going to the dinner dance with me."

Sasha clapped a hand over her mouth to smother her laughter. "Did you see my mother's face when I said it? I thought she was going to faint away."

Dwight smiled as he stacked dishes and serving pieces. "And I can't believe my mother did not have a comeback."

Carrying a platter of chicken, Sasha followed him into the kitchen. "Can you imagine what their reaction would be if we told them we were getting married?"

He went completely still and then set the dishes on the countertop. "No, I can't."

"Neither can I. The first time I married it was for all the wrong reasons, and I promised myself if or when I did marry again it would have to be because of love."

Dwight gave her an incredulous stare. "You weren't in love with your husband?"

"I tried to convince myself that I was, yet in the end, I knew I was deceiving him and myself."

"I know this is a very personal question, but did you marry him because he was a superstar recording artist?"

Chapter Five

Sasha's eyelids fluttered wildly. "No." Grant was not only charming, but he projected a larger-than-life persona she hadn't been able to resist.

"How long had you been dating?"

"A little less than three months. But even if I'd dated Grant for a year, I realized in the end that I wasn't cut out to be a celebrity wife."

"Maybe he couldn't accept that his wife was a celebrity in her own right."

Sasha's jaw dropped. She tried to speak but it was as if her voice locked in her throat. She did not want to believe she was that transparent, or maybe Dwight was just that perceptive. She nodded instead.

"Did he hurt you?"

"Not physically, but emotionally, where the scars weren't visible," she admitted as tears filled her eyes.

Taking a step, Dwight pulled her into an embrace, his chin resting on the top of her head. "It's okay, sweetie. He can't hurt you now."

Sasha buried her face against his shoulder and wrapped her arms around his waist. Feeling Dwight's warmth and strength, she felt safe, protected. The strong, steady pumping of his heart against her breasts had become a soothing salve as hers pounded a runaway rhythm. "My marriage was a mess."

Lowering his head, Dwight brushed a light kiss over her parted lips. "I don't want to ruin what has been a wonderful afternoon talking about *him* right about now."

Sasha knew he was right. The afternoon was as close to perfect as she could have wanted. His family had invited hers into their home, making her and her mother truly welcomed and a part of theirs. Dwight kissed her again, this time on the forehead.

Easing back, she smiled up at him, and she was rewarded with a dimpled smile in return from him. She dropped her arms, turned on her heel and returned to the dining room to gather more plates. Sasha had been ready to bare her soul to Dwight, to tell him things no other person knew other than her mother, if only to unburden herself. In the end, Charlotte had blamed herself because she hadn't set the best example for her daughter to follow. Both had married men who'd felt the need to control their wives.

Sasha and Dwight made quick work of clearing away the remains of dinner and storing leftovers in microwave glass containers with snap-lock lids. She'd just lined the buffet server with plates filled with an assortment of desserts when Charlotte and Victoria returned.

Forty-five minutes later, Sasha settled Charlotte in the Corolla, waiting until she secured her seat belt, and then rounded the compact car to sit beside her. They'd spent more than four hours with the Adamses and Sasha looked forward to going home and relaxing with the knowledge she would not have to get up early the following morning because the sweet shop was closed on Mondays.

"What did I miss while Victoria and I were gone?" Charlotte asked, as Sasha put the car in Reverse and backed out of the driveway.

"What are you talking about?"

"I asked Victoria if I could see her place to give you and Dwight some time alone."

Sasha's right foot hit the brake so hard the car lurched to a stop. "You did what?"

"There's no need to get your nose out of joint, Natasha. Even before you said you were going out with Dwight next weekend, I saw how he was staring at you when he opened the door. And anyone who isn't visually impaired could see what you've tried so hard to hide."

"And what's that, Mama?"

"That you like each other."

Easing off the brake, Sasha continued driving, her teeth clenched so tightly that her jaw ached. She'd wanted to scream at her mother, to remind her that she was an adult and did not need her as a go-between to help her attract a man. "I'm not going to lie and say I don't like Dwight, but you have no right to try to play matchmaker."

Charlotte stared out the side window. "I'm sorry. You can call me a meddling old fool if you want."

"Don't start with the guilt trip, Mama. I know you

want the best for me, but that's not going to happen until you let me experience life on my own, and to learn from my own mistakes and hopefully never repeat them."

"I know I never asked you, but do you want to get married again?"

Sasha pondered the question for several seconds. "If I found someone I loved and wanted to spend the rest of my life with—then yes."

Shifting slightly, Charlotte turned and looked at her. "You didn't see yourself when you came back to The Falls, Natasha. Not only did you look like the walking dead, but you were so angry that I was afraid to say anything to you. I know if I'd had a different temperament after you told me how Grant treated you, I would've driven to Nashville and—"

"Don't say it, Mama," Sasha said, cutting her off. "Grant is my past and you don't have to think or talk about what you'd liked or wanted to do to him."

"What I couldn't understand was why you didn't say something to me whenever we talked. If you'd given me the slightest hint of what you'd been going through with him, I would've told you to leave the son of a bitch."

"Mama! When did you start cussin'?"

Charlotte made a sucking sound with her tongue and teeth. "I did a lot of cussin' when your father was alive. It's just that I wouldn't let my kids hear it."

"So, you gave as good as you got?"

"Damn straight. Harold Manning knew I wouldn't cuss him out when our kids were around, so he knew when to start up with me."

"Why did you marry him, Mama?"

A beat passed. "Your father and I went out a few times, and the first time we slept together, he got me pregnant.

And when I told him, he insisted we get married. His folks never married, and that always bothered him. And if I hadn't married him, then you wouldn't be here. And that's something I've never regretted. I wanted and love all my children."

"Why didn't Grandma and Pops get married?"

"Your grandma's first husband refused to give her a divorce, so she left him and moved in with Pops. They had a bunch of kids and lived together as common-law husband and wife even if the state of West Virginia doesn't recognize it."

"The fact that you married Dad should've been enough for him."

"Harold was just an angry man, Natasha. After a while, I realized no one or nothing could make him happy. The first couple of years of our marriage I bent over backward to do whatever I could to make him not complain, but then I gave up. Either it was Harold's way or no way."

Sasha thought about what she'd had to go through to keep peace in her marriage. And like her mother, she had done whatever she could to make Grant happy, and despite his meteoric rise in country music, it was never enough for him. If she'd had this conversation with Charlotte before she'd exchanged vows with Grant, Sasha knew she would not have married him. However, she wasn't one to live with regrets, because it taught her what she would or would not accept if or when she became involved with a man again.

"You really like Dwight, don't you, Mama?"

Charlotte smiled. "What is there not to like, Natasha? He's gorgeous, intelligent and a wonderful father. You can tell in a single glance that he dotes on his daughter. Some men in his position would have a gaggle of women trailing after him. And you should count yourself among the lucky ones, because I believe you're the first woman from The Falls he's dated since Adrienne Wheeler."

"It could be he's not really into local women."

"Not into them how, Natasha?"

"Once burned, twice shy. Maybe he's afraid to commit to one again."

"Does that bother you?" Charlotte asked.

"No. I don't have a problem dating Dwight and not wanting more."

"What if it becomes more?"

"I can't and don't want to project that far into the future, Mama."

Sasha turned off into the driveway and parked beside the van with the sweet shop's logo painted on the front doors. When she'd left earlier that afternoon to drive to Dwight's house to share Sunday dinner with him and his family, she never could've imagined that he would ask her to accompany him to a local social event. But first they would start tongues wagging when they showed up together at the Wolf Den. And going out with Dwight had taken care of one concern for her: he was willing to date women out of his race.

Charlotte opened the passenger-side door. "I think I'm going to turn in early. Right now, I'm as full as a tick, and after a couple of glasses of wine I doubt I'll be able to keep my eyes open long enough to watch my regular shows."

"Make that two stuffed ticks." Sasha got out and plucked the bag with containers of leftover food Victoria had insisted they take home with them once she'd sheepishly admitted she had cooked too much and didn't want it to go to waste.

Charlotte slowly made her way up the steps to the front door. "What are your plans for tomorrow?"

"First, I'm going to sleep in late. And then I'm going to the bank to deposit last week's receipts. I also plan to stop by the newspaper's office to see if Langston is there to interview me for his Who's Who column. We've been playing phone tag for a couple of weeks."

"You don't plan to go into the shop?"

Sasha shook her head. Although she closed Sunday and Monday, she would occasionally go in and put up batches of yeast for bread or doughnuts or roll out piecrusts. "No."

"Good. It's time you stop working when the shop is closed, or you'll end up burning out."

"As soon as I put the food away, I'm going to change into my jammies, get into bed and set the TV to sleep mode."

True to her word, Sasha stored the leftovers in the fridge, cleansed her face of makeup and got into a pair of pajamas and slipped into bed. Picking up the remote on the bedside table, she flicked on the television resting on its own stand and settled down to watch a pre-programmed romantic-comedy movie.

Sasha finished totaling the weekly receipts and entered the amount into a bookkeeping program on the laptop linked to the desktop in the shop. After disbursing payroll and paying vendors, the business had yielded a profit for the third consecutive week, alleviating some of her former anxiety that the bakeshop would not be sustainable. She'd projected six continuous months of profits before contacting cooking schools to solicit their recommendations for an assistant pastry chef.

Gathering her tote, she walked out of her bedroom and headed for the staircase. The sounds of laughter from the audience of a morning talk show came from the kitchen. The results of a positive checkup from her cardiologist was good news for Charlotte. She'd volunteered to work longer hours, but Sasha rejected her suggestion. She wanted to wait until the fall before increasing Charlotte's hours.

"Mama, I'm leaving now."

"Okay, baby."

Sasha found an empty spot on the street far from the bank. Shopkeepers were sweeping and hosing down the sidewalks fronting their businesses. All the business establishments were shaded by black-and-white-striped awnings. She'd become a window-shopper in her own hometown, as she peered into the windows of the dry cleaner, Laundromat, pharmacy, hardware and department stores. As a child, the highlights of her Saturdays were when her mother went downtown, where they'd spent hours browsing and shopping for things they needed and a few they didn't. The residents of The Falls did not have to leave their town to shop, because everything they'd want was available in the four-block-long business district.

She walked into the bank and did not have to wait for a teller, who cheerfully greeted her. He'd just completed her transaction when Sasha heard someone call her name. Turning, she recognized a woman with whom she'd shared several classes in high school. Georgi, who was biracial, had inherited each of her parents' best traits. She had a café au lait complexion, delicate features with a sprinkling of freckles and natural curly reddish hair that she'd pulled back and secured in a ponytail.

"Georgi. How are you?" Sasha's smile faded when she stared at Georgina Powell's teeth. The gap that had been so much of her trademark smile was missing.

Georgina's large round eyes, the color of bright copper pennies, crinkled when she threw back her head and laughed. "I know you're shocked not to see the gap, but I decided to give myself a present for my thirtieth birthday, because that was the first thing folks noticed whenever I introduced myself."

Sasha managed to look sheepish. "I must admit it was very distinctive." Georgina had been an illustrator for their high school's newspaper, and she had always talked about becoming an artist, but knew that was wishful thinking because she was expected to work for and eventually take control of the department store that had been in the Powell family for more than four generations. It had started up at the turn of the previous century as a general store selling everything from feed, seeds, fabric and household tools to canned goods. It expanded for years until it stocked enough merchandise that residents did not have to seek out large box or chain stores lining the interstate.

"I heard a couple of months ago that you were back in The Falls, but I've been up to my eyeballs helping out my parents at the store that I don't even have time to breathe. Stocking shelves, keeping track of inventory and taking care of customers has become a bit overwhelming. You should know that now that you're running your own business."

"It can be somewhat daunting at times, but thankfully I have my mother, who has been a blessing."

Georgina leaned closer. "That's what I want to talk to you about whenever you have some free time."

"Do you want to give me a hint?" Sasha asked.

"I'm thinking of opening my own business here in The Falls."

Somewhat taken aback, Sasha went completely still. "You intend to compete with your parents for business?"

Georgina shook her head. "I definitely will not compete. My father has decided to downsize the arts-and-crafts section and I want to open a small shop featuring needlecrafts. I'm aware that it may be a dying art, but there are a lot of folks who still knit and crochet. I also plan to give classes for those who want to learn to quilt by hand or machine. I used to complain when my grandmother forced me to learn needlecrafts, but now I'm grateful that she did. When she passed away, she left me a collection of quilts dating back to before the Civil War."

"They have to be priceless." Sasha was unable to disguise the awe in her voice.

"They are. We'll talk about that another time. Right now, I need to deposit these receipts and get back to the store."

"Call the shop and let me know when you're available."

Georgina hugged Sasha. "Thanks, girl."

Sasha walked out of the bank, wondering why her former classmate wasn't pursuing her dream of becoming an illustrator instead of planning to open a needlecraft shop. Georgina wasn't just talented; she was gifted.

Reuniting with Georgina reminded Sasha that she

was still estranged from her hometown. She'd returned the summer before and today was the first time she'd strolled along Main Street and gone into the bank, because normally Charlotte did that.

Once Sasha had made the decision to return to Wickham Falls, she did not call and tell her mother. When she rang the bell and Charlotte opened the door, Sasha knew she'd looked vastly different than she had during her last visit, but she was also different inwardly. The first few weeks were a repeat of the one before: she slept, ate and watched countless movies. Then one day she decided she'd hidden enough and went into Preston McAvoy's office to file papers of incorporation for her proposed new business. With her distinctive red hair dyed a nondescript brown and her face hidden by oversize sunglasses, no one recognized her as the woman who'd been married to the Nashville recording artist who'd crossed over from country to pop and Southern rock. Sasha had managed to keep a low profile even after word spread that she'd filed a permit to open a shop in the downtown business district.

She knew her customers were curious as to why she had come back and even more so why she'd decided to divorce her superstar husband and give up what had been a glamorous lifestyle. Having her mother and Kiera man the front of the shop had saved Sasha from answering questions she had no intention of explaining.

She was certain being seen with Dwight would generate more than its share of gossip, but at this point in her life Sasha was past caring what people thought of her. It had taken years for her to come into her own, and now at thirty-two she liked what she had become: the captain of her own destiny.

* * *

Dwight drove onto the driveway to the Manning house and got out. He had questioned himself over and over if he was courting trouble dating his daughter's employer; the last local woman he'd dated he married, and despite his attraction to Sasha, he had no intention of marrying her or any other woman—at least for several years. He'd always mapped out his future carefully and it was only because of unforeseen circumstances that he was forced to modify his plans.

The door opened before he could ring the bell and he came face-to-face with the subject of his musings. The sensual scent of her perfume, which now he could recognize if he was in a room with dozens of women. Sasha did not even remotely resemble the women he'd been involved with since his divorce, but that did not detract from what he'd found so engaging about her. She'd occasionally exhibit a shyness whenever he looked at her too long, making him wonder if she'd had much experience with men. Kiera constantly talked about her in glowing terms, which only made her go up several points on his approval scale.

"You look very nice."

It was the only thing Dwight could think to say when he noticed the black stretchy long-sleeved T-shirt Sasha had paired with matching leggings and low-heel booties. The black attire, hugging every curve of her slim figure, made her appear even taller. She'd styled her hair in a ponytail and applied a light cover of makeup to her eyes and mouth. Sasha lowered her eyes, gazing up at him through long charcoal-gray lashes, a sensual gesture he'd come to recognize and look for.

"Thank you. I'll be right with you. I just have to get my jacket and keys."

Dwight turned his back rather than stare at the sensual sway of Sasha's hips in the body-hugging attire. He had an inkling that Sasha was totally unaware of how sexy she was, and because of this he had to be very careful not to cross or blur the lines going from friends to lovers. Sleeping with her would not only complicate their relationship, but it would also impact Sasha and Kiera's. He shook his head as if to banish any licentious thoughts.

"Ready." Sasha had returned, wearing a fatigue jacket. "It's an old one that belonged to one of my brothers."

A knowing smile tugged at the corners of Dwight's mouth. All former and present members of the different branches were required to wear military paraphernalia to take advantage of the advertised specials at the sports bar. "Let's go, Corporal Manning."

Sasha glanced down at her brother's name and rank stamped on the jacket. "Maybe I should exchange it for another one."

Dwight took her hand. "Please don't. Everyone knows you belong to a military family." He led her around the passenger side of the Jeep and assisted her up.

"Why did you decide to join the army?" Sasha asked as he got in and sat beside her.

He gave a quick glance. "I wanted to continue the tradition of serving that began in my family dating back to before the Spanish–American War. Some of my relatives were buffalo soldiers, and before that served in all-black regiments during the Civil War."

"What if you'd decided not to serve?"

Dwight put the vehicle in gear and drove down the

tree-lined street, heading in the direction of the local road leading to the Wolf Den. "That wasn't an option. I grew up listening to my father and grandfather trade war stories about Korea and Vietnam, and for me it was like watching a war movie. I'd heard the term 'shell shock,' but it wasn't until I was much older that I realized it was a form of PTSD."

"Why did you decide to become a dentist?"

"It really wasn't my first choice. When I'd enrolled in college as a premed student, I'd planned to become a pediatrician. It wasn't until my junior year that I decided I wanted to become a dentist."

"Do you like being a dentist?"

"I love it. I like the personal one-on-one contact with the patient sitting in my chair, and helping people achieve a healthy mouth, which is essential to overall good health, is very satisfying."

"Do you think Kiera wants to become a dentist?"

Coming to a stop at a four-way intersection, Dwight looked for oncoming traffic. "She hasn't said anything to me about it. Right now, all she talks about is learning to make fancy cakes." He knew he'd shocked Sasha with this disclosure when she emitted an audible gasp.

"Has she actually told you she wants to become a pastry chef?" Sasha asked.

"Not in so many words," he replied truthfully. Dwight didn't want to tell Sasha that his daughter talked nonstop about the customers that came into the sweet shop and about her employer.

"Would it bother you if she did choose a career as a pastry chef?"

Dwight shook his head. "No. I've asked my daughter what she wants to be when she grows up, and she always says she doesn't know. What I don't want to do is put pressure on her as to her career choice. I tell her that once she decides, it should be something she's passionate about. But what I will not do is support her if she wants to become a professional student because she doesn't know what she wants to be."

"Her wanting to learn to bake may be just a phase, but I'm willing to give her lessons once I hire an assistant. That probably won't be until the summer. Even if she elects not to become a pastry chef, she can always use it as a backup to supplement her income."

"Did you know that you were going to be a pastry chef when you graduated high school?"

Sasha paused. "That's a long story. I'll tell you about it at another time."

Dwight registered something in Sasha's tone that indicated it was something she truly did not want to talk about, and he was perceptive enough not to bring up the topic again. After all, they were still more strangers than friends.

He maneuvered off the local road and down a sloping decline to a path leading through a copse of trees before the landscape opened to a valley as the Wolf Den came into view. The mouthwatering aroma of smoked meats wafted through partially open windows of the Jeep. A smokehouse and newly erected red-painted barn were located behind the restaurant. The Den's owners had built the barn to double as a venue for catered affairs. It was the only business in town with a license to serve alcohol. The parking lot alongside the building was crowded with SUVs and pickups, and a few Harleys. He pulled into a reserved space bearing his name and rank.

Sasha gave him an incredulous look at the same time she undid her seat belt. "You get your own parking space?"

Dwight winked at her. "Only on Military Monday. As the highest-ranking officer in The Falls, I'm afforded the honor."

Her smile matched his. "So, rank does have its privileges."

He nodded. "Yes, it does." The owners had afforded him the privilege after town council members voted to host Community Week for residents to volunteer to give back or pay it forward. Dwight had elected to treat all active, retired and/or former military personnel free of charge, regardless of whether they had dental insurance. "Don't move. I'll help you down."

Sasha waited for Dwight to get out and open her door. He extended his arms and she slid off the seat as he held her effortlessly, her head level with his for several seconds, before lowering her until her feet touched the ground. Suddenly, she felt light-headed, as if she couldn't draw a normal breath because they were a hairbreadth away from each other. Being this close to Dwight made her feel as if she'd been sucked into a vortex that made everything around her vanish like a puff of smoke. Ripples of awareness eddied through her, and for the first time in a very long time she felt a longing that she wanted to be made love to. However, she knew realistically that couldn't happen. There was no way she was going to become physically involved with the father of her employee. It would not bode well for her, Dwight or Kiera if they decided to break up.

And in that instant, she knew it was best for them to become friends.

Friends without benefits.

"Let's go in so that we can give these folks something to talk about."

Reaching over her head, Dwight shut the door and then held her hand and led her out of the parking lot to the front of the eating establishment.

Chapter Six

Sasha had grown up listening to stories about the celebrated sports bar, but this was her first time stepping foot into the place that had earned the reputation of serving the best smoked meat in the county. The ear-shattering sounds of raised voices, the waitstaff shouting food orders and the deep, pulsing music from a heavy-metal band coming from hidden speakers were an assault on her senses.

A crowd of men and women were standing two-deep at the bar, where a trio of bartenders were filling drink orders. Although the legal drinking age in West Virginia was twenty-one, the owners of the Wolf Den had posted a sign stating they reserved the right not to serve anyone under twenty-three. More than a half dozen wall-mounted muted televisions were tuned to sporting events.

"Attention!" Everyone went completely still, and all manner of speech ended abruptly as they executed salutes. Sasha also froze when she saw everyone staring at her and Dwight.

"At ease, everyone." Dwight's voice, though low, carried easily above the music.

It suddenly dawned on Sasha the assembly had acknowledged him as a senior ranking officer. Going on tiptoe, she whispered close to his ear, "Does this always happen when you come in?"

Dwight lowered his head and pressed his mouth to her hair. "It started as a joke a couple of years ago and it stuck. Anyone who was or is a commissioned officer gets the spotlight." His hand rested at the small of her back. "Let me see if I can find a table before we can order something to eat."

Sasha glanced around the sports bar. Almost everyone wore an article of clothing advertising a branch of the military. She stared at a tray a waitress balanced on her shoulder filled with dishes of grilled meat and sides. The mouthwatering aroma of brisket, chicken, ribs and baked beans with pieces of burnt ends, collard greens, and macaroni and cheese wafted to her nostrils. Wrapping her arm around Dwight's waist, she moved even closer to him when the door opened, and more people came in.

"Doc Adams! Over here!"

Dwight craned his neck to see who was calling his name. He spied one of the owners beckoning him closer. Tonight Aiden Gibson, a former navy SEAL, was doing double duty as the pit master and bartender. Resting his hand at the small of Sasha's back, he shouldered his way through the throng to find two stools at the far end of the bar.

A network of fine lines fanned out around Aiden's blue-green eyes when he smiled. "I wasn't certain whether you would show up tonight. I'll have one of the waitstaff get a table for you."

Dwight seated Sasha and then reached over the bar and shook Aiden's hand. "Thanks for looking out for us. Aiden, I'm not certain whether you know Sasha Manning." He studied her delicate profile. "Sasha, Aiden Gibson. He happens to be one of the owners of this fine dining establishment."

Sasha extended her hand. "It's a pleasure to meet you."

Aiden cradled her much smaller hand in his. "I'm more familiar with your brother Phil, because he and I were in some of the same classes. Aren't you the cake lady everyone's talking about?" A slight flush suffused Sasha's fair complexion as she modestly inclined her head. "You and I have to talk at another time, because I'm thinking of adding a few items to our dessert menu. Now, what can I get you good folks to drink while you wait for a table?"

Dwight dropped an arm over Sasha's shoulders. "What do you want, sweetie?" The endearment had just slipped out.

She stared at the chalkboard with the day's specials and beers. "I'll have a Blue Moon."

He ordered Sasha's beer and a Dos Equis for himself. Minutes later, Aiden placed pint glasses of ice-cold beer on two coasters. Raising his glass, Dwight touched it to Sasha's, which was garnished with an orange slice. "Enjoy."

She took a long swallow of her icy brew, moaning softly. "That's nice."

Picking up a napkin, Dwight gently held her chin and blotted the froth off her upper lip. He leaned closer and brushed his mouth over hers, savoring the lingering taste of orange. "We need to make folks believe we're a couple," he whispered against her moist parted lips. Although not prone to displays of public affection, Dwight admitted to himself that he enjoyed kissing Sasha.

Sasha looked up at him through her lashes. "You're right." The two words were barely off her tongue when she leaned closer and kissed him on the mouth, the joining lasting almost five seconds. "I think that's a lot more convincing."

Dwight felt the flesh between his thighs stir to life, and he pressed his knees tightly together as he struggled not to become fully aroused. He cursed to himself when he realized he'd concocted a dangerous scheme that backfired. He'd convinced himself he and Sasha could see each other socially without a physical entanglement. Now it was apparent he was wrong because his body had just reminded him how long it had been since he'd been intimately involved with a woman; his last relationship, by mutual agreement, did not include sharing a bed.

Sitting straight, he saw Sasha staring back at him. It was impossible for him to read her expression. "Are you okay?"

A mysterious smile softened Sasha's mouth. "I'm more than okay."

And she was. Kissing Dwight, really kissing him, had assuaged her curiosity about the man whose image plagued her days and nights. She hadn't had a lot of experience when it came to the opposite sex, but after almost five years of marriage to a narcissist, she'd come to know what she did not like or want in a man.

Sasha knew she wasn't a girl, but a woman, who no longer entertained fantasies about finding her prince who would sweep her away and they would live happily ever after. Her grandmother had given her a colorful cloth-covered journal for her eighth birthday with a note for her to write down everything that had happened to her that day and every day thereafter. She told her that she had to be honest about her feelings, because the entries would provide a blueprint as to how she should live her life.

It wasn't until years later, when she unpacked the personal belongings she'd shipped from Nashville to Wickham Falls, that Sasha found the journals. She'd kept them because they were the last link between her and her grandmother; she sat in bed and read every entry. Her childish print gave way to a beautiful cursive along with drawings that hinted of the artistic ability she would eventually use when designing cakes.

When she compared Dwight to Grant, she realized they were complete opposites in appearance and personality. She'd found Dwight even-tempered, generous and affectionate, while Grant was critical, opinionated and selfish. It was only when Grant was in public or onstage performing for a crowd that he was able to morph into the charming, magnetic man women fantasized about and men wanted to be.

"Hey, Sasha. What are you doing here?"

She turned to find someone she hadn't seen since their high school graduation. Gregg Henderson had been her prom date. He wore a tan-colored T-shirt under a desert fatigue jacket. "What happened to 'how are you?'" she teased, smiling.

Gregg ran a hand over his close-cropped sandy-brown hair. His dark blue eyes in a deeply tanned face reminded her of sapphires. "Sorry about that." He leaned closer and kissed her cheek. "How are you?"

"I'm well. And how have you been?"

"I'm really good. I just finished my second tour, so I'm going to be stateside for a while. My mother told me about you marrying and then divorcing that country singer. What happened?"

Sasha's expression changed, becoming a mask of stone. "We decided to go our separate ways." She had no intention of giving Gregg the intimate details of her failed marriage.

"I'm going to be here for another couple of weeks, so maybe we can hang out together and catch up on old times."

She wanted to tell Gregg that there were no old times. He was the first boy to ask her to prom and she'd accepted. "I don't think that's going to be possible. When I'm not running my business, I try to spend time with my boyfriend." The moment she'd referred to Dwight as her boyfriend, Sasha knew for certain everyone in The Falls would know about it because Gregg's mother was an incurable gossipmonger.

"I didn't know you were seeing someone."

Looping her arm through Dwight's and resting her head on his shoulder, Sasha wordlessly confirmed to Gregg that she was seeing The Falls' resident dentist.

Gregg's eyes were large as silver dollars when he realized who she was talking about. "I suppose I'll see you around." Turning, he walked away, leaving Sasha staring at his back.

"You played that off quite well."

Sasha looked at Dwight, who appeared to have an intense interest in the plastic-covered menu. "I suppose you heard everything."

"Curious and wondering how you were going to handle him coming on to you."

"He really wasn't coming on to me, Dwight."

Dwight's inky-black eyebrows rose. "You think not? He was talking about catching up on old times."

"The old times was prom. He was my prom date and nothing beyond that."

"You didn't date him in high school?"

Sasha lowered her eyes. Dwight was asking a question that if she answered would open a Pandora's box of memories she'd put behind her. "I didn't date anyone in high school." He gave her an incredulous look. "I didn't want any entanglements when I knew I was leaving town following graduation."

She'd told Dwight a half lie. If she'd had a boyfriend, she knew he probably would've tried to convince her to stay. At the time she knew she had to put some distance between her and her parents before she had a complete mental breakdown.

"Why did you leave, Sasha?"

"That's a long story. One that I can't talk about *here*."

Dwight dropped a kiss on her hair. "Forgive me for prying."

"There's nothing to forgive, sweetie," she whispered, repeating his term of endearment. "I want to thank you."

"For what?"

"For masquerading as my boyfriend because I don't

need or want a repeat of what I just had with Gregg. I've discovered some men don't react well to rejection."

Once she'd appeared on the competition cooking show she was easily recognizable because of her distinctive laugh and red hair. At the time she didn't know whether men were attracted to her because she'd become a celebrity chef, or if they liked her for herself, which resulted in her deftly rejecting any offers to take her out. She'd had one serious relationship before Grant, which had ended badly. He had been one of her culinary school instructors. Almost fifteen years her senior, he did not deal well with rejection, and she was forced to move out of her apartment once he began stalking her. It ended only when she reported him to the police; the judge warned him that a subsequent arrest could result in his serving time in prison.

Dwight threaded their fingers together, bringing her hand to his mouth and kissing the back of it. "I think I'm going to enjoy masquerading as your boyfriend."

She gazed into a pair of dark eyes that reminded her of tiny cups of espresso. Light from pendants shimmered on the cropped salt-and-pepper strands covering his head, while casting long and short shadows over Dwight's exquisitely sculpted face. It wasn't for the first time that she wondered why some woman hadn't gotten him to fall in love and marry her, despite his pronouncement that he liked being single. Sasha was preempted from replying when a waitress came over to inform them she had an available table for them.

Dwight ordered for himself and Sasha. Once the dishes arrived and she bit into a succulent piece of smoked brisket, she said she now knew why the Wolf

Den was so popular with folks in The Falls and surrounding towns. He introduced her to men and women—some with whom she was familiar and others who were complete strangers. It was apparent she'd missed a lot during her fourteen-year absence.

The time was approaching nine when a waitress came over to the table to ask him if he wanted another beer. "No, thank you. But I will take the check."

Sasha touched the napkin to her mouth. "Is there anybody in town that you don't know?" she asked, teasingly.

"Very few. Remember, I've lived here all my life. Even when I went to college and dental school, I managed to come back in between semesters." He looked at something over her head. "There's something about Wickham Falls that keeps pulling me back whenever I'm away for any appreciable period of time."

"Maybe it's because you had a very happy childhood."

Dwight's eyes narrowed suspiciously. "And you didn't?"

Sasha's eyelids fluttered wildly. "It wasn't as happy as it should've been. My parents argued."

"What parents don't, Sasha?"

"Every day, Dwight."

He stood, signaled for the waitress and handed her three large bills. "Keep the change." Rounding the booth, he cupped Sasha's elbow, helping her to stand. "Let's go, Cinderella. I promised to get you home by nine."

Dwight escorted her out of the restaurant and into the cool night air. Sasha's mentioning her parents arguing every day was certain to negatively impact her attitude about relationships. Had she and her ex-husband quarreled so much that it had put a strain on their marriage until it resulted in divorce?

He wanted to tell Sasha that he and Adrienne rarely argued until it came time for him to set up his practice. Then it was relentless and uncompromising. What he could not and did not understand at the time was why she so vehemently objected when she'd known for years of his intentions. However, once they were divorced and she moved to New York and reunited with one of her college classmates, realization dawned for Dwight. Adrienne finally admitted that she'd had an affair with the man who would eventually become her second husband.

Sasha attempted to stifle a yawn as he drove out of the parking lot. "Sleepy or full?"

"Both," she admitted, smiling. "Thank you for inviting me to come with you."

"Anytime."

"How often do you come for Military Monday?"

"I try to make it at least once and no more than twice a month. I really like hanging out at the lake house."

"What you really like is fishing."

Dwight gave Sasha a quick glance. "Yup. It's the only thing I like better than dentistry." A beat passed, and then he asked, "Do you fish?"

"Some."

"How much is some, Sasha?"

"Just say I've learned to fly-fish."

Dwight's teeth shone whitely in the glow of the illumination coming from the dashboard. "Are you saying you've mastered the wrist action?"

"Some," Sasha repeated.

"We'll have to see how much 'some' you have if you ever decide to join Kiera and me at the lake."

"How about your mother? Does she ever join you?"

"She did when I first bought the place, but she's not much for roughing it."

"Does roughing it translate into bathing in the lake?" Sasha questioned.

"Nah," Dwight said, laughing. "The house has all the comforts of home with indoor plumbing, hot and cold running water, electricity, heat and air-conditioning. There are quite a few retirees who live there year-round."

"How secluded is it?"

"Just say you have to know where you're going to find it. Anytime you need a break and want to escape for a day or two, just let me know and I'll make it happen."

"It sounds tempting."

Dwight heard the hesitation in her voice and wondered if she thought he had an ulterior motive for inviting her. "The cabin has two bedrooms, and there's also a loft that sleeps a third person."

"I'll definitely think about it."

"My invitation comes with no strings attached, and because of this I promise you nothing physical can ever happen between us."

"Do you really find me so unattractive that I repulse you that much? I constantly overhear customers that come into the shop tell Kiera that she's a beauty just like her mother."

Dwight did not want to believe what had just come out of Sasha's mouth as his hands tightened on the steering wheel. "Your ex must have really done a number on you if you believe you're not an attractive woman, Sasha."

"Leave my ex out of this."

"Why?" he countered.

"Because I don't want to talk about him."

Signaling, Dwight maneuvered off the road and came to a stop where he would be out of the path of coming traffic. Shifting into Park, he unbuckled his seat belt and turned to look at Sasha. "We don't have to talk about him, but I think we need to straighten out a few details so you can understand where I'm coming from." Her eyes appeared abnormally large as she stared at him. Reaching over, he rested his hand on the nape of her neck, his fingertips pressed against the runaway pulse. "You don't have to concern yourself with me trying to get you to go to bed with me, and it's not because I don't find you attractive. But our sleeping together would only complicate things for both of us. My daughter works for you and the situation could become somewhat awkward if or when we broke up."

Sasha was mute for a full minute as she replayed what Dwight had just told her. She'd asked him if he'd found her unattractive because whenever she was out with Grant, he would compare her to other women he'd claim he found more beautiful. And to a small-town girl who rarely wore makeup and bought her clothes off the rack, Sasha had always believed she would never be able to compete with the more glamorous wives of the other recording stars. Even after she hired a dresser who selected her clothes and a makeup artist taught her what to use to enhance her best features, the insecurities lingered.

She did not want to talk about her ex-husband, because she couldn't. She'd signed a nondisclosure agreement not to divulge the details of their marriage because to do so could negatively impact the wholesome country-boy image his publicist had created for him. Only her mother knew, after she'd sworn her to secrecy, what she'd had to go through during her five-year marriage.

"I only asked if you found me unattractive because I know how everyone talks about how beautiful Kiera's mother is," she lied smoothly.

Dwight's fingertips feathered over the column of her neck. "It's not about how a woman looks on the outside, Sasha. Some women are like an apple—beautiful on the outside, but once you bite into it you discover it's rotten to the core. You're one of those rare finds who's beautiful inside and out."

Sasha didn't know if Dwight was telling her she was beautiful because he thought that was what she wanted to hear, yet there was something in his voice and reassuring touch that lessened her despair and filled her with a sense of strength she didn't know she had. Something unknown communicated that Dwight was good to and for her even if they never became lovers. He had proved that during the time they'd spent at the Wolf Den. She'd found him attentive and protective whenever a man appeared to express an interest in her. He would place a proprietary arm around her shoulders or kiss her hair, silently signaling she wasn't available.

She'd admitted to her mother that one day if or when she married again it would be for love, and having Dwight as a friend was a bonus, given her dearth of experience when it came to men. She'd slept with one man before

Grant, and if or when she slept with the next one, she prayed it would be her last.

Sasha rested her head on Dwight's shoulder. "You are so good for a woman's ego."

"It's about the truth and not my attempting to boost your ego, Sasha. I've been divorced a lot longer than you have, so it's going to be a while before you stop blaming yourself for what you did or didn't do."

A trembling smile parted her lips. "You think?"

"I know," he said confidently. "Now, it's time I get you home so you can get your beauty rest."

Sasha wanted to tell Dwight that not only was he good for her, but also good to her. He was the first man who'd treated her like an equal, and for that she was grateful. The man she'd given her virginity to would go into jealous rages and reprimand her like a father with a child whenever he'd believed she wasn't being attentive enough. And she did not want to think about Grant, who calculatingly found ways to emotionally abuse her because he'd believed there wasn't enough room in their marriage for two celebrities.

Dwight secured his seat belt and the remainder of the drive was completed in silence, and when he maneuvered into the driveway to her home, Sasha knew she wasn't the same person she'd been when she'd opened the door for him. She waited for him to come around and help her down.

"Thank you for a wonderful time."

Dwight angled his head. "Does this mean you want to do it again?"

Sasha smiled. "Of course. And I'll let you know when I'm ready to go fly-fishing with you and Kiera."

"That's a bet."

"Good night, Dwight."

"Good night, Sasha. I'll text you later in the week about when to expect me to pick you up for the dinner dance."

"Okay." She turned and walked up the steps to the house, unlocked the door, and then closed and locked it behind her.

"How did it go?"

Sasha turned to find her mother in a nightgown and bathrobe standing in the middle of the living room holding a glass of water. "How did what go?"

"Your date with Dwight."

Bending slightly, Sasha kicked off her shoes. "It really wasn't a date."

"I'm not so old that I don't know when a man comes to a woman's home to take her out that it's a date."

"All right, Mama. It was a date. And it was perfect."

"That's all I need to know. Good night."

Sasha watched her mother walk across the living room to the staircase. "Good night, Mama. By the way, do you want to know if he kissed me?"

Charlotte stopped halfway. "No. That's too much information. Don't stay up too late."

Sasha smiled. "I won't."

She'd planned to be in bed by ten. Her workday usually began between five and six in the morning and ended twelve hours later. And now that Aiden Gibson wanted her to bake for the Den, she knew hiring an assistant sooner rather than later was now a priority. As she climbed the staircase to the second story, she smiled when she thought about the hours she'd spent with Dwight. And she'd been truthful with her mother when she admitted it was a date and that it was perfect.

And as perfect as she found Dwight, Sasha realized she could not afford to lose focus. Not when she needed all her energy to grow her business.

Dwight sat up in bed with a mound of pillows cradling his back and shoulders, staring at the images on the flat screen. It was past midnight and he knew he should've been sleeping instead of watching the encore of basketball playoff games.

After dropping Sasha off, he'd come home to find a note from his mother that Kiera had decided to stay with her rather than have a sleepover with the neighbor's daughter. He wondered what Victoria had said or done to entice her granddaughter to sleep in the guesthouse. Dwight had given up completely lecturing Victoria about turning into the indulgent grandparent as she attempted to give or take Kiera whatever and wherever she wanted.

Against his protestations, Victoria had gifted Kiera with a pair of diamond studs, totaling two carats, for her sixteenth birthday. The earrings had been a gift to her from her husband for their twentieth wedding anniversary. He much would've preferred his mother give his daughter a strand of her pearls, but Victoria overrode him when she said it was her right to give her only grandchild whatever she wanted. Dwight had not missed his mother's backhanded reminder that her only child had elected to give her only one grandchild. However, it wasn't his mother or daughter that kept him from going to sleep but Sasha. He couldn't stop thinking about what he'd said to her about their not sleeping together.

Was he attracted to her? The answer was yes.

He'd asked himself did he like her, and again the answer was a resounding yes.

But the defining question was the probability of his sleeping with her. And if he were truly honest, his body said yes while his head said no.

Dwight realized his ambivalence about Sasha stemmed from two factors: she was his daughter's employer, and she lived in Wickham Falls. He wasn't bothered if they were seen together out and about because they were friends—without benefits. What he couldn't understand was Sasha believing he'd found her unattractive, and he wondered if she was conscious of the differences in their race, and of the fact that Adrienne, at the age of sixteen, had won a beauty contest.

Well, the quiet, talented redhead did not have to concern herself about her appearance. What she failed to realize was that not only was she cute, but she claimed an understated sexiness he found appealing.

Picking up the remote device, he turned off the television and rearranged the pillows, so he lay in a more comfortable position. Sleep was slow in coming, and when it did, he temporarily forgot about the sweetness of Sasha's mouth when they kissed; the subtle hypnotic scent of her perfume that had lingered in the Jeep when she was no longer there. But an image of the way she innocently lowered her eyes and glanced up at him through her lashes visited him in an erotic dream. It served as a reminder of how long it had been since he'd slept with a woman.

Chapter Seven

Sasha felt like the hamster she saw in a pet shop running around on a wheel until he finally collapsed from exhaustion. She was overtired and close to burnout. Even when she'd sat at Adele Harvey's bedside around the clock for three days, leaving only to shower and change her clothes, she hadn't felt this fatigued.

Aiden Gibson, as promised, had called her to place an order for six cakes: coconut cream, bourbon-pecan pound, German chocolate, chocolate-raspberry truffle, strawberry cheesecake and red velvet.

Langston Cooper had come by the shop to inquire when she would be available for an interview, and again she told him she did not have the time. She had also put off meeting with Georgina Powell with the excuse that if Georgi came by her house late in the evening, she would set aside time for them to talk. She had just finished decorating the last of three dozen cupcakes with colorful tulips for a mother who wanted to take them to school for her daughter's eighth birthday when Kiera entered the kitchen.

"Miss Sasha, there's a Miss Campos asking to see you."

"Tell her I'll be right there." She set down the piping bag and discarded the disposable gloves. Using Russian piping tips to create leaves and colorful flowers, she'd decorated all the cupcakes in less than ten minutes. Pressed for time, Sasha had called in her prior experience when she'd been a contestant in a timed competition.

Sasha walked into the front of the shop to find Nicole Campos sitting at one of the three bistro tables. She now could count on regular customers who came in most mornings to order coffee and the daily special. It seemed so long ago that she'd come to Preston McAvoy's office to retain the attorney to file an application to set up a corporation. She knew Nicole was just as shocked to see her as she was to discover that Nicole now worked for the law firm.

She took a chair opposite Nicole, immediately noticing obvious changes in the woman who'd attained the rank of captain in the Corps piloting Black Hawk helicopter gunships. Her face was fuller than when she last saw her, and her hair had grown out of the pixie cut. Even her tawny-brown complexion was darker, as if she'd spent time in the sun.

"Congratulations on your engagement." Word had traveled quickly around The Falls that Fletcher Austen and Nicole had gotten engaged. And she could count on her mother to keep her abreast of local gossip. Charlotte tended to talk to everyone who came into the shop.

Nicole's eyes went to the diamond ring on her left hand, as a slight blush further darkened her delicate features. "Thank you."

"Have you set a date?"

Nicole nodded. "Yes. That's why I've come to see you about a wedding cake."

"When do you need it?" Sasha asked.

Lowering her eyes, Nicole focused on her outstretched hands. "A week from this coming Saturday. I know it's short notice," she said quickly. "But Fletcher is insisting we marry before I start showing."

"You're pregnant." The query had come out like a statement.

Nicole nodded again. "I just completed my first trimester, and even though I'm willing to wait until after I have the baby to get married, Fletcher says he doesn't want to be labeled a baby daddy."

Good for him, Sasha mused. There were some men in town who had chosen not to marry the women who'd had their children, preferring instead to live their lives by their leave. Fletcher Austen, a former decorated soldier, had become a much sought-after bachelor once he returned to civilian life to work in his family-owned auto repair business.

"How many people are you inviting?" It would be the first wedding cake she would bake since opening the shop.

Nicole shrugged under the suit jacket she'd put on over a white cotton man-tailored shirt. "I'm not sure. Fletcher keeps adding folks to the list, so right now it's anyone's guess. Of course, our families are invited, but then he began contacting some of the people he served with. I didn't want to be outdone, so I invited some of my buddies from the Corps. He just told me this morning that he's also invited everyone who hangs out at the Den on Military Monday."

Sasha did not envy Nicole, and she wondered if Dwight had received an invitation. She knew what went into planning a wedding, but to continually add names to the guest list was certain to create premarital problems. "I need a ballpark figure, Nicole. Fifty. Seventy-five."

Nicole threw up her hands. "Make it a hundred. I'd rather have too much than not enough. I refuse to let this wedding stress me out. I intend to show up, say my vows, eat, dance, and then go to bed and sleep until nature or hunger force me to get up."

Sasha laughed. "Where do you plan to hold the wedding and reception?"

"Everything will be done at the house. We've already ordered a tent, tables, chairs, DJ, and the Gibsons are going to cater the food. I told Fletcher I want simplicity and not some catering hall where people have to get all dressed up."

"Come into the back with me, where we can talk about what type of cake you want." Sasha smiled at Kiera, who'd just handed a customer a box filled with an assortment of muffins she'd baked earlier that morning. Most days she was able to sell out most of what she'd made that day. "Are you certain you don't want something to eat?" she asked Nicole again once they were seated in the area she'd set aside as her office.

"I just ate, so I'm good for another few hours."

Forty-five minutes later Sasha had entered every detail for the cake for the Campos-Fletcher nuptials into the desktop. Nicole had chosen a romantic look of pale pink hearts and flowers on tri-level stands, positioned at six, twelve and nineteen inches in height. Each cake, eight, ten and twelve inches in diameter, would serve at least one hundred guests. It took Nicole longer to select the cake, and eventually she decided on red velvet and carrot, both with cream-cheese fillings, and a classic white with confetti sprinkles.

Sasha quoted a price and the attorney handed her a credit card, and then gave her the address where she and Fletcher were living together. She was certain the wedding guests would be surprised to find the new flavor combinations under the delicate flowers and buttercream and royal icings.

There had been a time when she'd baked cakes exclusively for weddings, baby and bridal showers, anniversary and retirement dinners. Most of her clients wanted over-the-top creations to outdo one another. Sasha walked Nicole to the door before returning to the kitchen, where she checked her inventory for what she needed to make the cake. Although she liked baking muffins, cookies and bread, it was creating theme cakes that proved both most challenging and most rewarding. She returned to the shop's office to email several cooking schools to solicit a possible apprentice to assist now that her workload had increased.

It was after ten on a Friday night when Sasha sat on the front porch with Georgina, listening to her friend pour her heart out about wanting to open her own business without incurring her parents' wrath. They were expecting her to take over managing the department store once they retired.

"I sort of dropped a hint the other day and my mother went ballistic, telling me that I'm ungrateful, and that she and my father have sacrificed everything to keep the store afloat when they've had to compete with some of the larger department stores that went up on the interstate."

"Did you say anything about opening a shop in The Falls?"

Georgina shook her head and closed her eyes. "No, because knowing my father, he probably would tell the landlord not to rent it to me. Don't forget the Powell name goes a long way here in Wickham Falls."

Sasha nodded. Georgina's father could trace his ancestry back to the early seventeenth century, when they sailed from Wales for the Colonies. They'd started out as pig and sheep farmers and as merchants following the Civil War, when they opened a blacksmith shop and then a feed store and general store.

"Have you thought about setting up a shop in another town?" she asked.

Georgina gave Sasha an incredulous stare. "Did you when you opened your bakeshop?"

Sasha wanted to tell Georgina their conversation had nothing to do with her. "No."

"Why, Sasha?"

"I only asked because you may have to deal with interference from your parents. Meanwhile, there's just me and Mama, who was 100 percent behind me when I told her about my plans. But if you're looking to challenge your parents to prove your independence, then do it."

A silence ensued until Georgina said, "You're right about me wanting to be emancipated. I'm thirty-two

years old and I've never left home. I can't find and keep
a steady boyfriend once they discover I'm still living
with my parents. One guy even told me that I was a child
trapped in a woman's body."

Sasha grimaced. The remark may have been cruel,
but she had to admit the man wasn't that far from the
truth. At her age, Georgina needed to demonstrate a
modicum of independence or she would spend the rest
of her life either resenting her parents or blaming herself
for not following her dreams. However, Sasha realized
it wasn't easy to find enough strength to go through
with changing one's life.

"What would you do if you were in my situation,
Sasha?"

"Do you have your own money?" Georgina nodded.
"The first thing I'd do is move out. Let them get used
to not seeing you except when you come to the store."

Running a hand over her hair, Georgina tucked a
wayward curl that had escaped the elastic band behind
her right ear. "You're right." She paused. "Maybe I'll
rent a place in Mineral Springs until I decide whether
I want to live there permanently or move back to The
Falls."

"That sounds like the beginning of a plan."

Sasha wondered if Georgina was serious about moving out of the house where she'd spent her entire life,
or if saying it aloud made it sound more convincing.
When most graduating seniors were planning the next
phase of their lives to either enlist in the military, enroll
in college, marry their high school sweethearts or seek
employment outside of The Falls, Georgina had known
exactly what she'd planned to do—work in Powell's Department Store. She knew Georgina's parents were dev-

astated when their eldest son died from meningitis at the age of thirteen, which shifted the future responsibility of running the store to his younger sister.

Georgina stood. "I've taken up enough of your time talking about my crazy life."

Sasha rose to her feet and hugged her friend. "Anytime you need someone to talk to, just let me know." She smiled. "This too shall pass." She waited until Georgina drove away before going into the house and locking the door. Charlotte hadn't wanted her to move so far away, but there was nothing she could do or say to make her stay. She still remembered her father saying, *If she wants to leave, then let her go. My boys left, so why not my daughter?*

She never regretted leaving The Falls, marrying and divorcing Grant or returning home. It was as if her life had come full circle, and in doing so Sasha was content with her new life. She didn't have all the answers for Georgina except to offer moral support. And when she looked back, Sasha realized she had been a lot stronger at eighteen than her friend was now at thirty-two.

The following night was the chamber dinner dance, and because Sasha had an appointment with the local salon to have her hair trimmed Saturday afternoon, Charlotte had volunteered to work until closing. Earlier in the week, Dwight had sent her a text indicating he would pick her up at seven. The chamber had chosen to hold the event at the newly constructed barn behind the Wolf Den rather than in the ballroom at their favorite hotel off the interstate.

It had taken her a while to select a dress for the semiformal affair among the ones she'd shipped back from Nashville. Those she'd worn when attending award ceremonies or social events with Grant she had donated to an organization set up to provide prom dresses to girls from needy families, and those with price tags she'd kept.

Sasha had admitted to Dwight that she was a country girl at heart, preferring going barefoot to wearing shoes. The only time she'd really dressed up was for prom, when Charlotte had driven her to a Charleston boutique where she could find a dress that had not come off the rack. She'd wanted only the best for her daughter's big night.

Now she was going to have another big night when she attended the fund-raiser as Dr. Dwight Adams's date. Sasha had been so busy during the week she hadn't had much time to think about her friend. And she'd come to think of him as her friend because she was pragmatic enough to know that friendship would be all they would ever share, no matter how much she wished for it to be otherwise.

Dwight knew he was gawking when Sasha opened the door. Like a butterfly emerging from its cocoon, she'd morphed into someone he wouldn't have recognized if it hadn't been for her hair and eye color. Smoky-brown shadow on her lids and red-gold waves floating around her face held him spellbound. How, he thought, could she have suggested that he did not find her attractive? But whether fresh-faced without a hint of makeup, or now wearing eye shadow, tangerine-orange lipstick, a hint of blush and the curls that were now loose waves, Dwight had been truthful when he told Sasha it wasn't about her looks but how they related to each other.

"You look incredible!"

The compliment had slipped out unbidden. The chocolate-brown off-the-shoulder dress with a revealing necklace was nipped at the waist and flowed out around her legs, drawing attention to Sasha's tall, slender body. His gaze traveled downward to a pair of brown, silk-covered strappy stilettos that put her close to his height of six foot two.

Smiling, Sasha held her arms out at her sides. "So, do I pass inspection, Major Adams?"

His smile was dazzling. "You're beyond anything I could've imagined, and I hope I don't have to rough up a few guys crazy enough to try to come on to my woman tonight."

Sasha's smile faded quickly. "Am I your woman, Dwight? I thought we were friends."

He took her hands, bringing them to his mouth and gently kissing the knuckles. "That, too. But, for the benefit of others, tonight you're my woman."

Sasha felt a chill sweep over her body despite the warmth of the late-spring night. Dwight didn't know how much she'd wanted to be his woman, girlfriend and lover if only to banish the pain she'd endured when married. But whenever she thought about a possible intimate relationship with Dwight, she did not want him to believe that she was using him to make up for what she hadn't had with Grant. Images of the many times when she'd argued with Grant only hours before they were scheduled to appear in public together came to mind and she shook her head as if to banish them.

Sasha forced a smile she didn't quite feel. She picked up the cashmere-and-silk shawl and small beaded evening bag off the table near the door. "I know it now." What she had to do was believe it. "I'm ready." And she was. Ready to enjoy whatever the night offered and her time with a man she was falling for when she'd told herself over and over they could not have a relationship.

Dwight rested his hand on the small of her back, leading her to where he'd parked his vehicle. He opened the passenger-side door and held her elbow until she was seated. She buckled her seat belt and looked out the windshield as Dwight slipped in behind the wheel rather than have him see her lusting after him.

When she'd opened the door, she was able to take in everything about his appearance in one sweeping glance, committing it to memory: the stark white dress shirt with monogrammed cuff links, charcoal-gray silk tie under the spread collar, tailored suit pants and highly shined imported slip-ons. She could avoid looking at him but there was no way she could dismiss his warmth or the sensual masculine cologne that was the perfect complement to his body's natural pheromones.

Sasha realized she was no different than some of the women in her Nashville social circle whenever they'd gossiped to each other about being horny and wanting to sleep with men other than their husbands. There had come a time when she'd believed some of them had slept with her husband once she moved out of their bedroom. Sasha hadn't missed the sly and surreptitious looks he'd exchanged with one woman, and it wasn't until their divorce was finalized that Sasha's suspicions were confirmed when they were seen coupled up together in public.

Dwight rested his right arm over the back of her seat. "Are you okay, sweetie?"

"Yes."

"You're rather quiet tonight."

"I was just thinking about a few things."

"Do those things have anything to do with *us*?" he asked.

"Some of them."

"Do you want to talk about *them*?"

Sasha knew what she was about to tell Dwight would either bring them closer together or apart. "Do you recall when I told you I didn't want to talk about my ex?"

"I do."

"Well, what I'm about to tell you I've only told one other person."

"Your mother?"

Sasha breathed out an audible sigh as she gathered the strength to reveal to Dwight what she'd sworn never to repeat. She'd told her mother because she had a right to know why she'd come back to Wickham Falls to start up a business, and why she wasn't the same as when she'd returned for the first time in seven years for her father's funeral.

She really didn't want to disclose the circumstances surrounding what people thought of as a fairy-tale marriage between the cowboy and the redhead. But if she hoped to have an uncomplicated relationship with Dwight, then she wanted him to understand her reaction to certain scenarios.

"Yes."

Dwight gave her a quick glance. "Why tell me, Sasha?"

"Because of how I feel about you."

He slowed the Jeep to less than ten miles as he approached the railroad crossing and then, after looking in both directions, drove over the tracks. "And that is?"

Sasha wanted to tell Dwight he wasn't making it easy for her to tell him that she wanted to be more than friends. "I like you, Dwight." Why, she chided, did she sound like an adolescent girl talking to a boy she had a crush on?

He smiled, the dimple creasing his cheek. "That goes for both of us, because I like you, too, Sasha."

"I mean I really like you."

"Are you trying to say you want us to be more than just friends? That we could be friends with benefits?"

The seconds ticked until it became a full minute. *Answer the man*, her inner voice taunted her. "Yes."

Dwight dropped his arm and met her eyes briefly in the glow coming from the dashboard. He wondered what it had taken for her to admit she wanted to engage in a physical relationship. He wasn't immune to Sasha. It was quite the contrary. There were nights when he woke up with an erection and in a cold sweat after he'd dreamed of making love with her. As a virile man in his prime, he'd always had a healthy libido, but since Kiera had come to live with him, he'd elected to remain celibate. He'd never slept with a woman in his home even before becoming a full-time father, preferring instead to entertain women at the lake house. And now that Kiera accompanied him for their fishing outings, even the lake house was off-limits for his clandestine liaisons.

"Do you really believe that I'm that immune to you, Sasha? We're both consenting adults, so sleeping together shouldn't present a problem except that…" His words trailed off.

Sasha placed her hand over his gripping the wheel. "Except that it would complicate everything if we decide to break up," she said, finishing his statement.

"Yes."

"But didn't you say we are adults?"

He nodded. "Yes, I did."

"Then as adults we should not have to resort to childish tantrums or play head games where we try to make each other's life miserable because we feel we've been wronged."

"That sounds good."

"You don't believe me, do you?"

Dwight came to a stop at the four-way intersection and waited for traffic to slow enough so he could drive across to the road leading to the Den. "I believe you, sweetie." And he did. Not only did he believe Sasha, but he also appreciated her candor. He'd dealt with women closer to his age than Sasha's and some of them made a habit of being evasive in the belief they were being mysterious, and it was a trait that annoyed him. "And you don't have to tell me about your ex-husband because I've made it a practice not to discuss Kiera's mother with women I go out with."

"Beginning now, talking about exes is prohibited," Sasha said in a quiet voice.

Dwight reversed their hands, his thumb caressing the silken skin and delicate bones on hers. He refused to talk about or bad-mouth Adrienne because he had always respected her as Kiera's mother. His daughter was the best thing to come out of their marriage, and that was something he'd never regretted.

He knew eventually he would be open to listening to Sasha talk about her ex, only because he was aware that she needed to unburden herself to someone other than her mother. However, he didn't want to become a substitute or a catharsis for her to exorcise her ex.

It had taken Dwight years to come to forgive Adrienne for her duplicity. He'd forgiven her for reversing her position to live in The Falls once he'd set up his practice, but what took much longer for him to accept was her admission that she'd slept with another man with whom she had attended college both while they were engaged and during their marriage.

He didn't want to speculate as to why Sasha's marriage hadn't survived the glare of the spotlight as one half of a very public couple. However, he knew what he felt and was beginning to feel about her had nothing to do with her past fame as the go-to pastry chef for celebrities but how she related to him and his family.

Dwight had made up a litany of excuses as to why he couldn't afford to become *that* involved with Sasha and he knew each one rang hollow. He'd told himself that he didn't want to date a woman in the same hometown as his, yet he'd taken Sasha with him to the Den for Military Monday and now she was his date for a local fund-raiser. He'd called her his woman, and to Dwight that meant she was very special—someone he wanted to see exclusively and protect.

He'd conjured up a few roadblocks, the first being she looked nothing like the women he'd dated in the past, but all of them had dissipated like a puff of smoke the first time she came to his home with her mother. Dwight found everything about Sasha refreshing, from her admission that she was just a country girl who'd left the glare of the spotlight in Music City to return to The Falls, and her resolute motivation to make her bakeshop viable.

And then there was Kiera. Any woman he dated had to accept his daughter because they were a package deal, and unknowingly Sasha had passed that test. Kiera tended to dominate their dinner table conversations when she could not stop talking about her boss and the fact that she was seriously thinking of going to culinary school to become a professional chef. When she'd mentioned her intentions to Sasha, the pastry chef told her she would bring her on as an apprentice to teach her the ins and outs of designing cakes. Sasha had also promised Kiera that she could begin giving her lessons in the summer during the days when the shop was closed, which had the teenager so excited she could hardly get the words out coherently.

Dwight was proud of the changes he saw in Kiera. She'd stopped complaining that she had nothing to do because she loved her part-time job at the bakeshop, while she'd managed to maintain her honor student status. Her friendship with the neighbor's daughter now included a few other girls in the neighborhood.

"What if we let things unfold naturally and see where it leads us?"

"I like that," Sasha said, smiling.

Sasha walked into the barn holding on to Dwight's arm over his suit jacket, not seeing the curious looks directed at them when she glanced around the building that was both rustic and ethereal. Strings of tiny white bulbs and gaslight-inspired chandeliers evoked a bygone era. Round tables, with seating for six, were covered with white tablecloths. Colorful Depression glasses and flatware with ornate handles were also in keeping with the designated time period. Her attention was drawn to a mahogany bar, reminiscent of those in old saloons, where several men had gathered to order their favorite libation. She estimated the barn could easily accommodate seventy-five to ninety for a catered event.

The woman checking their names off on a printout smiled up at Dwight. "Dr. Adams, you and your date are assigned to table four."

He returned her smile. "Thank you, Mrs. Nicholls."

"What are you thinking?" Dwight asked in Sasha's ear when they were out of earshot of the woman.

"This is the perfect place to hold a wedding or even prom, without the alcohol, of course."

"I think that's what the Gibsons were thinking about when they put up this place. Aiden said he had a long talk with his uncle about folks having to leave The Falls to have their weddings."

Sasha hadn't been back long enough to know who'd planned their wedding. The exception was Nicole Campos and Fletcher Austen, who'd arranged to host their nuptials at their home. "The Gibsons are very resourceful because they're able to provide the venue, food and alcoholic drinks."

The word *alcohol* was barely off her tongue when a waiter approached with a tray of flutes with a pale bubbly wine. "Champagne, miss?"

She smiled. "Yes, please."

Dwight took the flute from the man and handed it to Sasha before taking one for himself. He touched his glass to hers. "Here's to new beginnings."

"To a new beginning," she repeated in a soft whisper. Sasha took a sip of the wine. It was delicious.

White-jacketed waitstaff circulated with trays of canapés and hors d'oeuvres, while a young woman dressed in chef whites manned a carving station. It was Sasha's first time attending a Wickham Falls soiree, and it was

apparent it was on par with some of those she'd attended
and catered. Over the years she'd heard people complain
that The Falls was stuck in time, but Sasha never felt that
way because the residents had always looked out for one
another. They came together when someone lost their job
or a family member. The church's outreach did their part
soliciting donations of food and clothes for the neediest
families. And many of the businesses had survived despite the ups and downs of the nation's economy because
their motto was: live local, shop local. Members of the
town council were aware of their residents' resistance to
fast-food and chain stores and consistently voted down
their requests to build in The Falls.

Dwight's free arm went around her waist, pulling
her closer to his side. "Do you want anything from the
carving station?"

Sasha smiled up at him. She was beginning to feel
the effects of the champagne. "Yes. I'll come with you."

She spent the remainder of the cocktail hour sam-
pling prawns with an Asian-inspired dipping sauce, filo
tartlets with spicy cilantro shrimp, mint-marinated lamb
kebabs with a tahini-and-honey dip, and ginger orange
pork skewers. Sasha was impressed with the gourmet
selections prepared by cooks who were better known
for barbecuing, grilling and smoking meat.

Within minutes of Dwight excusing himself to speak
to the mayor, Sasha saw Georgina walk in. Her friend
was resplendent in a black body-hugging halter dress
and her hair tucked into a twist behind her left ear.
"You look fabulous," Sasha said, as she and Georgina
exchanged air-kisses.

"That goes double for you, Sasha. I love your dress
and hair."

"Thanks. Do you always attend this fund-raiser?"

Georgina shook her head. "No. This is my first time. My dad always comes alone, because Mom hates these gatherings. He decided to give me his ticket because he claims it's time I start to represent the business. And before you ask, I still haven't said anything to them about moving out. I want to find a place and sign a lease before I tell them."

Sasha had no intention of offering Georgina any more advice about her family dilemma. After all, blood was thicker than water, and she did not want to be labeled an interloper. "Do you know who you are sitting with?"

"Not yet. I'll be at the table with folks who don't have escorts. By the way, did you come with anyone?" Georgina asked.

Sasha glanced over at her date, who was talking to the mayor and several members of the town council. "Dwight Adams."

Georgina's jaw dropped. "You are dating Dr. Adams?"

She curbed the urge to laugh at Georgina's shocked expression. "Yes. Why do you look so surprised?" It was obvious her friend hadn't heard that she and Dwight were together at the Wolf Den for Military Monday. Sasha did not want to believe her former classmate's life was so insular that she hadn't been aware of the goings-on outside the department store.

"Did you know he's one of The Falls' most eligible bachelors? Of which we have very few," Georgina added. "And he can't seem to take his eyes off you."

Sasha glanced over her shoulder to find Dwight staring at her. A hint of a smile tilted the corners of his mouth and she returned it with one of her own. Overhead light glinted off the silver in his cropped hair, and the contrast between the shimmering strands and his mahogany complexion added to his overall masculine beauty.

She shifted her attention to Georgina, who had a strange look on her face. "What's the matter?"

"You and Dr. Adams, Sasha."

"What about us?"

Georgina was preempted from answering when Langston Cooper joined them. "Good evening, lovely ladies," he drawled, extending a glass filled with an amber liquid in their direction.

"Hello, Langston," Sasha and Georgina chorused in unison.

Langston took a sip of his cocktail, staring at Georgina over the rim of the old-fashioned glass. "I like what the Gibsons have set up here."

"We should've had something like this when we had prom," Sasha said.

"Word," Georgina drawled. "We had the prom from hell when the hotel had a power outage and their generator malfunctioned and everyone started yelling about wanting a refund."

Sasha and Georgina were entertaining Langston with the events following their aborted prom when she detected the fragrance of a familiar men's cologne; she turned to find Dwight standing a short distance away, seemingly waiting before interrupting their animated conversation. Excusing herself, she approached him.

Dwight took her hand, threading their fingers together. "They want us to take our seats because they're going to begin serving dinner."

She saw waiters filling water glasses, while a hostess

was directing guests to their respective tables. Sasha ignored the stares of those following her and Dwight as he escorted her to their table. It was the second time they were seen in public together and she surmised they were curious not only why she had returned to The Falls, but also why Dwight had attended the annual fund-raiser with her rather than his mother.

Dwight pulled out a chair, seated her, and then leaned over and pressed a kiss on her hair. Those sitting at their table, and others nearby, did not miss the tender intimate gesture of affection or Sasha's smile or when she covered the hand resting on her shoulder.

Chapter Eight

Sasha felt the strong, steady beating of Dwight's heart against her breasts as they danced the last dance of the night when the DJ played a slower love song after several upbeat tunes. She'd discovered something else about the man holding her close: he liked to slow dance.

A sumptuous sit-down dinner followed the cock-tail hour with dining choices of excellently prepared chicken, grilled bourbon salmon and rib-eye steak. As a chef, Sasha gave the Gibsons a top grade for taste and presentation.

"Did you enjoy your first chamber fund-raiser?" Dwight said, his mouth pressed to her ear.

"Yes. However, they could've done away with the long, windy speeches from the officers of the chamber, otherwise it would've been perfect." The waitstaff had been instructed not to serve the next course until after everyone stopped speaking.

Dwight's arm tightened around her waist as he spun her around and around. "They've been told for years to cut down on the number of speeches, but it looks as if everyone wants their fifteen minutes of fame at the expense of folks enjoying their dinner."

"I still enjoyed it."

"I enjoyed you more."

Sasha did not have a comeback because she believed she'd said too much during the drive over. She didn't want Dwight to see her as a desperate divorcée prowling for her next husband.

Sasha waited until she was seated and belted into the Jeep and Dwight had maneuvered out of the parking area to say, "I want to apologize."

He gave her a sidelong glance. "What for?"

"For being overly aggressive when I told you I wanted more than friendship when you'd already established that wasn't what you wanted."

Dwight stared straight ahead as he concentrated on driving. The silence inside the vehicle swelled to deafening proportions. "There's nothing to apologize for, Sasha. I said what I did because I didn't want you to know that I'd met a woman that had me rethinking the excuses why I didn't want to get involved in a serious relationship. But there was something about you that proved me wrong. I'd promised myself that I would never date another woman from The Falls, and that I couldn't commit to any permanence until Kiera left for college. And more importantly, a woman would have to accept that my daughter comes first in my life."

"And she should be first, Dwight. If I'd had a child,

then my priority would have to be my son or daughter." A beat passed before Sasha asked, "What did I do to make you change your mind?"

He smiled. "Nothing. Just don't change from being that unpretentious redheaded, freckle-faced country girl who makes incredible desserts and prefers going barefoot to wearing shoes."

"So, you like my freckles?"

"Every single one of them. Especially those on your cheeks."

Sasha's bubbly laugh bounced off the roof of the vehicle. "There was a time when I hated my freckles because kids used to tease me saying I had dirt on my face and other epithets referring to flies that I won't repeat."

"Kids can be cruel."

"And they grow up to become cruel adults."

Dwight registered a slight hardness in Sasha's tone, and he wondered if she was referring to her ex-husband. Was the smiling face of the hometown girl splashed across the glossy pages of entertainment magazines all for show? Locals couldn't stop talking about her because she'd married an A-list recording artist and was a celebrity chef to the rich and famous. The showplace mansion she shared with her husband had been featured in many of the popular architectural magazines. She had it all, and then she walked away from it all, refusing to answer reporters' questions. She subsequently disappeared from the public until she returned to where her ancestors had put down roots many generations ago.

He arrived at Sasha's house and walked her to the door, not wanting the night to end although they would see each other the next day for Sunday dinner. Dwight waited for her to unlock and open the door to cradle her face in his hands. Slowly, deliberately, he lowered his head and kissed her until her lips parted under his. He reluctantly ended the kiss. "Good night, sweets."

Sasha smiled. "Good night. And thank you for a wonderful evening."

"Thank you for being the perfect date. I'll see you tomorrow for Sunday dinner."

"Don't forget to bring your appetite."

"I won't."

Dwight waited until Sasha went inside before getting back into the Jeep. He'd wanted to tell Sasha that he was tired of lying—to her and himself. He'd made up so many excuses as to why he didn't want to get involved with her that he hadn't been able to come up with another one. Then there was the excuse that his daughter worked for her, and he didn't want to jeopardize Kiera's future employment if he and Sasha split up. And last was his vow never to date another woman from Wickham Falls.

Dwight felt as if his life was under a microscope the first time Adrienne Wheeler had agreed to go out with him. All the high school boys wanted to date her, and the girls wanted to be her. After they were spotted together at the movies, a collective groan went out through The Falls from guys who'd believed they still had a chance with the flirtatious young coed who'd been blessed with beauty *and* brains.

He recalled the plans they'd made for their futures, both agreeing to becoming engaged before heading off to college. Dwight married Adrienne within days of her college graduation. They'd wanted to wait until after he finished dental school to start a family, but it was as if nature had conspired against them, because despite taking precautions, Adrienne informed him she was pregnant. Becoming parents signaled a change in what had been an uncomplicated passionate relationship. Adrienne complained incessantly that she felt as if she was slowly dying in The Falls and issued veiled hints that it wasn't where she'd wanted to live her entire life like her parents and grandparents before her.

He'd believed he could give Adrienne what she wanted and needed to ensure a happy marriage; however, it wasn't until he saw her with her new husband that he had come to the realization that she truly loved her second husband in a way she could never love her first. Not only did Adrienne appear content with her life, but Dwight was happy for her; he'd made it easy for her to survive her second marriage by assuming full custody of their daughter.

Dwight whistled a nameless tune as he headed home. He'd deliberately avoided encountering Sasha for weeks until she came to his home for Sunday dinner. That encounter changed everything when he'd invited her to accompany him to the Den for Military Monday. He thought of her as a breath of fresh air with her easygoing personality and distinctive high-pitched laugh. What he really liked about her was that what you saw was what you got. There was no pretense or hint that she was anything other than what she'd professed: a country girl down to the marrow in her bones.

Charlotte opened the door and Dwight handed her a large box wrapped in silver paper and black velvet ribbon. "A little something for the house." Pinpoints of red dotted her pale cheeks, and it was obvious Sasha's mother hadn't counted on his bringing anything. "You can't expect us to bring dessert, especially not when Sasha's a pastry chef."

"I heard my name."

Dwight stared over Charlotte's head, his eyes briefly meeting Sasha's. Her transformation was startling from the woman wearing haute couture the night before to one in a seafoam-green surplice, cropped black slacks and matching ballet-type shoes. "I was telling your mother that there's no way we were going to attempt to make dessert and embarrass ourselves."

Charlotte turned and handed Sasha the gift. "Please take this." She peered around Dwight. "Where's Victoria and Kiera?"

"We'd intended to all come together, but they said they had to make a stop. They should be here shortly."

"I'm forgetting my manners. Please come in and rest yourself. As soon as your family gets here, we can sit down to eat. In the meanwhile, can I get you something to drink?"

"No, thanks," Dwight said, as he followed Charlotte into the enclosed front porch and sat on an armchair.

Stretching out his legs, Dwight closed his eyes and crossed his feet at the ankles. A satisfying peace swept over him when he thought about the path his life had taken since his last visit to New York City. He'd loaded up the rental car with Kiera's clothes, while she said her goodbyes to her mother, driving nonstop to Wickham Falls. His daughter was unusually quiet during the trip, and he'd suspected she was experiencing mixed emotions about leaving a city where she'd attended school and spent time with her friends. Kiera, like Adrienne, was a social butterfly, and she literally came alive in the presence of others. He'd suspected the confrontation between his daughter and her stepfather must have been quite volatile if she'd agreed to live with him in a town she referred to as lame with nothing to do.

Dwight had to remind her that she'd learned to drive in The Falls, and once she completed her junior year and passed her driver's test, he would get her a car. His promise had been the deal breaker. He'd taken her out in the Jeep, but Kiera claimed she preferred driving her grandmother's compact.

He'd voiced his concern to Victoria after Kiera was enrolled at the high school when she came home sullen and monosyllabic. Dwight knew she missed her mother, although he doubted whether she would admit it, *and* her friends. And it wasn't until she began working at Sasha's Sweet Shoppe that she'd become more animated, and talked nonstop about how she was able to convince the bakeshop's regular customers to order the day's special, or another pastry they were unfamiliar with.

His cell phone chimed a familiar ringtone, and he removed it from the pocket of his slacks. "Hello, Adrienne."

"Why didn't you tell me my daughter wants to be a cook?"

Dwight rolled his eyes upward. He knew by his ex's strident tone that the conversation was going to be less than friendly. "I didn't have to tell you if she told you."

"She can't be a cook!"

"She wants to be a chef, and that's very different from being a cook."

"I don't need you to tell me the difference, Dwight! You know damn well what I mean."

He sat straight. It wasn't until they were separated

that he had become aware of how argumentative Adrienne could be. It was as if she thrived on being confrontational. "If you're looking for a fight today, then I don't intend to verbally spar with you. Kiera has made up her mind as to what she wants as a career choice, and we agreed a long time ago that I would pay for her college, which lets you off the hook monetarily for any decision she makes."

"I thought she wanted to be a doctor."

"You want her to be a doctor, while I'm open to whatever she chooses to be."

"She told me she wanted to be a doctor until you started sniffing around that Manning girl's skirts."

A muscle twitched in Dwight's jaw when he clenched his teeth. "What did you say?"

"Don't worry, Kiera didn't tell me about you and Sasha Manning because lately she's been like a deafmute whenever I ask about you. Although all the Wheelers have left The Falls, I still have a few friends there who keep me up on the latest news."

The Wheelers had begun a steady exodus over the decades from Wickham Falls, until even Kiera's distant cousins were gone. "If you're so concerned about what's going on here, then you should've never left. Goodbye," Dwight said, abruptly ending the call. He knew if it hadn't been for Kiera, he would've cut off all communication with Adrienne. He was aware she was upset because their daughter had refused to give her any information on his private life, which had him totally confused when her focus should've been on her husband. The few encounters he'd had with the man over the years had been congenial once Dwight set the ground rules for how he wanted him, as a stepfather, to relate to Kiera. He'd been forthcoming when he warned Omar Johnson never to lay a hand on Kiera or there would be hell to pay.

At the time, Dwight didn't know what had transpired between Omar and Kiera until she finally told him that she'd overheard her stepfather tell someone he hated his wife's daughter and he couldn't wait to get rid of her, yet knew there was no way Dwight would go along with Adrienne sending their daughter to boarding school to save her marriage, because it had been apparent that Kiera wasn't the most important person in her life.

Generally, he ignored Adrienne and didn't let her get under his skin, but today was different, because it involved Sasha. And because Kiera refused to talk to her mother about him, Adrienne had contacted locals who'd told her what she wanted to know about his personal life. What he had never been able to wrap his head around was Adrienne's desire to know about the women he dated when she had recently celebrated her twelfth wedding anniversary with a man who obviously adored her.

Dwight detected movement out of the side of his eye and stood up. Sasha had come into the room without making a sound. "How much did you hear?" he asked her, not knowing how long she had been standing there.

Sasha saw Dwight's thunderous expression and wondered what had set him off. "What are you talking about?"

"Were you eavesdropping on my telephone conversation?"

"No!" The single word exploded from her mouth, as she struggled to control her temper. "And I don't appreciate you implying that I'm a sneak."

Dwight ran a hand over his face and then took a step and cradled her against his chest. "I'm sorry, babe. I had no right to take out my frustrations on you."

Wrapping her arms around his waist, Sasha leaned back and looked up at him. "I'll forgive you this time but try not to let it happen again." Her words, though spoken quietly, held a thread of hardness that indicated she was serious. She'd experienced enough of Grant taking his frustrations out on her to last her a lifetime. He'd expected every song he released to reach number one on the country chart. As the ultimate narcissist, he thought earning the number two spot made him a loser.

Dwight brushed his mouth over hers. "I promise, it won't happen again."

Her annoyance vanished with his promise and chaste kiss. "I came to get you because I need you to be my taste tester."

"Can you give me a hint what I'll be eating?"

"You won't be eating but drinking. I've been experimenting with mocktails. I have dozens of photos of cakes, along with signed releases from former celebrity clients, filed away because I plan to publish a coffee-table book featuring desserts and accompanying drinks."

Sasha looped her arm through Dwight's and led him through the living and dining rooms, where warming dishes lined a buffet table. Her mother had decided to serve a buffet dinner in lieu of a sit-down because the dining room table, unlike the Adamses', wasn't large enough to accommodate the dishes she'd prepared for her guests.

"Something really smells good," Dwight remarked.

Sasha smiled. "My mother is an incredible cook."

"Is she the reason you went to culinary school?"

"Yes and no. I'll tell you about that at another time."

Charlotte glanced up from slicing ingredients for a mixed citrus salad. "I suppose Natasha wants you to…" Her words trailed off when the doorbell chimed throughout the house. She set down a knife. "You kids stay here. I'll get the door."

Sasha rested her hand on Dwight's back, feeling the warmth of his body through his shirt. "I can't remember the last time I've seen my mother this excited to have company. Now that my brothers aren't stationed stateside, she doesn't get to see her grandchildren as much as she would like."

"Where are they stationed?" Dwight asked.

"Philip lives in Germany and Stephen was recently transferred to Guam."

"Has she been putting pressure on you to give her a grandchild that lives closer to home?"

She didn't want to tell Dwight that when she was married her mother had asked her constantly when she was going to have a baby, and she'd told Charlotte she wasn't ready to start a family, that she'd had plenty of time before her biological clock began winding down. And she still had time. At thirty-two, she estimated she had at least three or even four years before being considered high risk, although women were having their first child well into their forties.

"No," Sasha replied. "Mama knows this is not the right time for me to have a baby." She picked up a martini glass with tiny purple flower petals floating atop pale green sparkling liquid and handed it to Dwight. "I want and need your honest opinion," she said, as Dwight put the glass to his mouth. Sasha hadn't realized she'd been holding her breath until she felt a band of tightness constrict her chest. "What? What?" she repeated after he'd taken a deep swallow.

Instead of answering Sasha, Dwight drained the glass. "It's delicious. How did you make it?"

Sasha's smile was dazzling. "You really like it?"

"I did say it was delicious. So yes, I really, really like it."

"What did you taste, Dwight?"

"Lime, a hint of mint, tonic water and something sweet to offset the acidity of the citrus."

"It's lavender. I use it in cakes and frostings."

Dwight set the glass on the countertop. "I never would've guessed that."

"What wouldn't you have guessed?"

Sasha turned to find Victoria and Kiera smiling at them. Kiera cradled a bouquet of fresh roses in every conceivable hue nestled in baby's breath, and wrapped in cellophane, while Victoria held a shopping bag. "Oh, my word. The roses are beautiful."

"Grammie had to drive to Mineral Springs to get them, because the florist here didn't get his shipment of flowers for the week," Kiera volunteered.

Victoria handed Sasha the bag. "This is a little something for the house."

Sasha unwrapped the box and opened it to find an exquisite Waterford vase. It was more than a little something, but to refuse the gift would demonstrate ungratefulness. Folks in the South were raised never to come to someone's home empty-handed.

"Thank you. Mama and I really appreciate your generous gift."

Victoria waved her hand. "I should be the one thanking you for spoiling us when Kiera comes home every night with dessert." She spied the martini glasses and a pitcher filled with the fizzy green liquid. "That really looks exotic."

"It's a take on a green dragon without the alcohol. I wanted to make something Kiera can also drink."

Kiera, who'd busied herself removing the cellophane from the flowers and arranging them in the vase, glanced over her shoulder. "Daddy told me he would disown me if I was caught drinking before I reach the legal age."

"That would be one time when I would side with your father," Victoria said, as she gave her granddaughter a long, penetrating stare.

Kiera lowered her eyes and went back to concentrating on the floral arrangement, and Sasha knew the young girl probably counted on her grandmother as an ally to support her when she wanted something from Dwight. But apparently underage drinking was an issue that was not debatable.

Charlotte removed her apron and picked up the bowl with the salad. "Now that everyone's here, we can go into the dining room to eat. Tonight's menu celebrates the Big Easy with dishes I learned from my grandmother who grew up in New Orleans before she married Granddaddy and moved to The Falls."

Dwight waited until everyone had served themselves before he picked up a bowl and filled it with chicken-andouille gumbo and topped the steaming soup with long-grain cooked rice. He knew from the first spoonful where Sasha had inherited her cooking skills. He ate sparingly because he wanted to sample every dish:

shrimp étouffée, red beans and rice, stuffed pork chops with creole seasoning and jalapeño corn bread. Sasha's mocktail was the perfect complement to offset the incredibly delicious rich and spicy dishes. And he'd discovered he wasn't the only one going back for second helpings.

Everything was perfect from the floral arrangement in the crystal vase, to the delicious iciness of the virgin cocktail, prepared food and the company. It was the second time the Mannings and Adamses had gathered for Sunday dinner, and for Dwight, it felt as if they were truly family. Conversations segued from world and national politics to professional sports teams' playoffs and championship games, and the upcoming events at Kiera's school. She revealed she'd joined a committee to plan events for the following year's graduation. She said students in the junior class were currently involved in planning car washes and bowling fund-raisers to offset the cost of their senior trip.

"Has the committee decided where they want to go for their senior trip?" Sasha asked Kiera.

"The choices are New York, Philadelphia and DC. Someone mentioned taking a three- or four-day cruise, but most kids said their parents can't afford prom and a cruise."

"That is a lot of financial responsibility for parents," Dwight admitted. It wouldn't be a hardship for him to pay for prom and a cruise, but he couldn't say the same for families that weren't as affluent as his.

"This is when some of the civic organizations ought to step up and support our kids," Victoria said. "Dwight, I'm certain the chamber takes in enough with dues and their various fund-raisers throughout the year to at least underwrite the cost of prom, which would provide some monetary relief for parents paying for the senior trip."

"The Gibsons' donation to prom could be their new catering venue, which would put quite a dent in the cost of the tickets," Sasha added. She saw four pairs of eyes staring at her. "Did I say something wrong?"

"No, you didn't," Victoria replied. "In fact, that's a wonderful idea. It's about time the businesses in The Falls support our kids expressly when they want us to shop locally."

"Which we definitely do," Charlotte said in agreement. "I can't remember the last time I went to Mineral Springs or even Beckley for something I could get here."

Victoria touched her napkin to her mouth. "That does it. Charlotte, when you have some spare time I want you to help me get some of the ladies together. We need to spearhead a campaign to help our graduating seniors defray some of the cost of prom and their senior trip. Of course, it's too late for this graduating class, so it would have to be for next year."

Dwight leaned back in his chair, winking at Charlotte. "I want to warn you that my mother is as tenacious as a pit bull once she gets the proverbial bee in her bonnet. She will not stop until she forces someone to submit to her will."

Charlotte smiled. "If that's the case, then she has a sister in crime, because I don't believe in giving up easily." She suddenly sobered. "Being married to a man who couldn't stop beating his gums because everything had to be his way, or no way, prepared me to go the distance."

Rising slightly, Victoria reached across the table and

exchanged a fist bump with Charlotte. "We're going to make an awesome team."

"Grammie, I hope you won't embarrass me," Kiera said.

Dwight looked at his daughter and then his mother. "Did I miss something?"

Victoria lowered her eyes. "No comment."

His eyebrows rose questioningly when his gaze returned to Kiera, who appeared more interested in the food on her plate. "You don't have to tell me. But remember, what doesn't come out in the wash will always come out in the rinse." Dwight knew his mother was his daughter's secret keeper, and he'd come to respect their close bond. However, he trusted Victoria to come to him if she felt a situation would negatively impact her granddaughter.

"And keeping with the theme of the Big Easy, I decided to make bananas Foster for dessert," Sasha said, shattering the uncomfortable silence.

Kiera jumped. "Can I help you make it, Miss Sasha?"

Pushing back her chair, Sasha stood. "Of course."

Dwight rose to his feet. "Mom, you and Miss Charlotte relax while I put away the leftovers."

"Are you sure?" the two older women said in unison.

"Yes, I am sure."

"Natasha will show you where I keep the containers to store the leftovers."

Dwight smiled at Sasha's mother. "Yes, ma'am." Stacking plates and flatware, he carried them into the kitchen, setting them on the countertop. He glanced at Sasha and Kiera as they peeled and sliced bananas, and the single act of shared domesticity rendered him motionless for several seconds. In that instant he realized he'd never witnessed Kiera and Adrienne together in their kitchen. Whenever he went to New York to see his daughter, he always checked into a hotel and met her in the lobby of the high-rise building where she lived with her mother and stepfather. Even when he'd sat down with Adrienne and Omar to discuss Kiera's future, the meeting took place in a restaurant.

Dwight was certain Adrienne loved her daughter, and Kiera her mother, and while he'd accepted some blame that she wasn't able to grow up with mother and father living under the same roof, he'd trusted Adrienne to protect and raise their daughter properly and she had. Not only was Kiera a good student but she appeared to be well-adjusted.

He'd stored the food in the refrigerator and stacked dishes in the dishwasher when Sasha announced she was ready to serve dessert. Sasha ignited the pan with light brown sugar, melted butter, bananas, cinnamon and dark rum. He watched as she carefully spooned the sauce over the bananas until the flame burned out and immediately ladled it over scoops of vanilla ice cream. It was only the second time Dwight had eaten the dessert, but the former could not come close to what Sasha had prepared.

"Did you buy the ice cream from the Village Market?" Victoria asked Sasha. "Because this brand is delicious."

Dwight wanted to ask the same thing. The Falls' supermarket, although smaller than many of the area's supermarkets and warehouse stores, was stocked with everything the residents needed to stock their refrigerators and pantries.

"Natasha makes her own ice cream," Charlotte said,

smiling. "I love her vanilla because she uses the actual beans, but her pistachio is to die for."

Victoria set down her spoon. "Sasha, I know I'm not giving you a lot of notice, but can you make an assortment of desserts for my Ladies Auxiliary meeting this coming Wednesday? Although many of us don't need the extra calories, I'd like you to make enough ice cream to serve eight."

Dwight met her eyes across the table, and he wondered if she was feeling that his mother had put her on the spot. He was aware that she worked long hours to grow her business and she'd mentioned she was looking to take on an assistant, which would free her up to accept special orders.

"I can put together a tray of miniature desserts along with a couple of pints of gelato, which has a lot less butterfat than ice cream."

"We don't have classes on Wednesday, because teachers have professional development on that day," Kiera said excitedly. "Can I come in and help you, Miss Sasha?"

"I don't mind, but you'll have to ask your father."

"Daddy, pul-eeze," Kiera drawled. "Can I?"

His daughter gave a longing look she knew he could not resist. "Yes."

Kiera jumped up, rounded the table, wrapped her arms around his neck and kissed his cheek. "Thank you, Daddy."

He held on to her hands. "You're welcome, baby girl."

Kiera pressed her mouth to his ear. "I'm too old to be your baby girl," she whispered.

"When I'm in my nineties and you're seventy you will still be my baby girl."

"Stop it, Daddy. You're embarrassing me."

Dwight kissed the back of her hand and then removed her arms from around his neck. What his daughter failed to understand was that he'd missed so many years watching her grow up to become the young woman she now presented. Visiting with her three or four times a year wasn't the same as seeing the milestones in which she went from a toddler to an adolescent, and he'd had to rely on Adrienne to tell him about the physical changes in their daughter's body.

He had less than two years before losing her again when she attended college. By that time, she would probably have a boyfriend who would become the most significant man in her life. Dwight hoped, if or when she married, she would find a partner who would love and, more important, respect her. Sasha shared a smile with Kiera when she retook her seat beside her.

He didn't know if it was a passing fancy that Kiera wanted to become a chef because the baking bug had hit from working in the bakeshop, but if it wasn't then he intended to support her totally until she achieved her goal.

Chapter Nine

Dwight parked behind a pickup along the street opposite Fletcher Austen's house, where Fletcher was scheduled to exchange vows with Nicole Campos. He hadn't planned to stay long because he wanted to drive to the lake house later that night to stock it with provisions he would need for the coming months. He'd bought the property on a whim when one of his patients had left the prospectus in the office waiting room. A developer was putting up one- and two-bedroom homes in a gated community around a lake with picturesque views of tree-covered mountains, thick forested areas and twin waterfalls that flowed into the lake. All the properties had docks for boat owners who were able to store them on the premises during the winter season.

Dwight knew he didn't need another house, but once he closed on the property, he'd contemplated that it would be the perfect place to vacation and possibly live once he retired. However, retirement was still a long time away, and as a single father of a teenage daughter, his plans were on hold until Kiera was emancipated. He'd asked Kiera if she wanted to join him at the lake house for the weekend, but she declined because she had to finish reading *A Tale of Two Cities*, and write an essay on what Dickens was attempting to convey about the social and economic conditions of England during the time he'd written the novel. She'd complained because she was taking French as a foreign language and preferred reading about authors who wrote about French history.

Dwight saw the familiar white van that belonged to Sasha's Sweet Shoppe parked in the driveway. He smiled when he saw her coming out of the house. She wore her usual white tunic with the shop's name stitched over her heart and a pair of black-and-white-striped chef's slacks. Her recognizable red hair was concealed under a white bandanna.

"Fancy meeting you here," he teased.

"I just delivered the wedding cake."

His eyebrows rose slightly. "Are you coming back for the ceremony and reception?" he asked.

"No. I'm going home to put my feet up and do nothing more strenuous than inhale and exhale. I've been going nonstop all week."

"Why don't you hang out with me this weekend?" The invitation had rolled off Dwight's tongue so quickly that it had shocked him.

Sasha blinked slowly. "Where?"

He successfully bit back a smile when he realized she hadn't said no. "At my lake house. I'm going up there later tonight and plan to stay over until Monday night."

"Don't you have office hours on Monday?"

This time Dwight did smile. It was apparent she had remembered his office hours. "Not again until after Labor Day. Once I start spending time at the lake, I take off Saturday through Monday."

"It's nice when you can make your own hours."

"You can make your own hours, Sasha. You talk about going home and vegging out for the next few days because you're working too hard. What you must do is work smart. I've been where you are now. I tried running a practice with serving one weekend a month and another two weeks in the summer, plus going to New York several times a year to spend time with Kiera. It affected me mentally and physically."

"What did you do?"

"I restructured office hours and added a dental assistant to the existing staff. And now that I'm civilian and I have sole custody of Kiera, I've restructured my life."

Sasha angled her head, seemingly deep in thought. "Other than hire an assistant, how do you suggest I restructure my life?"

"Come with me to the lake house tonight. You won't have to do anything more strenuous than lifting a fork to eat."

She smiled. "Do you plan to go fishing?"

"Not this weekend. I went shopping to stock the pantry and the fridge, so the first order of business will be getting the place ready for the season."

"It sounds tempting."

"Look, Sasha, I don't want to put any pressure on you. I'm going to be here for a couple of hours. If you decide you want to join me, then send me a text and I'll swing by and pick you up." He lowered his head and kissed her forehead. "Take care of yourself, sweetie."

Dwight waited for Sasha to get into the van and back out of the driveway before he walked around the house to the back, where a tent had been erected to accommodate the guests who'd come to witness the wedding of a couple who'd grown up in Wickham Falls. Fletcher had joined the army and Nicole the Corps following their high school graduation. They'd recently reunited when Nicole moved back to The Falls to take care of her nephews while their father was treated for an opioid addiction stemming from the injuries he sustained in an automobile accident that had claimed the life of his wife and their unborn child.

Dwight and Reggie Campos were best friends in high school, and he had volunteered to be his sponsor, but instead of returning to The Falls to live, the former college assistant defensive football coach had elected to live in Florida, where he had undergone treatment in a private residential facility. When Fletcher had come by to give Dwight the invitation, he'd informed him that Nicole's brother, parents and nephews were coming to The Falls for the wedding, and Dwight was looking forward to reuniting with his old friend.

The invitation indicated casual attire, and in lieu of gifts the bride and groom had requested their guests make online donations to the Wounded Warrior Project. Both had completed several tours of duty. Nicole had piloted Black Hawk helicopter gunships. Fletcher was a Special Forces medical sergeant, whose career ended when shrapnel from a rocket-propelled grenade tore through his right leg, shattering bone and damaging muscle.

It became Military Monday on steroids as Dwight greeted and was greeted by the crowd of predominantly military people gathering under the tent from which came mouthwatering aromas of smoking and grilling meat. Chairs were set up theater-style in a clearing beyond the tent where the ceremony was scheduled to take place. It was the perfect afternoon for a wedding with midday temperatures in the low seventies and there wasn't a cloud in the bright blue sky.

Dwight applauded Fletcher and Nicole for hosting an informal barbecue wedding reception in their backyard rather than in the ballroom of a hotel. He recalled his own wedding, which quickly turned from a small intimate affair into something close to a televised celebrity production. Adrienne's parents were willing to jump through hoops to give their only daughter whatever she wanted, even if it meant withdrawing money from their retirement nest egg.

A wide smile split Dwight's face when he spied Reggie coming out of the house. His friend wasn't as thin as he'd been before leaving The Falls and there were flecks of gray in his cropped hair that weren't apparent during their last encounter, but he had to admit Reggie looked much healthier.

"Hey, buddy," he said, wrapping Reggie in a bear hug.

Reggie pounded Dwight's back. "Man, it's good to see you. I just got in last night and the first thing I asked Nikki was if she'd invited you."

"Even if she hadn't, I still would've crashed this get-together if only to see you." He held his friend at arm's length. His tawny-brown complexion was deeply tanned. "You look good, Reggie."

"I feel good, Dwight. I must admit that getting and staying clean is a daily struggle. But whenever I look at my boys, I know I can't go down that rabbit hole again. Nikki sacrificed too much for me to start using again."

"Your sister is an exceptional woman."

"That she is," Reggie said in agreement.

"How long are you going to hang out in The Falls?" Dwight asked him.

"We're just going to be here overnight. I have a job interview Monday morning to coach football at a Dade County high school. Even though I prefer coaching on a college level, I'll take what I can get to get back into the game."

"You have my number. Contact me once you get settled into a routine, and maybe we can get together to catch up on old times."

"I'd like that, Dwight. I just bought a three-bedroom condo overlooking the ocean, so I'm adjusting to opening my door and not walking out on grass, while the boys are adjusting well to their new school."

Dwight chatted with Reggie for a few more minutes until someone told Reggie he was needed inside. He thought about what his friend had said about how difficult it was for him to maintain sobriety. Reggie had been one of a growing number of people who began taking prescription pain meds and after a while found themselves addicted to the substances. At first members of the town council were in denial when they claimed Wickham Falls did not have a drug problem, but with a rising crime rate attributed to substance abuse, they were forced to act by agreeing to open and support a substance abuse clinic. Dwight no longer wrote out prescriptions but faxed them directly to the pharmacist to be filled. The pharmacy was installed with cameras and a silent alarm that went directly to the sheriff's office.

The wedding went off smoothly with an exchange of vows and rings, and it was followed by a buffet reception with tables groaning with food. A DJ spun upbeat tunes that had most gyrating to the music as they ate, drank and shouted to one another to be heard above the din. Dwight checked his watch after Nicole cut the cake and slices of each layer were handed out to the guests, and decided to leave because he wanted to reach the lake before it was completely dark. The three exquisitely decorated cakes were artistic masterpieces with the detail Sasha had lavished on the roses and leaves. He had no idea of how long it had taken her to decorate the cakes, but now he knew why she'd admitted to having gone nonstop all week.

He slipped away without saying anything to the newly married couple, who were dancing to a slow tune, and got into his vehicle. Reaching into the glove box, he retrieved his cell phone. He had one text message.

Natasha: I'm ready whenever you are.

Dwight smothered a laugh. It looked as if he was going to have a houseguest for the weekend.

Dwight: I'll pick you up at 8.

Sasha knocked softly on the door to her mother's bedroom to get her attention. Charlotte sat in her favorite chair, feet resting on the matching footstool, as she watched a James Bond movie she had seen several times.

"Mama, I just wanted to tell you that I'm going to be away for a couple of days."

Charlotte sat straight. "Where are you going?"

"Dwight invited me to spend the weekend at his lake house."

Charlotte's blue eyes grew wider, and then she smiled. "Good for you. Enjoy yourself."

"I'll try, Mama."

"Don't try, Natasha. Just do it."

She would have had to be completely dense not to figure out that Charlotte wanted her and Dwight together. Well, they were together, but as friends. They'd talked about letting everything unfold naturally, and that was what she intended to do.

She'd packed a bag with enough clothes to last her several days and was waiting on the porch when Dwight drove up. Sasha was off the porch before he came to a complete stop and walked around to the passenger side, going completely still when she realized he was the only one in the vehicle.

Sasha opened the rear door and placed her bag on the seat, and then got in next to Dwight. "Where's Kiera?"

Leaning to his right, Dwight pressed a kiss on her hair. "She has to complete a paper for Monday."

"So, it's just us?" she asked.

"You and me, babe. Do you think you'll be able to put up with me for a couple of days?"

"That can go both ways, Dwight. Do you think you can tolerate me for more than a few hours?"

"We'll see, won't we? Buckle up, sweetie."

Sasha fastened her seat belt. "How long will it take to get there?"

"About twenty minutes." Dwight shifted into Reverse and backed out of the driveway. "Why don't you take a nap? I'll wake you when we arrive."

"That's okay. I took a nap after I left Fletcher's place. By the way, how was the wedding?"

"Very nice. The ceremony went off without a hitch with Fletcher and Nikki writing their own vows. Everyone was raving about the scrumptious cake, so be prepared for your phone to ring off the hook because folks were talking about ordering from you."

Sasha exhaled an audible sigh of relief. She hadn't lost her touch. For her, cakes had to be more than pretty; they also had to taste good. "I need an assistant ASAP."

"Have you advertised for one?"

"Yes. I've contacted several cooking schools in and out of the state for a qualified candidate. At this point I'm so desperate that I'm willing to pay more than the entry-level salary for a new graduate."

"Have you had to turn away any orders?"

"One." Sasha told Dwight about a woman who'd decided to give her sister a surprise birthday party and wanted a specialized cake the following day. "I would've made the cake if I hadn't been committed to baking four hundred cupcakes for the Johnson County Schools' PTA bake sale."

Dwight whistled under his breath. "How long did it take you to make them?"

"It took me four hours to bake the cupcakes, and another two to frost and decorate."

"How much advance time did you get for the cupcakes?"

Sasha turned her head, staring out the side window. "Two days. I know they didn't give me much time, but I make allowances for nonprofits."

"Well, for the next two days you can put aside your whisk and pastry bag to decompress."

"I'm looking forward to it."

Sasha was anticipating a quiet, relaxed weekend with a gentle, compassionate man who made her believe in love. When she'd admitted to Grant that she loved him enough to become his wife, she'd believed they would spend the rest of their lives together. However, her fairy-tale world dissipated like a puff of smoke within days of their honeymoon when her new husband turned into someone she didn't recognize. When she questioned his mood swings, he dismissed it with the excuse that he tended to be temperamental when working on new music. She shook her head to banish all thoughts of her ex-husband. He was her past and she wanted him to remain in the past—even in her memory.

The sun had set, and it was difficult to discern the passing landscape as Dwight increased his speed. Stars dotted the darkening sky like minute particles of diamond dust on black velvet, and a near-full moon reminded Sasha of a wheel of creamy white cheese. Sinking lower in the seat, she pressed her head against the headrest as a gentle peace settled over her.

The trees lining the narrow road were taller and seemingly closer together until there was pitch-blackness if not for the Jeep's headlights. The hoot of an owl could be heard through the open windows along with the sounds of other nocturnal wildlife. Dwight shifted into a lower gear as the road seemed to rise out of nowhere, her ears popping with the higher elevation. A sprinkling of lights appeared in the distance and less than a minute later she saw lights reflecting off a large lake from houses ringing the water like a wreath. There were a few boats moored to docks leading from the homes to the water. A posted sign indicated all visitors must stop at the gatehouse.

Dwight's lake house was in a private gated community seemingly in the middle of nowhere.

"Do you own a boat?"

Dwight gave her a quick glance. "No, because I wouldn't get much use out of it." He tapped a remote device attached to the vehicle's visor, the gate went up and he drove through.

"What made you decide to buy property here?" Sasha questioned.

"I found it by accident."

She listened intently when he told her about finding the prospectus left by a patient in the waiting room that piqued his curiosity. The developer's original plan was for a retirement community, but the first couple of years he could only sell two of the dozen houses set on half-acre lots. Once he lowered the fifty-five and older age requirement and dropped the selling price, buyers were more receptive.

"I'm glad I bought in early because the value of the homes has nearly doubled."

"Do you plan to retire here?" She'd asked Dwight a lot of questions, but Sasha wanted to know more about the man with whom she would share a roof for two nights.

Dwight maneuvered along an unpaved road with LED pathway lights. "I'm still undecided. When I retire, I'm not certain whether I'll keep the house in The Falls, but if I do decide to continue to live there, then I'll give this place to Kiera to use it as a vacation property—but that all depends on whether she chooses to live in the state. After all, she is a city girl."

Sasha smiled. Kiera was a city girl who'd come to the country, and she was a country girl who'd left to go to the city. But she'd come back, and there hadn't been one day since her return that she regretted leaving a place she'd called home for almost half her life. She fled Wickham Falls at eighteen and returned fourteen years later at thirty-two and knowingly a lot more mature and hopefully wiser.

She was resolute when it came to her career, but still the proverbial babe in the woods when it came to her heart. Sasha had learned quite a bit about herself in fourteen years and that she had to stop letting her heart rule her head. Here she was with a man who had and was everything she wanted in a lover or husband and he continued to relate to her as if they were besties. It hadn't mattered that they'd shared a few kisses—chaste ones at that. She wanted more, and the more was the need to be desired.

Sasha didn't need to lie on a therapist's couch to bare her soul to get the answers to questions that had nagged at her for years. As the only girl in the family, she wanted her father to dote on her the way she saw Dwight act with Kiera. Even as a single part-time father, Dwight had exhibited more affection toward his daughter than her father had ever shown her in eighteen years. It was only after she'd ended her relationship with the cooking school instructor that she had come to the realization that she saw him as a father figure, someone to love and protect her.

She did not need a man to take care of her financially—that she could do for herself. What she craved was his being there for her when what she'd planned failed, while encouraging her to try it again or suggesting an alternative. She wanted to be able to pour out her heart and have him listen even if he didn't have the answers she needed.

"This is us," Dwight said, breaking into her tortured musings. "Wait here for me while I check inside."

Staring out the windshield, she saw a house that reminded her of pictures of chalets. Twin lanterns flanking the front door provided enough light for her to see the tall window over the loft area Dwight had mentioned. She got out and retrieved her weekender as Dwight walked up the path and opened the front door. Light illuminated the entire first story. He disappeared for several minutes, and when he reappeared in the doorway he beckoned her to come in.

Sasha's jaw dropped when she walked into the yawning space with high ceilings. French doors at the rear of the house offered views of the lake that appeared a great deal farther away than she'd originally thought. The interior was spotless with gleaming wood floors, and the faint aroma of lemon still lingered in the air. She jumped slightly when Dwight reached for her free hand.

"Come with me. I'll show you your bedroom and the bathroom. I have an en suite bath in mine, so that eliminates sharing one."

"Where's your bedroom?"

"It's at the other side of the house. The bath and bedrooms are the only rooms in the house with doors. The kitchen, dining area and the living rooms share an open floor plan. After you get up tomorrow morning, I'll give you a tour of the loft and the backyard. There's a path in the back that leads directly to the lake."

"How much land do you have here?"

"Each house is set on a half acre, which does provide us some privacy from our closest neighbors."

Sasha noticed it was the second time he'd referred to them as *us*. He touched a switch on the wall outside the bedroom and light flooded the space with full-size and twin beds. The vibrant colors of pink, red and lavender in a woven rug were repeated in the bedcovers, and pillow shams provided a radiant contrast to the bleached pine furniture. Floor-to-ceiling off-white lined drapery covered a wall of windows.

"This is very nice. I'm really going to enjoy sleeping here."

"The bathroom has everything you need, but if you're missing something, then let me know and I'll drive into town and pick it up for you."

Sasha turned and smiled up at Dwight as he stared down at her under lowered lids. What was going on behind those dark orbs? she wondered. Then another thought popped into her head. How many women, other than his mother and daughter, had he brought to the house on the lake? Had he bought this place to use as a rendezvous for his liaisons? After all, Dwight appeared to be a very virile man who did not lack for female attention. She'd noticed women staring at him whenever they were together, and first she thought they were curious, but after a while she noticed a coquettish smile, or a slight touch of their hair, and some were even bold enough to wink at him, all of which he tended to ignore.

"I'm good, Dwight. I brought everything I need with me."

"Good night. And try to sleep in as late as you want."

"Okay. Good night."

Sasha waited for him to leave before she closed the door. She'd showered and brushed her teeth before he came to pick her up, so all she needed was to get a nightgown out of her bag, put it on and crawl into bed. Three minutes later, she did just that, and within seconds of her head touching the pillow she was sound asleep.

It took Dwight three trips to unload the provisions he'd stored in the Jeep's cargo area. A large cooler was filled with perishables he stored in the refrigerator/freezer, and crates of dry and canned goods lined the shelves in a pantry tucked into an alcove of the kitchen.

He'd come to the house on Wednesday to remove dustcovers from the furniture, open windows to let out the mustiness, put clean linen on the beds, clean bathrooms, and dust floors and hard surfaces. This year he'd opened two weeks later than he normally would have now that Kiera was living with him. Becoming a full-time father forced him to rearrange his life where he no longer had to think only of himself and his mother, but also his child. He'd resigned his commission in the military, hadn't slept with a woman since he brought Kiera back from New York, and he had curtailed his visits to the lake because Kiera complained about the isolation. If she found Wickham Falls boring, then staying at the lake house was so mind-numbing that she felt more dead than alive.

He'd asked himself over and over what he was doing bringing Sasha to the place he thought of as his private retreat where he openly entertained women when it hadn't been possible in Wickham Falls. The town was too small, the residents too curious, and gossip that spread like a lighted fuse attached to a stick of dynamite made it impossible for him to date a local woman. That was before Natasha Manning came back to town. Not only were they seen together at social functions, but now he had invited her to a place no one, other than his mother and daughter, knew about.

And as much as he'd found himself attracted to Sasha, and wanted to sleep with her, Dwight knew that wasn't going to happen this weekend. He hadn't missed the dark bluish circles under her eyes or her slowed movements indicating she was close to complete exhaustion. He'd invited her to the lake for her and himself. Here she could do absolutely nothing more strenuous than sleep and/or sit and stare at the water. He'd planned to cook, watch a few old movies and while away the hours until it was time to return to The Falls.

Dwight retreated to his bedroom, closed the door, stripped naked and walked into the bathroom to shower and brush his teeth. Tomorrow was a new day and he looked forward to spending it with a woman who'd managed to slip under the armor he wore to protect himself from future heartbreak. He'd fallen in love with Adrienne, and despite their breakup and divorce, a part of him still loved her. And she knew that.

He'd tried exorcising her with other women but failed miserably. Dwight wasn't certain whether he was to blame or if it was because of Kiera that he still felt a connection with Adrienne. After all, they did share a child. What he found puzzling was why she hadn't had more children with Omar.

Turning off the water, he stepped out of the shower stall and dried his body. Walking on bare feet, he made his way into the bedroom and got into bed—alone. His last thoughts weren't of his ex-wife, but Sasha. Whenever she looked up at him through her lashes, the seductive gesture was nearly his undoing. His body silently taunted him over his self-induced celibacy.

Let everything unfold naturally. The very words he'd said to her flooded his mind as he adjusted the pillows under his head. One thing Dwight knew for certain. Once they made love there would be no turning back.

Chapter Ten

Sasha woke, totally disoriented. She'd lost track of place and time. Sitting up, she saw light coming through the drawn drapes and was suddenly aware of where she was. Her cell phone was still in the weekender, so she couldn't discern whether it was early morning or the afternoon. Swinging her legs over the side of the bed, she retrieved her cell phone. It was after ten in the morning. She hadn't slept that late since opening the shop. She scooped up the toiletry bag and walked out of the bedroom to the bath.

Peering into the mirror over the twin sinks, she studied her face. The puffiness under her eyes was gone but not the dark circles. She'd grown up angry because she'd inherited her mother's fair coloring, while her brothers had their father's dark hair, eyes and ruddy complexion.

Any other time she would have attempted to hide

the circles with concealers, but not today. What Dwight saw was what he was going to get—the unadulterated, freckles-and-all Natasha Manning. She decided to take a bath instead of a shower and it felt good just to relax in the tub until the water cooled and forced her to get out. Wrapping a towel around her body, she went back into the bedroom and closed the door.

She found Dwight sitting at a table on the patio at the rear of the house drinking coffee. He'd propped his bare feet on another chair, and she wondered why he hadn't chosen one of four chaises on which to relax.

She slid back the screen and stepped out into the brilliant morning sunlight.

"Good morning."

Setting down the mug, he came to his feet. Sasha swallowed an inaudible gasp as she stared at the magnificence of his tall, lean, muscular body in a black tank top and khaki walking shorts. It was the first time she'd seen him bare that much skin and it shocked her senses. How was she going to maintain a modicum of control when he blatantly put his body on display like that? He hadn't shaved and the emerging stubble only enhanced his magnetism.

Dwight approached her and cradled her face between his hands. "Good morning." Lowering his head, he brushed his mouth over hers. "You look pretty and well rested." She had selected to wear a pale pink crinkle-cotton seersucker sleeveless dress and a pair of matching ballet-type flats.

Sasha ran her tongue over her lips, tasting coffee. "I slept very well."

"Are you ready to eat breakfast?"

Her fingers curled around his wrists, pulling his

hands away from her face. Sasha didn't trust herself to be that close to Dwight. At least not until she found herself back in control of her runaway senses. He looked, smelled and tasted delicious.

"Yes."

"Do you have a preference?"

Sasha's lips parted as she flashed a wide smile. "I have choices?"

Dwight winked at her. "With me you'll always have choices. I don't believe in all or nothing."

She scrunched up her nose. "Bacon, eggs, toast, juice, coffee and fresh fruit." A beat passed as they stared at each other. "Did I order too much?"

"No, not at all. Do you want to eat inside or out?"

"I'll leave that up to you."

"This weekend is yours, Sasha. I'm your personal genie who will attempt to grant your every wish."

"Outside."

Dwight nodded. "That's what I'd hoped you would say."

"Do you need a sous chef?"

"No. I've got this."

"Kiera told me that you're a very good cook."

"My daughter is biased. My mother is a very good cook. And your mama can also burn some pots. I've been to New Orleans and her gumbo and red beans and rice surpassed any I've eaten there. I'm standing here jawing when I need to feed you."

Sasha took the chair Dwight had vacated. It only took a single glance to see why he'd bought the property. The outdoor kitchen also included a bar, pizza oven and fireplace. Outdoor furniture with all-weather cushions, a rectangular table seating six and two wrought-iron bistro tables, and a quartet of webbed recliners set the stage for casual dining and entertaining. The house and surrounding property was the perfect place in which to retire for someone looking for privacy and solitude.

"I could stay here forever." She sat straight and glanced around her. Sasha did not want to believe she'd spoken her thoughts aloud.

Dwight emerged from the house carrying a large picnic basket with plates, flatware, glasses and foodstuffs he needed to prepare breakfast. He'd made it a practice to use the outdoor kitchen. The exception was inclement weather. Even if temperatures dropped to the forties, he continued to cook outdoors.

Working quickly, he turned on the gas grill, and while the flattop heated, Dwight set the table and put out a covered dish with sliced melon. He'd bought several containers of sliced cantaloupe, honeydew and watermelon. He liked cooking, fishing and dentistry, but not necessarily in that order.

He'd admitted to Sasha that he liked being single; he'd also liked being married. He knew men who remarried within two years after their divorce, and others who'd professed never to marry again. He did not fit in either category. Dwight knew he would've remarried if he had found a woman he loved enough to want her to share his life and his daughter.

Dwight knew Sasha was special, that his feelings for her deepened with each encounter, yet he had no inkling how she felt about marriage. She'd admitted marrying a man she didn't love and that was something he couldn't fathom. If she wasn't pregnant, then why did she marry a man she did not love? He'd originally thought it might have been his celebrity status, yet she was also a celebrity in her own right.

They'd promised each other not to talk about their exes, but Dwight knew that couldn't continue if he hoped to have an open, honest and mature relationship with Sasha. Spending time alone at the lake house was key to them determining whether they would continue dating.

"How do you like your eggs?" he asked Sasha after he'd set a bottle of chilled orange juice on the table. Grasping the handle on a pole, he turned it until a white umbrella opened to shield the table from the intensifying rays of the sun rising higher in the sky.

She shielded her eyes with her hand when she looked up at him. "Scrambled."

Reaching down, Dwight eased her up from the chair. "Come sit under the umbrella. I hope you put on sunblock if you plan to sit outside or you're going to end up looking like a cooked lobster."

"I did apply sunblock, Dr. Adams."

A slight frown furrowed his forehead. He'd told her not to address him as Dr. Adams. "Did you bring a swimsuit?"

"No. I didn't know I needed to bring one."

He ran a finger down the length of her straight nose. "Remember to bring one the next time you come."

Her pale eyebrows rose slightly. "Will there be a next time, Dwight?"

"That will be your decision, Sasha. The invitation is an open one, so the ball will always be in your court." Not waiting for a comeback, Dwight turned on his heel and returned to the grill.

A short time later, he set a platter with fluffy scrambled eggs, crisp grilled bacon, buttered thick-sliced Texas garlic bread heated on the grill and mugs of steaming coffee on the table. He didn't know why but Dwight found food cooked outdoors always tasted better.

Sasha smiled at him across the table. "I could live like this every day."

Dwight also smiled. Sasha had given him the opening he needed for them to be frank with each other. "Maybe that can become a reality one of these days."

Propping her elbow on the table, Sasha rested her chin on the heel of her hand. "How?"

"We could eventually live together."

Sasha's hand came down as if in slow motion. She looked at Dwight as if he'd suddenly taken leave of his senses. "You're talking about us living together when we haven't even..." Her words trailed off when Dwight leaned forward.

"When we don't even know if we're compatible in bed," he said, completing her sentence while reading her thoughts.

"Yes, Dwight."

"Would you live with me if you found our lovemaking satisfying?"

A gamut of confusing emotions held Sasha captive as she tried understanding why Dwight was talking about them making love and living together when they weren't even friends with benefits. "No, Dwight, I won't live with you."

"Won't or can't?"

"Both."

"Why, Sasha?"

"Because I wouldn't live with you unless we were in love with each other."

"You admit to marrying a man you didn't love, so why not live with one you don't love?"

"I never said I didn't love you."

Dwight reacted to her admission as if he'd been stabbed by a sharp object.

"What did you say?"

A surge of strength came to Sasha she hadn't felt since the time she told Grant their marriage was over and that she'd filed for divorce. "You heard what I said, Dr. Adams."

"Stop calling me that."

"What? Dr. Adams?"

"Yes, dammit!"

"Don't cuss at me, Dwight."

"I'm not cursing at you, Natasha."

"Oh, now it's Natasha." She pressed her lips tightly together. "I tell you that I love you and now you're bent out of shape."

Leaning back in his chair, Dwight pressed his palms together. "I had no idea you felt anything more for me aside from friendship. I'm just shocked and pleased that we share the same feelings."

"You—you love me?"

"I'm falling in love with you."

"Is there a difference, Dwight?"

His expression softened when he smiled. "Yes. There is a big difference. You can love a movie, book or a car. But falling in love goes deeper where you are willing to compromise, make sacrifices and protect those you love unconditionally."

"Why me, Dwight, and not some other woman?"

Sasha could not believe she'd asked him why when it was enough to know that her feelings were reciprocated.

"Why not you, Sasha? Do you think you're unworthy of a man's love?"

"Grant felt me unworthy of being his wife. I'd just come off the cupcake competition, and although my team didn't win, I'd become an instant celebrity and attracted a lot of attention because of my hair and laugh. Grant came into the shop where I was working, and he turned on his country-boy charm. He came back a few days later and asked me out. I didn't want to believe that one of Nashville's fastest-rising stars was interested in me. We dated and it wasn't until after I became Mrs. Natasha Manning-Richards that I discovered he married me because he felt we would make the perfect celebrity couple. Once his publicist branded us as the Cowboy and the Redhead, the paparazzi began following us relentlessly. It was only when my star as a pastry chef began to rise that Grant showed his true colors when he attempted to sabotage my career. He insisted I tour with him and accompany him to the studio for recording sessions—time I needed to devote to baking."

Pushing to his feet, Dwight came around the table and sat next to her. "You didn't realize the man was as insecure and controlling as he was talented."

"It wasn't until I'd filed for divorce that my lawyer made me aware of that. The final straw was when he went on tour and left one of his security people at the house to watch me. I knew I'd become a prisoner. That's when I discovered he was tracking my cell phone and had installed cameras throughout the house to monitor my comings and goings. It took all my resolve not to expose him to the tabloids. He finally agreed to end the marriage when I did threaten to talk to a reporter. Grant had me sign a prenup citing I wasn't entitled to any of his earnings or property."

"You'd signed it?"

"Yes. What my dear husband didn't know was that he'd married a woman who didn't need his money."

Sasha knew what she was about to tell Dwight would probably shock him. "I left The Falls two months after graduating to accept a job in Tennessee. Mrs. Harvey, a childless former English teacher, sold the mansion where she'd lived with her late husband, moved into a smaller three-bedroom house in a gated community and advertised for a live-in companion. We bonded and I'd become the granddaughter she never had. Her library was filled with the classics, and because of the onset of senility and failing eyesight, she wanted me to read to her. That's when I fell in love with Dickens, Dumas, Shakespeare, Austen and Brontë. Just before she was confined to an assisted living facility, she asked me what I wanted for my future. And when I told her I wanted to become a pastry chef, she made it happen. Her wealth manager gave me a check to cover my tuition at The Art Institute of Tennessee in Nashville and to rent an apartment. Going to school in Nashville allowed me to visit Mrs. Harvey, although she no longer knew who I was. I'd just received my degree in baking and pastry when I got a call from Mrs. Harvey's lawyer that she'd passed away and I was to attend the reading of her will. She'd left me enough money that it could take me into retirement if I didn't squander it."

"So, it's not that you don't have enough money to keep the bakeshop viable, but whether the business can sustain itself."

"Exactly," she agreed. "I invested my inheritance in an account Grant knew nothing about. I also signed a nondisclosure not to reveal anything about our marriage."

Dwight pulled her closer. "Thank goodness you don't have to deal with that clown anymore."

Sasha rested her head on Dwight's shoulder. "You're right about that. I just can't believe I put up with him for five years before I came to my senses. I didn't fight with Grant because I didn't want to relive my parents' marriage. It's sad when your childhood memories are filled with your mother and father's constant bickering. One time I asked my mother why she didn't leave my father and she said she couldn't because she loved him."

Dwight ran his fingers under the wealth of thick red curls on Sasha's neck. "People fall in love for different reasons."

"You're right, Dwight. I knew you were special the night I came to your house to return Kiera's cell phone. When you gave me your jacket, I decided then you were special. And when you invited me to be your date for the chamber fund-raiser, I felt like the princess in a fairy tale who'd met her prince where they would live happily ever after. I haven't had a lot of experience with men, but those I've met always wanted something from me. You're the only one who wants me for me even though I'm a freckle-faced country girl."

"I don't think you realize how easy it is for me to love you. And there's no need to be self-deprecating because you're one of a kind."

Turning her head, she smiled at him. "I could say the same about you, darling. You're unlike any other man I've met or known."

"So, I'm your darling?" he asked, deadpan.

"You didn't know?"

Dwight smiled. "I didn't want to be presumptuous."

"You are my love, my darling and of course my sweetie."

Dwight pressed his mouth to hers. "How do you taste, Miss Sasha's Sweet Shoppe?"

"I don't know," she whispered. "However, I'm not opposed to offering you a little sample."

Throwing back his head, Dwight laughed loudly, startling a few birds perched in a nearby tree. "What if I want more than just a sample?"

Shifting, Sasha straddled his lap and buried her face against the column of his neck. "Don't you want to find out if you like the sample before you ask for a larger piece?"

Dwight gasped when he felt the press of her bottom as she gyrated against his crotch. He'd hardened so quickly he feared ejaculating before he could make love to her. "Don't! Please." He was pleading with her to stop and didn't care if Sasha knew the power she yielded at that moment.

Her response was to press her breasts against his chest as her hot, moist breath feathered in his ear. "What do you want, Dwight?"

He gasped again as one hand searched under the tank top, fingernails trailing over his breasts. "You, babe."

"How much do you want me?" she taunted.

Dwight had had enough teasing. Wrapping an arm around her waist, he stood up, bringing her up with him. Taking long strides, he managed to slide back the screen, walk into the house and shut it after him without dropping Sasha. He did not want to believe, and was pleasantly surprised, that Sasha was a seductive temptress under the prim and shy exterior he'd come to know. When he'd invited her to spend the weekend with him, his intent wasn't to make love with her, but to give her time to relax and rejuvenate from her hectic week.

He carried her into his bedroom and placed her on the bed. He drew the drapes and then returned to the bed and the drawer in the nightstand to take out a condom. What he and Sasha were about to share was too new for them to risk an unplanned pregnancy. Dwight smiled at Sasha staring up at him when he caught the hem of his tank top and pulled it up and over his head. His eyes searched her face for a hint of uncertainty but saw only confidence in the green eyes. Dwight took his time undressing, and when he was completely nude, he saw Sasha's expression change as her lips parted.

Sasha tried not to react to seeing Dwight's nakedness, but she couldn't believe that his body was as magnificent as his face. Lean and muscled, he was Michelangelo's *David* in mahogany instead of marble. She forced herself not to look at his erection when he slipped on the condom. Sitting up, she slipped the straps to the dress off her shoulders, baring her breasts. Dwight got into bed with her and kissed her as he removed the dress and underwear. Her mouth was as busy as Dwight's, slanting across his lips, jaw and ear. Her teeth nibbled at his exposed throat, staking her claim at the same time a deep moan rose from the valley of his wide chest.

Dwight wanted to take Sasha hard and fast because he had been celibate much too long—but he decided not to. She needed to be loved, to know that she was loved. Cradling her head in his hands, he increased the pressure of his mouth on hers until her lips parted and he took possession of her tongue. One hand moved from her head to a satiny shoulder and still farther to a firm breast. It filled his hand, the nipple tightening against his palm. His thumb drew circles around the areola, pebbling and increasing his own desire and arousal.

Shifting slightly, he raised his body, while hers writhed with an escalating awakening. Slowly, methodically, Dwight held her hands at her sides while he slipped down the length of her silken body until his face was level with the juncture of her thighs. The erotic essence of her body filled his nostrils when he buried his face against the silky down concealing her femininity. His hot breath seared her delicate flesh before it cooled with the sweep of his moist tongue.

Sasha wanted to tell Dwight to stop yet couldn't. Not when his rapacious tongue made every nerve in her body seem to be on fire; not when she felt herself falling over the edge where orgasms waited for her. Waves of ecstasy throbbed through her body. She gasped in sweet agony, and her fingers tightened on the sheet, twisting and pulling it from the confines of the mattress. She breathed in deep, soul-drenching drafts at the same time ripples of fulfillment gripped her. Arching, unashamed screams exploded from her parted lips as she gave herself up to the passion hurtling her higher than she had ever soared before.

The pulsating continued, faster and stronger until she abandoned herself to the liquid fire sweeping her into a vortex of sweet, burning fulfillment. The flames of passion had not subsided entirely when she felt Dwight's erection easing into her. She took him in, inch by inch. He moaned as if in pain, then began a slow thrusting, preparing her body to accept all of him.

Sasha moaned, her body opening and giving Dwight the advantage he needed as he rolled his hips, burying himself to the root of his penis. Her hot, wet flesh closed around him like a tight glove, and he knew it was helpless to hold back any longer. He rolled his hips again, each thrust deeper, harder. The sensation of her body opening and closing around him, pulling him in where he did not know where he began and Sasha ended, hurled him to a dimension he did not know existed. He had to let go of his dammed passions.

Sasha's soft sighs of satisfaction were his undoing. Listening to the throaty moans from her forced him to release the obdurate control on the passions he had kept in check and withheld from every woman since his divorce. Collapsing heavily on her slender body, he sucked in precious air to fill his lungs with much-needed oxygen. Dwight didn't know where he found the strength, but he managed to roll off Sasha's body, while at the same time savoring the pulsing aftermath of his own release.

The bedroom was silent as they lay side by side, eyes closed. Sasha reached for his hand, threading their fingers together. There was no need for conversation. Their bodies had spoken for them. She loved him and he loved her.

Chapter Eleven

Sasha did not want to believe life could be so perfect starting with the weekend at the lake house. She and Dwight spent more time in bed than out, talking and making endless love. He told her about his forensic psychologist FBI special-agent father, who lost his life when the driver of a tractor trailer had fallen asleep behind the wheel and plowed into his car.

He'd also disclosed that he might have contributed to the dissolution of his marriage; although he had not accepted a ROTC Guard/Reserves scholarship, he owed the army six years with two years remaining on active duty. He'd elected to fulfill the two-year commitment before enrolling in dental school, unaware that Adrienne was pregnant. He hadn't been there for her during the first year of Kiera's life; then he was gone again after he'd enrolled in dental school. Most of her immediate family had left The Falls, and Adrienne had made up her mind that she also didn't want to stay.

It wasn't until mid-June when Sasha was finally able to hire an assistant, a young man who was extremely talented. She suspected he was attracted to Kiera, who totally ignored him, and Sasha had come to believe Kiera resented his intrusion because it reduced the time they would spend together. With the additional help, she was able to fulfill more special orders from clients as far away as Beckley.

Her alone time with Dwight was infrequent because they were unable to get away to the lake more than once a month. Most of the time Kiera accompanied them, and the weekend before Kiera left to go to New York to vacation with her mother, Victoria and Charlotte also joined them. Kiera passed her driver's test, and Dwight had promised that when she returned in August they would go shopping for a late-model used car.

Sasha had just parked the van at her home when the front door opened, and her mother walked out onto the porch. Charlotte was now an official member of the Ladies Auxiliary, which was on hiatus until the fall, and she was looking forward to the induction ceremony. Charlotte's strained expression said it all: she was upset. Reaching for her tote, she got out, her pulse throbbing at the base of her throat.

"What's the matter, Mama?" She prayed her mother wasn't experiencing chest pains again. Reaching for her hands, she discovered they were ice-cold.

"I just got a call from Grant Richards."

"What the hell...?" Sasha paused, taking a deep

breath. "I'm sorry about that." She didn't want her mother to bear the brunt of her anger. "Why would he be calling you?" She knew there was no way he was able to call her because she'd changed her cell's number.

"I suppose he still has my number from when he came here for your daddy's funeral."

"What does he want, Mama?"

"He said he has upcoming concerts beginning next month in Charleston, Richmond, Virginia, and the DC area, and he wants to see you. He did ask for your number, but I know you don't want him to have it."

Sasha struggled to control her anger. "Not only don't I want to talk to him, but I also don't want to ever see him again."

"He did say he was sorry for how he treated you."

"And you believed him?"

A pained expression flitted over Charlotte's features. "He did sound remorseful."

"That's because he's a charlatan and a con man, Mama. He knows what to say to draw you in, and then before you know it, he's got you trapped in his web where he'll control every phase of your life."

"I thought by this time you would've forgiven him. It's not good to carry around so much hate."

Sasha threw up her hands. "I'm sorry, Mama, but I'm not you. You were a sponge, soaking up everything Daddy dumped on you and still you turned the other cheek."

Charlotte's eyes filled with tears. "That's not fair."

"What's not fair is becoming a receptacle for abuse. What really bothers me is that I told you what he did to me and you still want to welcome him into your home like he was the perfect son-in-law."

"Don't put words in my mouth, Natasha. I never said I was going to invite him here, so don't shoot the messenger."

Sasha knew her mother was angry when her face turned beet red. "I think we'd better end this conversation before we say something we'll later regret."

"Yes, we'd better," Charlotte shot back.

"I'm going inside to shower, and then I'm going to bed."

Sasha was still upset when she crawled into bed. She cursed Grant even though she knew he couldn't have done what he did to her if she hadn't given him permission. Too often she'd asked herself when had her ego surpassed her common sense because she'd gotten an A-list recording artist to choose her to become his wife from among the screaming, adoring women who'd risk life and limb to get close enough to touch him.

Her cell phone rang, and she knew from the programmed ringtone that it was Dwight. They'd made plans to go to the lake house after she closed on Saturday now that Kiera was away. She picked up the phone. "Yes."

There was a pregnant pause before Dwight said, "What's the matter?"

"Nothing," she lied smoothly.

"If nothing's wrong, then why does it sound as if you've lost your best friend?"

"Look, Dwight, I just don't feel like talking right now."

"If that's the case, then call me when you're in a better mood."

Suddenly the connection went dead, and she knew he'd hung up on her. Frustrated, Sasha threw the phone across the room, and it landed on the chair in the corner. Hot, angry tears pricked the backs of her eyelids, but she refused to cry. She'd cried enough because of two men to last several lifetimes. First it was because of her father, when she stayed on her young knees praying for him to change; and then it was because of Grant, who had used her to his advantage, then openly flaunted his infidelity with a woman who'd grinned in her face while she was sleeping with her husband. Sasha knew she had to get her head together before seeing Dwight again, because it wasn't fair to him to let her dilemma with Grant destroy her newfound happiness.

Dwight immediately recognized the number on the phone's screen, wondering why his daughter was calling him from the Dominican Republic. He tapped the speaker feature. "What's up, Kiera?"

"Daddy, can you come and get me?"

His stomach muscles tightened as he struggled not to panic. "What's the matter?"

"I was having a conversation with Mom when Omar called me an ungrateful little snot who should be slapped across the mouth after I told him I needed to talk with my mother without his interruptions."

Dwight closed his eyes as he whispered a silent prayer for patience. He did not want to believe the man to whom he'd entrusted his daughter's safety had threatened to hit her. "Put your mother on the phone."

"She went out."

"Then put Omar on the phone."

"He's out, too. I'm alone in the condo."

"Stay there, get your passport and pack your bags,

Kiera. And if your mother says anything, then tell her I'm coming to get you."

"What about Omar?"

"Don't worry about him, Kiera. I'll take care of him when I get there. Keep your phone on and charged in case I have to call you."

"Okay, Daddy. When do you think you'll get here?"

"Hopefully sometime tomorrow. I have to call the airline and see if I can reserve a flight."

Dwight hung up and scrolled through his phone for the number to an airline with departures to Punta Cana. It took him more than forty-five minutes to reserve a seat to the Caribbean island. He was scheduled to board a red-eye in Charleston for Miami, then take a connecting flight to Punta Cana.

He tapped the number to the bakeshop, hoping Sasha was in a better mood than she'd been a couple of days ago. He'd told her to call him, and she hadn't. While he'd been prepared to wait indefinitely, now he owed it to her to let her know he was going out of the country, and he hoped this would be the last time he would have to drop everything to rescue his daughter.

"Sasha's Sweet Shoppe."

Dwight hesitated. He still wasn't used to hearing a masculine voice answer the phone. Sasha's young assistant, Christian Weber, looked more like a male model with sun-streaked shoulder-length twists, a deeply tanned tawny-brown face and a tall, slender body. He'd noticed him staring at his daughter and he'd left it to Sasha to warn him that Kiera was much too young to date a twenty-two-year-old man, and that her father was overly protective of his only child.

"May I please speak to Miss Sasha."

"Miss Sasha is on the other line with a client. Would you like to leave a message?"

"Yes. Please tell her to call Dr. Adams."

"I'll give her the message, Dr. Adams. How's Kiera?"

"Kiera's well," Dwight lied. She wasn't well, and she wouldn't be until he brought her back to Wickham Falls.

"That's good. I know you don't want me to date your daughter but—"

"Look, son," Dwight said, cutting him off. "You and I will have to talk about Kiera when I see you. But right now, I need to speak to Miss Sasha."

"Right. I'll let her know as soon as she hangs up."

Dwight hung up, shaking his head. Right now, he had enough problems with Omar to even think of how to convince the pastry chef that his daughter was unobtainable and unavailable to him.

His focus was on Omar, who allegedly had threatened to hit Kiera. When Adrienne had informed him that she was remarrying, Dwight had been concerned about the man who was to become his daughter's stepfather. However, when he met Omar, the man reassured him that he would love and protect Kiera as if she were his own. Kiera had grown up calling Omar Dad, yet something had to have happened between them for her to refer to him by his given name. Something he knew annoyed the man.

His phone rang and Dwight answered it before the second ring. "Hello."

"This is Miss Sasha from Sasha's Sweet Shoppe returning Dr. Adams's call. Is he available?"

He smiled. The teasing woman with whom he'd fallen in love was back. "This is he. How are you, Miss Sasha?"

"I'm well, thank you. And you?"

Dwight sobered as he focused on why he'd called Sasha. "I have to fly down to the Caribbean to bring Kiera back home."

"She is sick?"

"No. It's more like we're having a family crisis."

"I'm sorry to hear that. When are you leaving?"

"I'm driving up to Charleston in a couple of hours. I plan to check into a hotel to get some sleep before taking a red-eye to Miami for a connecting flight to Punta Cana. I'll book a return flight once I get there."

"Do whatever you have to do to make certain Kiera's okay. Tell her I love and miss her when you see her."

Dwight went completely still. It was the first time Sasha had verbalized her affection for his daughter. "I will."

"I love you, Dwight."

He smiled. "I know that. I love you, too."

"Be safe."

"Thank you. I'll see you when we get back."

Dwight sat in the condo's living room staring at the man he'd expected to love and protect his daughter as her stepfather. By the time the jet had touched down at the Punta Cana airport, Dwight had become even more resolute that this would be the last time he would have to drop everything to extract Kiera from a hostile family confrontation.

He leaned forward, impaling the shorter, slightly built man with a long, penetrating direct stare. "When you married Adrienne, you promised me you would care for and protect Kiera as if she was your daughter. Now I hear you want to slap her across the mouth."

Omar ran a hand over his shaved light brown pate at the same time he forced what could pass for a smile. Omar Johnson had earned a reputation as a brilliant litigator, and when he graduated at the top of his law school class, prestigious law firms were lining up with lucrative offers to entice him to join them. As the CFO of a Fortune 500 company, Adrienne and Omar had become a super couple. They had a condo in a luxury Manhattan high-rise and the condo in the Caribbean with breathtaking views of the sea.

"I really wouldn't have hit her, Dwight."

"I'd hope you wouldn't because then I would have to get involved. And I can promise you, man-to-man, that it would be more than a slap that I'd inflict on you."

Omar's light brown eyes grew wider. "Are you threatening me, Dwight?"

"No. I don't have to do that because I'm taking my daughter home with me, and this will be the last time she will go anywhere with you."

"Have you forgotten I'm Adrienne's husband? There will be times when we'll have to be together."

"No, I haven't forgotten. What I want you to remember is Kiera's old enough to decide if she doesn't want to see you or her mother. And because I'm legally responsible for *my daughter*, I have the final say on what she can and cannot go or do."

"Kiera is not only your child, Dwight. She does have a mother."

Dwight's hands curled into fists. Only his military training kept him from leaping across the room and choking the pompous little man. "And you've been married to Adrienne long enough to have fathered a few kids of your own, so you can be a real dad and slap them in the mouth." He realized he'd hit a sore spot when Omar recoiled from the gibe.

"Daddy, I'm ready to leave."

He stood up when Kiera walked into the living room pulling two wheeled bags. "Do you have your passport?"

Kiera patted the cross-body bag slung across her chest. "It's in here."

Dwight picked up his carry-on, walked over to the door, opened it and let Kiera precede him out into the hallway. He didn't get to see Adrienne, who'd remained in her bedroom during his brief visit. When she'd returned his call, she claimed she did not have a problem with Dwight coming to get their daughter. There was something in her voice indicating relief that Kiera would be leaving.

He punched a button for the elevator. Dwight had hired a driver to take them to the airport for a flight back to the States. They had a three-hour layover in Miami before flying on to Charleston, West Virginia, where he would pick up the Jeep from airport parking.

"I think Mom and Omar are getting a divorce."

"That happens with married couples." Dwight had no intention of getting involved in his ex-wife's marriage.

"It doesn't bother you, Daddy?"

He gave Kiera a direct stare. "No. Your mother and her husband are adults who must work through their own issues. It's only when you're drawn into it that I get involved."

Kiera's eyelids fluttered. "They fight all the time, and I was sick of it. I really don't want to be with them ever again."

"You don't have to worry about that right now.

Maybe once they work through their problems, you may change your mind." Dwight didn't want Kiera not to have a relationship with her mother, but it was incumbent on Adrienne to stabilize her marriage or lose her daughter.

The elevator arrived and they stepped into the car. The doors closed and it descended quickly to the lobby. Tropical heat enveloped them as the automatic doors opened. Dwight's driver alighted from the air-cooled sedan parked near the entrance to the building and took their bags.

Dwight sat in the rear of the car with Kiera and stared out the side window. Under another set of circumstances, he would've enjoyed an extended stay in the beautiful tropical island. He was still smarting from Omar believing he had some legal claim on Kiera because he was married to her mother.

Stretching out his legs, he folded his arms over his chest and closed his eyes. He was leaving Punta Cana to return to Wickham Falls and Sasha. He'd thought a lot about her during his stay, and the depth of his feelings for Sasha shocked him. Dwight realized they had reached a point where their relationship had to be resolved with permanence.

Sasha walked out of the kitchen when she heard the doorbell. Charlotte had gone out and she was alone in the house. She opened the door and felt her legs buckle slightly when she stared at the man she'd believed she would never see again.

"What are you doing here?"

He smiled and laugh lines fanned out around the

large hazel eyes with lashes women paid a lot of money to affect. "What? No 'hello, Grant'?"

Sasha's eyes narrowed. "You didn't answer my question. What are you doing here?"

Grant Richards ran his fingers through thick wavy brown hair. "May I come in?"

She glanced around him to see if he'd come with someone, but there was a lone pickup parked in front of the house. "No." Sasha opened the door wider and stepped out on the porch.

Grant stared at her bare feet. "You still don't like to wear shoes."

Leaning against the door frame, she crossed her arms under her breasts. "I know you didn't come here to talk about my feet. Say what you have to say, Grant. I am busy."

"How's the bakeshop?"

Sasha was quickly losing her patience with the man who'd made her life a living hell. She lowered her arms. "Goodbye, Grant."

He caught her upper arm. "Don't go, Sasha. I came to tell you that this will be my last tour."

She stared at the tanned hand on her arm until he released her. "What you do with your life is your business."

Grant's shoulders slumped under the untucked white shirt he'd paired with well-worn jeans and his signature black snakeskin boots. "This will be my last tour because I've been diagnosed with the onset of ALS. Earlier this year I woke up and found it hard to even walk to make it to the bathroom. At first I thought it was muscle cramps, so I applied ice and then heat, and when they went away, I forgot about it. Then a couple of months later I experienced weakness in my right hand and again I ignored it. The day after I signed up for the upcoming tour, I tripped and fell and ended up in the hospital for a battery of tests. That's when I was told I had ALS."

Sasha couldn't believe what she was hearing. "You have ALS and you're still going on the tour?"

"Yes. Instead of singing, playing guitar, while dancing around the stage, I'm going to sit on a stool and just sing. I'll explain to everyone when the show opens that I had an accident and hurt my legs and back, so they're going to get to see a very different Grant Richards."

"I don't understand, Grant. Why aren't you taking care of yourself? What if you fall and seriously injure yourself?"

He angled his head. "That's a chance I'll have to take. I want to go out while I'm still on top." He sobered quickly, shocking Sasha when his eyes filled with tears. "I really came here to apologize, and I'm ashamed of what I did to you."

She averted her head because it pained her to see him cry. "I'm over it, Grant. I've moved on with my life."

"But I can't move on with mine until you forgive me."

Her gaze swung back to him. "You want me to give you absolution?" Sasha's heart turned over when tears streamed down his face. She never would've believed the narcissistic man who never gave a whit for anything or anyone but himself was asking for forgiveness.

She knew it took a lot of strength and courage for Grant to come to her when he knew his days were numbered by a disease that would eventually confine him to a wheelchair before it claimed his life.

Taking a step, she wrapped her arms around his waist and rested her forehead on his shoulder. "I forgive you, Grant," she said.

Grant cupped her chin in his hand, lowered his head and brushed a kiss across her parted lips. "Thank you, baby."

Sasha reached up and blotted his tears with her fingertips. "You take care of yourself."

He nodded. "Now I don't have a choice. No more chasing women and all-night parties."

"Do you have someone who will take care of you?"

"My mother. She's the only one who knows besides you and my manager. After this tour, the world will know the whole story. I'd like you to keep this between us until my manager makes the announcement."

"Okay, Grant," she promised.

He gave her a weak smile. "You take care of yourself. And make sure the next man you take up with will appreciate everything you have to offer him. It wasn't until you left me that I realized you were one badass woman, and you were the better half of the Cowboy and the Redhead."

Turning on his heel, Grant walked off the porch and got into the pickup. Sasha didn't wait to see him drive off. She also didn't see the man sitting across the street in the Jeep watching the interaction with her ex-husband.

Chapter Twelve

Dwight didn't want to believe what he'd just witnessed. He'd come to Sasha's house to talk about wanting to marry her; however, it appeared as if she was still involved with her ex-husband as evidenced by the kiss they'd shared. He wondered if she'd made up the story about his controlling her life when they were married to elicit sympathy as the victim or maybe to shift the blame from herself to him because she'd been the villainess.

He started the Jeep and headed back to the main road, wondering why he'd always chosen the wrong woman to give his heart to. When he slipped an engagement and then a wedding ring on Adrienne's hand, Dwight had believed it would be forever. However, forever ended when she decided to marry the man with whom she'd had an affair while she and Dwight were engaged.

It had become an instant rerun with Sasha. She'd married and divorced Grant Richards, labeling him a monster and saying she never wanted to see him again, yet she couldn't resist locking lips with him on the porch of her home, where anyone walking or driving by could see them.

Perhaps, Dwight mused, he was destined to remain single. Not being committed to a woman and living his life by his leave was satisfying and uncomplicated. His only responsibility was Kiera and planning for her future.

He drove aimlessly until he found himself pulling into a parking space at the Wolf Den. It was Military Monday and there was always a steady stream of active and former military coming and going. He walked into the sports bar, waiting for his eyes to adjust to the dimmer light, and took a seat at the bar. The lunchtime crowd was gone and there were quite a few empty tables and booths.

Aiden Gibson came from the back carrying a keg of beer. He set the keg on the floor and extended his hand. "Welcome back, stranger. How long has it been?"

Dwight shook Aiden's hand. "It's been a while."

"A while? The last time I remember you coming in was with a redhead who bakes the most incredible cakes that we sell out of them whenever they're listed on the chalkboard with the day's special." Aiden paused to hook up the keg. "What are you drinking?"

"I'll take anything you have on tap."

Aiden picked up a mug, tilted it and filled it with a golden foaming liquid, and then set it on a coaster. "Why do you look so down in the dumps?"

Picking up the mug, Dwight took a long swallow. "Do I?"

"Hell, yeah, you do," Aiden countered. "I'm willing to bet that it has something to do with a woman.

Sasha?" he asked when Dwight did not deny or confirm his assumption.

"Women," Dwight said under his breath. "Can't live with them and can't live without them."

Resting his elbows on the bar, Aiden leaned forward. "You seem to have done quite well as a bachelor."

Dwight's dark eyes met Aiden's blue-green ones. "True, but things change when you meet someone you really care about."

"I know what you mean, buddy. I thought I'd never fall in love again until I met Taryn. Even though she is an amazing woman and mother, it's not all sunshine and butterflies. Every once in a while we have our ups and downs, but it only makes our marriage stronger."

Dwight took another sip of the cold brew. "You're preaching to the choir, Aiden."

"If you know, then why the long face, Dwight?"

"It gets a little sticky when there's a third person in the relationship." There was no way he was going to tell Aiden that he saw Sasha kissing her ex-husband.

Aiden grimaced. "That does make it a little messy."

"I can think of another word to describe it. Enough talk about me. How are your kids?"

"They're all good. Taryn is still homeschooling the girls until they get to middle school, while Daniel believes all he has to do is scream to get what he wants."

"How old is he now?"

"Two."

Dwight smiled. "There's a reason why they're called the Terrible Twos."

"Didn't your daughter graduate this year?"

"No. She still has another year." He had a Wednesday morning appointment with a dealer in Beckley to purchase a car for Kiera. He'd asked the dealer to order the same make and model, but a different color, as the one Victoria drove. Kiera was anticipating getting the car a week before the start of the new school year, and he knew she would be surprised when it arrived earlier.

Dwight picked up a menu and ordered the daily special of baked chicken, garlic mashed potatoes, roasted asparagus and corn bread, along with another glass of beer. He made it home to find Kiera in his kitchen sitting on a stool between Sasha and her grandmother.

Kiera jumped and came over to hug him. "Hi, Daddy. We were waiting for you to come back so we can all eat together at Ruthie's."

Smiling, he dropped a kiss on Kiera's chemically relaxed hair. She'd taken out the braids and had the stylist relax her thick natural hair, set it on large rollers and trim the ends. Using a round brush and blow-dryer, she blew it out until it hung in stick-straight strands halfway down her back.

"I'm going to have to take a rain check, sweetie. I already ate at the Wolf Den."

Sasha swiveled on the stool. "You went to the Den without me?"

Dwight stared at the woman he wanted to hate for her duplicity yet couldn't because he'd found himself in too deep. "Sasha, will you please step out on the porch with me? I'd like to talk to you about something."

"Are you going to ask her to marry you?" Kiera asked in a loud voice.

"Kiera Robyn Adams, mind your manners!" Victoria scolded. "How many times have I warned you to stay out of grown folks' business?"

Kiera lowered her eyes. "Sorry, Grammie."

"It's your father and Sasha you should be apologizing to."

"I'm sorry, Daddy. Miss Sasha."

Dwight nodded to Kiera. "Apology accepted."

Sasha slipped off the stool and came over to him. "I'm ready to talk whenever you are."

Cupping her elbow, he escorted her out of the house and onto the porch. Dwight waited for Sasha to sit on the cushioned love seat before dropping down beside her. "Is there something you want to tell me?"

Shifting, Sasha turned to look directly at him. "What's going on, Dwight?"

He blinked slowly. "That's what I want to know, Sasha. What's up with you and your ex-husband?"

"Say what?"

"Say what," he repeated. "I came by to see you earlier this afternoon, and to say I was shocked is an understatement when I saw you locking lips with Grant Richards. I thought you never wanted to see him again. What's next, Sasha? A reconciliation?"

"It's not what you think!"

"No, Sasha. It's not what I think but what I saw."

"What you saw is not what you think, Dwight."

He closed his eyes. "Please don't tell me what I think. Right now, my thoughts are saying that I don't trust you. And I've made it a practice not to deal with women I can't trust."

"I want you to trust me when I say I can't tell you why Grant came to see me and why he kissed me."

"Can't or won't?"

"I can't. At least not now."

Dwight extended his legs, crossing his feet at the ankles. He knew what he was going to tell Sasha would forever affect their relationship. "I think we should stop seeing each other until you can be truthful with me. Meanwhile, feel free to date other people." He pushed off the love seat. "Please excuse me. I'm going inside."

Sasha sat, numbed by what had just transpired between her and Dwight. He had just broken up with her. She had no idea he had seen her with Grant, and she'd promised her ex-husband that she wouldn't say anything about his physical condition.

She wanted to keep Grant's secret, and she wanted to keep her man. This was the second time Grant wanted her to shield him from the public. The first was the non-disclosure when she was legally bound not to reveal the details of their marriage. Now he'd asked her not to talk about a disease that would eventually rob him of the ability to walk, talk, feed or relieve himself.

Pulling her legs up and tucking them under her body, she closed her eyes and pressed her head against the back cushion. She'd walked away from Grant to start over, and when she least expected it, he'd walked back into her life to control her once again. When she'd opened the door to find him standing on her porch, her impulse was to close it and leave him standing there. Even before he'd revealed his diagnosis, she'd noticed the slight trembling in his right hand—something she didn't remember when they lived together. He would periodically complain of fatigue, which she attributed to nonstop touring and too many late-night parties.

Sasha opened her eyes and smiled. She wasn't ready to give up Dwight Adams, not when she'd waited all her life to find a man who loved her for herself and not what she could do to enhance his life or image. Dwight lived and worked in Wickham Falls, which meant he wasn't going anywhere, and neither was she. She returned to the kitchen, smiling. "It looks like it's just us ladies tonight."

Victoria walked over to her and placed her hand on Sasha's arm. "Are you all right?"

"Of course. Why would you think I'm not?"

The sweep hand on the wall clock made a full revolution before Victoria smiled. "Nothing. We can leave as soon as I get my bag."

Dwight stood up when he heard the approaching car. This was the second time Kiera had broken curfew. He'd given her the car a month ago, and during that time he rarely saw her when she didn't have classes or work at the bakeshop. He'd warned her the next time she came in after midnight she would forfeit her right to drive the car for a month. He watched her as she got out and then stopped when she saw him leaning over the railing to the porch.

"I'm sorry, Daddy, that I'm late but I had to drop my friend off home. We had to wait before we could get a lane at the bowling alley."

"Where does your friend live, Kiera Adams?"

"Mineral Springs."

"Is this friend a girl or a boy?"

Kiera placed her foot on the first step. "It's a boy but I swear I'm not doing anything with him."

"Are you dating this boy?"

Kiera took another step. "Not really."

"Either you are, or you aren't."

"We've seen each other a few times."

"You're dating a boy from another town and not once did you think of bringing him home so I could meet him." Dwight didn't want to tell his daughter most kids from The Falls did not date kids who lived in the Springs because of a football rivalry going back at least a couple of generations.

"Miss Sasha met him."

"You introduced your boyfriend to your boss and not your father." Dwight had not seen or heard from Sasha since the day he confronted her about her ex-husband.

"Miss Sasha is like a mom and I wanted her to let me know if she liked Enrique."

"Miss Sasha isn't your mom, Kiera."

"I know, but she could be my stepmother if you married her. Why did you stop dating her, Daddy?"

Dwight held out his hand and Kiera dropped the car fob on his outstretched palm. He had no intention of discussing his relationship with Sasha with her. "You'll get this back when I get to meet the boy who's responsible for your breaking curfew and losing your driving privileges."

Kiera stomped up the steps and went into the house, slamming the door behind her. His daughter mentioning Sasha was a reminder of how long it had been since he last saw her. Dwight knew he was being a hardnose, because he didn't want a repeat with her of what he'd had with Adrienne.

He went inside and flopped down on a chair in the family room. Being a parent was hard. Being the parent to a teenager was trial by fire. Dwight picked up the remote device and flicked on the television, channel surfing until he found a show featuring entertainment news.

He sat straight up, his eyes glued to Grant Richards's image when it filled the screen. The man was chairing a news conference in which he was announcing his retirement from the music scene. Dwight did not want to believe what he was hearing. Grant had been diagnosed with ALS, and he had sworn his mother, manager and ex-wife to secrecy that they would not reveal the debilitating disease until after he completed his last tour because he did not want to disappoint his loyal fans.

Dwight buried his face in his hands. When he'd asked Sasha to tell him about the encounter with her ex, she said, *I can't. At least not now.* He didn't want to believe he'd lost the woman who'd made him plan for the next day and years to come.

He knew it was late, but he was past caring. He had to know if he had a second chance to make things right. Picking up the phone on the side table, Dwight tapped Sasha's number.

"Hello."

He knew he'd woken her. "Sasha."

"Yes, Dwight."

"Can you forgive me for being a selfish, jealous fool?"

"There's nothing to forgive, darling. I know you had a right to feel the way you did, but I'd promised Grant that I wouldn't tell anyone about his condition because it wasn't mine to tell."

"I know that now."

"Dwight?"

"What, babe?"

"I love you so much."

"I love you more. Can you do me a favor?"

"What?" she asked.

"Will you marry me?"

Sasha's distinctive laugh came through the earpiece. "I thought you'd never ask."

"Is that a yes or no, Miss Manning?"

"Of course it's a yes, Dr. Adams."

"What size ring do you wear?"

"A six."

"Tomorrow we'll go ring shopping before we officially announce our engagement."

Sasha laughed again. "Do you want a long engagement?"

"No. Do you want children?" he asked.

"We already have a daughter, so a son would be nice."

Dwight hadn't thought about fathering more children until he fell in love with Sasha. And if they did have a child together, it would be raised as an only child because Kiera would be so much older than her sister or brother.

"When do you want to start trying for a baby?"

"Tomorrow. And I've always wanted a Christmas wedding."

It was August and if Sasha got pregnant right away then she would be at least three months along by the end of the year. "Are you sure you want to walk down the aisle with a belly?"

"Yes. As long as it's your baby in my belly."

"You keep talking like that and I'm going to come over there and take you to a motel where we can make up for lost time."

"Come on over, darling. I'll be waiting on the porch when you get here."

Six Months Later...

Sasha walked out of the bathroom, her eyes meeting her husband's. What she'd expected was confirmed. She was pregnant. They'd been trying for a baby since the day before he slipped a ring on her finger, but with no results. They'd exchanged vows during a winter wonderland–themed wedding in the barn behind the

Wolf Den. Her brothers and their families had come in for the event, and she and Dwight took a weeklong honeymoon on St. Thomas, returning more in love than when they left the States. Kiera hadn't changed her mind about becoming a professional chef when she'd sent off applications to top culinary schools.

Dwight pushed into a sitting position as he looked at her. "Why are you smiling?"

Sasha slipped into bed next to him. "You did it. We're pregnant."

Throwing back his head, Dwight howled like a wolf. "Congratulations, Mama!"

Straddling his lap, she pressed her breasts to his bare chest. "Congratulations to you, too, Daddy!"

Sasha could not believe all her dreams had come true. She'd married a man she loved, she was carrying his baby and she could claim an incredible stepdaughter and mother-in-law. And Sasha's Sweet Shoppe had earned the reputation of offering some of the best desserts in Johnson County.

* * * * *

MILLS & BOON

Coming next month

HER TWIN BABY SECRET
Therese Beharrie

He laughed. Gave in to the urge to tuck her hair behind her ear as he'd seen her do earlier.

She exhaled. 'What are you doing, Benjamin?'

He dropped his hand, looked at her face. 'I don't know.'

'You do know.'

'No, I don't.' He smiled. Almost as soon as he did, it vanished. 'Except for right now. Right now, I'm contemplating how to get you to kiss me again. I'd say it's an appropriate response to how incredible you look.' He shook his head. 'I was staring earlier because I didn't have anything to say. You're so beautiful. And this dress is…and your hair, your face…' He shook his head again. Offered her a wry, possibly apologetic smile. 'I'm sorry. I think the last couple days have officially caught up with me.'

Her expression was unreadable, but she said, 'It's been a rough couple of days.'

'Yeah.'

'Because of me.' She paused. 'I'm sorry.'

'You don't have to apologise. You already have, at least.'

'Right.' She leaned back against her door, which he realised only now she hadn't moved away from. 'This hasn't been easy for me either.'

'I know.'

'A large part of it is because you get on my nerves. A lot,' she added when he frowned.

'That seems uncalled for considering I just gave you a bunch of compliments.'

'You want acknowledgement for that?'

'A thank you would nice,' he muttered.

'You're right.'

'Sorry—could you say that again?' He patted his pocket, looking for his phone. 'I want to record it for posterity.'

'This, for example, is extremely annoying. But at the same time, I can't stop thinking about the kiss we had the other day.'

He stilled.

'Which gets on my nerves, too. An interesting conundrum. Am I annoyed because I'm attracted to you? Am I annoyed because you annoy me but I'm still attracted to you?' She exhaled. It sounded frustrated. 'I don't have answers, but I keep asking these questions. Then, of course, you do something decent, like pretend to be my boyfriend even though you have no reason or incentive to. You stand up for me in front of my brother, which I found disturbingly hot. In the same breath, you act stupidly, and tell your mother—your *mother*—that I'm your girlfriend. Which, tonight, we have to rectify.'

She shook her head.

'Honestly, Benjamin, these last few days have been the most frustratingly complicated of my life, and I'm an entrepreneur with a crappy family. And I'm *pregnant,* about to become a single mother. Complicated is the air I breathe. But you make things...' She trailed off with a little laugh. 'And still, I want to kiss you, too.'

Continue reading
HER TWIN BABY SECRET
Therese Beharrie

Available next month
www.millsandboon.co.uk

COMING SOON!

We really hope you enjoyed reading this book. If you're looking for more romance, be sure to head to the shops when new books are available on

Thursday 23rd January

To see which titles are coming soon, please visit

millsandboon.co.uk/nextmonth

MILLS & BOON
MEDICAL
Pulse-Racing Passion

Set your pulse racing with dedicated, delectable doctors in the high-pressure world of medicine, where emotions run high and passion, comfort and love are the best medicine.

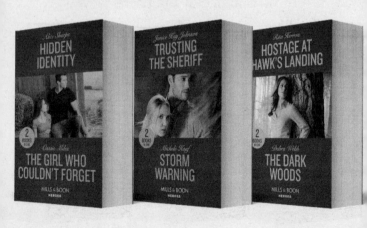

MILLS & BOON
Desire

Indulge in secrets and scandal, intense drama and plenty of sizzling hot action with powerful and passionate heroes who have it all: wealth, status, good looks... everything but the right woman.

Six Desire stories published every month, find them all at:

millsandboon.co.uk/Desire

LET'S TALK
Romance

For exclusive extracts, competitions
and special offers, find us online:

facebook.com/millsandboon

@MillsandBoon

@MillsandBoonUK

Get in touch on 01413 063232

For all the latest titles coming soon, visit
millsandboon.co.uk/nextmonth